Ghost
Image

Joshua Gilder

Simon & Schuster

New York · London · Toronto · Sydney · Singapore

SIMON & SCHUSTER
Rockefeller Center
1230 Avenue of the Americas
New York, NY 10020

SIMON & SCHUSTER and colophon are registered trademarks
of Simon & Schuster, Inc.

Designed by Lauren Simonetti

Manufactured in the United States of America

ISBN 0-7432-2312-8

To my wife, Anne-Lee

A scar is permanent. That is why a skilled plastic surgeon will try to hide it—in the crease of an eyelid, in the fold beneath the breast, along the hairline or behind the ear. If you're lucky and have the right genetic makeup, the scar may be almost indiscernible to the naked eye. But it is always there. It never goes away.

Ghost
Image

Prologue

It was Stern's idea, originally, that I keep a diary, a record; that I write it down as I remember it and as it happens to me. "Just get it out. Get it down on paper. You need to *objectify* things, Jackson," he told me. That's one of Stern's favorite words, "objectify."

Stern is my psychiatrist, my shrink. He's also my colleague, a member of the teaching staff at the hospital where I work, which is why I can afford to see him—the administration subsidizes the therapy of those residents who feel they need it. No doubt a prudent precaution. Medicine is a stressful occupation.

"You never need to show the diary to anyone," he assured me. It would be just for our sessions together. Only Stern would see it. But even that isn't possible any longer. It's gone too far beyond that now.

I remember in the beginning, when I first started therapy, I thought Stern would be my deliverance from this constant fear; from this past that pursues me and still has the power to reach out and pull me back. Like one of those bad dreams when you're on the border of consciousness, trying to wake up. Therapy would be the door that led out into the world everyone else seemed to inhabit, the one where normal people live normal lives. In time, I thought, I would be able to walk through that door and be free. Instead, week after week, it just led me right back to Stern, the dispassionate dissector of people's souls, slouched in his chair as if he'd never moved from the spot, like some gargoyle watching over a dark cathedral.

Stern believes that I became a doctor to try, in some symbolic way, to get close to my father. He was a cardiac surgeon who died, somewhat ironically, of heart complications a while after abandoning our family and the crazy wife, my mother, who had become such a burden to him. Very possibly, Stern is right, but as with so much he says, I feel it somehow misses the point.

"It's more like this," I tried to explain, and I told him a story from when I was a medical student, the first time I observed microsurgery. Some guy drinking beer with his buddies had chosen to demonstrate his new power saw, which very cleanly sliced off the first and second fingers of his right hand. Fortunately, his drinking companions were sobered up enough by the sight of his fingers flying through the air that they were able to pick them up, wrap them in a T-shirt and put the bloody package in a beer cooler, alongside the remains of a six-pack of Coors. It took eight hours to put the fingers back on, the plastic surgeon in charge hardly moving the whole time, hunched over the microscope through which he could find and reassemble the almost invisible tendons, arteries and veins. "Like sewing together pieces of thread," he told us. I hardly moved the whole time myself. I just stood there, fascinated, though I could see little of what was going on through the crowd of students and residents who had come into the operating room to observe. It seemed like a miracle to me: that we could reattach this man's fingers, make him whole again. That fate could be undone, mistakes rectified. That you could have a second chance.

I suppose that's what I've been looking for. A second chance.

It's a good thing to believe, to have faith in something. Stern, despite his detached, clinical persona and the air of cynicism he likes to project, is a believer. He believes in reality; he is a disciple of reality and its curative powers. He takes it as a given truth that we can and should reconcile ourselves to the way things are, a process he equates with "progress." As in "We're making progress now, Jackson." That's why he wanted me to write things down: "Get it down on paper. Get it out of the realm of fear and fantasy, back to something real, something concrete that you can work with."

It's almost endearing, this faith he has in reality, as if the more we have of it the better off we will be. "*Objectify* things," he tells me, as if that will make it better. As if anything could. But I don't believe that anymore. Lately, I've come to wonder if it doesn't just make it worse.

Chapter 1

The blade cut smoothly through the translucent skin covering her eye. Little drops of blood bubbled up along the line of the incision.

Taking the forceps, I pulled back on the skin—delicately, like peeling a grape—reaching under with the scalpel to sever the connective tissue holding it in place. The nurse followed behind with an electrical bovie device to cauterize the bleeding vessels. It made a zapping sound—like those gadgets that hang in the backyard to electrocute mosquitoes—followed by a sizzle and the smell of burnt flesh.

"Yummy!" said Henning. "Barbecue!"

Henning was a first-year resident, an intern. He was bright and a quick learner, but like many medical students, he'd had his nose buried in a book since he was a small child and his social development had suffered accordingly.

A final cut and the skin pulled free: a crescent shape, like a quarter moon. I plunged the scalpel vertically through the muscle surrounding the eyeball—Henning made an "ouch" sound and drew in his breath—and fatty tissue welled up through the incision.

"Henning," I said, "get ahold of her arm, would you. I think our patient is trying to grab the scalpel."

Because it was a relatively short procedure, the woman we were operating on was sedated but not put all the way under. It's safer that way, and the patient doesn't feel anything, but the nerves still react to the pain.

Henning and the nurse wrestled her arm down, strapping it under the Velcro restraint, while the anesthesiologist gave the woman another "cocktail" through the IV tube. In less than a minute, she had calmed down again.

"So," said Henning, "is this one of your movie stars?"

In fact, she was an aspiring actress, and had been for almost three decades now, not a star; which is why she came to be operated on at the Residents' Clinic, where the rates were a fraction of what they would be with a private doctor. The procedure would remove the bags from her eyes and give her another decade or so to aspire.

"Yeah," I said, "it's Marilyn Monroe, back for her thirty-seventh face-lift."

"Looking good, Marilyn," pronounced Henning.

The real stars all went to Brandt, Dr. Peter Brandt, the head of Plastics here at San Francisco Memorial: Hollywood actors of both sexes, escaping the L.A. media; politicians' wives from Washington, hoping to erase the effects of too many campaigns with too much stress and too much junk food; and, increasingly, large numbers of foreigners spending their newly gotten wealth to "westernize" their ethnic features.

They'd made Brandt one of the most highly paid plastic surgeons in the country, and with the recent attention to his new start-up venture, Genederm—a biotech company growing genetically manufactured skin in the laboratory—he'd become something of a media celebrity as well. As Brandt's chief resident, studying with him on a special two-year fellowship, I basked in his reflected glory, as well as the rumors, all true, that he was pulling strings to get me a coveted position on the faculty at Memorial.

"Ah, Jackson—" Henning began, as I moved over to work on the other eye.

"Yes?"

"Can you get me a date with our patient here?"

"She's twice your age, Henning."

"I'm not prejudiced. Anyway, I saw her in prep. She's a fox."

"Sorry, Henning. Hippocratic oath. We're not supposed to do anything detrimental to our patients."

The operation proceeded methodically. I sutured the incision above her eye, then moved down, cutting along the almost invisible line between the outside of the lower lid and the lashes. Henning, though ostensibly watching me closely, soon became absorbed in other thoughts. The anesthesiologist sat by her machine, reading a book. The nurses stopped hovering, and stillness fell over the operating room.

There is something about delicate work that sets my mind free. Those days, in any case, I was always thinking about Allie.

———

I hadn't known her long before I made up my mind to propose. I had tried once, when we were at the beach, desperately struggling to get out the words, without success. I don't know whether Allie sensed my turmoil, but she gave no sign of it. She just sat there calmly, her eyes looking out to the sea, her knees tucked up to her chest and circled by her arms, moving her bare feet back and forth until they were buried in the sand.

And I just sat there, too, gazing at her extraordinary hair as the wind blew it about her face and she would grab it and try to push it back. There were masses of it, and it never seemed to be under control. She complained about it all the time and carried a can of hair spray wherever she went. It was one of the things I loved about her, the way she was constantly trying to mat her hair down with spray, then giving up and putting on a cap—with this great clump of curls sticking out behind in a kind of ponytail—or, when she was trying to look more sophisticated, putting a bandanna over her head and tying it tightly in back. It was the wet air of San Francisco, she said, that made her hair so impossible. Once, when we were downtown and she was having a particularly bad hair day, we happened to be passing a Hermès store, so I went inside and bought her a scarf. It was tan, with a pattern of little red balloons that made her look innocent, even schoolgirlish, and from then on she wore it all the time.

———

I tied the final knot in the suture at the corner of the patient's eye, and the nurse clipped it with her scissors.

"We're about through here," I said loudly.

Henning woke with a start. Like all first-year residents, he'd developed the ability to catch up on his sleep while standing over an operating table. He reached up to rub his eyes awake, then realized he had on sterile gloves, so just shook his head violently.

"Put some cold compresses on her eyes to keep the swelling down," I told him, "and take her down to recovery, would you? I've got to get moving."

"Yes, boss," he said. "Sure thing."

The scrub nurse gave me a look of surprise—usually I'm the last one out of the operating room—then went back to helping Henning with the compresses. The circulating nurse untied my smock in back, and I turned around as she unwrapped me.

"Put some more cold compresses on when you get there," I called to Henning as I banged through the door. With any luck, I'd be with Allie in less than an hour.

She'd be waiting for me at my apartment, as we'd arranged, surprised to see me so early; not ready yet to go out. That was fine with me: I liked to lie on the bed and watch her get dressed and put on her makeup, that look of intense concentration followed by a little frown in the mirror when it was all complete. The sight of her stepping into a dress, or tucking in her shirt and zipping up her jeans, was almost better than watching her take off her clothes—not erotic, exactly, not particularly graceful, either. Just practical, unself-conscious and feminine. I'd come to memorize those movements, the way she would step into her shoes while buttoning her blouse, squeezing her feet in while walking over to pick up her handbag, then turn to me and announce she was ready. Sometimes, when I was very late, and the fog and damp had settled over the city and I showed up at the door at midnight, Allie would pull on her pants, tuck in the nightdress she'd been sleeping in and put on a leather jacket. Then we'd walk to the diner and order a beer for me and a hamburger, onion rings and milk shake for her, no matter how soundly she'd been asleep just minutes earlier.

—

I was in the shower, washing the hospital smell from my hands and out of my hair. The sound was muffled, almost drowned out by the noise of the running water—three short beeps, a high-pitched summons on my pager. So faint I could have missed it. But I didn't.

Chapter 2

I opened my locker, searched through my clothes for the pager and pushed the button. It was the Control Center. For all they knew, I'd left the hospital and was out of range. I was no longer on call; I didn't have to answer the message.

Still dripping from the shower, I walked to the telephone on the wall and punched in the number for Control.

"It's Dr. Maebry. You beeped?"

It was probably the patient I had just operated on. The sedation would be wearing off and she'd need reassurance. I'd stop by on the way out and be driving home in ten minutes.

"It's the ER," the voice said. "The helicopter is bringing in a trauma case from Marin. Severe burns and lacerations. Lieberman wants you there."

Damn. "Why here, why not Marin County? They've got a trauma center."

"Apparently, there's been a pileup in the fog on the freeway north of the bay and they're overwhelmed."

I looked at my watch. It was almost six-thirty. "What about Anderson? Isn't he supposed to be on call now?" Anderson was the other plastics resident at Memorial.

"He's still in OR, doing a rhinoplasty."

"Jesus. He started at two o'clock." Only Anderson could take over four hours on a nose job.

"Anyway, Lieberman asked for you specifically."

I had started my training in emergency medicine before I switched to plastics. Lieberman, the head of the ER, liked that. And we had worked well together on a couple of cases.

"It's nice to feel wanted."

"They've already landed," the operator said. "They're on their way to Trauma now," he added, then hung up.

I grabbed a new set of greens, pulled them on and headed down the hall, thinking of the clothes that clung to my damp body and the green booties that never fit properly over my running shoes, about how I was going to be late for Allie and how much I sometimes hated being a doctor. I skipped the elevator, took the emergency stairs, cut between the buildings and came around through the ambulance loading dock.

Later in the evening the ER would heat up, when the Saturday-night parties reached the drunken, aggressive phase and the knives came out and old animosities were settled with guns. Now it was almost peaceful: The unhurried movements of the orderlies getting ready for the night ahead. The woman wearing jogging clothes, standing by the admitting window holding a baby in her arms (Did she run here? I wondered). The surfer sitting in one of the outer cubicles, his dreadlocks still wet and a gash in his forehead, warily eyeing the needle in the hand of the intern before him. The nurses gossiping over coffee as I made my way to the door of the Trauma Room in the back.

I could already sense it when I was still outside: the invisible vortex that surrounds trauma cases, sweeping you up in a series of actions and reactions that follow one another without interruption—without thought, almost—until you're deposited, bleary-eyed and disoriented, on the far shore of the crisis. I'd come to dread that feeling; it was one reason I had left emergency medicine: the constant fear that everything was on the verge of spinning out of control, that as good as you were, as hard as you tried, it could all go suddenly, terribly wrong. I should call Allie first, I thought, let her know I would be late. But there wasn't time, and my feet had already pulled me inside.

The sour odor of gasoline and wet ashes pushed into my nostrils, the familiar smell of burn victims.

Lieberman was presiding: a calm, steady presence. He looked, I thought, like those pictures of weightless astronauts, every movement purposeful, deliberate, as if it required the utmost concentration. Eight or nine people surrounded the table. The nurses were focused, busy, hooking up the monitors, placing a cuff around the patient's arm to check the blood pressure. The ER resident was saying something in Lieberman's ear; off to the side, pushed back from the knot of hovering bodies, was an intern, his face looking slightly green. It's August, I realized, the beginning of the rotation. He's just started.

" . . . hyperventilating, probable carbon monoxide poisoning. She'd been vomiting, so we intubated her . . ." The paramedics were standing behind Lieberman, rattling off the critical information. "A lot of blood loss from the scalp wounds. Possible cervical trauma, so we put on a hard collar. She's comatose. No surprise, considering."

Lieberman gave a series of orders while a nurse called out the vital signs and the resident opened up a saline infusion into the IV.

"Let's get a tube in her stomach in case she starts to vomit again," Lieberman said. "And let's start getting some X rays in here," he called in a loud voice, turning his head toward the X-ray room. "C-spine first, I want to see if there's any damage to the vertebrae before we turn her."

The resident hunched over the patient, feeding a tube through the nose and into the stomach; the radiology technician arrived at the other side of the table, pulling the X-ray camera along the overhead rack and into position above the patient's neck. Lieberman stepped back to give him room and noticed me for the first time.

"Maebry, glad you're here. I want you to look at these burns—no," he said to the technician, "do the head next, then the chest, check for broken ribs." Then back to me: "Also the lacerations. And facial fractures. As you can see." He gestured toward the bloody mass of the victim's face, so swollen and disfigured it was barely recognizable as human.

The nurses were cutting away what was left of her clothing and peeling off the larger pieces of debris from the body. I could see the greasy opening of the wounds beneath, clotted with blood and pieces of charred fabric and flesh—it was hard to tell one from the other. The burns ran across the left side of the chest area and up the neck. It looked as if the ear had been partially burnt off, but I couldn't get a good view because the X-ray technician was in my way.

"What was it," I asked, "a car accident?"

"Nope," said one of the paramedics. "We got her out of a construction site up in Marin. Probably a domestic." "Domestic" was shorthand for a fight between a homeless couple: one gets mad at the other, beats them or tries to light them on fire while they're sleeping. It's not infrequent.

"There are no homeless in Marin," said one of the nurses.

"There are homeless everywhere," said the paramedic. "Anyway, looked like someone rolled her up in a carpet and torched it. Smells like they used gasoline, too."

"This is no bag lady," said the nurse, cutting away at the nylon stocking that had partially melted and adhered to the skin. "Look at these shoes." She took one off and pointed inside. "Gucci."

A nurse from the Control Center stuck her head in the room and called to Lieberman that the resident was needed on another case.

"No way!" Lieberman shook his head. "Impossible. Not going to happen."

"Sorry, Doctor, they're sending the overflow down from the pileup in Marin and we're short."

Lieberman winced, still shaking his head. "Yeah, yeah, yeah. Okay." He looked at the monitors. "She seems pretty stable for now. Go ahead," he said, waving the resident out the door. He turned to me: "Remember your ER medicine, Maebry?"

The tech was moving the X ray down the body to the chest, and I stepped forward to get a better look at the head injuries. I guessed by the swelling that the trauma was several hours old, at least. The worst was on the left side, where I was standing with Lieberman: the eggshell-thin bones that support the eye had been crushed, and the entire side of the face was sunken in, the eye deeply recessed. The nasal bone was crushed as well, and the fleshy part of the nose torn and lacerated.

Blood was smeared across the forehead, but there were no fractures there as far as I could see. That was a good sign: the brain might have escaped the worst trauma. I leaned over to look at the other side of the face, where the swelling was less severe. I didn't see any fractures there either, only minor lacerations, but it was hard to be sure because it was covered with debris and thickly caked with blood, as if the victim had been lying on that side and the blood had pooled around her face, congealing over her eye and clotting in her hair. I noticed without thinking about it how fine the hair was. A scarf had fallen to the side and was stuck by the dried blood to her face. I pulled the stiff fabric carefully away to check underneath.

"Pretty fucking brutal, hunh?" Lieberman said by my side.

It was a tan scarf, covered with tiny red balloons.

The nurses were reading off the vital signs, a staccato of figures, hypnotic in their repetition. I was trying to concentrate, but it was as if the entire scene was receding into the back of my mind, somewhere deep, where I didn't want to follow. Lieberman was telling the radiology tech to get X rays of her pelvis and also her right arm. Something about a compound fracture.

Often the mind doesn't see what it doesn't want to see, what it can't let itself see. It shuts down and refuses to process the information. You stare and try to make sense, but the image before your eyes has no meaning—until you notice one thing, one small visual clue, like a scarf with tiny red balloons, and your perspective shifts and snaps into place.

The swelling was less advanced on the right side. I looked down at the features I had gazed upon so often before, every curve, every line and expression, committed to memory. The nurse came up with a sponge and began to wipe away the blood and dirt.

It's not Allie, I told myself. It couldn't be. Just a patient, a stranger, another emergency case. In a few hours I'd be through here; I'd forget about it and go home. Allie was waiting for me in the apartment right now, growing cross because I'd been delayed again. I could see her sitting there in the big straw armchair, with two sweatshirts on and wool socks, wrapped in a blanket because the fog was heavy and she got cold easily, especially her feet. They were always cold; when my feet bumped against them under the covers at night, they made me shiver. Occasionally, she would have to get up and run hot water over them to warm up, and I'd sit with her and we'd talk. We'd talk through the night, sometimes, until we were too sleepy to talk anymore.

I realized I had to call her immediately. I had to leave the Trauma Room and use the phone out by the desk. I had to talk to her, now.

I heard everything from far away, as if through a tunnel. The respiratory therapist calling out something. Lieberman saying my name in my ear. Then voices yelling.

The voices became louder, violent, like the panic rising inside me. I tried to look up and felt Lieberman's hand grasp my arm. Someone was swearing and pushing in front of me. "Maebry! Get out of the way! For Christ's sake, Maebry!" It felt as if I were asking a question over and over but couldn't come up with the right answer. All I could think was how impossible it was, how I had to call her, I had to. I have something important to say to you, Allie. Something very important. But how can I? How will I ever be able to tell you now?

Chapter 3

The voices again, communicating something urgent. I could hear it in their tone.

Numbers. A nurse was calling out numbers. They must be blood pressure readings, I thought.

" . . . a hundred and ten . . . five . . . dropping . . ."

I was back against the wall, watching the people before me as if it were a play and I couldn't follow the plot. Lieberman was moving about rapidly, the nurses were ripping off the last pieces of clothing on Allie's body and throwing off the sheet they had placed over her for modesty's sake.

"She's hemorrhaging!" Lieberman shouted. "Do you see it? Do you see any blood?"

" . . . ninety-five . . . still dropping."

"Nothing, Doctor. No blood. I don't see anything."

"Nothing here."

"Okay. Okay. X rays?" Lieberman called out. "Hello!" he yelled at the door the tech had disappeared through. "Do we have the fucking X rays! I want an X ray of her spine before I lift her!"

A nurse ran out quickly and came back shaking her head.

"No X rays? Great. Okay. Fine. Great." He was calm again. "Okay, we can't wait. We've got to move her anyway." Two nurses came forward and put their hands under the limp body and half lifted, half rolled her while Lieberman crouched down and ran his hands along her back feeling for blood.

"Nothing here." They let her down and Lieberman started poking at her abdomen to check for internal bleeding.

" . . . ninety . . . eighty-five . . ."

"What the hell?"

I looked over and saw the intern, who, like me, had backed away from the table, and I thought, absurdly, that he'd just taken a bath. His hair was wet against his forehead, and a dark patch of perspiration ran down the front of his greens.

"Eighty . . . dropping."

"EKG?"

"Normal, Doctor."

"Are you sure?"

"Normal, Doctor."

Lieberman whirled toward the rhythm strip of the EKG and stared at it with such intensity that my eyes followed his. It was completely normal. Electrical pulses were passing through the heart in a steady pulse, just as they should, but the muscle wasn't beating.

Lieberman grabbed at his collar, realized he didn't have his stethoscope on him and leaned over, pressing his ear to the burnt flesh on the left side of the chest. "Sounds like it's underwater." He dove with his hands toward her neck, his fingers feeling for the jugular vein. "The blood is backing up." He looked around at me. "Maebry?"

I tried to concentrate.

"Maebry? What do you think? Cardiac tamponade? That's my guess."

Yes, I thought to myself, he's probably right: the heart was bleeding into its surrounding sac, slowly building up pressure, squeezing itself to death.

"Yes," I heard myself say, as if coming out of a trance.

Lieberman didn't wait for my reply. He'd already called for a needle, and a nurse was slapping a syringe into his hand while he felt for Allie's ribs, finding the right spot.

"Slowly, slowly," Lieberman said to himself as he pushed the metal point through the skin and under her breastbone, guiding it toward her heart. I could see his hand shaking. "Slowly. That's it. There." He pierced the engorged sac and blood welled into the syringe. We all waited for the nurse to read out the pressure.

The silence lasted too long.

"It's dropping, Doctor."

"What?"

"Dropping . . . sixty over fifty . . . forty . . ."

"Damn it all!"

14

Simultaneously, we heard the EKG emit a steady wail and the nurse call out, "It's gone."

Allie's heart had stopped.

Lieberman began pumping violently on her chest. "Let's jump-start her, guys! Maebry!" he yelled at me. "You want to help out here?"

His voice pulled me forward. He was up on the table hunched over her now. The nurse pushed the crash cart up. Like an automaton, I took the paddles and placed them on either side of Allie's chest. I counted to three loudly to give everyone time to stand back, and Lieberman jumped away just before I pulled the trigger. Every muscle in Allie's body convulsed as the electrical current shot through it.

"Nothing," said the nurse at the EKG.

"Again!" Lieberman called. "Turn it up!"

I counted to three again and pulled the trigger. Allie's right leg kicked off the table with the convulsion, and two nurses grabbed it and thrust it back in place.

"Nothing."

"Again!"

"One. Two. Three." I pulled the trigger and waited.

"Nothing. No response."

"Epinephrine!" The nurse handed Lieberman the syringe and he injected it. "Again. Do it now!"

"Nothing, Doctor."

"Again!"

With each jolt, Allie's body would writhe under me and her right leg would splay off the table. Lieberman shouted at the nurses to strap it down, but there was never time and they would frantically try to wedge it back on the table while Lieberman pumped rhythmically on her chest between shocks. Then I'd count to three and everyone would jump back as I pulled the trigger. I lost track of how many times. Each action repeated in sequence, like choreography—"One, two, three. Now! One, two, three"—a clockwork dance, slowly winding down.

I heard Lieberman behind me saying that it was enough, the EKG was flat, she was gone. He was telling me to stop and the nurses were standing back, not even trying to rescue the leg that dangled off the side of the table.

I shocked her again, and another time. Each time Allie's body spasmed in a ghoulish imitation of life, and each time the nurse looked at the EKG and said "Nothing," but now the sound in her voice was saying "Stop it, it's futile."

"Forget it, Jackson," Lieberman said. He wasn't pumping anymore. "Enough."

I looked up as if pulling my head from under water. I'd seen it before in the ER: the intense focus on the patient, so sharp one moment you could feel it, the next moment dissolving into apathy. Some still looked at her but with little interest; others gazed off in another direction or went through the motions, but their movements were now slack. It's over, they were saying with their eyes, the tone of their voices, the way they held their bodies. In their minds they were clearing the table for the next patient. This one—Allie—was history, and they were already forgetting about her.

"It's flat, Jackson," said Lieberman. I could hear the relief in his voice. He'd tried. Done his best. He stood next to me, his arms at his sides. "It's no use."

"Give me the thoracotomy tray," I said. "I'm going to open her up."

No one moved. The nurse drew her hand back from the tray and looked from me to Lieberman.

"This isn't going to work," Lieberman said. "Forget about it, Jackson. We don't do this anymore."

I reached over and grabbed a scalpel.

"It's not protocol, Jackson!"

I ignored him and cut a large incision down the middle of her chest. Then I took the circular saw and cut lengthwise down her sternum. The saw screamed as it churned through the bone.

"She's not going to make it," Lieberman yelled over the noise. "They never do."

"Give me the spreader," I called to the nurse.

Lieberman glanced from me to the nurse to Allie.

"Okay! Fine!" he said. "Let's do it!" The nurse handed Lieberman the spreader, and he helped me insert it in her chest and ratchet it open. I pushed the soft pink tissue of the lung out of the way and could see Allie's still, unbeating heart beneath.

"I'll do it," Lieberman said, but I already held her heart in my hands, squeezing the muscle to force blood through her veins, counting to myself to keep it rhythmic, not too fast, not too slow.

One. Two. Three. I squeezed Allie's heart between my fingers. One. Two. Three. I counted and squeezed again, forcing the blood to circulate. I can do this forever if I have to, I thought. She's not going to die. She can't. It's impossible.

Lieberman told me to get out of the way. He had the interior paddles in his hands, ready to administer a shock directly to the heart.

"Let me in, Jackson!"

I held her heart and waited, then pressed the muscle between my fingers one more time, willing life back into it.

Allie, I pleaded silently. *Please . . .*

"Jackson!"

I was about to stand back, but then I felt it: a jump. A quickening, like a baby's first movement in the womb. With my fingertips still on the muscle, I felt it again, stronger.

"I've got something, Doctor," the nurse called out. The monitor registered the beats, irregular and weak, as if they might give out at any moment. Then louder, stronger.

"Okay," said Lieberman. "Okay."

I stood back amid the bloody sheets and littered remains of sterile packages, gazing into her open chest, watching her heart beat inside its cavity. Strong, steady, insistent; the rhythm of life.

Chapter 4

It was early April, almost four months before. The weather was warm for that time of year, the evening free of fog, and as I drove down the peninsula, the wind off the ocean ran through the long grass like a giant comb, creating waves of light green color that swept up and over the surrounding hills.

Brandt's biotech company, Genederm, was celebrating its fifth anniversary in the home of one of its partners. I'd been held up by an operation and was running several hours late, but the house, a large, modern steel-and-glass construction nestled below the Woodside hills, was still crowded with partyers. I saw Brandt as soon as I entered, towering above the surrounding humanity on the other side of the living room, deep in conversation with someone else in a suit. His wife, Helen, was by his side, looking as usual too beautiful for ordinary surroundings, her face a study in perfect proportions, her lips slightly parted in semidetached repose. She noticed me, smiled and gave a wink, but my path was solidly blocked by bodies and elbows and wineglasses. I soon found myself flowing with the currents of the crowd to the other side of the room, then through a pair of open glass doors and out onto the lawn, where I searched for a table that might serve drinks.

The property was a gently sloping expanse that ended some two hundred yards away at a stand of giant, peeling eucalyptus trees. The lowering sun cast their long shadows back across the grass to where I stood. The sound of laughter and female voices followed.

"Harder! Harder! Don't stop!"

I saw two women—in their late twenties, I guessed—bending over a beer keg. One was reading the pressure gauge, the other frantically working the handle up and down. I walked toward them.

"Harder, girlfriend! Don't stop now! Keep on pumping!"

"I can't! I'm exhausted!"

"Just a little more. Don't give out on me!"

"Okay, that's it, try it now." The one at the pump stood back, brushed aside the sweaty hair that clung to her brow and held out a plastic cup.

Her friend stood up with the nozzle and pointed it her way. "You look like you need to cool off," she said, pressing the lever and squirting the other woman in the face. They both yelped and laughed some more.

Too high-spirited for me, I thought. I probably would have turned the other way, but the one with the nozzle noticed me and said hello.

I introduced myself as she tried unsuccessfully to appear sober. "I'm Paula," she said.

Her friend had taken the hose and was intently filling her cup. She took a sip and then looked up. "And I'm Allie," she said. Her lips parted in a wide, round smile framed by beer suds.

There was an awkward moment when I realized that my hand was in the air to shake hers, which was still holding the beer cup. Her smile got even bigger. She reached out with her other hand and gave mine a playful jerk without letting go. "Pleased to meet you, ah . . . ?"

"Jackson," I said. "Jackson Maebry," I added, because I couldn't think of anything else to say.

"Pleased to meet you, Jackson Maebry," she said, jerking my hand again. Her eyes were light green and varied, her skin so pale it glowed in the reflected light from the house.

"I'd offer you a beer," she said, "but it's all foam. Paula screwed it up by pumping too hard." She released my hand to flick some suds in Paula's direction.

"I work with Dr. Brandt at Memorial," I explained unnecessarily, still at a loss for conversation.

"All hail the great and glorious Brandt!" Paula declaimed loudly, lifting her cup to her lips before she realized it was empty. Allie lifted her glass to her lips, too, and more suds ran down her cheeks. The setting sun outlined the curve of her legs through the light summer dress she wore.

"I guess we all work for Brandt, sort of," she said. "Paula and I are in public relations at Genederm."

Paula tried again to take a drink from her empty cup. "I think," she said, "that we need something in liquid form. Jackson, what would you like, a beer? Wine? This is California, you don't get any other choices."

I chose beer.

"You guys stay here," she said. "There's beer in bottles back at the house." She walked away toward the lighted glass doors and I turned back to Allie. It took a few seconds before we realized we'd been left alone with each other.

She looked down and self-consciously adjusted one of the straps of her dress.

"I never could get the hang of these things," she said, indicating the beer keg. "Guess I didn't spend enough time partying in college." For an instant she appeared completely sober, even sad. The change was so sudden I started to laugh. At that, her eyes widened and she smiled again. "But as you can see, I'm making up for it now."

Her curly blond hair was held by three or four barrettes and combs, the brightly colored plastic ones they sell in drugstores. They would have looked ridiculous on anyone else. Large drops of moisture were still clinging to the down on her upper lip. Other drops had fallen onto her neck and were pooling in the hollow of her collarbone.

"Am I drooling?" she asked me with a look.

I realized I had been staring. "A little. You spilled some beer." I reached out and wiped it from her neck with my fingers.

"Excuse me?" she said, knitting her brows crossly and making me wonder what the hell I thought I was doing. Then she laughed. "You're blushing."

I could feel the heat rising into my ears. "It's too dark to see if someone's blushing," I objected.

"It's not that dark. Anyway, I can feel it." She brought her hand up to my face and touched me lightly. "You're burning," she said softly. She held her hand gently to my cheek for a short time, then took it away. Too soon.

"I think I need that beer," I said, rubbing the spot where I could still feel her touch.

"We'd better go get some over by the pool, then," she declared, stepping gracefully to my side and taking me by the arm, seeming completely sober again. So changeable, I thought. "Paula's probably been captured by her guests," she explained, giving me a little tug forward. "Probably forgotten all about us. She's the hostess, you know. Lady of the manor."

The lawn ended after a few steps, and we were soon making our way through the long grass of the surrounding field, already damp in the evening air. Allie paused, resting one hand on my shoulder for balance while she slipped off her shoes. She held them loosely by her side, a single finger through the straps, and steered me with her other hand toward the pool, a fair distance away at the other end of the house.

"Paula owns this place?" I asked, wondering how many millions she must be worth. "She seems awfully . . . young."

Allie laughed. "In more ways than one. Actually, she's a little older than me, twenty-nine—or so she says. She's married to Brian Luff, the money behind Genederm. She has this thing for younger guys. Older guys, too. Anything that's reasonably humanoid in appearance, if you want to know the truth."

"Paula's husband is *younger?*" I said, feeling out of my league.

"He developed some software or something for the commodities markets and made buckets of money."

"Apparently."

A few other guests strolled about the property, some distance from us. We watched quietly as the sun finished setting behind a far ridge of mountains, the elongated shadows of the eucalyptus trees deepening until they became absorbed in the general blackness of the landscape. For a brief while the sky above the horizon remained brightly lit by the receding sun, then rapidly closed up in darkness. Allie shuddered ever so slightly and pulled close to me.

We turned back to the lighted house.

Allie spoke first. "So you work with Peter at Memorial?" she asked. "Dr. Brandt," she added, when I appeared confused. I wasn't accustomed to people calling him by his first name.

I told her about my job and she told me about hers—she arranged interviews for Brandt and helped handle the press for Genederm. I listened more to her voice than to the substance, barely catching the words as they brushed by me, soft and light like her hair, which, if I leaned slightly toward her, was close enough to smell.

"What made you choose plastic surgery?" she asked.

Inwardly, I sighed. It was a question I was often asked, generally with the unspoken subtext "Why waste training and resources on people's vanity when there are so many real medical needs that go unaddressed?" I wasn't in the mood to be serious, so I gave my usual flip answer. "The money," I said.

She didn't laugh, but then it wasn't all that funny. "I was joking," I explained, realizing I'd made a misstep.

"Oh." It was the least inflected "oh" I had ever heard, like the dull sound of a door closing shut.

I took a deep breath and gave her the serious answer, starting with my father the surgeon, and how I'd always assumed without much thinking about it that I'd be a doctor, too; getting most of the way through medical school before wondering what the hell I was doing there; deciding to drop out but then deciding it was too late to change direction; taking my residency in emergency room medicine and leaving in my second year.

It crossed my mind that I wasn't coming across too well in my own description—indecisive, weak. A wimp, in fact. It was one of the reasons I didn't like to talk about myself. It was too unflattering.

"Why did you quit ER?" she asked.

Because I couldn't stand the pressure, I thought.

"Too many people died," I said. That was true, too. Close to the truth.

She glanced at me skeptically, in case I was joking again.

"Not because of anything I did," I hastened to add. "Or anything I didn't do. Not most of the time. I was pretty good, actually. You end up saving a lot of lives, and that's great; but the others . . . It's just the nature of the work."

"It's the nature of life," she said. "At least you were trying to do something about it."

"Yeah, well, that's the upside."

"I thought doctors got used to that," she said. "People dying."

"Maybe some do. I didn't. Anyway," I went on quickly, trying to lighten the conversation, "in plastics your patients don't die. Usually."

"That's good to hear!" She laughed this time. "And that's it, the whole reason?" I could feel the pressure of her hand on my arm, the slight pull encouraging me to go on.

So I told her more: about watching that man's fingers being sewn back on and what a miracle it had seemed. About giving people a second chance. Rectifying mistakes. Making things right. Undoing fate.

"Maybe that sounds a little grandiose," I said, afraid that I was coming across badly again. First a wimp, now just another pretentious surgeon.

"What?"

"You know, like I'm trying to play God or something."

"Oh," she said, as if her thoughts were a long way off. "Well, you know what they say: if you're going to play at being God, you better know the rules."

We were at the edge of the terrace now, the pool a glowing rectangle of aquamarine amid the crowd.

"Here we are," she said, suddenly bright and cheerful again. She released my arm and gestured in the direction of the bar, only ten feet and about twenty or thirty bodies away. It was a gesture, I realized unhappily, that also meant the conversation was over. We'd arrived at the object of our stroll and her duty was fulfilled.

"There's a bar here," she said. "You can get a beer if you want."

I was being dispatched. No doubt about it.

"Great." I tried not to appear too disappointed, and was beginning to say, "Well, it was very nice to meet you," when I realized that Allie was still looking up into my face and smiling. Apparently she saw something amusing there.

"What? Am I blushing again?"

"No. It's just that you're so—so—what's that word?"

"I'm not sure. Handsome? Charismatic? Sexy?"

She shook her head. "That's not it."

"I was afraid not."

She laughed. "It's your face, its moods. You seem so restless, so—what *is* that word?" She stamped her foot in frustration. "Like you're always changing . . ."

"Changeable?"

"Yes, that's it!" She seemed very pleased to have the exact word, and repeated it to herself. "Changeable."

"You know," I began, "it's ironic you should say that. As a matter of fact—" But I didn't get to say "As a matter of fact, I was just thinking the same thing about you," because at that moment a big, round, smiling face appeared next to us, and Allie, exclaiming, "Brian!," jumped to embrace the roundish body it was attached to. The front of Allie's dress pressed up against the little polo pony embroidered on his shirt as her lips came up to meet his cheek.

"Brian, this is Jackson," she said, partly disengaging herself but keeping an arm wound gracefully around his waist, holding him close. "Jackson, this is Brian, who I told you about. Jackson is Peter's chief resident at Memorial."

"Hey, that's great!" Brian said, switching the beer bottle he was holding to his left hand and shaking my hand with several energetic pumps. He appeared even younger than I'd expected—a boy, really, pleased but awkward in Allie's half-embrace, uncomfortably conscious of the beautiful head that was now resting on his shoulder.

She was probably like that with everyone, I told myself, naturally friendly and flirtatious. It doesn't mean a thing. Not with Brian—he's married. Not with me.

I hadn't been paying attention to the conversation and realized Brian was talking to me.

"So what do you think?" he asked. "How much?"

"How much?"

"Liposuction!" Brian grabbed the roll around his middle and contemplated the bulge. "How much do you think you'd have to vacuum out of that one? Two, three quarts?"

"More like a pint," I estimated. "Possibly a bit more."

"That's all? Suck out a pint of blubber and a whole lifetime of beer consumption erased, just like that. Man, the miracle of modern medicine!" He finished his beer. "So, what does it look like—you know, the stuff you suck out? I mean, is it liquid or what?"

"Not really. It's more congealed. Like chicken fat."

"Really? Raw chicken fat or cooked chicken fat?"

Allie lifted her head off Brian's shoulder and straightened up. "This is fascinating, guys," she said. "I'd really love to stay and discuss it, but I'm sure I've got something else I have to do, like, ah, powder my nose."

"Powder your what?" asked Brian.

"It's an expression, kiddo," she laughed. "Used in *polite* society when discussing things such as, say, bodily fluids." She gave him a final hug, and with a short "Bye now" to both of us, she slipped off into the crowd. My eyes automatically followed until her form was swallowed up among the other guests.

"Great girl," Brian said, gazing after her, too. "Needs a boyfriend, though," he mused. "A real one." He refocused on the empty bottle in his hand. "And I need another beer," he said as if it were a natural association. "How about you, Jackson? You look empty-handed."

I followed him to the bar, where we hoisted a couple of beers and Brian was soon claimed by other guests. I got another beer and drifted off to the side of the bar, staying within reach of the liquor and wondering vaguely if there was anyone else there I knew. Unfortunately there was: my fellow resident Anderson, who looked extremely pleased to have found someone to talk to.

"Great party," he said, coming up to me and standing, as was his habit, too close. He was somehow both short and lanky, and his arms constantly moved about, as if he didn't know where to put them. "So how's the star of the OR?" He called me that all the time, even around other doctors. It was embarrassing.

"Hi, Anderson," I said, stepping back but finding myself trapped by the bar. "How's it going?"

"Like shit," he exclaimed. "Brandt is always busting my balls for some reason. Unlike you, Chief, who can do no wrong in his eyes. Not that I'm complaining."

I grabbed yet another beer as he elaborated on his woes.

"I mean, he's really pissed because this skin graft I did gets infected and we have to readmit the woman to the hospital and pump her full of antibiotics. But it's not my fault."

"Definitely not," I agreed.

"I told her not to take the bandages off."

"It's just so unfair," I said.

"Ah, yeah, it is," he said, confused that I'd stolen his line. "It's damned *unfair,* that's what it is."

We were distracted by a sudden burst of loud voices from the direction of the pool, followed by whoops and hollers. When I looked over, I saw Allie standing in the middle of the commotion. Her clothes and hair were soaking wet, and she was hugging her shoulders, either in modesty—her thin dress was now practically transparent—or from the cold. I guessed she'd fallen in, or jumped.

The people gathered around her were all chattering loudly and laughing. One of the men started to drape a sports jacket around her, but Allie shook it off angrily. He didn't seem to notice—he was as inebriated as everyone else—and tried again to lay the jacket on her shoulders. "Don't touch me, asshole," she shouted, flinging the jacket to the ground. Then she lunged forward and pushed another woman standing by the side of the pool. It was one of those girl-type pushes, with both arms fully extended, ineffectual. The woman pitched back but kept her balance, and Allie hit her again with both hands. This time her fists were clenched. The woman remained upright and tried to laugh it off but was clearly shaken. She shrugged her shoulders and flipped her hair to the side, and I saw it was Paula.

"Bitch!" Allie spat at her, not loudly, but intensely enough to cut through the relative quiet that descended on the scene. Brian soon arrived with a towel, wrapped it around Allie's shoulders and walked her back toward the house, Allie yanking violently at the plastic combs that had become tangled in her wet hair. The bystanders dispersed into the general party and the clamor of voices rose again to a dull roar.

"Wow! A catfight. You don't see enough of those." It was Anderson.

I decided it was time to go. I said good-bye to Anderson—who was still goggle-eyed at the scene he'd just witnessed and mumbled, "Unh? Oh, sure, Jackson"—and went into the house to use the bathroom before the drive home.

I was splashing cold water on my face and trying to figure out which towel to use—the real ones or the expensive-looking paper towels that didn't absorb anything—when I heard voices through the door to the adjoining room. It was Brian, saying something comforting, and Allie, crying. I turned off the water and listened but couldn't really make out what they were saying, just something about having drunk too much and how it would be better in the morning. I wiped my hands on my pants and exited quietly.

For some reason I didn't go home. I went outside and waited my turn at the bar again. I got a couple of beers and walked out across the lawn in back of the pool, where I found a hammock hung between two orange trees. I sat on the canvas edge, rocking back and forth, wondering what I was waiting for and why I didn't just leave. I finished one beer and started on the other. I decided I'd leave when the song was over, then decided that the music was a tape loop and would probably never end, but just sat there anyway, hunched over, sipping my beer, staring at the ground. I'd been in that position for some time when I saw two bare feet stop in front of me.

"You've been chosen as my designated driver." I looked up to see Allie holding two drinks in her hand; her hair was still wet and she was wearing sweatpants and a sweatshirt, which I presumed belonged to Paula. "I guess that means you can't drink this." She raised one of the glasses and drank it down in a few gulps.

"Brian made them," she said, looking woozily at the empty glass in her hand. "We broke into the liquor cabinet. I don't know what it is, but he says that anyone who has more than one isn't allowed to drive for a week. That was my second. This is my third." She raised the other glass to take a sip, and the sweatshirt rode up her body, uncovering the line of her hips above the sweatpants.

"Are you waiting for someone?" she asked.

"Me? No, I—"

"Push over," she said. I felt her body slide next to mine as she sat down and leaned back, lifting her feet from the ground. The hammock pitched backward and then forward, and we both rolled together awkwardly in the middle. She pushed against my shoulder, then squirmed around, her feet still dangling off the end, until she was comfortable. When we'd regained balance and were lying together in the middle, she lifted her glass and took a drink and sighed. Miraculously, it was still practically full. I had spilled most of my beer on my jacket.

"Poise," she said, "a lady must always retain her poise." She sipped her drink. "I fell in the pool. That's why I'm wearing this." She snapped the elastic drawstring of her pants.

"I saw. What happened with Paula?"

"You noticed that?" She grimaced to herself. "Kind of embarrassing."

"Sorry—it's none of my business."

"That's okay. I'm the one who made a public spectacle. Let's just say that, deep down, Paula appears normal enough, but on the surface she's a deeply disturbed individual."

"Don't you mean that the other way around?"

"Hunh? Which way around? Anyway, it was my fault it got out of hand. I was probably drinking too much. Or not enough." She finished her drink and stretched her arms over her head, dropping the empty glass on the lawn.

"Any beer left?" she asked.

"A little." I gave her the bottle and we lay there for a while, not saying anything.

"So that's okay?" she asked. "Driving me home?"

"Sure."

She squirmed closer. I adjusted my arm so that it lay around her shoulders, and she lifted her head to help me get in position. "Much better," she sighed. After a long silence, she said, "Actually, I lied to you earlier. I never went to college."

"Oh?"

"Are you shocked?"

"Very," I said.

She twisted her head around to see my face. "Oh, you're kidding." She lay back on my arm. "Did you have many girlfriends in college?"

"No, not really."

"Working too hard?"

"That would be a good excuse."

"What about high school?"

"I was kind of shy."

"Hmmm," she breathed out softly.

"I think you're the girlfriend I always wanted in high school," I said, intending it as a joke and then suddenly worrying that she might take it the wrong way. Then I wondered what was the right way to take it.

She didn't respond for a beat, then said, "That's nice."

When I thought she wouldn't say anything more, she added, "I want to be the girlfriend you never had in high school."

She fell silent again, then said simply, "Jackson." After a while she said it again, "Jackson," like she was trying out the name to see how it sounded. Soon I felt her body lose its tension and her chest began to rise and fall in a deep, regular rhythm. Another moment and she was snoring lightly, the edges of her nostrils vibrating as she exhaled.

I took the beer bottle from her hand and laid it on the grass and held her tighter. For all I knew, it might be my last chance.

In time, the party began to thin out, the talk and laughter receding from around the pool as if it were being wrapped up in little packages and carried away. About a half hour after my arm had fallen asleep and lost all sensation, Allie woke from her doze and raised her head. "Where did everybody go?" she asked, blinking her eyes into focus.

I helped her up, and she walked groggily inside with me. There were only a few stragglers left, everyone operating at half speed. Brian was splayed out on the sofa, his round head lying back on the cushions like a cannonball, his eyes closed. He roused himself when I sat down next to him, said, "Hey, Jackson," slapped his hand on my knee and then fell back asleep. Allie went off to find her shoes and came back empty-handed, wedging herself in on the sofa between Brian and me.

From what I could tell, Allie and Paula had made up, the way women do after even the worst arguments, and now appeared to be fast friends again. Paula brought in an extra pair of sneakers and knelt before Allie to put them on, Allie languidly stroking Paula's hair as she laced them up. "Such beautiful, straight hair," Allie sighed, caressing her cheek now. "You're so good to me, Paulie."

Paula finished and got up, saying she'd be right back. She returned with a mug and handed it to Allie.

"What's this?"

"Kahlúa. You'll like it," Paula said. "Drink up."

"It's coffee," Allie protested, but drank the contents. Paula went into the kitchen and brought back another cup for Allie and one for me.

Before we left, Paula wanted to take the remaining guests upstairs to see her three-year-old daughter. Allie grabbed my hand, and we followed along behind, tiptoeing into the room, not turning on the lights. We all stood around the little figure, buried deep in the blankets, barely visible in the triangle of light that slanted in from the hallway. The women all cooed how cute she was, and then we tiptoed back out and down to the foyer to say our good-byes.

On the way out Paula took me aside to speak privately. "Take good care of her," she said, clearly meaning more than the ride home. I nodded an "of course." "You two make such a great couple," she pronounced in a stage whisper, loudly enough to be heard by Allie and Brian, who were exchanging a farewell kiss by the door.

———

We drove silently on the empty highway leading into the city, and when we got into town, I asked Allie where she lived.

"Berkeley," she said.

"We missed the turnoff about half a mile ago."

"That's okay," she said. She was sober again, sitting up in her seat with her legs crossed at the ankles and her hands in her lap; looking positively demure, I thought.

"Cute kid," I said. "Paula's daughter."

"Unh." She shrugged noncommittally. I thought we'd dropped the subject when she added, "You know, she's not Brian's child."

"What?"

"Well, she may be, but Paula doesn't know for sure. She was having an affair when she got pregnant, and it could have been either one. If you ask me, the child doesn't look much like Brian."

"You're kidding?" I asked with a short laugh.

"No, I'm not." She laughed, too, but her laugh was even shorter than mine.

"Does he know?"

"No, of course he doesn't." Then she turned to me. "And you can't tell him, either."

"Jeezus," I said, "I hardly know the guy. What am I going to say? 'Hey Brian, have you had your child's DNA tested recently?'" Allie didn't respond. "Jeezus," I said again. "And she's kept this a secret from him for three years?"

"Almost four, if you count the pregnancy." There was something in the way she said it; so matter-of-fact. Her voice was opaque, like the low-hanging sky above the city.

"How could anyone live with a secret like that?" I asked.

She didn't answer. I looked over to try to gauge her mood, but her face was turned to the window. All I could see was her featureless reflection in the black glass.

Chapter 5

I stared for several minutes into the shadows before I realized I was awake. Allie's shrouded figure lay before me, lit only by the yellow light of the streetlamps seeping through the blinds. The duty nurse must have seen me sleeping and turned off the lights. I walked over and switched them on. My watch said it was five-thirty in the morning, about eleven hours since I had been called down to the emergency room. An eternity.

I walked back to Allie's bedside and checked her vital signs. Blood pressure, respiration, blood oxygenation, all within tolerable ranges. Heart rate: 115. Fast but okay.

Allie was in there somewhere under all that damage. Unconscious, thank God, her mind drawn into its inner core, where there is no awareness or pain. We should be home together now, I thought, in bed, in my apartment, I lying beside her, watching, as I often did, the morning light slowly illuminate her face. Sometimes, while she slept, I would trace the fine lines of that face with my fingers, as if only by touching her could I convince myself that such beauty was real.

The respirator whined as it filled her lungs with mechanical breath, followed by a click, then silence as the machine replenished its air.

I reached out to touch her face again. It was now completely unrecognizable. The swelling had continued so that the head looked too large for her body, her features grotesquely distorted or hidden under the hard, glossy surface of bruised purple skin. A series of black stitches ran from her nose along her upper lip and under the dressings that covered her burns. Several other black lines crisscrossed beside her left eye and over her brow. The work of a steady hand, I thought. Somehow, some part of my mind had taken over and done what it was trained to do.

As soon as Allie had been stabilized, we took her to the OR, where a cardiac surgeon sewed up the puncture wound in her heart. An orthopedist removed the bone splinter that had done the damage and fastened the sternum together with wire sutures. The shattered bones in her face couldn't be operated on until the swelling went down, but I sutured the lacerations to bring the torn skin into alignment and minimize scarring as it healed. The nurses debrided the burnt areas, scraping off the layers of dead and charred flesh until it began to bleed, a sign that they had reached living tissue. The third-degree burns—the really bad ones—would never grow new skin. Only scar tissue would form, hard and unyielding.

After the wounds had been prepared, I called down to supply for several packages of frozen cadaver skin, which we laid in strips across the wounds and covered with bandages. In time, the cadaver skin would separate and come off; until then it would protect the raw tissue from infection. The orthopedist then cleaned and bolted the compound fracture of Allie's arm with a steel plate. The bone had split in two and pierced the skin several inches below the elbow—probably broken, I realized, as Allie had tried to ward off the blows that rained down on her face. An image forced itself on my mind of Allie cowering before the assault, her cries steadily weaker until finally, unconscious, she fell silent.

I'd seen many terrible injuries in the ER, but the worst were usually car wrecks, mangled bodies extracted from twisted steel; the violence impersonal, unintentional. This was personal, horrifyingly intimate. Someone had intended each blow. How many blows had there been, I wondered, before she blacked out? How many more while she lay on the ground unconscious? What kind of rage could make somebody do that, over and over, and not stop even as she cried for help? What kind of terrible, uncontrolled rage?

A call for another doctor crackled over the intercom, jolting me back to the present. The greatest danger to Allie now was what was happening inside her head. The CT scan showed no immediate internal damage, but the battering had bruised the brain, like an egg yolk shaken inside its shell, and it was swelling just like her battered skin. The neurosurgeon had drilled a hole in her skull and put in a "bolt," a gauge that enabled us to monitor the pressure inside. I examined the readout: a steady increase. Allie was being given diuretics to expel fluids and extra oxygen through the respirator in an attempt to control the swelling, but it didn't seem to be working. Not well enough, anyway.

As I had done every hour, I pulled back her right eyelid—the left was swollen shut—and shone a penlight into her eye to check its reflexes. Normally, the iris would close up like a camera lens; no response would indicate a critical buildup of pressure. I angled the beam into her pupil and it retreated sluggishly before the light, like an animal wounded on the highway. If the swelling continued, her brain would be crushed against the inside of the skull as if it were in a vise, and there was nothing that I or anyone else could do about it.

I checked the vital signs one more time and walked out of the room.

There was someplace I needed to go.

As I approached the nurses' station, the duty nurse looked up from her papers and smiled.

"Long night?" she asked sympathetically.

"Yes," I said, but it came out hollow and dry, barely audible. I cleared my throat and tried again. "Yes. A long night." I looked at the bank of computer screens displaying the vital signs of the patients in the ICU. They were all active, meaning the ICU was full, probably with casualties from the freeway pileup in Marin. It was why Lieberman had agreed to put me in charge of Allie's case. He had more critical patients than he could handle.

"I'm going down to radiology for a while," I said. "You'll beep me if anything changes?"

"Sure will, Doctor."

"Anything at all."

"Anything at all, I promise."

The elevator rumbled up and the doors ground open. I hit the button for the basement, clanked to the bottom and walked out past the back entrance to the morgue and in through a door beneath a sign saying RADIOLOGY/FILES. The front room was empty, but in the back I found the technician on duty, sitting in his chair with his feet on the desk, earphones on and eyes closed. I put my hand on his shoulder and he gave a start, then dropped his feet to the floor and reluctantly removed the earphones. He didn't seem pleased.

"I need to take a look at the Sorosh file," I said.

He made a show of looking at his watch and moved slowly over to the long cabinets by the wall. "Guess it's pretty vital, huh?"

"It's Sorosh." I spelled it for him. "Alexandra Sorosh."

"When did she come in?"

"Last night. Saturday. Admitted to the ER about six-thirty."

He pushed the drawer shut and walked back to the desk, rummaging through a stack of folders that looked no more neatly arranged than the papers in my office.

"We did the CT around seven-thirty or eight."

He rooted around some more and pulled out Allie's file. I leafed through the papers. "I need the film from the CT," I said.

"If it's not there, it hasn't been printed out yet. It's probably still in the machine." I followed him to the small room, half filled by a computer, where I had stood the night before as Lieberman and the neurosurgeon on call tried to see what was going on inside Allie's head. Through the window was the table on which she had lain, and the gaping hole of the CT scanner that surrounded her head.

The computer powered up, and the tech brought up the files. He clicked on the menu, and an X ray of Allie's head appeared on the screen. About thirty lines transected the image, indicating the many cross-sections the CT had taken of her skull. I asked the tech if I could take over and adjusted the controls to move down through the vertical axis, past the successive cross-sections, until I came to the worst damage, the crushed bone of her cheek and the bony orbit around her left eye.

"Man, that must hurt," the technician exclaimed, bending toward the screen and opening his eyes wide. "What happened to her?"

"She was assaulted," I said, trying not to think of the violence recorded in front of me.

"By who, Mike Tyson?" He let a vacant whistle escape his lips. "Whoever it was must have had a real hard-on for her."

"Jerk," I said under my breath. I concentrated harder on what I was doing, clicking through the images until I came to the one of her lower jaw.

I had noticed it the night before. Lieberman had, too. A thin lucency in the CT. A pale line running through her jawbone, suggesting a fracture. What had really caught Lieberman's attention, however, was an indistinct shape beside it.

"Looks like there might be some hardware in there," he said. He held a magnifying lens over the shape, but a filmy shadow obscured that part of the CT, and he still couldn't make it out. The radiologist couldn't tell, either.

"Maybe it's an artifact," I suggested, meaning a ghost image produced by the scanner. As advanced as the technology was, it wasn't perfect, and reading a CT still required a lot of experience. Often you wouldn't know for sure what was going on until the patient was opened up on the operating table and you could see with your own eyes.

Whatever the case, the fracture—if that's what it was—hadn't been displaced. The bones were still in alignment. We weren't setting her facial fractures that night anyway, so we quickly moved on to look for other injuries that demanded our immediate attention. Now, with more time, I zeroed in on the image and instructed the computer to magnify it. It was a long process, and the tech, clearly getting bored, left the room and asked me to lock up when I was done.

I still couldn't be certain. It could have been a piece of "hardware," as Lieberman had called it, a metal plate used to set a severed jawbone in place. But a metal plate would have come through much more clearly, a solid white square on the CT. This was too murky, and faded off into the shadows.

Clicking back to the earlier image, I zeroed in on the other side of her jawbone. Another lucency, possibly another fracture, glowed faintly in the same place as on the other side of the jaw, but the shadows here were worse and the shape even more indistinct.

It was possible, I thought, that Allie had had an accident. She might have broken her jaw and never told me about it. These lucencies, however, appeared too symmetrical—one each, on either side of her lower jaw—and they were too straight, too perfectly healed. A normal break would not be so smooth: bone "scars" much the way skin does. There would be calcifications around the healed bone, bumps and ridges, like when two pieces of steel are soldered together. These breaks were clean, the kind of cut produced by the high-speed electric saws orthopedists and plastic surgeons use to sever bone. But if she'd had an operation, the surgeons would have needed to hold the bones in place with metal plates, and none were visible. Just those ghostly images, indecipherable.

There were only two possible explanations: an accident or major surgery, and neither made sense, neither explanation jibed with what

I could see on the CTs. And if she'd had an accident, if she'd had surgery, why hadn't she ever told me?

What were you keeping secret, Allie? I wondered. Why is it that even as I watch over you lying comatose in the ICU, I can somehow feel you slipping away from me?

I switched off the computer and watched the image collapse into a bright star in the center of the screen, then vanish with a snap.

Chapter 6

I put two quarters in the machine in the doctors' lounge, pressed the button for coffee, black. I watched the brownish liquid leak into the paper cup, then carried it around the corner to the mail room, rummaging through the leaflets, notices and announcements stuffed in my message box while I drank. The only personal item was a card from Krista, an old girlfriend who worked as a nurse in the hospital. I knew it was from her by the large loopy lettering on the envelope. That and the fact that she left a note for me weekly. The card was a picture of San Francisco Bay, the view from a restaurant we'd sometimes visited. On the back she'd written, "Thinking of you, always."

I tossed it away with the rest of the papers, got another tepid coffee from the machine, then walked over to the phone and dialed zero.

"Switchboard."

"This is Dr. Maebry. I left a message last night for Dr. Brandt saying I needed to talk with him if he calls."

"Yes?"

"I'm just checking in."

"He hasn't called, Doctor."

"I think he's at some conference in L.A. You're sure he didn't leave a forwarding number?"

"He's not on call. We have the number of the doctor who's covering for him. Do you want that?"

"No. You'll beep me if he does call in?"

"It's right here on the message board, Doctor."

I said thanks and hung up.

I had no good reason for being so anxious to speak to him. The critical issues in Allie's care all had to do with her heart and her brain, and Lieberman was on top of those. I'd left a message for Palfrey, the head of neurosurgery, to check on her during morning rounds. The burns were under control; disfiguring, but not life-threatening. Still, I wanted to talk to Brandt, run through the case with him. Get his reassurance.

"You idolize him," Stern had said to me during one of our early therapy sessions.

"I *respect* him," I said.

He waved his hand as if to brush away the response. "It's more than that, Jackson. The way you talk about Brandt, it's with a kind of reverence, almost as if he were a god."

I said that was ridiculous, but when Stern was spinning one of his theories, it didn't matter much what I said. He'd pass it off as "resistance" or "denial," something I engaged in, he said, "to an unhealthy extent." His theory at that moment was that Brandt was a father figure to me, "a replacement for the father who abandoned you and then, well . . ." He made a nervous little cough. "Died."

Stern might have been right, but I wasn't going to tell him so. He could call it resistance, but I hated the feeling I got with him that everything stood for something else, that nothing was as it appeared to be. I'd follow him down his labyrinth of reasoning and come out in the end with nothing—nothing but one more of Stern's theories, which gave him such satisfaction but always seemed to leave me with so much less than I'd started with.

I got another cup of coffee from the machine and called Brandt's home number. There were several rings, and then a blurred female voice answered at the other end.

"Yeah?"

"Mrs. Brandt?"

"Who the hell—" She practically gargled the words.

"This is Jackson." It took a moment for the name to register. "Jackson Maebry. I work with Dr. Brandt at the hospital . . ."

She groaned, and I could hear her turning over in bed. "Sure. The protégé." That was the pet name she'd adopted for me the first night I'd had dinner at their house.

"I hope I didn't wake you," I said, looking at my watch. It was barely seven on a Sunday morning.

She made an unsuccessful attempt to clear her throat. "Well, I'm not entirely awake yet, so if you make it quick, I can go back to bed and sleep this thing off."

"I need to talk to Dr. Brandt."

"Sorry, Jackson, the early bird usually catches the worm, but he's not here." There was more rustling on the other end and the clinking of glass. I heard her drink something, then give a muffled gasp of relief as whatever it was took effect. Her voice was smoother when she spoke again. "He's at some conference for his skin business. In Los Angeles, I think. He's been there all weekend. I don't expect him back until late tonight, or maybe tomorrow. I'm not sure."

"Do you have his number, or at least the name of the hotel? It's urgent."

"Yeah. It always is." She took another drink. "I don't have the number, Jackson. I just don't keep track these days. What about the hospital?"

"They don't have it. It's probably down on his secretary's calendar, but she keeps that locked up tight on weekends. Listen, if he calls in, would you be sure to have him page me at the hospital?"

"It's not likely," she said, "but if he does, I will. What's so urgent?"

"It's a patient. She's been in an accident." There was no response. "Alexandra Sorosh," I explained. "She works in public relations at Genederm. You may have met her there. She's a friend and . . ." And what? I wondered. "I—I just thought Dr. Brandt should know."

There was still no response. I imagined her searching for aspirin, or another bottle of whatever it was she was drinking, the receiver lost in the bedclothes. "Hello?" I said. "Mrs. Brandt?"

I was about to apologize again for the early hour and hang up when she came back on the line. "What kind of accident?"

"Actually, it was an assault. Someone attacked her." There was another silence. "It happened sometime yesterday," I continued. "She was brought into the ER last night about six-thirty. I was on duty—"

I heard a loud crack, the neck of a bottle brought down too hard on a glass's rim. "Shit!"

"I—I was on duty," I repeated, "when she was brought in. She had severe trauma to the head and fractures of the ribs and sternum, a piece of which punctured the heart, causing a cardiac tamponade. Sort of a heart attack. She's stable now, but the edema—"

"Dammit, Jackson! I'm not a fucking doctor. Is she alive?"

"Yes, sorry. She's passed the critical stage. She's in the ICU now." There was no sound at the other side of the line. I wasn't sure if I should continue, or if she was even listening. "Mrs. Brandt?" I said.

I waited through another long silence. Then I heard her hang up.

Chapter 7

It was about a month after I first met Allie.

I got back from the hospital late Friday evening; not too late to go out, theoretically, but I'd fallen asleep with my clothes on and woken up the next morning around ten with Allie already dressed, tugging at my arm and complaining about how hungry she was. I put on shorts, a T-shirt and loafers, and she pulled me out the door and down a couple of blocks to our diner, where I watched her consume her usual cheeseburger and onion rings, this time with a Diet Coke. Afterward, we walked over to Golden Gate Park and lay down on the big lawn—I lay, as Allie sat—beside a giant oak tree. You could smell the sea in the distance.

A few couples with blankets dotted the lawn, and over near the road a large Hispanic family had set up for a picnic with so much equipment I wondered briefly how they'd carried it all there. My "week's" duty at the hospital had turned into a long ten days, one operation following another with no real time off and barely enough sleep between shifts to add up to one good night. My plan was to lay my head in the shade of Allie's lap—I had her turn so her shoulder blocked the sun—and sleep as long as I could.

As she adjusted her thighs under my head to get comfortable, I saw a colored marking on her ankle, but it was immediately hidden from my view as she crossed her legs.

"What's that, Allie?"

"What's what, Jacko?" She called me "Jacko" when she was feeling playful, "Jack off" when she was mad. She reserved my full name for serious conversations or, with a completely different inflection, moments of tenderness.

"*That.* On your ankle. A tattoo?"

She lifted her leg and turned her ankle so I could admire it.

"Like it? I had it done yesterday. It's a heart with barbed wire wrapped around, and it says 'biker chick' underneath."

I couldn't see it clearly without lifting my head, but it looked more like the typical butterfly tattoo. "It's a butterfly, right?"

"Actually, it's a *dragon*fly. Kind of pretty. Don't you think so?"

"I can't believe you got a tattoo. What are you going to do when you're sixty years old and have to explain this to your grandchildren?"

"They'll think that Grandma was a wild and crazy dame. Anyway, you can just zap it off with that new procedure you have. Like that guy, the wrestler you did."

She was referring to one of my patients, a professional wrestler who had come in to have the name of his first wife removed from his forearm. A year later he came back with a new name in its place and wanted that removed. He said he was getting back together with his first wife.

"The procedure isn't that great, Allie. It takes months and still leaves a mark."

"Don't get so serious, Jacko; it's not really a tattoo. It's body paint. I had it done at this place off the Haight. It just lasts a couple of weeks. If you don't wash."

"Lovely."

"I got another one, too. But I'll only let you see it if you're a good boy. It's up here, on my leg." She bent over me, and I could see her smiling upside down. "Wanna see?"

This time I lifted my head as she slowly drew up her dress and opened her legs. There, as high up on the inner thigh as it was possible to get, was another "tattoo." This one was a heart with two cupids floating on either side, holding a golden banner inscribed with my name: "Jackson."

"Pretty ornate," I said.

"That's your response!" She pushed my head away. "Here I have myself practically *branded* with your name—"

"I thought it was just paint."

"Okay, painted with your name, and all you can say is 'pretty ornate'! How totally unromantic can you get?"

"It's beautiful," I said, moving closer. "Beautiful. I just need to get a better look."

She pushed my head away again and laughed and straightened her dress. "Down, boy. I'll let you look later. Lie down again and get some sleep. You should rest up after the week you've had. You'll need it later."

I laid my head back in her lap. "By the way . . ."

"Yes?" she said.

"I mean, that *is* pretty intricate, the design and all."

"It's mine. I drew a sketch of what I wanted."

"Very talented. But what I mean is, it must have taken a long time to, ah, paint."

"It did, almost an hour. I was drinking piña coladas the whole time. They have a bar there, even videos if you want to watch. It's really *neat.*"

"Neat," I said. "But, well, so who was the . . . artist?"

"I don't remember her name."

"*Her* name?"

"Yes, *her* name."

She moved her legs together and moaned slightly. "She was *sooo cute!* She said she liked doing me so much I could come back and have another one done free. Anywhere I wanted."

"You're such a tease, Allie."

"Only with you, Jacko. Only with you."

She ran her fingers through my hair and talked of plans for our two days off. That afternoon she said she'd buy some fresh cilantro for the dinner she wanted to prepare (when I told her I hated cilantro, she adjusted the menu). Then we'd go out dancing at this new club she'd heard about. Allie loved to dance, and I loved to watch her.

"And other things, too," she said.

"And other things, too," I agreed.

"And maybe we can go down to the beach later and take a jump in the water," she said.

"We didn't bring bathing suits," I said sleepily.

"We'll swim in our underwear; no one will notice."

"Great idea," I said. Then remembered: "You're not wearing underwear."

Through half-closed eyes, I saw the children around us running on the lawn. It was one of those moments of pure contentment before sleep, when the sounds get farther and farther away, then seem to become detached from their source and drift through your mind like music.

"Wait, don't move." I felt her fingertip on my eyelid. "There," she said, and I looked up. "An eyelash to make a wish on."

I blew the lash from the end of her finger and realized she had blown at the same time.

"I thought I was supposed to wish," I said.

"No way. Then you could just pluck your own lashes and wish anytime you wanted."

"Oh."

I adjusted my head and drifted off.

I was almost asleep when I felt a wave of anxiety pass through me and imagined myself falling. I woke up with a start, Allie's body stiffening under me. A loud wailing resounded in my ear, as if someone had just switched on a siren. I turned my head to see a child's contorted face and an array of uneven teeth in a mouth that was as wide open as it was possible for a mouth to be. My first thought was astonishment that any noise could be so loud.

I realized it was one of the children belonging to the Hispanic family, a young girl whom I'd noticed even from a distance had Down's syndrome. I had seen her earlier, twirling around on the grass, her ponytails sticking out like helicopter blades. The wailing continued at a high pitch, with only momentary pauses for the child to gulp down air, until her mother rushed over and scooped up the dangling body. She apologized to us and carried her daughter away, murmuring soothingly to her as they went, "*Mi angelita, mi angelita.* Don't cry, my little angel."

I lay my head back down and kidded Allie, "What did you do, make a face at her?"

"That's not funny," she said. Her voice was suddenly cold. She got up so abruptly that my head hit the ground. I stood up, too.

"What happened?" I asked, confused by her reaction.

"How should I know?" she answered sharply. She brushed at her clothes in an agitated way and pulled ineffectually at her hair to get it out of her face. "Let's go," she said.

"To the beach?"

"No. Home. I want to go home." She walked away without waiting for me, her body moving awkwardly with each step, as if out of rhythm with itself.

I gathered up my shoes and ran after her. She was moving quickly, and we were at the corner of the park before I could make her turn around and face me. Tears were rolling down her cheeks.

"What is it?" I asked.

No answer.

"What is it?" I repeated. "Tell me."

The sun was hot by the street, the air still. A lone pine tree cast a sharp shadow over the sidewalk but gave no shade.

"The child had Down's syndrome, Allie. I'm sure it's nothing you did."

"I know that, Jackson," she said.

Three teenagers with Boogie boards passed by, gawking at the emotional scene and laughing together as they moved on. Allie looked away and wiped the tears from her face. "Let's go home, Jackson. Please."

I took her hand and we walked side by side along the burning sidewalk, past the compact houses of the Sunset District. It was dark inside my apartment, and Allie curled up on the unmade bed. I got a glass of water and offered it to her, but she shook her head.

"A beer?" I asked.

Another jerk of her head.

I lay down beside her and stroked her hair.

"Will you always love me, Jackson?" she asked.

"Yes," I said. "Always."

"No matter what?"

"No matter what."

"You don't have to, you know."

"Yes, I do."

"I mean, if you ever want to stop. Stop loving me. That's all right."

"Allie . . ."

She began to sob, clenching the material of my shirt in her fists and burying her head against my chest. She cried for a long time, her body shaking against mine. When there were no more tears, we lay together silently. We stayed that way late into the afternoon, her hands still clasping my shirt.

"Maybe we'll see a movie," I said later.

"Maybe," she said without inflection.

"Maybe walk along the beach at sunset, then go to a movie."

"Okay."

"We'll watch the sunset, get a cheeseburger and onion rings at the diner, then go to the movies."

"That would be nice."

"And we'll buy Twizzlers and bite off the ends so you can drink your Coke through them like a straw." She did that sometimes.

Her mouth smiled, but her eyes didn't.

I brushed the hair back from her forehead. "So tell me," I said, "what did you wish?"

"Wish?"

"With my eyelash. What did you wish for?"

"It's a secret, Jackson." Her voice was weary and she seemed far away. "That's the point about secrets. You never tell."

Chapter 8

I was still in the doctors' lounge, staring blankly out the window, when my beeper startled me out of my stupor. I jumped up, spilling my coffee, and called the Control Center, worried it might be about Allie.

"Maebry here. Is it the ICU?"

"No. Front desk just called."

Relief. My heart began to slow to a normal pace. "A Detective Rossi is here to see you. From the Marin County police department. They sent him up to your office."

The relief vanished. I had been hoping the police would talk to Lieberman and skip me. I got another cup of coffee, then decided against it and threw it in the hall trash as I walked the quarter mile or so of corridors to the surgeons' offices. The light in the central room over the secretaries' desks was off, but I could see the detective through the open door to my office, standing at the window facing out.

He was an immense man. His body seemed to fill up the space in the tiny office, and his broad shoulders visibly strained against his sports jacket, a brown-checkered affair that he'd clearly bought at some specialty shop selling extra-large clothing. His head was tilted back, as if he was looking at the ceiling a few inches above to make sure he'd fit underneath. Black skin glistened through his closely cropped hair as I switched on the overhead light.

"Hello," I said as I walked in.

He turned, and I saw he was holding a plastic bottle of nasal spray up to his nose, his eyebrows raised in mid-inhalation.

"Hello," he said, pulling the bottle from his nostril. "My name's Rossi. Detective Rossi."

Deep blue eyes looked out from his broad face. I wasn't sure I'd ever seen a black person with blue eyes before. Not blue like that.

"Hope you don't mind my coming into your office. The door was open."

"Of course, no problem. I'm Dr. Maebry."

He took a step forward to shake my hand, then realized he was still holding the nose spray. He transferred it to his other hand, reextended his arm across the desk to me and practically swallowed my hand in his grip. "Sorry, I've got a terrible cold." He put the tip of the nose spray back in his nostril and inhaled. "It's this damned city. I can't get used to the weather."

"Where are you from originally?" I asked.

"Toronto," he said, and gave a short laugh. "But at least in Toronto you know what to expect."

There was only one chair for visitors, and it was covered with folders. I scooped them into a pile, dropping several on the floor in the process. He watched silently as I gathered them up with the others and put them atop another pile on my desk. I offered him a seat. The chair creaked as he sat down.

He put the bottle away and withdrew a leather wallet and notepad from his inside breast pocket. The objects looked minuscule in his hands.

"Just a formality," he said, opening the wallet and holding it out for me to see. "We're supposed to make sure we identify ourselves properly."

On one side was a picture with his name, on the other a metal badge. I'd never seen one outside the movies, but it looked real enough. I nodded, and he tucked the wallet away again.

"I wanted to talk to you about the . . ." He looked at his notebook. "The Sorosh case. The assault and battery that was brought in last night."

"Anything I can do to help."

"I'm with the precinct detective squad in Marin. I'll be handling the case, since the assault happened in our jurisdiction. Unless the victim dies; then Homicide will take over. And, of course, if rape is involved, the sex crimes unit will get involved, and there'll be troops of social workers in here. But I guess you're accustomed to all this."

"Yes. No," I said. "Not really. Not like this."

"They told me you assisted in the ER."

"That's right."

"So you were on duty there?"

"Not exactly. We don't have a plastic surgeon permanently on duty in the ER. Most hospitals don't. If one's needed, they just get the doctor on call or whoever's available. I had just finished an operation and was available."

"You were in the ER when they brought her in?"

"I got there a few minutes later."

He took a series of Polaroids from his notepad and started thumbing through them. "Not exactly the sort of thing you want to frame and put on the wall," he commented. I could see from across the desk that they were pictures of Allie taken in the Trauma Room.

"Does that about capture it?" Rossi asked, handing me the photographs. I looked at the pictures for the first time. The flash and the garish colors of the cheap film made the wounds seem even worse. The room tilted out of balance. I carefully laid the pictures back down on the table. "Yes. That pretty much captures it."

"Did a nurse take these, or was it one of the uniformed officers?"

"It was a policewoman—the one who picked up the Vitullo kit." The Vitullo test is frequently administered in the ER to test for the presence of semen in the vagina and other signs that might indicate rape.

"Yeah." He consulted his notebook again. "The lab is closed on Sunday, but we should have the results of the Vitullo back tomorrow or Tuesday, depending on the backlog. Were there any injuries suggesting rape?"

"I don't think so. I'm afraid I was focused on other things." In fact, I'd left the room during the procedure. It had been too long since Allie and I had made love for anything to show. Otherwise, I didn't want to think about it. "You might want to ask Lieberman. He was in charge of the trauma team."

"Right. Dr. Lieberman. He's supposed to be in later today." Rossi was consulting his book again. "I need to talk to him. In the meantime, maybe you can tell me something about the injuries." He splayed the pictures out on the desk with his fingers.

I took a deep breath. "The . . . patient," I began, "had multiple contusions on her face, head and neck, with fractures apparent on her frontal bone—that's here, above the orbital rim—above the eyes, in other words. Her maxilla and zygomatic arch—basically the whole side of her face—also show multiple fractures, as well as the bony orbit of her eye, which looks pretty well shattered." Rossi listened with little expression as I ran through the long list of injuries; once in a while he made a notation in his book, sometimes squeezing the wide bridge of his nose and crossing his eyes as if that would help clear his congestion.

"How recent would you estimate the wounds were?" he asked when I had concluded.

"Not too old. The swelling was new. From the look of the bruises, I'd guess it couldn't have been more than six or seven hours."

"Uh-huh. That's what it looks like to me." He put down his pen, fished out the nasal spray again and took a snort. "Actually, I don't think it's a cold, I think I'm addicted to this stuff."

"It happens. You might want to try laying off for a while."

"Yeah. I should. So the assault was probably sometime in the afternoon. What's her condition now?"

"Cardiacwise, she seems stable. She crashed in ER, but we got the heart pumping again, and there's no major structural damage. Her heart's basically in good shape. The biggest problem, what we can't predict, is brain function."

"Right, the coma. Any idea when she'll come out of it and I can talk to her?"

"I'm hoping she'll come out of it in the next day or so, but there's really no telling when." I didn't say "or if."

"And then there's also the question of what shape the person is in afterward—animal or vegetable, right?"

"Yes. That's right." Inwardly, I cringed. It was one of the things I'd been trying not to think about. Allie might recover from the coma but never speak or walk or feed herself again.

"One of the nurses, I think she's on the trauma team . . ." Rossi consulted his notes. "She told the uniformed officers that you appeared to know the victim. She said you called her by name. Allie, right?"

The intense blue of his eyes was unnerving. I hadn't realized I'd spoken her name aloud. I ran my hand through my hair and tried to collect myself. "We were acquainted," I said.

Rossi was quiet, waiting for a fuller explanation.

"Allie does public relations for Genederm. It's a biotech company in Palo Alto. Dr. Brandt, the chief of plastic surgery here, is one of the original founders. We met at a company party a few months ago."

"Brandt. I've heard of him. He's the guy on TV, right? 'Plastic surgeon to the stars'?"

"He's interviewed a lot."

"Do you have any idea why she was up on Mercurtor Drive?"

"I don't know where that is."

"Up in Marin. They're putting up a couple of new houses on one of the bigger lots. Sure to be expensive. Was she thinking of buying a house?"

"I don't think so. She never mentioned it."

"According to her driver's license, she now lives across the bay, in Berkeley."

"She rents an apartment there. Genederm started out in Berkeley, near the campus."

Rossi patted his pockets for the nose spray and inhaled it like a man gasping for air.

"According to her driver's license and Social Security information, she's twenty-seven years old, born in Carpendale, California."

"I think so." The truth was, I didn't know where she was born. We'd never discussed it.

"Any parents? Family?"

"No. She was an only child. Her parents died some years ago." Allie almost never spoke of her family, but I knew that much.

"Well, I guess that's it," Rossi said, flipping through the pages of his notebook. "Is there anything else you think I should know?"

I wondered if I should tell him more about Allie and me, but it hardly seemed relevant, and I didn't want our relationship dragged into the middle of a police investigation. "Nothing I can think of," I said. "I was just wondering . . ." I hesitated to ask. "Do you have any idea what happened?"

"Not yet. It was definitely an assault of some kind." Rossi gathered the pictures off the table as he spoke. "Probably not with a knife. The wounds are too jagged. My guess is that the assailant hit her with one of the tools that was lying around on the construction site, possibly a claw hammer or a jagged piece of metal. We've got several things in the lab now, testing them for prints. The broken arm is congruent with her trying to fend off an assault. But the weapon must have been pretty heavy or hit it just right. It's tough to break an arm, even a woman's."

I could tell he was visualizing the scene just as I was, but to him it was only professional curiosity.

"And what about the burns?" I asked. "The paramedics said something about a carpet."

"It looks like whoever attacked her rolled her in some carpeting that was on the construction site and doused it with gasoline. I suppose they had some idea of trying to destroy the evidence—the body, that is—but they didn't stick around to see that the fire caught. Probably panicked and ran. Most carpets these days are flame-retardant—fire code—the material probably saved her life. Without that, she would have been . . ." He shrugged.

"Do you have any leads?"

"We're checking on the construction guys who found her, but they look pretty clean. Doesn't look like a robbery. Her purse was lying there at the scene, with about two hundred dollars in cash." He shrugged again. "There are a lot of psychos out there."

He contemplated the nose spray and decided against another hit. "Well, thanks for your time," he said. He put his notebook, pictures and nose spray back in his jacket pocket and rose to leave, seeming to fill the room as he did so.

"One more thing," he said as I stood up to say good-bye. "Did she have any enemies you know of, anyone who might do something like this?"

"No. Absolutely not." The idea seemed absurd.

"Right. Well, here's my card in case anything comes to mind."

He handed me the card. I looked down at it and he was already through the door. He stopped then and turned his head. "I can always reach you here?"

"Most of the time. The switchboard can page me at home if you need me." He walked through the outside office and disappeared down the hall with steady, unhurried steps.

I turned toward the window. A thick fog bled the light out of the day. My office looked out over the entrance to the hospital, and I could see swallows flying listlessly in the wet air, perching on the metal supports of the glass canopy that covered the front walk. Every summer, several of them would get inside the canopy and become confused, thinking they could fly directly up into the sky. I would watch as they battered themselves against the plate glass, finally falling down dazed or dead on the pavement below, visitors stepping gingerly over their small carcasses until the janitorial crew came and swept them up. I'd written several memos to the administration suggesting they fix the problem, all of which were ignored.

I opened my desk drawer, rummaging through papers and pens, canceled checks and patients' insurance forms that I hadn't completed. Underneath were scattered photos, before-and-after pictures of patients I'd operated on, and at the bottom a photo of Allie I had taken shortly after we met. She had just come from a business meeting, and I couldn't believe at the time how good she looked in her pin-striped business suit, cut low, with no blouse underneath. I made her pose by the car with her briefcase, and she was rolling her eyes and telling me it was silly and I should hurry up and take the damned picture. Her hair was momentarily held back with combs, and I could see her small, delicate ears, the oval of her face, its features appearing somehow fragile and impermanent in the light.

I reached in the back of the drawer and pulled out the small box with the engagement ring I'd bought for Allie. I took out the ring and put it in the change pocket of my wallet.

My eyes turned toward the window again and I saw Rossi striding across the parking lot, his massive bulk moving easily, confidently, secure in the knowledge that nothing would ever be big enough or foolish enough to get in its way. I couldn't shake the image of him sitting across from me—those blue eyes that took in everything but never changed expression. I shuddered slightly at the thought.

He made his way to the other side of the lot and got into an old Ford Taurus that looked about two sizes too small for him. It took a while to start, then he drove off the same way he moved: calm, deliberate, as if he had all the time in the world.

A swallow flew under the glass canopy and fluttered anxiously against the glass. I pulled the string on my blinds and let them fall shut.

Chapter 9

I t was past nine in the morning by the time I got down to the ICU. The shift had changed and there was a new duty nurse. I explained I was the doctor for the patient in room three.

"Yes, Doctor. I've got instructions to beep you if there's any change."

"Right, thanks."

"There's been nothing since I came on. Diane's the nurse for rooms three and four. She's in there now, changing the bandages."

"Now? I left instructions that I was to be present."

"Maybe she just wanted to get a jump on the day," she said, smiling.

I swore to myself and went quickly to Allie's room. Dressed only in her standard white uniform, the nurse I took to be Diane was leaning over Allie's bed, beginning to remove the bandages from the burn wounds—a procedure that requires sterile clothing.

"Are you doing a dressing change?" I asked, trying to control the anger in my voice.

She looked up, and I could see that she was assessing whether I was a doctor or an intern and how much she had to defer to my authority. She cocked one of her well-plucked eyebrows.

"Of course I am."

"This is supposed to be a sterile dressing change. Those burns are extremely vulnerable to infection."

"I didn't see an order for that," she said, giving her head a little jerk of defiance. Not one of the hairs in her large hairdo moved out of place.

"I wrote it myself yesterday. I also wrote that I wanted to be present. In any case, you should be able to see for yourself that these are third-degree burns. This side of Bangladesh, that's a sterile dressing change."

"I didn't . . . I . . . It's very busy this morning. The ICU is full, as you may have noticed, and I didn't have the time—"

"Great," I interrupted. "If the burn gets infected and the patient becomes septic, I'll be sure to write up that you didn't have the time to do a proper dressing change."

She took on a wounded look. "You don't have to talk to me like that!"

I breathed deeply and made an effort to collect myself. "Okay," I said. "From now on, sterile dressing changes. Okay?"

She averted her eyes and wouldn't answer.

"Look," I said, "why don't you just get a sterile gown on and we'll do the dressing change. I want to examine the wounds anyway." Without speaking, she walked around me and out the door.

I went to the foot of the bed and unhooked the clipboard with the chart. There it was: "Sterile dressing change, twice a day." I'd even underlined the word "sterile," and had noted that I was to be there so I could examine the wounds while the bandages were off.

I covered Allie's burns with the old bandages and got a sterile gown for myself from the cart in the hall. Diane was gowned, chatting with the duty nurse as if there was all the time in the world.

"Ready?" I asked.

She turned, frowning, and walked by me into the room with her head down, like a recalcitrant schoolgirl unwillingly accepting a lecture from her teacher.

Inside, I slowly and carefully peeled back the gauze and examined the wounds. The burns on Allie's arm, running up her side and over her breast, were mostly second-degree. The blisters were already peeling off to expose the raw, red tissue underneath. We'd leave those alone to heal by themselves, though the skin would never return to normal. The third-degree burns weren't as extensive as I'd feared, concentrated mostly on her shoulder and neck and the side of her head. The cadaver's skin we'd laid over it for protection had done its job: it was already beginning to separate, the tissue below appearing gray and leathery, the charred ends of the blood vessels speckling the surface. The ear, too, had been badly burnt and damaged. It wasn't possible to tell how much could be saved. When it came time, we would have to cut the dead skin away and try, to the best of our ability, to patch the areas with skin grafted from other parts of her body. We'd likely have to construct a new ear, or parts of one, as well.

Diane cleaned the wounds and swabbed them with antibacterial ointment. When the new dressings were on, I took out my penlight and pulled back the lid from Allie's right eye. The reflex was even more hesitant than before. I checked the monitors: the pressure inside her head was still increasing.

"Retinal reflex sluggish," I said, and Diane noted it on the chart, then hung the clipboard on its hook at the foot of the bed.

"Thank you," I said. She snapped off her gloves and walked out of the room.

—

The hospital outside the ICU moved at a leisurely Sunday pace, mostly visitors roaming the hallways, carrying flowers and baskets of fruit, trailing children holding "get well soon" balloons. I had no patients other than Allie and spent most of the day in my office not doing my paperwork, stopping by the ICU every hour or so and calling the switchboard often enough that after a while the operator wouldn't even wait for my question before telling me Brandt hadn't called in.

Along about dinnertime, it occurred to me to call my home number in case he'd tried to reach me there. The machine picked up and I heard my own voice. "This is Jackson Mae—" I dialed in the code, and the tape rewound on its spool with a whir that seemed to go on forever. There must have been ten or fifteen minutes of tape rewinding. My heart sank.

It might have meant there were a lot of messages, but that was unlikely—not many people called me at home. The few people I knew in San Francisco were other residents from the hospital; we'd get together once in a while for a beer, but we had little in common except the shared isolation imposed by constant work, and all we knew to talk about was medicine and hospital gossip. It hardly seemed worth the effort, and our schedules were so busy anyway that we rarely had the chance.

The tape slapped to an end, and the automatic clock announced, "Saturday, six-thirty-five A.M."—shortly after I had left for the hospital the day before. As I suspected, it was my mother calling from her home—my old home—in Princeton, New Jersey. She had begun talking before the beep, and the first thing I heard was an endless barrage of words tumbling rapidly past each other with hardly a pause for breath. She was in one of her manic phases.

It happened periodically, most often when she went off her medication. My mother would have an "episode," as Stern calls it, a temporary break, and these phone calls were generally one of the first indications. If we could get her back on her medication, she'd usually calm down; sometimes, however, nothing could stop her downward cycle once she began it. She'd have to be hospitalized until the medication kicked in and the sickness had run its course. For a time. Until the next episode.

She was speaking as if I were there, on the other side of the line, and was several minutes into her monologue before she realized something was wrong.

"Jack! Jack! Are you there?" But she didn't wait for an answer, just barreled on. As usual these days, it was about the neighbors, on whom she'd developed a paranoid fixation: they were spying on her, looking in the windows, watching her undress. Every time this happened, I'd desperately search for some rational response to calm her anxiety, explaining that the neighbors' house was more than twenty yards away and in the summer the bushes blocked the view, but she insisted they could see in. When I suggested she draw the curtain, she would jump without pause to some other complaint.

This time it was about the neighbors' children, who, she was convinced, were sneaking into her garden and defecating there. She had seen them at night, running across the yard, and then she had gone out and found it, she said. They had been put up to it by their parents, who wanted my mother to move out because they had always envied her and wanted the house for themselves. "I've heard them talking about it," she was saying. "They think I can't, but they leave their window open at night and I can hear them when I'm lying in my bed."

I could hardly bear it. I knew what she must look like, the lines in her face that had grown deeper with the illness even as the skin had shrunk back tight around her skull. She had always been small and thin in a typically Waspish way, but for years I had suspected her of being clinically anorexic, and the cigarettes that she chain-smoked—I could hear her drawing compulsively on one now—had dried her out and made her brittle.

"They want to drive me out of my house, and it's all I have since your father left me." She launched into a tirade about Father's "girl-friend," the woman he married after he moved out and divorced my mother. That had been almost eighteen years ago, and she still talked as if it were happening at that moment. I heard her call my name again, "Jack! Jack!" as if I might have been sitting silent all this time on the other end of the line. She'd always called me Jackson before, until a few months ago. We'd been very formal growing up, my brother, sister and I, addressing our parents as Mother and Father. They in turn called us by our full names. But now my mother had started calling me Jack and calling herself by her nickname from college, Lilly, as if she were flirting.

The pen I was holding in my hand snapped. I looked down and saw that I'd covered my message pad with deep lines: angular scratches of ink, traced and retraced, scored one on top of the other, until the entire paper was almost obliterated in black. As I pulled my hand away, a piece of the pen came with it, the jagged end of the plastic embedded in my index finger. I pulled it out and, as I had nothing else to wipe my hands with, smeared the welling blood across the paper.

The monologue continued, but I didn't try to follow it, just waited for it to be over. Then, as suddenly as she had begun, she stopped, and all I could hear was the faint static of an open line and her irregular breathing. She must have forgotten to hang up the receiver, distracted by some other phantom in her mind. I waited a full minute for her to come back on, then threw the receiver back down in its cradle in disgust.

Chapter 10

I t's all right to hate your mother, Jackson," Stern once said to me. We were discussing one of my earliest memories: Mother in a long summer dress, walking across the porch to where I sat on the floor playing with my blocks. She bent down and I opened my arms to her as she picked me up; but then I realized she wasn't looking at me and her face was completely blank. The next moment, she held me over to the side and dropped me, then kept on walking out the door into the garden. I think I must have been in her way.

"We all have these feelings," Stern said.

I wonder.

It was only later that I began to understand what was going on in our household; why, particularly, Father was rarely home. At first I romanticized his absence: he was a hero, a heart surgeon. He was saving people's lives; the hours he worked demonstrated his commitment to his patients, how desperately he was needed at the hospital. Then he got sued for malpractice in the death of a young girl with a weak heart.

In retrospect, I assume the case was baseless (and, indeed, several years later it was settled out of court), but Mother somehow got it into her head that he was guilty and would rave at him, accusing him of killing that little girl. She would be at the sink or the stove preparing Sunday dinner (the only evening that Father was home), and we—Father, my brother, sister and I—would be, as usual, waiting for what seemed like hours for Mother to serve. To this day I don't know what she was doing in there, through the swinging doors of the kitchen; invariably, the roast or lamb would be burnt, black and shriveled, almost inedible. We would wait patiently at the table, trying to pretend nothing was wrong. And then we'd hear the clank and the cries from the kitchen and Mother howling, "How could you, how could you? That poor girl!" The scene repeated itself many times over the years, and I got to know the gesture well. The first two or three times, I rushed in to see Mother flinging down the sauce spoon or ladle, or whatever she held in her hand, bringing her arm up across her brow and weeping without tears. Many years later, I saw Vivien Leigh play Blanche DuBois in the movie version of *A Streetcar Named Desire*. I thought: That's just like my mother.

Father would try to calm her. He never got angry then. He'd speak reasonably, reassuringly, as if he didn't take it personally. Like a professional, a doctor. Only later, when he got her upstairs to the bedroom, would there be more crashing, and yelling from both sides. We'd hear slamming doors and Mother screaming hysterically, "You killed her! You murderer! Get away from me!" The worst Father would say was "Oh, Lilly, *please*! I'm tired of this!" Though after it had been going on for several months, he changed. Then he would say, "Shut your mouth, will you? Will you just shut your mouth!"

It's strange the things that fill you with shame, but those words do, for some reason, more than my mother's lunatic accusations: Father saying, "Shut your mouth, will you?"—reduced from his proud bearing to talking like a child. It makes my flesh crawl when I think about it. That and one final image: the blackened roast, which I would then retrieve from the oven. I'd get my younger brother and sister some cereal and milk and I'd scrape the burnt food into the trash. I've never told anyone about that, that final thing. Not even Stern. I've told him almost everything else, but I couldn't tell him about the roast.

"It's not a definitive diagnosis, schizophrenia," Stern said. "I've talked to her doctor, Jackson. He doesn't know for sure."

"What about the medications?"

"He's just covering all likely bases."

We spent most of our time discussing this issue: how much my mother's behavior indicated schizophrenia and how much could be attributed to mere hysteria, neurosis and other character disorders.

"Hysterical behavior often imitates schizophrenia," he said.

"She hears voices," I said.

"Well, it's a symptom. Sure."

It was an important issue, because schizophrenia is almost certainly an inheritable trait. If my mother had it, it was only a matter of genetics—random currents in the gene pool, the luck of the draw—whether she passed those genes on to me. I'd looked into the family history on my mother's side: an old Wasp family that seemed to have more than its share of frail, "neurasthenic" women like my mother, and eccentric men who never did much with their lives and usually ended up dying alone in shabby, dirty apartments. How many would today be diagnosed as schizophrenic I couldn't be sure, but I'd calculated the odds that I'd inherit the disease at about 50 percent.

"You've already passed the most dangerous years," Stern would tell me. He was trying to be reassuring, but the truth, which he couldn't conceal, was that he didn't know. And if I had it, there was little he or anyone else could do. "Most people with the disease suffer their first episodes in the teens or early twenties." But not all. It could "blossom," to use Stern's strangely appropriate word, at any time—like a poisonous flower whose seed was slowly germinating inside me. That was my fear—the fear that kept me coming back to him, searching for a reassurance I knew he couldn't give.

Chapter 11

About eight o'clock that evening, I went down to the ICU to check on Allie. As I passed the central desk, the duty nurse informed me that Dr. Brandt was "in with the patient." From the door, I could see his tall figure stooping over Allie's bed.

"Dr. Brandt! Hello!" A feeling of relief filled my body. I wouldn't be alone with this any longer. He'd make everything right.

"Jackson," he greeted me, "I called in and got your message. I took a plane up as soon as I could." He brushed the white locks of hair back from his forehead as he looked up. His face was drawn with fatigue, his eyes registering deep anxiety. I'd seen him like that only once before, when he had particularly bad news to tell a patient.

"It probably wasn't necessary to disturb you," I said, coming up to Allie's bedside and standing beside him. "I just thought you should know. She works at Genederm and—"

"Of course. I'm glad you called."

We stood together, looking down at her. The only sign of life was the gentle rise of the blanket over her chest as the respirator pumped air into her lungs. I thought of telling him about Allie and me. I could have used the support, but I didn't want him pulling me off the case because he thought I'd be too emotionally distraught to handle myself professionally.

"She's been in a coma the whole time?" he asked.

"She was unconscious when they found her." I checked the monitors. "Her edema is bad. Her heart's okay and everything else seems stable. But the pressure inside her skull is high, and building."

He looked at the pressure monitor. "Damn," he said under his breath. "And I suppose the neurosurgeons can't do anything for us."

It was more a statement than a question, but I shook my head no.

"You've got Palfrey on the case?"

"I called his office. He comes back on duty tomorrow."

"It seems like a cliché," Brandt said, sighing, "but you never expect this sort of thing to happen to someone you know. Do they have any idea who—how this happened?"

"There was a detective here. I spoke to him. They don't have any leads yet."

"Good Lord," he muttered, shaking his head. Then he stood straight, took a deep breath and slapped me affectionately on the back.

"Well, there's nothing more we can do now," he said. He told me to go home and get some sleep, I looked like I needed it; and, as he reminded me, the schedule called for me to assist him on an operation the next morning.

—

The sun huddled low over the ocean as I walked across the parking lot to my car. The engine started up, surprisingly, on the first try, and I drove down the quiet streets of the Sunset District to my apartment, a couple of blocks from the beach. Usually I loved these times in the evening, before the fog advanced up the hill from the ocean, when the sky was open and the air was perfectly clear. Today it just felt empty, as if the city had been hollowed out; and all the buildings, the cars moving by and the people walking in the streets only accentuated the emptiness of it all.

The neighborhood is called the Sunset District because it sits on the western edge of the San Francisco Peninsula, where the steep hills of the city level out into a kind of saddle that opens on to the Pacific Ocean. When I first moved there, Sandra, my landlady, took me into the bedroom of the two-room apartment she had remodeled from a garage attached to her house. She had used it originally as a sculpture studio, but she was tight for cash and so decided to rent the space out, advertising it as having an "ocean view." She stood me in a corner of the room and pointed out the window to a patch of water visible between the neighboring buildings.

"You can see the sunset through there," she said. "In the summer, at least. It's too far south later in the year. It's blocked by the 7-Eleven."

There were many evenings I would lie in my bed after a twenty-four-hour-or-more shift, too exhausted to take off my shoes but too strung out to sleep, waiting for the sun to appear. It would already be swollen when it came around the corner of the convenience store, its rim poised for the briefest moment above the water before sinking rapidly out of sight, leaving nothing visible but the flickering blue image of the television across the alley, invariably tuned to *Wheel of Fortune*. Other nights—the majority of them—the fog came in early and heavy and I couldn't see anything. Even the wooden fence outside the window would be no more than a shadow. On those nights I would turn on my space heater, which burns kerosene and blasts a jet of hot air into the room, pull up my wicker armchair and sit there as if in front of a fireplace, waiting for the apartment to get warm enough so that I could go back to bed.

I parked my car on the street and walked the few steps up the path to my door. I could hear Sandra's worn-out vinyl record of *Whitebird* playing in the adjoining house. She was a child of the sixties, but these days the only drugs she took came in half-gallon sizes with the label GALLO on them. Behind the curtains, the lights were not yet turned on, and probably wouldn't be; it was almost nine, and I guessed Sandra had already put away her sculpture for the day and was well on her way to being passed out on the couch.

My apartment was just as I had left it, which I realized was what I had been dreading: the bed carelessly made, Allie's T-shirt balled up by a pillow, left from the last night she'd slept over. Under the covers at the bottom of the bed, I knew, were the wool socks she would push off awkwardly with her toes when we were making love and her circulation finally got going. It didn't seem right that it all should be as it was, unchanged. As if everything weren't different now.

The screen saver on my computer mindlessly spun out its endless geometrical shapes in the dark. Out of habit, I opened the refrigerator and stood before it examining the contents: a piece of pizza that had shrunk over time to half its original size, a carton of milk and a cereal box that I must have absentmindedly put away with the milk. I hadn't eaten in over a day and was thinking in an abstract way that I probably should. My mind was walking through the steps of getting a bowl and spoon, pouring in cereal and milk and sitting down to eat, but I didn't move. Then I heard a bang at the door and the sound of a ten-year-old voice calling my name.

I'd forgotten about Danny.

"Yo! Jack!" The door burst open and Danny's boyish frame rolled across the floor on his skateboard, his cap turned around backward and an oversize Giants baseball shirt hanging down to his knees. He hopped off the board, slammed down on the back with his foot and caught the front with his hand.

Danny was Sandra's son. The father was never mentioned and, at any rate, didn't seem to be a factor anymore. When Danny saw my car outside, he'd often come by and we'd watch a game on TV.

"What's up, Jack?"

He flopped on the couch, picked up the remote from the floor and started surfing through the stations. "You wanna watch the game?"

I swung the refrigerator door closed.

"Where are your helmet and knee guards?" I asked with an attempt at authority. I had once caught him doing thirty miles an hour on a steep hill and had taken him in my car to buy a full set of wrist, elbow and knee guards and a helmet. He would never wear the wrist or elbow guards, for some reason, but I thought I had a chance with the others.

"I took 'em off outside."

"Sure."

He found the game and was soon insulting the opposing team's pitcher.

"It's important," I said.

"Uh-huh," he said. The batter struck out, and Danny let loose with a series of ten-year-old epithets.

I gave up on the safety lecture and sat down next to him.

"So is Allie coming over later?" He said it while still looking at the TV, as if it were no big deal; a ten-year-old using all his self-control to not let it be obvious how much he cared.

"No," I said, "Allie's not going to be here tonight."

He tried to hide it, but I could see the disappointment in his face. He started flipping aimlessly through the channels.

"How about some pizza?" I said.

"Yeah!" His eyes lit up.

"Why don't you go to Raimondo's, okay, and get us one?" Raimondo's was farther away and didn't deliver, but we both agreed they had superior pizza. I gave him a twenty and he dropped the skateboard on the floor, jumped on it and rolled to the door.

"Pizza!" he shouted, and skated out.

"Put on your helmet!" I shouted after him.

Danny had known Allie about four months now, since she started coming over to my place regularly. The first time they met, he had rung the doorbell, surprised that the door was locked when my car was parked outside. Allie had opened the door and said, "Well, hello, and what can I do for you?"

He had shrugged at the patronizing tone and looked at her as if she were clearly an interloper.

"Is Jack in?" he asked, and then, seeing me, he started to walk past Allie, hesitating halfway, unsure. Allie told him to come in. We were just about to eat, a special dinner that Allie had prepared, but she sensed the relationship between Danny and me, even though I hadn't mentioned him to her yet, and asked if he wanted to join us. "Okay, sure," he said. He was almost silent during dinner, answering Allie's questions in monosyllables; but later in the evening, sitting on the couch and watching a game on TV, he warmed up. At first he sat, as only children can, like an awkward doll that had been placed there, his arms straight at his sides, leaning a little away from her; but Allie, as it turned out, knew about baseball and soon impressed him with her knowledge. By the end of the game he was leaning the other way, asleep on her shoulder.

We were like surrogate parents to him. With me he resolutely played the part of a tough kid, but after the first couple of visits, he attached himself to Allie and wanted to be next to her constantly. Once we took him to a game at Candlestick Park, and on the way back to the car he let her hold his hand. I remember his looking up at her—I forget what she was saying—and laughing. It wasn't his macho, Arnold Schwarzenegger laugh, or the mocking laugh he gave when a friend fell off his skateboard—"Tough balls, fuckface!"—it was a normal child's laugh. And it occurred to me—coming as something of a surprise—how easy it can be to make a child happy.

I had hoped I would think of some way to break the news to Danny, but by the time he got back with the pizza, I still hadn't thought of anything.

"What's the score?" He threw the box next to me on the sofa and started ripping off the top, simultaneously grabbing a slice and the remote and switching back to the game.

"Danny," I began, "Allie's not coming over tonight."

"Yeah?" he said around a mouthful of pizza, still expressive enough to be sarcastic, as in "No kidding, you already told me that." But I could see he was also wary. When adults repeated themselves, it usually meant bad news.

"What I mean is, she's not well." He looked at me and stopped chewing. The way he looked would have been funny in any other circumstance, his eyes wide and mouth so stuffed with pizza he couldn't close it all the way.

"Whaddaya mean? She's sick? She's got a cold?"

"No, Danny, she's been injured." The look in his eyes was almost panic. How could I have gotten into this without figuring out what I was going to say? "She's in the hospital right now, but she's going to be fine. She's going to be all right."

Every word took an immense effort to bring out, as if it weighed a ton, but as soon as I spoke, it sounded insubstantial, unbelievable. "We're taking very good care of her. She's going to be just fine." I was repeating myself again.

"Your hospital?" he asked after a moment.

"Yes, she's in Memorial."

"Can I see her?"

There was no way on earth I was going to let him see her. "This isn't such a good time, Danny. Maybe later."

He didn't say anything. After a while I saw his Adam's apple move up and down as he swallowed.

"Later, okay, when she's feeling better. I promise."

He didn't argue, just stared down at the half-eaten slice of pizza he held in his lap. I felt as if I'd ruptured something between us. I wanted to reassure him, but somehow I knew anything I said would just make him more suspicious of me.

"I'm going to sack out, Danny," I said. "I haven't really slept in almost two days and I'm exhausted." I got up from the couch and put my hand on his head, but he didn't move. He didn't look at me, just said okay. I lay down on my bed on the other side of the divider without bothering to undress, and a few moments later I heard him turn off the TV, then close the door behind him as he left.

He'd never left in the past before the end of a game. I wondered if he'd go back to his place. He hated going home until he was sure his mother was completely unconscious for the night. Usually I'd find him curled up on the couch the next morning, using his jacket as a blanket. Even when Allie stayed over, he'd sleep there—though she'd tuck him in with a real blanket—and she and I would make love softly, so he wouldn't hear. I remember joking, "Is this what it's like when you have kids?" and she put her hand over my mouth and kept it there, telling me to be quiet with a fierce look that dissolved only when her head fell back and she collapsed against me.

I buried my head in the pillow and could still smell Allie there, the smell she had when she was sleeping, which was so different from when she came over after work in her business suit, or when she'd been on the floor doing her exercises, or when we'd spent a day at the beach. She swore that she always used the same perfume, but it smelled different, too. It was like everything else about her, so hard to catch hold of.

I pulled my head from the pillow and threw myself over on my back. I'd denied it to myself, but the truth was that no matter how close I got to Allie, there was someplace inside her that she never opened up to me. I thought of the endless nights when we would lie in bed together and, like two children, talk through the early hours of the morning, as if the night were our special universe and nothing else existed, or mattered, but us. We had talked and talked, but she would never tell me about her past—no more than the most minimal details.

I had never asked her because I felt she didn't want me to. I had let her reticence constrain me, and also the fear that I might find out something I didn't want to know. The usual things lovers are jealous of, but maybe also something I couldn't handle. And because of that, I had never broken through to her. I had let so much go by, so much of her that I might never know now.

I sat upright in bed, knowing sleep was futile. In the darkness on the corner table, the message light on my answering machine blinked on and off. Glad for the distraction, I reached over and pressed the button, bringing the machine to life. It was the end of my mother's message. The tape had stopped when I hung up and now resumed where it had left off: the sound of her heavy breathing and fumbling on the other side of the line. I sat there for several minutes waiting for it to be over, taking a perverse satisfaction in letting the tape run, as if each moment was further proof of how crazy she was. God, I hated it when she got like this. I reminded myself to call my brother and have him check up on her. He wouldn't want to. He only went near the house under duress from me or if he needed money.

I was about to hit the stop button and erase the damn thing when there was a clatter on the other end and the buzz of blank tape. Mother must have realized she was still holding the receiver and hung up. I expected the machine to turn off, but as I lay back down, I heard another beep and the automatic voice on the machine announcing, "Saturday . . . seven-twenty-nine . . . A.M."

Then Allie speaking.

"Hey, Jacko. Are you there? Pick up." It was her morning voice, about an octave lower and even softer than usual. She must have called me right after my mother hung up, and I hadn't realized there were two messages on the machine.

"Hey, babe, it's me. Your one and only. Your goddess of earthly delights. Remember?" She waited for me to pick up, then continued. "So I guess you're not there? Already at work. I was hoping to catch you before you left." She said the last with a pout in her voice and then became more serious. "I wanted to talk to you, kiddo. I wanted to tell you not to worry. You worry too much sometimes, you know that?"

I caught my breath and lay absolutely still. "There's nothing to be jealous of, really. It's just . . . It was a beautiful ring, darling. It was a lovely proposal, and you were so sweet . . ."

Sweet. I cringed at the word.

"No, I mean it. I know you hate that word. It was beautiful. But it's just too early. Give it time. I mean, how long have we known each other? Four months?"

Four months, five days, I thought to myself.

"Don't be angry, darling, please. You scare me when you lose your temper like that, like you're someone else and I don't know you anymore. It's not at all what you think. I'm not ashamed of you, Jacko, how could you even think that? I just don't want people to know yet. I don't want them gossiping about us. You know how small this town is. It's better this way, it's just our secret. Yours and mine."

She snuffled back her tears. "God, this is silly. I'll be holding you in my arms again before you even get this message. We're still seeing each other later today, just as we planned? Can't wait, lover. Don't worry. Everything will be fine. Be patient, darling. I love you!" The machine came to the end of the message, clicked loudly and stopped.

I took out the ring—the one Allie had handed back to me, unwanted—then stuffed it back in my wallet. I went to the bathroom, got a couple of sleeping pills from the cabinet and swallowed them without water. The face reflected in the mirror looked strange. I turned my back so I wouldn't have to see.

Allie was wrong. It had been my fault. My suspicions, my jealousy. My anger. It was the worst fight we'd ever had. Terrible, like a nightmare.

I couldn't even remember what I had said, the specifics, the accusations, the threats. I hardly knew what I was saying at the time. But I remembered the fear, the panic at the thought of being abandoned. I remembered feeling out of control, the desperation of trying to stop and not being able to. The anger turning into overwhelming sadness and still not being able to stop.

I'd told myself afterward that it was just a fight, like all lovers have, though I knew it wasn't true. I'd pushed it from my mind, convinced myself that the next time we met, we would laugh about how silly it all was. Next time . . .

My head felt fevered. I splashed cold water on my face, but it didn't help. I knocked two more pills from the bottle, swallowed them and lay back down on my bed to wait for the drug to take hold.

We all count on there being a next time, another day. It's only fair. I had the right to expect it. At least that much. Just one more day. Everything would have been all right then. She had forgiven me, she said so. She said it on the recording.

In time the pills did their work. The anxious roar of voices inside my head became muted and dull, like when you close a window on a busy city street, and I could feel myself being dragged down into sleep—descending, as through a long corridor, past the dark chambers of memory into a bottomless well of regret.

Chapter 12

I woke suddenly in the dark of early morning, my heart racing despite the lingering effects of the drug. The digital clock glowed: half past four. The sheet was twisted in a knot around my legs; my shirt dripped with perspiration.

I untangled myself, dressed in dry clothes and walked around the block to the 7-Eleven, where I drank a full pint and a half of coffee. I filled a second large cup and wandered out onto the beach, where the surfers, their boards already planted in the sand, crouched inside their parkas and waited for the first light of day. I sat and shivered in the wet sea air, drank my coffee and waited for my head to clear.

The night nurses were still on duty when I got to the ICU, another hour to go before the morning shift started at seven. I checked Allie's monitors. The intercranial pressure was still dangerously high. Her retinal reflexes had been taken every hour and were marked off neatly on the chart, line after line, with the notation "Sluggish, nonresponsive." I opened the blinds so that if the sun finally burnt through the fog, it might find its way into the room.

In the cafeteria, the kitchen staff was banging around large stainless-steel trays, each filled to the top with jiggling masses of scrambled eggs and crusty wedges of ham. I grabbed two pieces of cold toast hardening under the infrared lamps and poured another Styrofoam cup full of coffee. Henning, the intern, was sitting in the mostly empty dining room with Crockett, one of the orthopedic surgeons on staff, who was reading the paper while plowing into a huge helping of the scrambled eggs I'd passed up.

Henning gestured in Crockett's direction as I sat down with them. "We're thinking of reporting Crockett to cardiology for rampant cholesterol intake," he said.

"What you don't realize, Henning," Crockett responded without looking up, "is that cholesterol is a vital component in sperm production. This," he said, taking another bite, "is the breakfast of champions."

"A lot of good it would do me," Henning remarked. "I haven't been out of this hospital in the last two weeks."

Crockett's real name was Jerry Crocker. He was in his late forties and had been passed up once already to head his department because even among surgeons he was known for being high-strung. He'd gotten his nickname one day in surgery when the control room kept calling to ask when the operating room would be free. There had been complications with the surgery, and the situation was getting tense. The fifth time the phone rang, Crocker shouted furiously, "Turn that damned thing off!" and hurled his scalpel at it. The blade missed the phone but stuck about half an inch deep in the wall. The operating room burst into applause, and from then on the staff started calling him Davy Crockett, soon shortened to simply Crockett. Which, of course, he loved.

"I can't wait until I'm a real doctor," Henning continued, "then I can make the really big bucks, drive a Mercedes convertible and get all the hot chicks, like Crockett here."

"It's a BMW, and I'm married, but if you want the big bucks, you'd better go into plastics, like Maebry. Real medicine's all going to be managed care sooner or later, and then we'll all be working on salary for the government or the insurance companies and bureaucrats. But the rich will always be willing to pay for a nose job."

"Not that plastics isn't real medicine, of course," said Henning ironically.

Crockett slapped the paper against the table and swore loudly.

"Stock market down?" asked Henning.

"What? No." Crockett grunted. "Listen to this. You know the guy they just picked up for the rape and murder of that missing child?"

Henning shook his head. I hadn't heard of it, either.

"Of course not, your generation only reads the comics."

Henning sheepishly folded the comics lying next to his tray and slid them down into his lap.

"It was on TV," Crockett continued, "maybe you saw it there. Her parents have been on the news a lot. Offered a reward. Anyway, they just caught the killer. Turns out he's got seven prior arrests, three for rape or molestation. He was out on parole when he raped this child, mutilated her body and dumped her in a ditch, and the prison officials say it's not their fault, the prisons are overcrowded. The judge, it says here, refused to be interviewed—I'm not surprised—but released a statement to the press saying that, get this"—he read from the paper—"'all appropriate sentencing guidelines were followed in the case.' That makes me feel much better."

He dug back into his breakfast, talking as he chewed. "You know what they used to do to murderers like this guy? It was called drawing and quartering. Of course, society was less civilized back then. Now we just let these lunatics free to torture and kill innocent children. And the politicians do nothing about it." He grimaced at the forkful of eggs poised halfway to his mouth and dropped it back on the plate as if it were one of the offending politicians. He pushed away his tray and leaned back. "If I were running for office, do you know what my campaign slogan would be?"

"I can imagine," said Henning.

"I'd print up bumper stickers that said: 'The Death Penalty Is Not Enough!' Like it?" He repeated it with satisfaction: "'The Death Penalty Is Not Enough!' Damn, that's good! And then underneath, in italics, it would say, *'Bring Back the Rack.'* I bet you I'd win, too."

"No doubt," said Henning.

"Think about it: how many of these animals are probably wandering loose at this moment in the great state of California alone? I mean, do we breed them here, or do they just come for the sunshine and nice weather?" He looked at his watch and swore again. "Let's go, Henning," he said, pushing back from the table. "We're first up in the OR. Time to go sharpen the saws."

"It's an amputation," Henning explained to me. "Diabetic. His foot's already been taken off, but the gangrene has spread up to his knee. It's not my rotation, but I've never seen an amputation before."

"Live and learn, Henning," Crockett said as they strode off. "Live and learn."

After they left, I went to the trash and fished out the paper Crockett had thrown away. It was folded open to the weekend crime report, most of which was devoted to the capture of the murderer that Crockett had been reading about. To the side, however, was a small notice. It didn't mention Allie by name, just reported that a twenty-seven-year-old Berkeley woman had been assaulted and brutally beaten in Marin and was now in a coma at Memorial Hospital. The police, it said, were investigating a promising lead.

Rossi had said the day before that they didn't have any.

—

Brandt's secretary, Eileen, smiled when I got to his office. "He's on the phone," she said, "but go ahead in. He said he wanted to see you as soon as you got here."

Brandt was standing behind his large mahogany desk, one hand clutching a phone to his ear, the other holding a folder that he waved in the direction of a chair. The TV was tuned to the morning business report, the mute sign showing in the corner of the screen, the remote lying in easy reach next to a row of messages overlapping in a perfectly straight row. From experience, I knew he would answer each one in order, from top to bottom, then discard it.

He tossed the file onto my side of the desk, then ran his fingers through his white hair to push it back from his brow.

"Hold it a moment," he said into the phone, "it looks like they're reporting on the conference." He picked up the remote and struggled with the buttons for several seconds before he got the sound working. He had long, elegant fingers—classic surgeon's hands—that didn't yet show the arthritis that on some days made them stiff and awkward. His eyes turned to the screen, and I opened the folder he had thrown on the desk. It contained copies of Allie's CT scans.

"No, nothing," he sighed a few moments later. "All right. Yes, yes. We'll talk then. Good-bye." He hung up the phone and wrestled with the remote again to turn off the TV. I looked back down at the folder. He was embarrassed by his slight disability and didn't like people to notice.

"Amazing," he said, falling back in his chair. "They interview me for forty-five minutes and don't use a word." He massaged his temples to help clear his mind. "So! More importantly, I talked to Palfrey in neurosurgery. He didn't sound too optimistic, to be honest. The edema is bad, and the damage may well be irreparable. One hates to say it, but . . ." he shook his head, "it might be better for her if she didn't wake up."

My heart sank. I realized I'd been hoping for some kind of magical reprieve from Brandt. It was irrational. I knew the seriousness of the injuries, but his words shook me anyway.

"What about the burns?" he asked. "I didn't want to take the bandages off last night. How bad would you say they are?"

I described their location and severity, and the fact that much of the left ear had been destroyed and would have to be reconstructed. We then turned to the CTs. I moved around to stand beside his chair as we examined the images and discussed various reconstruction techniques. I pointed out the mysterious lucencies and shadows on the jaw that seemed to suggest earlier trauma.

"Could be a hairline fracture," Brandt said. "Doesn't look like surgery. Probably just an artifact produced by the scanner. We won't really know until we operate—if we get the chance."

We were interrupted by Eileen buzzing on the intercom. The operating room had just freed up, she said, and the Valontes baby, whose cleft palate we were repairing that morning, was prepped and waiting for us in the OR.

"On schedule?" Brandt remarked. "That must be a first." He stood, exchanging his suit jacket for a white doctor's smock, and strode out of the room, shouting some last-minute business to Eileen as I followed.

Though Brandt had already described the operation to the parents, he made a point of stopping in the waiting room to reassure them again. It appeared that the entire extended family was there; Filipino, I guessed, all dressed in their best clothes, even the little children, five of them, who sat in a row on the couch in jackets and ties, their legs dangling above the floor. He greeted the young parents, and as the other adults—grandparents, great-grandparents and cousins—gathered around, he patiently reexplained the procedure and answered questions he'd answered many times before. For the nine months of their baby's short life, the parents had had to feed her with a dropper, gently squeezing the milk down the back of her throat drop by drop. Within a few days, Brandt told the mother, her child would be able to feed normally from a bottle and soon would begin to put on weight. The mother embraced Brandt and the father shook his hand, more or less simultaneously, and the children, sensing the general lift in spirits, began chattering and chasing one another around the room before we were out the door.

"I never get over it," Brandt said when we were outside, as if thinking aloud. "A few hours, a simple operation, and you've completely changed someone's life. And they wonder why surgeons have God complexes."

A short while later we were scrubbing up at adjoining sinks. "I hope you'll be able to make it tomorrow night to our dinner," he said to me. "Helen's counting on you being there."

I had forgotten. It was the Brandts' yearly party for his colleagues at the hospital. I was hardly in the mood, but I couldn't refuse. "Wouldn't miss it for the world," I said.

"Good," Brandt said as he thrust his hands into the gloves held for him by the nurse. "Perhaps we can sneak away at some point in the evening. There's something I want to discuss with you."

—

Inside the OR, the tiny baby lay at the head of the operating table, a special infant-size breathing tube taped to her mouth and her little outstretched arm strapped down for the IV. Brandt operated and I assisted, cutting two diagonal flaps of skin in her palate, which we would then stretch across to cover the opening. Brandt's hands were clearly giving him trouble today, and after a while he let me take over.

It was a difficult procedure, working inside the small space of the infant's mouth. It demanded my full concentration, but I had to make an effort to remain focused. At one point, I hit a vein that wouldn't stop bleeding and had to stand back while Brandt and the nurse cauterized it and suctioned out the pooling blood.

"A lot of blood for a little baby," Brandt joked when they were done. "Okay, Jackson. Ready to continue?"

"Ready," I said, but I wasn't. I gazed into the baby's mouth, at the dark cleft behind, and I remembered. The feeling of futility and loss. The images that had chased me from sleep earlier that morning.

"We're almost there," Brandt said. "One more flap and we can start sewing the little one up."

I made the incision, and as the blood welled up behind my scalpel, I could see the dream of the night before as if it were projected inside my head. Allie was sitting before the mirror, brushing her hair with all the movements I knew so well: the careful strokes, the bend of her neck as the brush caught and pulled against the tangles, the steady look of concentration she would get whenever struggling with her hair.

It was the change in her eyes I noticed first.

"It's too damned hot in here," I said, and called for the nurse to wipe my face. But I held my head down so she wouldn't see, so no one would see, the tears mixing with my perspiration.

It was all happening again. The change in her eyes—from help-lessness to fear. Then horror as her hair fell out in large clumps, charred and bloody patches of skin coming with it, sticking and tan-gling in the bristles. The worse it got, the more desperately she pulled at the brush. "Oh God! Jackson!" her voice wailed over that hollow space between us. "Oh God! What's happening to me?" And all I could do was watch, unable to respond to her pleas. Unable to help. "Oh God! Stop it! God! Oh God! Please stop!"

Chapter 13

He put his hand on my arm. That was something my father rarely did, touch me. In my memory he's wearing his white hospital coat, but I know that can't be right. We were in his apartment, the condo he rented after he moved out of the house and got the divorce.

I jerked away and called him names. What does one say to one's father at fourteen? The worst I could think of, I'm sure. But as much as I wanted to hurt him, I already knew he was just trying to save himself—to escape from his crazy wife, the scenes and hysteria, the whole shameful vortex of twisted emotions that was our family life.

We all tried to escape, in one way or another. My mother into her insanity. My sister into an ashram that would allow her to see members of our family only with a "spiritual adviser" present; my brother, in and out of drug-treatment programs his whole life.

We all did it. I could forgive him for that.

"Perhaps what you couldn't forgive," Stern once suggested, "is that he left you behind."

Yes, I agreed. Then shook my head. "No."

"Clearly—"

"No, listen to me, Stern," I said, understanding then what I couldn't have at fourteen. "It was worse, much worse than that. Listen to me. Try to follow. There *was* nothing to forgive, or at least forgiveness wasn't the point. Don't you get it? One of the people he was trying to save himself from was me."

That's what made it so bad. I could understand and forgive all I wanted, but it wouldn't help. Because if my father was right—if he was right about me—how would I ever be able to save myself?

Chapter 14

The afternoon was taken up with examining patients in the Residents' Clinic and trying to contact Palfrey, the neurosurgeon on Allie's case. "The only thing to do now," he said when I finally reached him, "is wait and see." I wondered how many times a day he said those words to anxious family members.

Afterward I went down to look in on Allie myself. I checked the monitors, examined the bandages, then opened the chart to make a few notations. It was all in order, except for the record of her retinal reflexes. The column of hourly notations ended at one-ten P.M. It was now after five. I pulled back Allie's eyelid and shone my penlight in her eye. The contraction had slowed noticeably since the morning. The swelling continued. I turned off the light and let the lid close over Allie's uncomprehending stare.

The duty roster at the control desk showed that Diane was the nurse assigned to Allie's room. The one I'd had the run-in with the day before. I found her sitting on the couch in the nurses' room, a *Cosmopolitan* magazine open in her lap. She didn't look up as I approached; her attention was absorbed by what she was reading.

"Excuse me, Diane?"

She raised her eyes unwillingly from the astrology forecasts.

"Are you still assigned to room three, Ms. Sorosh?"

She nodded a yes warily, as if it were a trick question.

"Could I talk to you about something here in the charts?" I could hear my voice rising and tried to contain it.

She sighed, indicating it was a terrible imposition. "I'm on my break now," she said, and turned back to her magazine.

I spoke as calmly as I could. "It's noted here that the patient is supposed to have her retinal reflexes checked every hour." Diane made no response, other than clicking her long, bright red fingernails together. "But there doesn't seem to be any notation after one-ten. That's four hours ago."

"It's been very busy here" was all she said.

"Does that mean the exams weren't made? Or did you just forget to record them?"

Again no response, just the clicking of those nails. "Excuse me!" I said, my patience running out. "I didn't hear your answer."

She didn't say anything. She simply flipped a page and continued reading as if I weren't there. At that moment I lost it.

"Goddamn it!" I yelled, all the frustration of the last two days breaking through. "Stop reading that fucking magazine and listen to me!" I grabbed the magazine and hurled it to the floor. She cowered back on the couch and let out a little yelp. "Do you have any idea how important this is?"

She stared up at me in dumb astonishment, her mouth gaping. The page she'd been holding had torn off in her hand, and she clutched it now in front of her body as if it might give her some protection.

"You idiotic little—" I kicked the end table with my foot, sending it crashing against the wall. I could feel the adrenaline coursing through my body, sweat beading on my forehead and the palms of my hands, tears of rage forming in my eyes, my heart hammering uselessly against the inside of my chest. I turned away and tried to calm down, holding my head between my hands and waiting for the pounding rush of blood in my ears to subside. After several deep breaths I was able to straighten up and look around. That's when I saw him: a large figure standing down the hall at the entrance to the ICU. Rossi.

I rubbed my eyes and ran both hands through my hair, but when I looked again, he was gone, seeming to leave a huge vacuum behind. I gazed at the magazine at my feet for a moment, then picked it up and held it out toward Diane. She cowered farther away and wouldn't take it.

"We'll talk about this later," I said, my voice still shaking. I dropped the magazine on the couch beside her and walked out to the hallway to find Rossi, assuming he had come to speak with me. I went as far as the elevators and through the double doors to the adjoining wing, but there was no sign of him.

By the time I got back to the ICU, Diane had disappeared. I decided there was no point in trying to find her. I checked the duty roster again and saw that, as luck would have it, she was on for a double rotation that night. In fact, she was marked down for night duty the rest of the week. I called the paging desk and asked them to beep the head nurse for me. When she called in, I explained the problem and asked if another nurse could be assigned to Allie.

"We're understaffed," she told me. "Diane and some of the other nurses are working double shifts." When I insisted, she said she would "see what could be done," which I knew would almost certainly be nothing. Short of writing a complaint to the administration—which, under the best of circumstances, would take several weeks to be acted on—there was nothing I could do officially to solve the Diane problem.

I hung up and called the paging desk again.

"Is Krista Generis on duty?"

"It says here she's in oncology. Do you want me to page her?"

"No thanks," I said, "I'll just call."

Krista was with a patient, and it took her a while to come to the phone, but her voice was as bright and friendly as ever.

"Jackson, how nice to hear from you. It's been so long!"

I'd never been able to adjust to her implacable cheerfulness. Even now it grated on me. But she was a good nurse—one of the best in the hospital—and there was no one else I could ask to do such a big favor.

"Yes, it has, I'm sorry—"Already I was apologizing, which is what I remembered doing through most of our relationship. I started over. "Yes, it has been a while. How have you been, Krista?"

"Good, Jackson. I've been *good.*" She overemphasized the last word, as if giving herself a little pep talk. "To what do I owe the honor of this call?"

"It's about . . . well . . . the fact is, it's too much to explain over the phone. I was wondering if I could come by to see you."

"Sure. It's pretty slow here this evening. Come anytime."

When I got to the oncology ward, Krista was tucking in a patient in one of the semiprivate rooms. She patted down the sheets, deposited a syringe she had just used in the red "sharps" container and came over to me with a big smile on her face. She gave me a hug, then leaned back and looked into my face.

"It's nice to see you, Krista," I said.

"Nice to see *you,* Jackson. What is it, four months since we last talked? Funny how two people can work every day in the same hospital and never run into each other."

"Ah, I've been meaning to call . . ." I said, disengaging from her embrace. We began walking down the hall side by side. She was holding my arm.

"I know, I know. You've been busy. I have, too. You're looking good, though."

"I doubt that."

"Actually, you look pretty tired, and your hair is a mess, as usual." She laughed and tousled my hair. "You shouldn't hide that sweet face of yours. When was the last time you got a haircut?"

"I don't know. A few months."

"Looks like it. Why don't we go to the nurses' lounge? I don't think anyone is in there now."

Krista turned off the TV in the lounge and poured us each a cup of coffee. "Kind of like old times," she said, putting the mugs on the table and sitting next to me on the edge of the couch, which I knew folded out into a temporary bed for nurses who needed to catch a few moments' sleep during long night shifts. We had often made use of it in the past, as well as many others around the hospital, depending on where Krista was stationed at the time.

She put her hand on mine and gave me a knowing smile. "Don't worry, Jackson. I know we're just friends now. We are, aren't we? Friends?"

"Of course, Krista," I said.

She squeezed my hand in hers. "I'm *here* for you, Jackson," she said, focusing on me with a look of concern. "I want you to know that."

"Thanks," I said lamely. "I mean, yes, that's really great. You were always good to me."

It was true, in fact. She'd been an excellent girlfriend, constantly bringing me little presents to commemorate some anniversary in our two- or three-month relationship, cooking meals for me and leaving them in my refrigerator at home when I was on a long shift and we couldn't get together. She'd even clean my apartment and do the laundry.

I lowered my gaze to break eye contact and couldn't help but notice how good she made the otherwise shapeless blue pants and blouse of her nurse's uniform look. Pretty, sexy and nice, I thought. And yet I had never felt anything for her aside from physical attraction, and that passed quickly enough. I thought I would feel something in time, but it just didn't happen.

"Krista," I said, squeezing her hand back, "right now I need to ask you a favor."

"Shoot."

"I've got a patient down in the ICU. Comatose. Generalized edema of the brain. She coded in the ER and we revived her."

"What happened?"

I answered indirectly, describing the injuries but not mentioning the assault. "The thing is, I'm not so sure about the nurse they've got assigned to her. You know what the nursing staff is like here. Half are angels, like you—"

"Flattery will get you everywhere."

"It's true, you're a great nurse. But some of the others, well, you know. I've asked for this one to be reassigned, but that could take weeks. I was wondering if, in the meantime, you could keep an eye on my patient. Check in every once in a while. See that things are being done properly."

"That's no problem. Of course I will."

"Thanks, Krista," I said. "That's really a load off my mind." I closed my eyes and let myself feel a moment of relief.

"Pretty special patient?" she asked.

"What?" I raised my head.

She wore the same fixed expression of sincere concern. "Is she a friend of yours?"

"Ah—yes. That's right. A friend. Her name is Allie Sorosh."

"Allie Sorosh," Krista repeated, as if considering the name. "Sure, I've seen her around here."

"I don't think—" As far as I knew, Allie had never come to the hospital. "You may be thinking of someone else."

"Oh, no. The one with the beautiful curly hair." Krista sighed. "I've always wanted curly hair, mine is so straight and *bo-oring.*"

She still had my hand gripped in hers. I extricated it to reach for my coffee, the tenth cup or so I'd had that day. The only effect it had was to increase the buzzing in my ears, as if the volume had suddenly been turned up on a loudspeaker.

"You remember seeing Allie here at the hospital?"

"How could I forget? It's not every day you see someone so beautiful."

I placed the cup back on the table and Krista gathered up my free hand again, cupping it in one palm and patting it gently with the other. "Don't worry, Jackson," she said. "I'm here for you. I'll always be here for you."

I stared down at the fake Oriental rug beneath our feet, a violent pattern of sharp angles and spikes that made my head spin.

Chapter 15

By six P.M., I was crossing the Golden Gate Bridge. My road map, which had served mostly as a floor mat in the year since I'd come to San Francisco, was still legible enough for me to locate Mercurtor Drive, up beyond Sausalito and through Mill Valley. Even with the rush-hour traffic, I was soon climbing up the steep, winding ridge of mountains that run along the coast, the shallow, green water of the northern bay behind me.

I came to a dead end and turned into what was clearly a construction area, a bulldozed road leading in, rutted and muddy from heavy machinery and littered with building materials. The site was deserted; only a cement foundation, now filled with water, had been finished.

I got out of my car and walked up a second bulldozed road to the top of the property. Two other houses were there, much further along toward completion. One had orange phosphorescent tape strung across the unfinished doorway. When I came closer, I could read the warning in black letters: POLICE LINE DO NOT CROSS.

There wasn't a soul in sight. I looked around quickly to be sure I was alone, then ducked under the tape to get inside. The floor was bare plywood. Exposed pipes and wires still ran overhead. It was an enormous house, with a foyer big enough to play basketball in and a living room that was a full two stories high, windows stretching from floor to ceiling on one side and a balcony running along behind. I wandered around the rooms on the lower level but found only what one would expect in a house under construction: wood shavings, scuff marks and the footprints of workers' boots in the piles of sawdust that lay about the floor.

I held on to the banister and climbed to the second floor, walking the length of the balcony to what was clearly intended as a master bedroom. I entered through the double doors and stood in the middle of the large, empty space. Tall windows framed a view of mountains and sky beyond. The evening sun lit the ceiling white and projected my shadow against the back wall but left the floor in darkness.

That's what I thought it was at first, just part of the darkness. A shadowy patch under the windowsill. I blocked the sun with my hand, and as my eyes adjusted, I made out an irregularly shaped stain on the plywood boards. Brownish. The color of dried blood.

There was a lot of it, I saw, when I came closer. The stain covered a large area of the plywood floor and the bottom of several panels of plasterboard. The panel under the window was missing, and it was evident that a large quantity of blood had flowed through the opening and down into the wall. Five feet or so above, a fine pattern of droplets radiated up and out—the kind produced when an artery is severed in the OR and the blood sprays up in a crimson mist. Parts of the floor were blackened as well. Charred by fire.

This was where it had happened. Three days earlier. Where Allie had been . . .

It was impossible to finish the thought—as if a door had suddenly banged closed in my head, leaving me confused and disoriented. I found myself staring at my right hand, which was covered with some kind of black powder, like the toner used in photocopiers. Left over from when they'd dusted for fingerprints, I realized.

"Stupid!" I said to myself. I wiped my hand against my pants but only smeared the cotton and left my fingers black.

What was I doing here? What did I think I'd find? I looked at the blood and burnt wood and desperately wished I hadn't come. I felt soiled, physically disgusted with myself. I kept trying to wipe my hand, but the stain wouldn't come off. I found the bathroom and started frantically turning the faucets, but the water hadn't been turned on yet, and the plumbing only made an arid gasp as I wrenched the handles open. I had to get out. Leave this feeling behind.

I hurried down the stairs and walked outside. The evening was deepening, and shadows were already turning blue. I could feel the cold air coming inland from the ocean and shuddered at the thought that it would soon be dark. Just leave, I said to myself. Get out of here. Just go home.

"Dr. Maebry?"

I started and turned around, then started again when I saw Rossi coming around the corner of the house. Even in the open air he appeared huge.

"Dr. Maebry?" He stood just a few steps away, the lowering sunlight caught in his blue eyes.

"Hello, Detective." I had an impulse to extend my hand but realized again how filthy it was and stuffed it in my pocket instead.

"Can I ask what you're doing here?"

"I'm . . . I . . . I just came by . . . to take a look." Rossi glanced around the house and then back at me without saying anything. I began to explain: "You mentioned that the attack on Allie—Alexandra Sorosh . . . You said that . . . you mentioned that it happened at a construction site on Mercurtor—"

"This is a crime scene, Doctor. You're not supposed to go wandering around crime scenes. That's why we put the tape up."

"Right. Of course. Sorry. I—I just wanted to see where it happened." He said nothing. It occurred to me that he might have followed me here. Observing me the whole time. "This is it, isn't it?" I asked, as naturally as I could. "This is where she was attacked?"

He nodded.

"How come no one was working here? Where were all the construction people?"

He took out his nasal spray and squeezed it into each nostril, then rubbed the bridge of his nose. He walked beyond me, then turned so the sun was at his back. I could no longer see his expression.

"They stopped temporarily," he said. "Some zoning issue. People around here aren't too keen on development." He looked around again. "It's pretty deserted here most of the time."

"How did they find her? Who would have known she was here?"

"The contractor came by to check on something. It was lucky, I guess. She could have been in there for days without anyone noticing her." He turned his head up at the second story of the house and snorted into a handkerchief to clear his nostrils.

"Do you know any more about what happened?" I asked.

"She was attacked. With a hammer, and then lit on fire."

"I know. That is, you told me. Not the hammer, that wasn't certain, but . . . what I mean is, do you have any idea who did this?"

"We're working on it, Doctor. We're working on it."

—

Rossi walked me back to my car, and as I was trying to start it—the air was already getting wet, and the ignition wouldn't catch—he leaned down to my window and said he wanted me to drop by the station house the next day. There were some things he wanted to go over with me.

"What things?" I asked.

"Just some questions you can help me with."

I asked him if he wanted me to bring the medical records and X rays.

"No. We've already got copies of those," he answered. "So, say around five?"

I said I thought I could make it.

"Great." He slapped the roof of my car. "See you then."

He watched as I backed up to turn around, my wheels getting caught in the mud for a moment; then I jerked forward and drove out through the gate. I glanced back from the road. He was still standing there, looking at me.

Chapter 16

I stopped at a gas station to wash my hands before I got to the bridge. It was a coincidence, I told myself. He probably needed to check on something and just happened by while I was there. Of course that was it. Why would Rossi be following me?

I turned east after the park and drove toward the hospital. I was at least half an hour late for my appointment with Stern, but I knew he wouldn't leave. Workaholic that he was, he had another patient scheduled after me at nine. Monday was his late night, but he was rarely out of the office before eight on other evenings, and he started at six-thirty in the morning, seeing patients who couldn't get off during the day. He worked Saturdays as well, and wasn't averse to scheduling on Sundays if a patient was having a crisis, which in his line of work was fairly often.

I assumed he didn't see much of his family (I met them once at a hospital function: a thin wife and two young daughters with blank eyes, one of whom Stern carried until she began to cry, then gave back to her mother) and whatever free time he did have appeared to be devoted to reading. He told me once that he needed very little sleep—three or four hours a night and he was fine—but there were gray rings under his eyes that had grown steadily blacker and more unhealthy-looking in the year I'd known him. Of course, that may have been simply from the emotional toll of listening to other people's problems fourteen hours a day or—what I suspected—a creeping sense of futility at his inability to do much about them. I once asked him what he estimated his cure rate to be.

"We no longer really talk of 'cures' in this profession," he had responded. "At least not 'cures' as they are commonly understood. You know what Freud said?" I shook my head. "Of course not, they don't teach Freud any longer in medical school, do they? How the mighty have fallen! Freud said that the purpose of psychoanalysis is to take miserable neurotics and turn them into normally unhappy members of society."

"Kind of a low hurdle," I said.

"Yeah," he sighed. "Not low enough sometimes, I'm afraid."

I had told him about Allie in the beginning, when our relationship was new and I was eager to share the news with someone, but I'd come to regret it. Talking about love to Stern, I decided, was like describing a beautiful painting to someone who was color-blind or telling a joke to someone with no sense of humor. The words I spoke and the words Stern heard were the same, but somehow they took on a different meaning in the transmission. "I love her," I'd say, meaning, like all lovers, more than I could possibly explain: that her love for me was like some extraordinary reprieve, or pardon from my sickness and fear. For the first time I had something good, something truly good and beautiful to hold on to. I had her love. And even more miraculous, an even greater gift, I loved her, too, without questions or doubt, and that love was more real than all the history, all the disappointments and twisted anger that I had taken for the elemental fact of me. When I was with her, I told Stern, I'd sometimes think—it would just occur to me—yes, it can be like this. I can be happy, too. But then Stern didn't believe in happiness. He'd said so. At least not for me.

"I *love* her," I'd repeat, hoping somehow I could make him understand, but to Stern, every emotion, every desire or hope, was interesting only to the extent that it provided material for his analysis. Even as I spoke, I could see him mentally categorizing the information content of what I said, storing what he thought was "interesting" and discarding the rest.

"You don't believe in it, do you, Stern?" I asked him one time. "Love, I mean. It's just another Freudian neurosis of some kind, right? What would you say, 'an idealized libidinal impulse,' something like that?"

"Actually," he said, considerably more interested now that the subject had reverted to theory, "Freud never said that love per se was neurotic. In fact, he seems to have believed in it as some sort of irreducible human emotion." He thought for a moment, then added, "Of course, deep down, Freud was really a romantic at heart." He shrugged, as if to indicate that even great men have their failings.

After every session I'd swear to myself that I wouldn't go back, but I always did. I might skip a session or two, but I always went back eventually. Hating Stern for having this hold over me. Hating myself for being so weak.

———

The hospital parking lot was almost empty that late in the evening. Stern's office was across the street in one of the buildings where many Memorial doctors had their private practices. The room in which he saw his patients had one of the best views in the building, straight down the hill to the sea, but Stern preferred to keep his blinds closed, and even when it was still day outside we would sit in relative darkness, each surrounded by the little circle of yellow light cast by the lamps standing beside our chairs. The only other light came from a picture lamp mounted on the wall that shone on his various diplomas: University of Chicago undergraduate, University of California at San Francisco medical school, the American Psychiatric Association and the American Psychoanalytic Association. Stern was nothing if not well educated.

He had left the door ajar, and when I knocked and pushed it open, he looked up from the book he was reading.

"Hello, Jackson. Glad you could make it."

I apologized for being late.

"No problem here," he said, carefully placing a bookmark inside the volume and laying it on a side table. "I was just reading a biography of R. D. Laing," he continued as I sat down. "He was all the rage in the sixties, believed it was society that was crazy and that schizophrenics were the truly sane ones. It's amazing how quickly these people become dated." He frowned and pursed his lips, the idea clearly troubling him. Soon, however, a happier thought occurred: "Of course, society *is* crazy. He was right about that." He chuckled, then cleared his throat to announce a change in subject. "So what's up? You've been late a lot recently, Jackson, when you haven't canceled."

"I was with a patient," I said, not wanting to go into the events of the last days. What good was there in telling Stern? What could he do about it, anyway? Which of his theories was going to help me now? Freud, Jung, behaviorism or Gestalt—or his latest enthusiasm, Jacques

Lacan? He knew them all, and the fact that none really worked for his patients never undermined his basic faith, which was that life was ultimately a mystery to be solved, that someday he would find the hidden key to it all, unlock the secret and make it intelligible. He assumed that knowledge led inevitably to understanding, and once we understood, everything would be okay. But there was no understanding that could explain this trauma and make it go away. Nothing that could make it not have happened.

He sat there staring into the corner of the room, blinking, expecting me to go on. The antique clock on his desk ticked loudly in the silence, its hands pointing to twenty to nine. A twenty-minute void to be filled.

So I told him.

It didn't take long. Just the facts of Allie's assault, as if I were reading a news story about someone else. When I finished, the room was silent again. But Stern was looking at me now, his professional demeanor shattered, his eyes bright with alarm.

"Jesus Christ, Jackson!" he said.

I didn't say anything more. It took him several minutes to collect himself. Then he said: "Jackson, we need to talk about this." He paused. "Jackson?" he repeated. "We really must talk about this."

But I didn't answer. He seemed so very far away. Too far to hear. Too far to reach.

Chapter 17

I didn't go home. I couldn't face that bed again. Not yet.

I drove around until I came to a kind of no-man's-land between neighborhoods, empty streets lined with low-built warehouses, garages, Chinese laundries and fast-food places, the sort of area one never notices, just passes through on the way to somewhere else. I parked my car underneath a dingy sign with broken neon lettering saying TIFFANY'S BAR AND GRILL and walked inside.

It was the kind of bar that would fill up at five o'clock with tired-looking men who had punched out for the day and needed a few drinks before going home to their families. By the time I got there, only the hardened regulars remained, scattered around the cavernous interior, hunched over their drinks and not even watching the TV above the cash register. I sat at the bar and drank silently with the rest. Two twenty-dollar bills pushed to the far side of the counter served as a signal to keep the drinks coming.

At least I could be sure I wouldn't run into anyone I knew. The last yuppie who ventured in here was probably having car trouble and needed to use the phone. It had become a running joke with Allie and me that whatever bar or nightclub we went to, the bartender would greet her by name and usually give us free drinks.

"Do you know every bartender in this town?" I asked the third or fourth time it happened.

"San Francisco's a small town," she answered.

"True."

"The girlfriends and I used to hang out a lot," she said.

"I guess so."

"But that was before."

"Before when?" I asked.

"Before you," she said, pinching my cheek. Then she added, "They're just *friends,* Jackson."

How long ago had that conversation been? A month? Two?

I drank methodically, like the other patrons there. Neither slow nor fast. Deliberate. In step with the alcohol, one drink at a time, in perfect synchronization. A forced march into oblivion.

———

The sun was coming up. That's what woke me. Plus the pain in my neck and shoulders.

My head, I slowly realized, was wedged between the car door and the back of the driver's seat. It took some doing to dislodge it and pull my cramped body into an upright position. Stiffly, as if my whole upper body was in a cast, I craned my neck and shoulders around to locate the neon Tiffany's sign. It wasn't there.

I groaned. Partly it was my throbbing head. Even more the realization that I'd driven here—wherever here was—and had absolutely no recollection of it. "Idiot!" I said, slapping my forehead. It was a weak, halfhearted blow. It hurt anyway. I tried to remember one scrap from the last five hours. One shred of memory. I couldn't. One of these days I was going to get a major DUI, maybe even have my medical license suspended.

"Idiot!" I repeated. This time it was more fatalistic. I'd told myself the same thing so many times before, and it never seemed to make any difference. I didn't know what direction to take, so I just drove straight until I found a street I did know and navigated to the hospital from there.

Fortunately, the morning shift hadn't come on yet and the halls were fairly deserted. I went to the locker room and took a long hot shower, then turned the water to cold until I was chilled through. After I dressed, I put on a white hospital jacket to hide the rumpled state of my clothes. Several cups of coffee later, I was more or less okay.

When I went to check on Allie, I found that the pressure readings on her chart showed a slow but steady decrease. I rechecked to be sure. Slow but definite. The swelling was going down. "Thank God," I said out loud. But no sooner were the words spoken than my head began to throb again. It's not over yet, Jackson, I said to myself. Not nearly over.

———

By the afternoon the pressure had come down enough that Palfrey took Allie off the respirator. When I spoke to him, however, he was still noncommittal. It was impossible to know how much brain damage there had been and when—or if—she would come out of her coma. "All we can do now," he said again, "is wait and see."

My duties that day were largely routine. Rossi called in the afternoon to confirm our appointment and give me directions to police headquarters in the Hall of Justice, or the Hall, as he called it. I said I'd be there in an hour.

I thought of dropping by to see Krista on the way out but decided to phone instead. She was as cheerful as ever. I asked if she would keep an eye on Allie again that night. She said she was on night duty the rest of the week and it was no bother. I thanked her and we hung up after agreeing to get together soon. "I can tell you need someone to talk to," she said.

—

The street in front of the Hall of Justice was tightly packed with police cars, and I had to park a couple of blocks away and walk back. Inside, I expected to see a policeman at a high wooden desk, but it was just like any other institutional building in a big city that had to deal with the public: I was directed through a metal detector and pointed toward the receptionist, who sat behind a thick Plexiglas window and studiously ignored me as I searched for those little boreholes one usually speaks through. Eventually, I knocked on the Plexiglas and she pointed—still without making eye contact—to a phone at the end of the counter. I would have gotten a better connection calling Siberia.

"I'm here to see Detective Rossi," I said over the crackling line.

She mumbled something indecipherable.

"Excuse me? He said he was in the General Works office?"

She mumbled louder and pointed over my shoulder. There was a directory some twenty feet away, affixed to the marble wall.

I took the elevator to the fourth floor and followed the signs to room 411. No one answered when I knocked, so I opened the door, which swung inward. It crashed midway into something on the other side.

"Slowly!" barked a voice from inside.

"Sorry," I said, coming around the door and finding myself practically face-to-face with a somewhat overweight, thirtyish-looking man, his polyester shirt mostly untucked from his pants and a gun holster on his belt. His drooping eyes rolled in dismay when I let the door go and it banged shut again. "Sorry," I repeated. "I didn't hit you, did I?"

"No, I make more noise when I'm hit."

The "reception area" was a tightly cramped space, set off by temporary but apparently long-standing partitions from the rest of the office. A large gouge in the side of the desk testified to frequent collisions with the door.

I told the man I had an appointment with Detective Rossi.

"Oh yeah. Maebry, right? I'm working with Rossi on the case. His liaison, you might say, with the SFPD." He shook my hand. "I'm Mulvane. Take a seat. I'll get the big guy."

I sat in a large wooden chair beside the door, waiting.

"Dr. Maebry."

Rossi's looming figure threw me off balance as I stood, and I fell back down in the chair. I made it to my feet on the second try.

"Thanks for coming down," he said, simultaneously shaking my hand, opening the door and steering me out into the corridor. "They're lending me a desk here while I'm on the case. Unfortunately, the interview rooms here are taken right now, but there's one in Homicide we can use." He let go of the door, and it banged closed behind us. The sound jarred on my nerves.s

"Interview room?" I asked, suddenly aware of how anxious I was.

"Just a quiet place we can talk."

I walked with him down the hall, acutely conscious of his massive shoulder moving alongside me, a good distance above eye level.

"I'm afraid I had an ulterior motive in asking you to come down here," he said after a moment.

"Oh?" Two officers led a woman in spandex and a large, dirty sweatshirt by us. As they passed, I noticed she tried to keep her hands hidden under the sweatshirt. She was wearing handcuffs.

"The truth is, I can't stand hospitals." He laughed. "I must have gotten it from my dad. He was convinced that if he ever went to a hospital, he'd never get out alive. Damned if he wasn't right, too. When we finally got him into one, he was dead within twenty-four hours."

"What did he die of?"

"Pancreatic cancer, I think, though by then it had spread all through his body."

"Sounds like a preexisting condition," I said.

"Yeah, that's what the doctors told him, but he didn't believe it." Rossi smiled. "He was one of those stubborn immigrant types, you know? Real superstitious. Couldn't stand the sight of blood, either. I inherited that from him, too. Last time I gave blood I passed right out, actually fell out of the chair. They had to pick me up from the floor. I'll never do that again. It was the joke of the department for months. It's probably why I never went into Homicide, too much blood. Here we are."

He pushed open a door and led me through a room crowded with desks, coat hangers and files. A couple of guys whom I took to be detectives looked up as we walked past but didn't speak. Rossi opened another door at the back, and I went in first.

"We can talk in here without being disturbed," he said, motioning me to a seat at a Formica table with chipped edges. There were no windows in the room, just air ducts high on the walls and bright fluorescent lights running down the spine of the ceiling. Rossi sat down opposite me and flipped through his notepad, abandoning the effort at small talk.

"So," he said at last, then shifted in the chair. "So." He cleared his throat. "As I said, we're just trying to assemble some information, see if we can find out what happened."

"Sure. Of course. Anything I can do," I said.

He was silent again, as if contemplating my answer.

"Do you have any leads, any suspects?" I asked.

"Well . . ." He pulled at the knot of his tie and moved his neck around in his collar to get more room, his eyes on me the whole time. "You see, Doctor, a lead and a suspect—those are two very different things. You've got to follow a lead a long way before you actually arrive at calling someone a suspect."

"What about this guy they picked up in Oakland for the murder of that girl? It said in the newspaper that he was tied to other murders. Isn't he a suspect?"

"Yeah. The psycho. We're talking to him now, but he's got some new guy from legal services. Fresh out of law school. Real gung-ho. The perp's not saying much."

"But do you think it could have been him?"

"Could be," he said, as if considering the possibility for the first time. "Different MO. Ms. Sorosh wasn't raped, for one thing."

Thank God, I thought. I hadn't wanted to ask. Hadn't wanted to know, really.

"That doesn't necessarily mean he wasn't the assailant," Rossi continued. He took out his bottle of nose spray and plugged it into a nostril, talking all the while. "Some guys are real rote, it's like they have a formula. Others are more improvisational. Depends on their mood." He squeezed the bottle and inhaled hard. "Damn! One day it's my left, another my right, some days my whole head feels clogged up."

"It's the nose spray," I said.

"Yeah, I know. You told me. Gotta get off this stuff. So," he said again, "we just feel that if we could get to know more about Ms. Sorosh—her friends, who she spent time with, that sort of thing—it might help us in the investigation."

"You think it could be someone she knew?"

"We're just trying to get as much information as possible, Doctor. We're really not at the point that we think anything yet." He took out a tissue and blew into it several times, examined the result briefly before stuffing it back in his pocket. "Nothing. It's like cement in there. Anyway, from what we can tell, Ms. Sorosh got around a lot. Sort of wild."

"What the hell does that mean?" I was surprised at my own anger.

Rossi raised his palm placatingly. "Please. No offense intended, Doctor. We're not into blaming the victim. We just have very little to go on, and in cases like this, where there are no eyewitnesses, you have to start with the victim. That's all."

"Sure, okay. Okay," I said.

"We looked through her apartment in Berkeley—with the victim in a coma and all, the judge gave us a search warrant. She seemed to hang out at a lot of clubs in town. There were several invitations and matchbooks from the Asylum Club."

"It's a dance club. She liked to dance."

"Kind of a rough place, I hear. Lotta drugs. We also found men's clothing in her closet. It's hard to tell the difference these days, but this didn't look like something a woman would wear. Wing-tip shoes, ties, that sort of thing."

I'd rarely been to Allie's apartment—we usually got together at my place—and I'd never worn wing tips in my life. I knew the two ties I owned were still in my closet at home.

"And," he said, clearing his throat, "there were drugs there, too.

Not in huge amounts, mostly marijuana and something our lab is checking on—looked like Ecstasy to me—and some prescription drugs, mostly Alprazolam—"

"Alprazolam?" I said.

"Generic name for Xanax," Rossi explained. "It's a benzodi-azepine, like Valium or Halcion—"

"No," I said. "I know that, of course. I mean . . ." I meant I hadn't been aware she'd been taking drugs. Not really.

"Yes, well, the point," Rossi said, "is not the drugs. She was clearly a recreational user. We don't approve, of course, but in this town, it's not one of our first concerns." He paused, as if expecting me to say something.

"I don't know what I can tell you," I said. I felt confused, unable to process all the information.

"You mentioned that you and Ms. Sorosh were acquainted?"

"Yes. We . . . we were friends."

"Friends?"

"Good friends."

"How good?" His tone didn't change, but his blue eyes focused more intently on mine. I looked away to avoid his gaze.

"Do you have any coffee?" I asked. "I could use some."

"Sure. In a moment. You were saying?" He waited a beat, then prompted me again. "Doctor?"

"We . . ." I tried to find the words. "We had . . . a relationship."

"You were having a sexual relationship?" he said, a slight inflection on the "sexual."

"You don't understand—" I stopped. I could hear how defensive I sounded.

"Understand what?" he said evenly.

"We were going to get married. I mean, not right away . . . we'd only known each other a few months, but . . ." My mind returned to Allie's message on my answering machine. I struggled to come back to the conversation. "Look," I said. I took my wallet out of my back pocket and fumbled for a moment, opening the change compartment. "I was going to give her this." I held out the ring for Rossi to see. "Here," I said, making a gesture of handing it to him. He didn't move. His hands remained still, resting on his notepad, his eyes expressionless.

I thought of Allie handing it back to me. Rejected. *No, Jacko, it's too soon.*

"You were going to see her on Saturday?" Rossi continued.

I nodded.

"When we were in your office the other day, I noticed Ms. Sorosh's name marked on your calendar. It was lying open on your desk. I assume it was her name. Allie, right?"

"Yes. We were going to meet later at my place. In the evening."

"The calendar was marked for noon."

I reddened, as if he'd tripped me up somehow. "Right. I wrote that down a while ago. We were going to get together for lunch, but we rescheduled."

"Why?"

"I can't remember. We just did. There was more time in the evening."

"So there wasn't any reason? No appointments or anything. You just rescheduled?"

"No. I mean, yes. There was just more time—"

"And you were in the hospital all day?"

"Yes—I mean, most of it. I had a hole in my schedule in the middle of the day, you know, the time we'd planned to meet. I drove down to the beach and took a nap. I'd been on call most of the week, I'd hardly slept . . . It was a nice day. I . . ."

Rossi put down the notepad. The chair creaked as he pushed back and stretched. It was an abrupt movement for him, and I thought he was ending the interview. I began to put the ring back into my wallet.

"Can you tell me about her other friends, people she knew?" Rossi asked.

"There were the other people at Genederm. She's friends with Paula Luff and her husband, Brian. Paula works there in public relations with Allie. Brian's one of the owners." It occurred to me I should call to tell them about Allie.

"Luff . . . Luff . . ." Rossi was flipping through his notes. "Right. We spoke with them. Said they hadn't seen her in a while."

"I think that's right." Of course they already knew. They would have found out at work, if not from Rossi.

"Any other friends? People she saw frequently?"

I didn't really know any of Allie's other friends. "There were people at the clubs we'd go to. Everyone there seemed to know each other, but I never really got their names."

"None?"

There was a Barry, I remembered, or maybe it was Bart, and a Mike and—I had no idea what their last names were and couldn't even bring to mind what they looked like. All I could remember was that they all seemed younger than I was, fashionably dressed, much more self-confident and better-looking. I used to wonder what Allie saw in me.

"No. Sorry."

"What about the clubs she liked to go to? Do you remember any of those?"

I named a few, then thought for a moment and added a couple more.

Rossi made a note on his pad, got up from his chair and came around the table to stand in front of my chair.

"Did you ever prescribe her drugs, Doctor?"

"No. I wasn't her doctor. We were just friends. I mean—"

"Did you ever give any to her?"

"No, of course not." I looked up at him and then down again at the wallet I was still holding in my lap. "No."

My "no" hung in the air, and though I didn't raise my head, I could feel Rossi's eyes boring into me.

"Well, okay, then," he said at last. "I guess that about does it. Thank you for coming down."

I put the wallet in my pocket as I stood up. Rossi was squinting at me—dubiously, I thought, but it may have been his sinuses.

"Am I a suspect?" I asked, unable to return his look.

He opened the door to usher me out. "Doctor, we're simply gathering information. Examining every angle. That's all. Sorry if the questions seem rough. It's just part of the business."

"Oh. Okay," I said, conscious of having to squeeze by him. "Will you let me know if anything develops?" He looked perplexed for a second. "You know, if you find anything out."

His lips drew back from his white teeth, and I realized he was smiling.

"Yes, of course, Doctor. We'll let you know."

Chapter 18

I ran a red light on the way home and almost cracked up my car.

Rossi said I wasn't a suspect, but every question he asked pointed back at me, and he seized on every little thing I said and did and made it sound suspicious. I thought of those blue eyes again. You wouldn't look that way at someone if you didn't think they were guilty. It was crazy. I was a doctor, for God's sake, a surgeon. I helped people, I didn't hurt them. I'd never been in trouble with the law before. I had to fight the urge to call Rossi at the station house and explain why I clearly shouldn't be a suspect. It didn't make sense. He had to see that.

—

When I got home, I tried to make myself presentable for the Brandts' dinner party. It was about the last place I wanted to be, but I couldn't disappoint Brandt. If I could avoid talking to anyone, I thought, I might be able to get through the evening.

As I did periodically, I got out the nicer of the two sport jackets I owned, and lifted the plastic dry cleaner's bag to examine the blood-stain that would probably never come out. I happened to be wearing the jacket during an emergency procedure at the hospital. I should have thrown it away, but I hung it back in the closet and took out my blue blazer instead. I ironed a pair of already worn khaki pants on the kitchen counter, got a tie and clean oxford shirt from the drawer and found my loafers under the bed. I usually wore running shoes at work, and the loafers were the only proper shoes I owned. There were any number of innocent explanations for the wing tips found in Allie's closet. They might have belonged to someone Allie dated before we met. Or . . . what? Any number of innocent explanations, I said to myself.

Before I left, I phoned Brian and Paula's house, feeling guilty for not having called them before. I'd seen them a couple of times in April, shortly after the party, each time in the city. It had all been extremely friendly; I got on well with Brian, and Allie and Paula were as tight as conspirators. But we'd dropped out of touch during the summer. I assumed it was our busy schedules. Allie never mentioned anything.

The housekeeper answered the phone. She spoke only Spanish, but after I repeated "Mrs. Luff" and "Paula" several times, she said, "*Sí,*" and put down the receiver. I was still waiting several minutes later, wondering if I had dialed the wrong number, when Paula came on another extension. She was breathing heavily, the unmistakable grinding sound of a StairMaster in the background. "Hello?" she gasped into the phone.

"Paula, it's Jackson, Jackson Maebry."

"Oh," she said after a moment. The StairMaster came to a halt, and I could hear Paula catching her breath.

"Paula, I'm—I'm calling about Allie."

"Yeah," she answered distractedly. I could imagine her wiping away the sweat with a towel. "What's up?"

"She's—" Didn't Paula know? Rossi had said he'd interviewed her. "She's in the hospital. I'm afraid she's had a bad accident—I mean, she was attacked by somebody and beaten very badly. She's been in a coma for several days." I paused after each sentence, expecting her to say something, but she didn't. She didn't seem to react at all. "I thought Rossi—the detective on the case—I thought he told you."

"Yeah, we spoke. So how is she?"

"She's in a coma," I repeated. "Unconscious," I explained, thinking maybe she didn't understand. "It's pretty serious." Her reaction, or rather lack of one, confused me. "I mean, we're hoping for the best, but her head injuries are severe. I thought you might want to visit her or . . . or something."

"But she's in a coma, right?"

"Yes, she is."

"Look, I'm sorry, Jackson, but it doesn't sound like there's much I can do."

"Well, no, I suppose not . . . I thought you . . . I mean—no, there's not really anything to *do* right now. We're basically just waiting—"

"Okay," she said. As far as she was concerned, that seemed to settle the matter. "I'm afraid I have to go, Jackson. I've got an appointment, and if I miss this, it will be a week before they can fit me in again. I've really got to run."

"Okay," I said, "bye," but she'd already hung up.

I sat holding the phone until it started beeping, then I hung up, too. I felt as if I'd missed some crucial bit of information without which nothing made sense. I'd known people to respond strangely to bad news; it happens all the time in the ER. Anger, denial, laughter even. But nothing like this. Nothing so cold.

I considered trying to reach Brian at his office, wondering if he might be able to explain what was going on with Paula. But the conversation had unsettled me, and I wanted to put it out of my mind. Besides, I told myself, it was late. Brian was probably gone for the day.

And then I thought: Brian must know about Allie, too. And he hasn't called, either.

—

As I left my apartment, I noticed Sandra's door was open and leaned inside to say hello. She was sitting in her studio—most of what was originally the living room—wearing her usual clay-spattered overalls and tie-dyed T-shirt, her gray hair gathered up in a bun and large hoop earrings with amethysts hanging from her ears.

She invited me in and cleared off a stool by her workbench. I was in no rush to get to the party—all that was required was that I make an appearance, and the later I arrived, the shorter it would have to be—so I sat beside her as she poured me a mugful of the wine she was drinking.

"So what do you think of my latest creation?" she asked, unwinding a wet rag from a mound of clay on the bench. It appeared to be a human figure of some kind, but so mangled and disjointed that I couldn't tell for sure.

"Is it finished?" I asked.

"Either it's finished or I am," she said. "You don't like it, do you?"

"No—I mean, yes."

"That's all right, Jackson, I can't make up my mind, either. It's either a work of unsurpassed genius or it, like, *totally sucks,* as Danny would say." She threw the wet rag over the sculpture and refilled her mug.

"Speaking of Danny, have you seen him recently?" I asked.

"Not the last few days. He's been staying out later and later and leaves before I get up in the morning." I wondered how she knew he'd been there at all. "I can tell when his bed has been slept in," she added in answer to my unspoken question.

"I think he's upset," I said.

"Why? What happened?" She was suddenly worried. It must have been the tone of my voice.

I explained about Allie. I said I thought Danny was taking it hard. I wondered why Sandra was so shocked. She didn't know Allie well. Then I realized it wasn't just shock, it was compassion. Then I realized it was for me.

"Jackson, why didn't you tell me?"

Her face had a look of such overwhelming sorrow that I thought to myself, almost abstractly, how deeply, deeply sad it all in fact was. I tried to say something, but my voice caught.

She opened her arms and embraced me, holding me tight as I sat there on the stool. And then I cried.

After several minutes, she stood back and I made an effort to straighten myself up. "Sorry," I said.

"Sorry for what, Jackson?"

"I didn't mean to cry," I said.

She took a clean towel from the bench and dried off my face. "I think you've got a lot more of that to do before you're finished."

Chapter 19

I parked near the summit of Pacific Heights and walked the half block downhill to the Brandts'. From the street I could see through the large-paned windows of the homes, brightly lit and perfectly decorated like set pieces in a play about domestic happiness. I'd often gone for long walks at night as a child. I'd run away from the screams and banging doors and wander the neighborhood looking through the windows of other people's homes, imagining that everything there was as clean and bright as it seemed, with no terrible secrets or hidden shames.

I rang the Brandts' front doorbell and straightened my sport coat, thinking that I probably should have worn the tie. The door was opened by a young male with a ponytail, tuxedo pants and a black vest with no shirt underneath. I followed him into the foyer.

Most of the guests had already arrived and were now gathered in the living room, talking volubly and juggling drinks and hors d'oeuvres while several more young bodies in vests moved about carrying silver trays.

"Jackson! How nice!" It was Helen, her heels clicking on the marble floor as she came across the foyer. She looked as elegant as ever in a short black dress that clung to her hips as she moved, a pearl choker around her neck and her hair—a whitish blond that appeared completely natural—pulled back in a French braid.

"Thanks, Rudy," she said to the young man with the ponytail as he drifted away.

"Sure, Mrs. Brandt," he said.

"They're members of a dancing troupe. They have a catering company that helps them pay the bills. Cute, isn't he?" she said, eyeing him from behind.

"Very," I said.

"Not your type, I guess. So how's our little protégé tonight?" She took my arm in hers and gave it a squeeze.

I said I was fine.

"No, I don't think so." She pulled me closer, making a little moue as she peered into my face. "You look tired. Is Peter still working you too hard?"

"Not really," I stammered. I never quite knew how to respond to Helen, and the more flustered I became, the more she would flirt.

"Yes he is, I know it," she insisted, leaning closer still. "What are these under your eyes? Circles! That's not good advertising for a plastic surgeon, Jackson."

"I guess not," I said, my attention drawn, as she expected it to be, to the top of her low-cut dress, which fell even further open as she leaned toward me.

She was generally assumed to be one of Brandt's greatest creations and was, in fact, strikingly beautiful—to an almost disconcerting degree. Whenever I found myself near her, however, I couldn't help trying to figure out how old she really was. From what I'd been able to piece together, she was probably somewhere in her late forties or early fifties, but all the usual signs by which one determines age were missing. She could have passed for a young thirty, but even a thirty-year-old would have had more wrinkles. It was as if her face had been partially erased; the only evidence of her real age, if one was quick enough to notice it, were the hands with which she now held me, long and graceful and carefully manicured but no longer those of a young woman. No one has yet invented a way to do hand-lifts.

"I'll have to have a talk with Peter," she said, drawing herself so close that her hips pressed against mine, "tell him to lighten up on you."

I babbled something incoherent, and she laughed and broke away. Having accomplished her objective of reducing me to complete confusion, she told me to "go mingle," gave me a little shove in the direction of the crowd and went off to the kitchen to take care of something. I found the buffet table, took my food over to an ottoman in the corner and sat down to observe the company. The men were all dressed in dark suits—which, in San Francisco, meant they were either in finance or were wealthy doctors; the women, like Helen, all wore the same style of short, tight dress that could have become so universally fashionable only in the age of liposuction.

An hour or so after I arrived, the doctors who had to be up early the next day began to leave. I spied Brandt at the door, seeing a couple out, and went over to say hello as they walked away.

"Jackson!" he greeted me enthusiastically. "I was wondering if you'd make it. Come, let's escape to my office and get something to drink, shall we." He put his hand on my shoulder and we walked back through the living room, Brandt nodding and saying hellos as we worked our way past the milling guests. Helen noticed us as we went by and frowned in his direction.

"Don't keep him too long, Jackson," she said to me, forming her mouth into a tight smile. "The other guests will be jealous."

"Just a little business talk," Brandt responded, without altering his stride. We made our way to a flight of stairs, and Brandt ushered me down ahead of him, through the hallway to his office.

Because of the steep slope of the hill on which the house was constructed, even the lower level had an unobstructed view over the neighboring rooftops to the black water of the bay below. Far out in the darkness, the halogen lamps of a lone cargo ship cast a colorless halo in the wet air.

"Make yourself comfortable," Brandt said, gesturing to one of two large armchairs arranged opposite his desk. The other was occupied by a very shaggy golden retriever curled up on the cushion.

"Hello, Burton," Brandt said, rubbing him behind the ears. The dog lifted his head, and a large tongue lolled out and licked back affectionately. "He's very old and entirely deaf," Brandt explained, giving him a pat and walking over to a small bar by the desk. The dog descended to the floor and lumbered after him, leaning against Brandt's leg as he fixed the drinks.

"Martini all right with you?" Brandt asked.

"Always," I said as he emptied an ice tray into a glass pitcher, then poured the gin and vermouth by eye, dropping olives now and then into the dog's waiting mouth. The dog would chew them for a while, then dribble the mauled pieces on the floor before picking them up again and swallowing with difficulty.

"Very old," Brandt said, stroking his head.

Several photographs lined the wall, mostly of Helen: publicity shots and rehearsal pictures that appeared to be from the late sixties or early seventies. Two of the pictures were framed magazine covers, one from *Esquire,* in which she wore bright red lipstick and held a cigar to her mouth—the headline was A POCKET GUIDE TO THE LIBERATED WOMAN—the other from *Playboy*, in which she wore only a pair of black mesh stockings, her hands cupped coyly over her breasts as she lay upside down, looking up at the camera and crossing her legs like rabbit's ears. The curious thing was that she didn't look particularly younger in the photographs, just altered in some indefinable way.

Brandt poured out two glasses and tasted one. "Perfection!" he announced, handing me mine and taking his seat.

"Excellent," I agreed, feeling myself relax even before the drink took effect. The other residents at Memorial, I knew, thought Brandt too demanding, that he was often capricious and arrogant; but perhaps because I was the beneficiary of that capriciousness—for some reason, he'd liked me from our first interview—I'd always felt at ease and comfortable with his authority. There was something protective about him. Secure. I wondered briefly what Stern would make of that, then took another sip of my martini and decided I really didn't give a damn.

Brandt made a significant-sounding "ahem" and I looked up from my drink. "I mentioned yesterday," he said, "that I had something important to discuss with you."

I nodded.

"First off, you should know that I talked to the hiring committee at Memorial. They still have to sign the paperwork, but I think we have you lined up for the position as attending surgeon in plastic surgery when your fellowship ends next year."

"Thank you," I said. "I'm honored that you think so well of me." We'd spoken of the possibility, but he was now announcing that it was as good as official. "Attending" meant that one had the full rights and privileges of surgeon at the hospital. It was a highly coveted position in plastic surgery at Memorial. It as much as made one's career.

Brandt raised his glass and clinked it with mine. "You deserve it, Jackson. You're a good surgeon."

He "ahemmed" again. "But there's something else I wanted to bring up." He settled deeper into his chair. "I've been looking for someone to join me in my private practice. Someone younger with whom I can share the workload and, perhaps in time, if he wants, to take over much of the practice for me. There are so many other demands on my time. Memorial never lets up. And Genederm is only going to become more of a commitment. What I'm saying is that I'd like that person to be you, Jackson."

"I— Do you think I'm qualified?" I said, unable to mask my surprise. Most of the work at the hospital was reconstructive surgery; I had relatively little experience on the cosmetic side.

"No." He laughed. "I'm not saying we start you out cold. I'd like you to come work with me, assist me on the more extensive operations, maybe take over the less delicate ones with my supervision."

It was as if someone had waved a magic wand and every professional ambition I'd had was suddenly realized: a prestigious position at Memorial and a partnership in one of the most lucrative practices in the country. A few days ago I would have rushed home to tell Allie the good news. Now it seemed almost unimportant.

"I'd be thrilled," I said.

"Good. It's settled." We clinked our now empty glasses and Brandt got up to mix another batch at the bar. "You know what makes a really great martini?" Brandt said, looking around to feed an olive to the dog, who had fallen asleep on the rug by the door.

"The gin?"

"A common misconception," Brandt said, popping the olive in his own mouth. "Gin—even the best gin—is basically swill, after all. It started out as the cheap drink for the lower classes in London. It's the vermouth that transforms it into that exquisite thing called a martini. The secret," he said, turning back to me with the pitcher in hand, "is getting just the right proportions. In other words, it is an issue of *art.*"

He sat back down and poured us each another drink. "Did I ever tell you that I originally did my residency in cardiac surgery?" I shook my head. "I did, four years of it. But I realized I wanted to be more than a plumber unclogging stopped-up pipes."

I smiled politely. It was an old joke.

He laughed. "Okay, you've heard it before, but it's true. Most of medicine is really just a trade. It's memorization and rote response. You know that from your ER training. When someone comes in with internal bleeding in his abdomen, there are certain steps you take, a certain procedure you're trained to follow. You don't make it up as you go along. There may be a lot of technique involved, craft even, but there's very little creativity.

"It's different with plastic surgery. Plastics is the only field where the doctor is more than a trained technician. At least the best are. In plastics you're dealing with the whole person, with his image of himself. His desires. His dreams. You have to be more than a doctor. You have to be an artist." He thought for a moment. "The only difference is, you're working on living tissue. You're molding life. There's nothing in this world like it. Nothing." He'd been contemplating his drink all this time but now turned his eyes up to me. "That's what I see in you, Jackson. You're an artist."

I took a long draft of my martini, embarrassed by the compliment. "Most plastic surgeons aren't, as a matter of fact. They may think of themselves as artists, but they're really just technicians. Every nose they do is the same, as if it came off an assembly line or was copied from the most popular model of the time, no matter how inappropriate it is to the rest of the face." I thought of Anderson, the resident who took four hours on a simple nose job, and every one came out looking like Kate Moss.

"I'm not just talking about Anderson," Brandt said, and we laughed again. "Only a minority, a small minority, of plastic surgeons can see the unique beauty in each face and enhance it, improve on nature. Correct God's mistakes, as it were, and evoke the true beauty dormant in a person's face. That's the challenge, that's what makes it so damned interesting."

At that moment, the door opened behind me and I heard a pained yelp from the dog.

"Damn it, Burton!" It was Helen. She gave the dog a kick with one of her high-heeled shoes as he struggled to his feet. "Peter, really!" she exclaimed, kicking at the dog again to get him moving. "I don't know why you keep that beast. He's old and blind and his breath smells horrible. We should just get rid of him." Burton slunk over to Brandt's chair, wheezing from the effort, and leaned his head against his master's leg. "There, there, boy," Brandt murmured, softly stroking the dog's fur.

"Sorry to break things up, gentlemen," Helen said as she bustled around the room, "but the guests are leaving, and one of our distinguished medical matrons seems to have left her purse somewhere." She tossed the pillows about on the couch, then strode back to the door and flipped a switch, bathing the room in a harsh white glare from the overhead lights. Like last call in a bar, I thought.

"Do you like to sit in the dark?" she asked crossly, turning on the remaining lamps as she searched. "You're going to make yourselves blind and not be able to operate anymore. What would your patients do then?" Her voice was impatient, unnecessarily loud. "You're at the end of your career, Peter, but Jackson's still young. He's got many years ahead of him. He should take care of himself."

She gave up on the purse and came up behind my chair, running her hand over my hair as if brushing it in place. Brandt simply sipped at his drink without responding and continued patting the dog's head; much, I thought, as Helen was patting mine. The blazing lights sharply reflected our little scene in the window. I saw Helen glower at Brandt and then jerk back her hand with a gesture of frustration.

"Well, the purse isn't here," she huffed, walking to the door. "I guess Mrs. Vice Chairman will just have to do without her Valium fix until she gets home." She twisted her head around for one last look at Brandt as she exited. "It might be nice if you made a final appearance before they all left," she said, closing the door with a bang.

Brandt put his hand under the dog's chin and stroked it lightly. "Here, Burton," he said, "how are you, boy?" The dog shivered and made little coughing sounds as if something was caught in his throat. Brandt held up the drooping head and gently pried his mouth open, holding down the tongue and peering inside.

"Nothing there, Burton," he said, closing the dog's mouth and stroking his muzzle. "Probably neurological," he whispered up to me. "And he's got cancer. I checked. Inoperable." He held the dog's head again on both sides and turned it so he could look him in the eyes. "You're just getting old, boy. Just getting old."

Chapter 20

When I got home, I found the door to my apartment unlocked and Danny asleep on the couch in front of the TV. He'd let himself in and, I saw, had a bowl of cereal for dinner. I left a note under Sandra's door to let her know Danny was with me, then came back and put the milk away and turned off the TV. Danny lay there not hearing a thing, not so much curled as tightly wound up, his arms crossed and his hands like fists before his face. I carried him to my bed, where I laid him down and took off his shoes. I got his head on a pillow and covered him, still coiled in a fetal position, with the blankets. The temperature had dropped in the night, but there was less moisture than usual in the air, so I didn't turn on the space heater, just put on a heavy sweatshirt and sat in a chair by the bed. I crooked my head against the cushion and, in the neon glow from the 7-Eleven sign, watched Danny, his face half buried in the pillow, taking in short little gulps of air through his open mouth.

"What? Yes? Who is it?" I thought at first I was at the hospital and speaking into the phone, but then I heard it still ringing and jumped up and grabbed the receiver. "Yes? Hello?" I said, still not sure where I was.

"Jackson. It's Krista. Sorry to call so late—"

A rush of adrenaline cleared my mind instantly. "Is it Allie? What's wrong?"

"Nothing, Jackson. I think she may be coming out of her coma. I called neurosurgery—"

"I'll be right there," I broke in, then said, "Thanks," before I hung up. It was still dark, and I had to turn on the light to see the clock. A few minutes after one in the morning. I went to the bathroom, splashed water on my face and got a clean shirt from the closet.

"Jackson?" It was Danny, who'd been woken by the noise and the light. "What's wrong? What's going on?" There was sleep and pleading and panic in his voice.

"Nothing, Danny. I just got a call."

"From the hospital? Is it about Allie? Is she all right?"

"Yes, she's okay," I said, as reassuringly as I could. "But I've got to go now." I grabbed a jacket and started toward the door.

"Are you going to the hospital to see Allie?"

"Yes."

"Can I come?" He was sitting now, looking up at me.

"Go back to sleep," I said. I tried to put the blankets around him, but he didn't lie back down.

"I want to come with you."

"Later, Danny, not now."

"Why can't I come? Why can't I see her?"

"It's the middle of the night. Go back to sleep. Everything's going to be okay." I turned the light off, but he just sat there, not moving.

—

The bright lights of Allie's room angled out into the darkened hallway. Inside, Krista stood by the bed with a man who introduced himself and explained he was the neurosurgery resident on call.

"She's coming around?" I asked, looking down at Allie. She lay perfectly still; there was no change that I could see.

"I just got here," said the resident. "Apparently the nurse noticed some spontaneous movement a couple of hours ago."

I looked at Krista.

"That was Diane," she said. "I only just came by and called you." Diane should have called me herself. I had left instructions to be notified immediately if there were any signs of consciousness.

"Has there been any movement since?" the resident asked.

Krista shook her head. "Not that I've been able to see."

"She's had basic reflexes this whole time?"

I said yes, and he flipped the covers off her legs, took one of her feet in his hands and ran the closed point of his pen across the sole. Her leg jerked back. "Good," he said. "Involuntary reflexes okay. Let's see how she responds to noxious stimuli."

He moved up to her shoulder, found the spot he was looking for and dug his knuckle in hard. Allie stirred slightly, as a sleeping person might when poked in the middle of the night.

"Let's try this again," the resident said. He straightened Allie's arms out above the covers and dug his knuckle in harder.

"Her arms moved," said Krista.

"Nonpurposeful," answered the resident. "She's only reacting in a general way. What I'm looking for is if she responds to localized stimulus. See if she reaches to the source of the pain, that sort of thing." He took her hand and pressed his pen against the nail of her second finger. Again a small movement, but she didn't try to draw her hand away. "Definitely nonpurposeful," he said. "Are you sure the other nurse said she was moving by herself?"

Krista raised her eyebrows again. "That's what Diane said."

"But she's reacting to pain," I said. "That's one of the stages of recovery, isn't it? It means she's coming out of the coma, right?"

"Could be. Yes."

"Could be or is, dammit?"

He started at the tone. "Sure, it sometimes is. Definitely. Maybe." He looked at the pressure monitor. "How long has she been out?"

"Since Saturday. Sometime in the afternoon."

"A long time," he said with a shrug.

I took Allie's hand in mine and leaned down to her ear. "Allie," I said loudly, clasping her hand in mine. "Allie, can you hear me?"

Nothing.

I said her name again, very loud this time. "Allie, can you hear me?"

At first I wasn't sure, I was gripping her hand so hard, but I loosened my grip and spoke her name again. "Allie."

It was faint, but there was no mistaking it; I could feel the pressure on my hand as she squeezed back.

"I felt something!" I was almost shouting. "She squeezed my hand."

"Uh-huh," grunted the resident, as if to say his diagnosis had been confirmed. "Nonspecific reflex."

———

I sat through the rest of the night by Allie's bed, dozing on and off, waking whenever Diane would bustle in to turn the patient. Allie's limp body would fall, unresisting, into whatever position she was placed, lying so motionless that the darkened hospital room seemed almost animated by comparison. The neurosurgery resident was right, I concluded. Allie was still in a deep coma and not coming out of it.

Then, just before the first light of day, I heard a low sound, like a rush of air. It was so soft I thought at first it was coming from outside. I turned on the light to be sure.

"Allie?" I thought I saw her move, but it might have been a trick of my eye, caused by the light flashing on. I went back to her bedside and repeated, "Allie."

An almost imperceptible tremor ran through the corner of her right eye. And then, slowly, it opened. She stared at the ceiling, her expression immobile. I leaned over so that I was in her line of sight.

"Allie? Are you awake?"

She made another sound, halfway between a whisper and a rasp, as if someone were drawing sandpaper across her vocal cords. The breathing tube had left her hoarse, and her battered lips made it difficult for her to form words. But I understood what she was saying. She was speaking my name.

"Jackson."

I squeezed her hand. "I'm here, Allie."

She tried to say something else.

"What, Allie?"

"I could . . . really use . . . a beer."

It came out "eer" because she couldn't pronounce the "b," but I knew what she meant. I laughed, it was so unexpected.

"There's no beer, Allie. Let me get you some water." I poured some into a cup and let it drip slowly into her mouth so she wouldn't gag. She cleared her throat and grimaced.

"It's the breathing tube, Allie. Your throat is sore from the intubation. It will hurt for a while." She didn't seem to take in the information.

"What time . . . ?" she asked. She said it as if she was slightly cross, the way she did when, after a late rotation, I would wake her in the middle of the night.

I looked at my watch. "About five in the morning."

"Go . . . to slee . . . p, Jacko . . . better in . . . the morning. Sleep now . . ." Her hand began to move and then smoothed the bed sheet, as if she was caressing it. Caressing me. "You . . . worry . . . too much . . ."

Her eyelid was flickering now, giving up the effort to stay open.

"I love you, Allie," I said, hoping she would hear it before she fell back asleep.

"I . . . love . . . *you*," she whispered. Soon I heard her snoring. And for that moment I actually believed that everything really would be better in the morning. Just as she said.

Chapter 21

Lieberman came by for early rounds, handing me one of two large cups of coffee he'd brought along. He looked like it was going to take a lot more than coffee to get him going. I gestured for him to follow me out into the hallway and closed the door behind us.

"I saw that new neuro intern in the cafeteria," he said, fumbling with the lid of his cup. "He mentioned you'd been up all night with the patient, and that she may be regaining some motor reflexes— Not like me, damn it all!" he exclaimed. "Look at this! The coffee's so hot the plastic lid is practically fused on!"

"Give it to me," I said. I peeled off the top and handed back the cup. Lieberman was the type of person who only came alive in a crisis situation; outside the Trauma Room he generally looked like he was about to fall asleep on his feet.

"It's not just motor reflexes," I said. "She woke up and was talking last night."

"Really?" He craned his head around and looked through the glass at her sleeping form. "She knew where she was? Aware of her surroundings and all?"

"No, but she was coherent."

"Oh." He took two big gulps of coffee, added some cold water from a pitcher on a cart nearby and finished it off. "You're going to drink yours?"

I peeled the top off my cup and handed it to him.

"We're going to have to operate," I said. "Go in and start putting her back together. The sooner the better."

"I don't know, Jackson." He shook his head. "She seems stable. Her heart's pretty strong, actually, considering it was just a few days ago you were giving it a Swedish massage in the ER. I'm just not sure I want her undergoing another major operation so soon."

"We've got to. If we wait too much longer, the broken bones will start to fuse and we'll have to break them apart again to set them right." I didn't even want to think about it.

"What does Palfrey say?"

"He hasn't been here yet today. I want your go-ahead."

Lieberman peered inside his cup, as if estimating its caffeine content and judging it inadequate. "Let's see in a couple of days, okay? We can't do anything before then, anyway. Right?"

"Right."

"Right," he repeated. "If you're so eager to operate, we could always use you down in the ER."

"Sure," I said, "maybe I'll drop by again sometime."

Lieberman went in to examine Allie. When he came back, I was leaning against the counter of the nurses' station with a newspaper spread out before me, not really reading it. He came and stood by my side, finishing his coffee. "Okay," he said. "If it's all right with Palfrey, I guess it's all right with me."

—

Palfrey arrived as Diane and I were completing the dressing change. I told him that Allie had woken up during the night.

"I mean, obviously that's a good sign, right?" I asked.

His wispy hair and scraggly eyebrows gave him a look of constant bafflement, and he had a way of considering every question as if it were the first time he had ever been asked such a thing. "A good sign, generally speaking. Certainly not a bad one."

He tested her reflexes much as the resident had, then stood by her head. "Allie," he said slowly and distinctly, "can you lift your arm? Point at the ceiling for me?" Allie tried to move the arm with the cast, but it was too heavy. He took her other arm and laid it out straight. "No, this one. Move this arm, Allie. Try to lift it up toward the ceiling." Her hand came several inches off the bed and quavered in the air. "That's wonderful." He took her hand and laid it back down. "Thank you, Allie." He pulled the covers up and raised his bushy eyebrows.

"You're right," he said. "She's coming around."

"Is she aware of what's going on around her?" I asked when we were outside.

"Minimally. Coming out of a coma is much like coming out of anesthesia. It can take a while. There may be ups and downs."

"How long before she's fully conscious?"

Palfrey sighed noncommittally. "A couple of days. A couple of hours. It's hard to say."

"Can we operate then?"

"Well . . ." he considered. "Putting her under again so soon . . . All else being equal, I wouldn't want to." He looked back in the direction of Allie's room and shook his head. "But all else, I suppose, is not equal. Yes, if it's important. Once she's fully woken up, if it's not contraindicated."

"What about . . ." I hesitated before asking the next question. "What about brain damage?"

"Well," he began, "the MRI didn't show any hemorrhaging. That's good. There's a good chance she'll regain most or all motor function." For Palfrey, that was an optimistic assessment. "And you say she spoke to you, so there's probably no speech impairment."

"What about memory?" I asked.

"That's another matter. Especially when someone's been out this long." He adjusted his bow tie, then noticed a few flakes of dandruff and brushed them away. "That detective on the case, what's his name?"

"Rossi," I said.

"Yes, Detective Rossi was asking me about that. The fact is, we don't really understand how memory works, or what it is, really. I told him it's like the memory on a computer—a crude analogy, but the best I can think of. When information comes into the brain—experiences, sights, sounds—it's held in what you might call the short-term memory center before being stored, more or less permanently, in long-term memory. I guess you'd call that the hard drive. Trauma interrupts the process. It's sort of like turning off your computer before you've saved a document. It vanishes." He made a little "poof" sound and snapped his fingers.

"How much vanishes?" I asked.

"You mean retrograde amnesia? Before the trauma?"

"Yes."

"It's hard to say. She's been out how long now, four days?"

"Since Saturday."

"That's a long time. Her memory could be wiped out for days, weeks, even a month or more before."

"Would it ever come back?"

"Might. Some often comes back, we don't know why or how. It's unpredictable. The further away from the trauma, the more likely that it will resurface, but it may not be consistent."

"What do you mean?"

"It may be spotty, fragmented. And memories closer to the trauma may be wiped out forever. Did you ever get a concussion?"

I shook my head.

"I did once. I was on the bicycling team in high school and had a bad accident during a race. Some people who saw me fall say I wasn't unconscious for more than half a minute at most. That was almost fifty years ago, but to this day I have no memory of it. The last thing I can remember was the two-mile marker, which was about a mile before the place I fell."

He paused for a moment and then continued. "That's what I explained to the detective, though I don't think it pleased him very much. It's very probable she'll never remember the precipitating event itself."

"You mean the attack?"

"Yes," he said. He looked back at Allie's room and sighed, brushing several more flakes of newly appearing dandruff from his tie. "Maybe that's not so bad, everything considered."

No, I thought to myself. Maybe not.

Chapter 22

I'm not saying denial is *always* a bad thing," Stern said, carrying on one of his dialogues with himself. "We all have to engage in denial to some extent or another, just to get by. It's a survival mechanism."

Stern was in one of his talkative moods, perhaps because I had been so mute since I walked in. He had convinced me to schedule an extra session during my lunch break, "given the importance of the, ah, material that has come up." As usual, once I got there, I regretted having come.

"Remember studying epidemiology in medical school?" he asked. "I do. We all got this textbook, I think it was called *Getting to Know Infectious Diseases,* and it had these four-color photos of people with every disease imaginable—actually, some of them are pretty *un*imaginable—and they showed them in the beginning, middle and advanced stages. So you read the symptoms, and they all start with fatigue, dizziness, disorientation, muscle aches. And you're a medical student. You haven't slept a full night since before you can remember, you live on coffee and junk food and you're under constant stress. You don't have to *imagine* the symptoms, you *have* them. Every disease you read about, you have the symptoms. But curiously, it isn't the common diseases—like heart disease or cancer—that are so frightening. It's the rare diseases, the ones for which there's no cure because only one tenth of one percent of the entire population ever contracts them, and so it just isn't economical to try to find a cure. And really, one tenth of one percent—that's only one in a thousand. What are the chances that you could have caught it? What are the probabilities?

"But then you read on in the book, and you realize that there are literally thousands of these rare diseases, and so the probability that you'll get one is really quite high—it's a certainty, in fact, unless some poor schmuck somewhere gets them all. Maybe there's something wrong with that reasoning, but to this day I haven't figured out what.

"You look around and you see all your professors and classmates going about their lives perfectly normally and you wonder: How can they do it? How can they keep up this facade of normalcy? Don't they know what's going to happen to them? It's like that science fiction movie where the aliens come down to earth and impose world peace, which is nice, except that periodically they eat humans who they randomly select off the streets. 'Gee, Dad is awfully late coming home from work!' And everybody goes along with it and pretends nothing is happening because *there is nothing they can do about it.*"

"Like me and schizophrenia," I interjected.

"Ah—?" He was momentarily confused by the interruption but didn't let it distract him from his train of thought. "The point is, they—the other doctors—they know, too, of course. And you realize they've just all found a way to cope. Some doctors become infectious disease specialists 'because it's so interesting,' they will tell you, but it's really because they have to look the monster straight in the face and stare him down, or they know that they will never again sleep at night. Others go into psychiatry because it's not catching. At least that's what we think at the time." He laughed at his own joke, then reestablished his serious tone. "What I'm saying is that everyone develops some sort of mode of denial. It's what enables us to function, to keep the terrors at bay, so to speak. The issue, Jackson"—and here he looked at me—"the issue is when denial becomes counterproductive"—he weighed his words for a moment—"even destructive."

He gave me a significant look as if expecting me to respond. When I didn't, he continued. "You're avoiding this, Jackson. You're quiet and withdrawn in our sessions. I can hardly get a word out of you."

When I still didn't speak, he gave an exasperated wave of his hand. "You see? Not a word! This is exactly what I'm talking about."

"I didn't know you'd finished your speech."

"Come, Jackson, let's be adults, shall we?"

"Look," I said. "I just don't see how it's going to help to talk about it. How is it going to make any difference? What happened to Allie just happened. Nothing's going to change that."

Stern sighed. "It's not just since the . . . incident." That's what he called it, the incident. "It was before that, too. You were canceling appointments. Coming late. You refuse to deal with these blackouts you've been having—"

"What blackouts?"

"Precisely!"

"I don't know what you're talking about."

"Really? That time you woke up in some alley with everything stolen—"

"Somebody must have put something in my drink. I was mugged. That's hardly—"

"And the time you came here at six in the morning and couldn't remember where you'd been for the last two days?"

"I was drunk. It happens."

"Quite a lot, in your case." He shifted in his seat, suppressing his frustration. "Listen, Jackson, the drinking isn't the problem in itself. It's a symptom. You've got to start dealing with this denial, the issues you're repressing."

"What issues?"

"Clearly something is bothering you."

"*This* is bothering me," I said irritably, "this therapy, or whatever we call it."

He nodded his head. "Go on."

"The thing I can't stand about psychoanalysis is the way it institutionalizes paranoia. There's always a hidden agenda. By definition. That's what the subconscious is, isn't it? A hidden agenda that you conceal even from yourself, a mystery that one can solve like some kind of crime novel, gathering up all the clues and then wrapping everything up neatly in the end. But what if there's nothing to solve? What if it can't be solved? What if some things are just bad? Really bad. And there's nothing to do about it."

He waited for me to continue, but I had nothing more to say. A claustrophobic silence descended on the room. Only Stern's antique clock kept up its inane *ticktock, ticktock,* the sound unbearably amplified by the stillness surrounding it.

"Can't you turn that damned thing off?" I snapped at him. "Get an electric clock like a normal person?"

Stern shook his head. "Total denial," he said to himself. Then to me, "You can't keep this up forever, Jackson. You know that."

Chapter 23

I stopped in Allie's room as often as I could between rounds and other unavoidable duties. The swelling around her eye and the whole left side of her face had gone down considerably, but otherwise there were few encouraging signs of her recovery.

It wasn't until evening, shortly after I'd waved away a dinner cart, that I sensed a change. I was sitting by her bed reading. I looked up from my magazine and noticed she was awake.

"Allie?"

No response.

"Allie?"

"Jackson?" she answered, unsure, confused.

"I'm here, Allie. I'm right beside you." Perhaps it was the reassuring bedside tone. She looked at me doubtfully, then glanced around the room, taking it in. She was fully conscious now, trying to make sense of what she saw.

"You're in the hospital, but everything's going to be okay."

She tried to sit up, then lay back with a groan.

"It's better if you lie still, Allie."

"It hurts . . ." It was both a statement and a question: Why does it hurt? What's wrong with me?

"I know it hurts," I said. "We'll give you something for the pain."

"Why . . . hospital. What . . ."

"It's all right," I said soothingly. "It's all right."

She struggled and asked again, insisting on an answer, "What . . . happened?"

"You were in an accident, Allie." I said it slowly and calmly, as if it was the most natural thing in the world. "Do you remember anything?"

She shook her head as much as the bandages would allow and, aware of them for the first time, lifted her hand to feel.

"Don't, Allie," I said, taking her hand.

"Accident? What . . . ?"

"You got a blow to the head that knocked you unconscious. You've been out for a while, but it's okay now."

Her body stiffened. I could feel her hand tighten in mine, and her gaze darted around the room again. When it came back to me, it was desperate.

"It's okay," I repeated. "It's going to be okay."

She pulled her hand away from mine and started grabbing at the bandages and touching the hard, swollen bruises on her face.

"Don't, Allie." I took her arm, and despite her weakened condition, I had to hold on tight to keep her from struggling free.

"My . . . face?" She stared at me with such sharp panic that I was taken aback and let go of her hand. She began clawing at the bandages, and I had to grab hold of her arm again and wrestle her down.

"Don't, Allie, lie still now."

From deep inside her came a high, wailing sound. "Oh God . . . no!" She twisted her body around, trying to escape from what I was telling her, escape from her bed and bandages. Escape from me. "Oh God!" she shrieked, a sound of absolute terror. "No . . . !"

I called for the nurse, trying to sound in control, but there was no response, so I yelled as loudly as I could out into the hall, holding on as Allie's body writhed in my grip.

"Yes, Doc—"

I heard the nurse behind me and called out over Allie's cries for two milligrams of IV Ativan. "And five milligrams IV Haldol," I yelled after her.

It seemed to take forever for the nurse to bring the medications and hook up the syringe to the IV, fumbling with the connection and finally injecting the sedatives. I held Allie still so she wouldn't tear the IV needle out of her arm.

"It's going to be all right," I said over and over. "It's going to be all right."

Before long, Allie's body went slack and slumped back into the bed. "No . . ." She was sobbing now, each gasp caught in the middle by the sharp pain from the wound and sutures in her chest, still thrashing her head from side to side.

"Give her two milligrams of IV morphine," I told the nurse. "Do you really think that's necessary?" I heard her ask. I looked up. It was Diane. She was on double duty, I remembered. "Jesus Christ!" I barked. "Just do it!" When she was done, I told her to leave the room.

Slowly, Allie's gasps began to subside into a low, continuous moan. "No . . ." Allie's head lay still on the pillow, her gaze once again on me, weakened by the drugs but still bright with fear.

"It's going to be all right," I said as her vision glazed over and her breathing became more regular. "It's going to be all right," I repeated, over and over again, long after she had drifted into unconsciousness and could no longer hear me.

Chapter 24

I got a couple of sleeping pills from my locker and lay down on a deserted cot in the outpatients' ward, but an hour later my heart was still racing. My thoughts were running around in circles, fixated on one split-second image like a video loop of a few frames played over and over. The terror in Allie's eyes. The same terror, I thought, with which she'd looked at her attacker.

By three o'clock in the morning, I gave up on the idea of sleep and wandered the halls, drinking coffee from the machine, finally ending up back in Allie's room. Her sleep became increasingly restless as the drugs wore off, and she sometimes cried out or moaned. I wondered if she was replaying a similar loop inside her head, buried deeper than memory, a sickening rush of panic and horror.

I spoke to her then, tried to calm her. Sometimes she appeared to be conscious for a brief moment, but I wasn't sure how much she was taking in. Palfrey arrived a little after seven for morning rounds. She woke up then, and he went through the drill with her, testing reflexes and asking her questions, which she answered in complete sentences. Her mind was working, but her voice was dull and flat, without affect.

Afterward I spoke with Palfrey out in the hall.

"She's doing very well," he said.

I described the night before and said I was worried about how she was taking it emotionally. I could hardly ask him about what was bothering me most: her reaction to me.

"It's not uncommon for patients with severe head injuries to experience anxiety and depression—a whole host of mental problems, really," Palfrey said. "It's a physiological reaction, probably, having to do with the brain chemistry being so violently disrupted, though we don't really understand the causes of it. And, of course, there's the difficulty of adjusting to one's, ah, altered circumstances."

"What do you mean, a whole host of mental problems?"

"Bipolar disorders, psychotic episodes, paranoid delusions and the like."

"I thought most of that was hereditary."

"Well, for some the disposition probably is. But a bad head injury can certainly precipitate it. I once had a patient—a construction worker—who'd been hit on the head with a pipe. He was convinced we were aliens who had abducted him to do sexual experiments on human beings. Funny how these delusions so often follow the same pattern—"

"Funny."

He could see I wasn't amused.

"I'm not saying that will happen, of course. She's just going to have to go through a period of healing. Both her body and her mind. There's little we can do, medically speaking." I knew what he'd say next, and he did. "We'll just have to wait and see."

—

The nurses from the morning shift came in a short time later with their artificially bright chatter, elevating the bed so Allie was partially sitting, and setting up a line with a manual control so she could administer the painkillers herself, in small doses, as needed. We changed her dressings, Allie watching us move around her, fully aware now but withdrawn. She could open her left eye halfway, but as the orbital casing was shattered, it was now misaligned, and keeping it open for too long made her dizzy.

After the nurses left, I asked if she wanted anyone to come by. Should I contact any friends? Family?

"No," she said.

Hesitantly, I asked about Paula and Brian. Allie simply closed her eyes. I didn't want to push it. Given Paula's bizarre reaction over the telephone, I assumed something had gone wrong between them, but Allie gave no indication of what she was thinking.

"Danny would like to see you," I said after a moment.

"No!" she said. "I don't want him to see me like this." She took several deep breaths—wincing from the pain. More calmly she added, "Tell him I miss him. I'll see him later. Okay?"

"Okay."

We were silent for a while, then she spoke.

"I want to know," she said.

"What, Allie?"

"I want to know about the accident."

I tried to dodge the question. "The important thing at this point is to rest. You shouldn't worry yourself about it now, there'll be plenty of time later—"

"Tell me," she insisted. The tone of her voice said, *I know you, you're keeping something from me.*

"You don't remember anything about it?"

"No. I don't think so. No."

At least she had been given that blessing, I thought with relief. Her mind had blacked out the horror of the attack.

"Tell me, Jackson."

She was going to find out anyway, I decided. It was better that I tell her.

"Allie, it wasn't an accident." I chose my words carefully, leaving out the brutal details about the hammer and rug, but said she'd been hit on the head and suffered a coma. "There were some . . . lacerations, which we sewed up, and burns. You have a compound fracture of your right arm, a few broken ribs, a fractured sternum, and we, ah, well, we had to perform CPR in the emergency room." I gave as optimistic a prognosis as I could, but I saw the shock registering in her frozen stillness.

"When?" she asked after some time.

"Last Saturday, about five days ago."

"Five days," she repeated, as if trying to make sense of it. "Who? Who did it? Do they know?"

"No, not yet. You don't remember anything . . . anything at all?"

She shook her head.

"What about before?" I asked. "We were going to see each other that evening. Do you remember that?"

She didn't say anything, and I thought she hadn't heard.

"We were meeting at my place," I prodded, "after I got out of the hospital."

"No, I don't think so," she said after a while.

"You had some kind of deadline. A sales prospectus or something. You had to finish it by Monday."

"No," she said, and gave her head a short jerk to the side. I could see the questioning was making her anxious, but for some reason it became terribly important to me to find out exactly how much she could recall. I thought back over the week before, trying to come up with some kind of marker that would fix a point in her memory.

"Remember watching *Pillow Talk*?" It was a Doris Day movie, her favorite.

"Sure, I remember that," she said. As soon as she answered, I realized we had seen it many times together, the last—the time I was thinking of—when we came back from Point Reyes. That had been two weeks before the assault, almost three weeks ago now.

"When we went to the beach, at Point Reyes, and came back and rented the movie . . . You said you wanted to see it again because it was so happy, and we were so happy then, too."

She didn't respond.

"We rented the movie and we ordered Chinese takeout and I got some kind of fried kidney thing by mistake. It was really awful. So we had pizza instead?"

"I'm not sure. No."

"The day we went to Point Reyes. To the beach? Allie . . ."

She turned her head away. I was being too insistent. Too loud.

———

My morning was taken up in surgery—first a skin graft on a lung cancer patient whose radiation therapy had left large burn wounds on his chest, then a call to the ER to stitch up a bicycle messenger who'd guessed wrong about which way a taxi was turning. In between I called Brandt's office to set a time for Allie's operation, but Eileen, his secretary, said he had been called away suddenly on Genederm business and hadn't left a forwarding number. I called Brandt's home number. No one was there, so I spoke into the answering machine, explaining that Allie had come out of her coma and except for a bad case of amnesia, she was in reasonably good shape. We had the go-ahead from Lieberman and Palfrey to operate as soon as Monday, if Eileen could fit it into his schedule. If he could call me back at the hospital, I added, I'd like to set up a time to preview the operation with him.

After the ER, I got a cup of coffee and tried to eat something in the cafeteria, then walked back to the ICU to check on Allie. When I turned the corner, I saw Rossi standing with Palfrey outside her door. I wondered how Rossi knew that Allie was out of her coma, then realized he'd probably phoned in to the nurses' desk and been told.

"Dr. Maebry," Rossi said by way of greeting.

Palfrey nodded and pulled at his bow tie, looking as if the slightest gesture from Rossi would whisk his frail body away. "Detective Rossi would like to ask Ms. Sorosh a few questions," he explained to me. "She's awake now, and—"

"I'm not sure this is the best time for an interrogation," I said, surprised at my own vehemence. "She's very anxious and confused right now. It's not only the physical trauma. We have to consider the emotional shock as well."

"Only a few short questions," Rossi said. He addressed his words to Palfrey, who was staring at the ground.

Palfrey ahemmed. "She *has* just come out of a long coma. She's bound to be disoriented . . ."

Rossi shifted on his feet. "I understand that, Doctor," he said, "but it's important to find out what Ms. Sorosh remembers of—"

"She doesn't remember anything," I broke in. "Not for several weeks."

"I'd like to ascertain that for myself," he said, his gaze still fixed on Palfrey. It was the first time I'd heard Rossi sound impatient, as if things weren't moving fast enough for him.

Palfrey shrugged. "I can't see that it would do much harm, Jackson, really," he mumbled, still staring at the floor. "If we keep it as brief as possible and try not to upset the patient too much . . ." His voice trailed away.

"Good," Rossi said decisively. I'd been overruled. Rossi moved toward the door, and we began to follow. "I'd like to speak with her alone," he shot back over his shoulder.

"Oh yes, well, I suppose so," Palfrey murmured apologetically, stepping back and almost knocking into me. "Well, well," he sighed as Rossi disappeared inside Allie's room. "No harm, I suppose . . . So, Jackson," he asked to change the subject, "have you scheduled the operation?"

"I've been trying to reach Brandt. I'm hoping for Monday." I was peering through the door but could see only Rossi's huge back bending over the bed.

"Oh yes. Brandt," Palfrey said. "He's as good as they come." He adjusted his bow tie and sighed again. "Well, well."

I began to feel self-conscious spying on Rossi, so I walked over to the desk nearby to reexamine Allie's chart, which I knew by heart anyway. After a few minutes, Rossi reappeared.

"Any luck?" Palfrey asked.

"Nothing," said Rossi, glancing in my direction. "She doesn't remember a thing."

"Yes, well, as I was saying—" Palfrey began.

"And you think it may not come back. Her memory of the assault?" Rossi asked.

"Well, you can never be certain. But so close to the trauma, very likely not, I'm afraid."

Rossi gripped the bridge of his nose and flexed his brow, as if the information was giving him a migraine.

"You might say it's a defensive mechanism of the brain," Palfrey continued, "blotting out the—"

"Yeah," Rossi grunted. I could hear his teeth grinding. "You might also say it's pretty goddamned convenient for whoever attacked her."

Chapter 25

Allie's depression deepened as the day wore on, as if the more her mind healed, the more aware she grew of the reality of her condition. Though I successfully resisted her entreaties to look at herself in the mirror, she had managed to convince a nurse to bring one to her bedside. As shocking as the sight must have been, however, it gave a false impression. Her burns, which would be the most difficult to deal with, were still covered by bandages, and the bruising on her face hid more than it revealed about the damage inside.

I tried to cheer her up, talking in a general way about what we planned for the operation and about its chances for success, but she would only say "Yes, Jackson" or "Sure, I know you're going to do your best" or simply "Okay, fine," as though it no longer mattered what I said or she didn't believe me. Or it just wasn't worth the effort to hope anymore.

"You're lying to me," she said finally. There was no anger when she said it. Just resignation. Somehow that was worse. "It can never be fixed. I know that."

"That's not true, Allie. There's a lot we can do . . ." I went on, and she let me talk, but she wasn't listening.

"I'm always going to have hideous scars on my face," she said when I'd finished. "People will stare at me in the street. 'Look! There goes the freak,' they'll say."

"Allie, that's not true—"

"Even people I know won't be able to look at me when we talk, not directly. They'll pretend not to notice, but their eyes will be moving all over the place trying not to look—gawk—at the freak."

"Don't say that, Allie."

"Why shouldn't I? It's true. Even children will laugh. I bet even Danny will be disgusted when he sees me."

There were tears on her cheeks, and I bent over to wipe them dry.

"Don't," she said, turning her head away. "Don't touch me."

She lay there, rigid and unmoving, as if her body was warning me not to get too close. There were no sobs; even her breathing was barely audible. Just tears, silent, continuous, glistening on her bruised skin and wetting the pillow by her head. Then, after a few minutes, they stopped.

"Why, Jackson?" she said.

"Allie?" I didn't know what she was asking.

"Why?" she repeated.

Did she want to know why this had happened to her? I wondered. And what was I supposed to say? That it was a senseless, random tragedy? Bad luck? There was no reason for it, no purpose. There was no meaning, nothing I could say that made sense.

"Allie, these things—" I began. I was about to say "these things happen," but stopped myself. I could think of nothing but platitudes.

"Why does he hate me so much?" she asked when it was clear I wouldn't go on. I thought she must be talking about her attacker. She said it as if she knew the person.

"Who, Allie?" My heart clenched, waiting for the answer.

"What did I do to make God hate me so much?"

"God?" I said, taken aback.

"Why has he always hated me?"

"Jesus, Allie," I objected, "God doesn't hate you." It just burst out of me. But I repeated myself, thinking I was being comforting. "God doesn't hate you, Allie."

"No?"

"Of course not." When she was silent, I said it again: "Of course not."

"Really?" she said dismissively, as if it wasn't worth the effort to talk to me anymore. "How would you know, Jackson?"

Her body seemed to draw even more tightly into itself, away from me, away from the world; as if by force of will, she could contract herself into a single, solitary point, and there vanish.

Chapter 26

Brandt called back later while I was in my office. I'd gone there to be alone and try to think things through.

"Sorry, Jackson. I just got back into town and got your message. You're in the office late."

"Paperwork," I replied, looking at the untouched stack of insurance forms and office memos in front of me.

"So Alexandra's come around," he said. "That's great news." We discussed her condition briefly.

"And her heart's still strong?"

"Yes, fine."

"And Palfrey has given us the go-ahead to operate?"

"He said it would be okay."

"Well, then, maybe we can do a little something about the other things, eh? You say the amnesia is bad?"

"Pretty bad, I'm afraid. She doesn't remember anything for three weeks or so. Palfrey says she'll probably never remember anything about the assault itself."

"Anyway, it's great news she's out of the coma." He said he'd call Eileen and make sure she allowed time on his schedule. "The worst thing is the waiting and not being able to do anything. Now we can start putting her back together again."

I agreed. We said a few more pleasantries, wished each other a good night and hung up.

The nursery rhyme "All the king's horses, and all the king's men" ran through my mind. As much confidence as I had in Brandt, the thought of the operation filled me with dread. I could only think of all the things that might go wrong. And all the things that would never be put right again.

—

I went home after that to get a change of clothes and must have dozed off on my couch. I woke late and it was after morning rounds by the time I made it to Allie's room.

I was surprised when I got there to find her raised up in bed. "Hi, Allie. You're sitting up. That's great."

"Hi, Jackson." She sounded almost like her old self. Almost. There was an unnatural brightness in her eyes. I checked the chart to see if she had a fever, but the nurses had taken her temperature just moments before and it was normal.

"Peter came by," she said.

"Peter? Oh, Dr. Brandt."

"He just left. We talked about the operation."

"Oh, good."

"Yes. He told me all about it. The whole thing."

It may have been my imagination, but I felt like she was reproaching me for not having explained it well enough.

"He said," she continued, hardly pausing to catch her breath, "that from the look of the X rays, my injuries won't be hard to fix."

"Allie," I began. "The CTs show a lot, but—" One could never see the full extent of the damage on CTs; the injuries appeared bad enough, but we might find when we opened her up that they were even worse than we had expected. And then, of course, there were the burns—skin is much less forgiving than bone, and its defects are all on the outside and visible—but I wasn't going to bring that up now. "You can't see everything on the X rays."

"*He* could," she insisted, angry with me for doubting. "*Peter* could!"

"Okay, Allie." The last thing I wanted to do was argue with her. "There's every reason to be optimistic." It sounded unconvincing even to me, and I caught a flash of anger in her eyes.

"He knows what he's talking about, Jackson." She spoke rapidly, as if there wasn't enough time to get all the words out. "He said he was going to fix it, fix everything, make it all like it was, as good as new, he said."

I knew Brandt never would have said anything like that, even if he was trying to raise her spirits. It's foolish to give a patient false hope.

"Allie, I think what he was trying to say was—"

"It's his field, Jackson. He's an *expert*. He said he could make it like it was. As a matter of fact, he said he could make it even better than it was!" she declared.

I began again, trying to be more positive. "We're going to do everything we possibly—"

"Better!" she insisted. "He's going to make me look even better. He said so. He said that if I wanted, he'd put in implants."

"Implants? You mean—" I tried to make sense of what she was saying. "Sure, we may have to use some implant material where the bone is fractured—"

"No! Cheek implants. To make me look like Michelle Pfeiffer."

"I'm not certain that's such a good—"

"Peter said," she interrupted me, "that if I wanted them, there was no problem. I've always wanted high cheekbones."

This was crazy. Just to fix the damage would be a marathon operation. We had the OR scheduled for six hours, but any number of problems, unforeseen now, might keep it running longer. It was a hugely complicated, delicate procedure, and to add anything unnecessary only increased the risk of something going wrong.

"Peter said so," she continued. "He said that I'd heal in a few months, and all this would be behind me; I could forget about it and get my old life back. Peter *said* so," she repeated like a mantra. "Peter said it would be like it never happened."

"Okay," I conceded, not wanting to upset her any more.

"Like it never happened," she said again, daring me to contradict her. She reached for her water glass and took a drink. The water spilled from her swollen lips, and when I dabbed them with a napkin, she winced in pain.

"Sorry," I said.

"Peter can do it, too, because he's the best there is. The best in the whole country. You said so yourself. He'll make it just like it was, even better than it was."

There are some things, I thought, even Brandt can't fix.

"Peter said so," she repeated.

"Yes, Allie, even better than it was," I said, the words echoing falsely in my own ears.

Chapter 27

I found Eileen outside Brandt's office. She told me that Brandt had just left, but if I ran, I might catch him in the parking lot. I got there as he was throwing some papers into the backseat of his Mercedes.

"Dr. Brandt."

"Hello, Jackson." He smiled broadly, glad to see me, as always.

I took a moment to catch my breath.

"Need a ride?" he asked kindly. "That Honda of yours give out again?"

"No, thanks, it's working for the moment. I wanted to discuss something with you."

"Is it urgent, Jackson?" He looked at his watch. "I was supposed to be in Palo Alto for an investors' meeting ten minutes ago."

"It's about Alexandra Sorosh."

"Right. We're scheduled for Monday, first thing. Get some rest this weekend." He gave me a fatherly smile. "It's going to be quite an operation. I think you'll find it very interesting."

"Yes, I'm looking forward to it," I said untruthfully. "I just wanted to ask—" I hesitated before going on. I'd rushed there without really thinking what I would say. It now seemed as if I was challenging his judgment. "I . . . I was talking with, ah, Ms. Sorosh, and she said that you'd been by to go over the operation with her."

"Yes, earlier this morning. Sorry I didn't tell you, but it was the only hole in my schedule."

"No. I mean, that's fine. She's in an emotional state, of course—"

"Understandable, considering. She's been through a terrible shock."

"That's just it . . ."

"Yes?" He was getting out his keys, folding his coat and laying it neatly on the backseat so it wouldn't wrinkle.

"What I mean is—as I say, she's pretty emotional, so she may not be getting things quite right, but she said that you had talked about putting in cheek implants."

"I mentioned it as an option. Yes?" His white hair blew in the wind and he swept it back from his forehead, waiting for me to continue.

I wanted to say that Allie was in no condition to make such a decision, but felt suddenly self-conscious. "Do you really think it's such a good idea?" I asked. It came out weak, hesitant; I wondered if it was even audible.

"I wouldn't have suggested it if I didn't," he said firmly.

I found myself looking at the ground. "The reason I ask is, I mean, it's a complicated operation . . ."

"It certainly is, but I think I've got it under control."

"Yes, I know, definitely. But is it really such a good idea to add another procedure if it's not necessary?"

"What's necessary," he said with some irritation, "is that the patient feel good about the results. I believe I can guarantee that."

"Right, of course," I said. "I was just wondering. Just wanted to get your thinking, you know, with Allie—the patient—so emotionally . . ." I let the sentence trail off and stepped back, trying to withdraw from the conversation, but he continued it.

"Ms. Sorosh will be going through—what's the expression?—a lot of changes over the next few months, including at least two skin grafts and an ear reconstruction—at least two major operations after this one. As confident as I am about the results, she will never look entirely the same, and it may not be possible to completely erase the evidence, visually speaking, of her injuries."

"Yes, I know."

"Implants are a minor issue if they can help her adjust to her new appearance."

"Right. I see. That makes a lot of sense."

I glanced up at him. He gave a tight smile. The lecture was over. "Don't worry so much, Jackson. It's normal to be nervous before a big operation such as this. Trust me, everything's going to go just fine."

He swung the back door shut and got in the driver's seat as I was mumbling something to the effect of "Yes, of course, I'm sure . . ."

As he backed up, he lowered his window and leaned out.

"Are you sure you're feeling well, Jackson? You look a bit under the weather."

"No, I'm fine, really. Just tired."

"Well, be sure to get some rest this weekend. Monday's a big day."

He drove out of the lot and I walked back to the hospital, a chill wind drying the perspiration on the back of my neck.

Chapter 28

The weekend passed, somehow. I checked on Allie periodically during rounds on Saturday, but she wasn't in the mood to talk and, after my third visit, told me she wanted to be alone and rest. I spent Sunday morning in the hospital library studying up on the procedures we'd be using, but I'd been in enough operations like it to know what to expect—and to be thoroughly dreading the next day.

Danny came by the apartment in the afternoon to watch the game on TV, bringing along a couple of martial arts videos he'd rented. I told him about the operation and promised again that he would see Allie later. He seemed to accept it but was quiet all afternoon. When the game ended around six, I said I was going to bed. I took two of the three sleeping pills remaining in the bottle then fell asleep to the sound of gunfire and explosions on the TV.

I got up Monday morning before daylight and mixed a quarter cup of instant coffee crystals with lukewarm water so I could drink it without waiting. A second cup enabled me to locate my bathing suit, get it on and make my way to the ocean. Even the surfers hadn't arrived yet. I dove into the icy water and forced myself to stay in until the cold had penetrated to my bones. After a shower and another cup of tepid coffee, my head was reasonably clear. I was as ready as I was ever going to be.

I got to the hospital early, but Brandt had already been by to see Allie, and the anesthesiologist had ordered her sedation. She was barely aware of my presence, but I stayed by her side while she was transferred to a stretcher and wheeled down to the OR. I took her hand as the anesthesiologist injected a shot of sodium pentathol into the IV to put her under. He told her to count backward from a hundred.

She murmured something indistinct but somehow urgent. I bent down to hear.

"Everything's going to be fine," I said, thinking she was anxious about the operation. "Just fine."

This time it was hardly even a whisper, but I understood. A single word. "Peter."

And then she was out.

———

The prep room was already packed when I arrived. A typed announcement of the operation had been pinned on the OR bulletin board, and despite the early hour, some fifteen to twenty medical students and residents had come to observe. They clustered around Brandt at the light box as he clipped up transparencies of Allie's CTs and began to explain the procedure we were about to perform. Anderson was there, eagerly worming as close as possible to the front of the crowd. Henning was standing at the back of the group and nodded to me discreetly as Brandt talked.

"This is a frontal view of the patient," Brandt said, pointing to the first CT. "As you can see, the damage is quite extensive. There are also burns that will require major reconstructive surgery, but in this operation we will be dealing only with the fractures to her facial bones."

He snapped up several more transparencies, taken from different angles.

"Until we get inside, we won't know the full extent of the injuries, but even on the CTs we can see extensive fracturing of the frontal bone, LeFort fractures of the maxilla, here"—he outlined them with his pen as he spoke—"as well as complex orbito-zygomatic-maxillary fractures."

He turned to the students. "In English, that would mean what, exactly?"

"One hell of a mess?" Henning said.

Brandt laughed. "Well put. Who says interns aren't as bright as they used to be?" Everyone laughed with him.

Brandt continued, pointing to the first injury. "What it means is that the bone right above the nose has been shattered into several fragments. Even on the CT you can see one large piece that appears completely detached and free-floating."

With his pen, he pointed to a fragment about the size of a quarter on Allie's brow. "There are several other pieces clearly visible. Here. Here. And here. If there's not too much splintering, we may be able to assemble them in place and build a bridge of plates—we'll be using titanium microplates—across the forehead to hold it rigidly in place."

He pointed to a CT that showed a side view of the orbital bone around Allie's left eye. "This, as I'm sure you all know, is the bony orbit, the socket in which the eyeball rests. It has clearly been badly splintered. The bones of the brow, and these here, on the side—the orbital rim—are also fractured in several places. As you'll see when we get to the patient, the entire structure has collapsed."

He took down the first set of CTs and put up another.

"This shows you the overall picture again. It's vital in a complex facial procedure such as this to completely expose the area of her injuries, so you have a full view of the facial bones and can assess the overall pattern of the fractures and how they relate to one another."

"Completely expose?" asked Henning.

"He means peel her face off," Anderson explained.

"Crudely put," said Brandt, "but yes, we have to peel the face down so we can see everything at once. The first and most crucial thing is to repair this structure here"—he outlined the bones that form the outside of the face, from the cheek up around the outside of the eye—"the zygomatic arches and the orbital frame. These bones give the face its basic shape and volume. They are, as it were, the foundation on which the other bones rest. You have to get that foundation right from the beginning, make sure the placement is perfect, then build on it.

"We will then be going up through the mouth to get at this evident fracture of the maxilla, directly above the roots of the upper teeth. We will also be checking on these lucencies in the lower jaw to see what they indicate. At the request of the patient, we will be adding prostheses—implants—to the cheekbones." He explained that it would be easier to achieve a better symmetry that way, considering the massive damage the patient had incurred. "And Henning," he added, "you will be in charge of the music."

"Oh, great!" said Henning.

"You can choose any selection you desire, as long as it's Mozart."

"Oh, great," Henning repeated, with considerably less enthusiasm.

"Well," Brandt concluded, "the patient will be prepped by now. Let's everyone who needs to get scrubbed."

My hands were visibly trembling as I held them under the hot water, and little nervous twitches, like jolts of electricity, ran down my arms. Brandt was at the other sink and didn't see, and by the time I'd dried off and held my hands out for the nurse to glove, they were still again.

Brandt stood by the door to let me go through first. "Relax, Jackson," he said with an encouraging smile. "You look like you're going to a funeral." I forced a smile in return. "This is the kind of operation that makes our business worthwhile," he continued, exuding his typical self-confidence.

I made myself smile again and walked on quickly.

Allie lay unconscious on the table, fully prepped, the bandages removed from her face. The scrub nurse arranged the instruments neatly on their trays—the scalpels, forceps and drill bits to make holes for the screws—while Brandt carefully checked the microplates to be sure we had all we needed. We had been assigned the third operating room, the largest and most modern, with a small amphitheater above for interested spectators. I could sense figures coming and going overhead and feel their curious stares on my back as I leaned over the operating table. I tried to shrug it off, but the feeling stayed with me.

"All right, everybody," said Brandt. He was manipulating the breathing tube where it came out of Allie's mouth. "It's very important in an operation such as this to wire the breathing tube securely to the patient's molars, so we have full flexibility. See?" Brandt twisted the tube down, then took the wire being offered by the nurse.

"That," said Anderson to Henning behind me, "is so the tube doesn't get in the way when they take her face off."

"Jackson," Brandt continued, "hold her mouth open, will you?"

I took Allie's head in my hands and gently tilted it back so that her mouth gaped open, then carefully pried her jaw farther apart as Brandt reached in and began twisting the wire around the tube and twining it around her back teeth.

"There, it's secure. This way we have full access without worrying about the tube coming out or getting in the way." He pulled the tube down and yanked on it to demonstrate. "I find it also makes things easier if we suture up the eyelids. Would you do the honors, Jackson?"

I took the curved needle offered by the nurse and sewed while everyone watched. I could feel the tremor returning to my arm, but I concentrated hard on what I was doing, and it passed. With my hands occupied, I was able to shut out my anxieties and focus only on the operation. For that moment, at least.

When I was finished, several black knots held Allie's lids shut.

"Okay," Brandt said. "We're going to start with a coronal incision—here." He traced a line from ear to ear across the top of her skull. "And then we'll work our way down, separating the skin from the connective tissue that holds it in place. Nurse? Scalpel, please." She laid it in his hand. "All right, then. Let's cut."

He made the coronal incision, and then, as I eased the skin back with a retractor, he used the scalpel to cut through the connective tissue underneath. The nurse followed along with the suction device, clearing the area of blood. I cauterized the bleeding vessels with a bovie.

"We have to be very careful not to damage the facial nerve," Brandt said as he worked. "As you can see, it's protected here by a layer of fat. More suction, Nurse. See that, everyone? Lay back the skin, Jackson, so we can all get a better look."

I did. By now the skin from Allie's hairline to her brow had been cut loose and it fell back in a flap over her eyes.

"As I said, you want to be very careful here," Brandt continued. "It's the nerve that gives the face its expression. If you slip and cut it, well—"

"You've screwed the pooch," said Henning.

"Yes, you might say that. This whole section of the face would be paralyzed, and there's little you can do to repair it." Brandt continued dissecting, and I peeled the skin back as he did so, until the entire top half of what had been her face lay exposed.

"Here," said Brandt, "you can see the extent of the fracturing." He took a retractor and poked at the fragments of her frontal bone, the skull above the bridge of her nose. They looked like shards of pottery on display in a museum, roughly assembled to approximate their original shape. "Notice how much more damage there is than we could see in the CT. This fragment, for instance"—Brandt poked again at one of the larger pieces—"has become completely detached.

"Nurse," he said, "let's get a picture of that for the books. My camera's in my bag."

The circulating nurse went over and rummaged through the bag but came up empty-handed. "Sorry, Doctor," she called back. "It's not here." Anderson quickly piped up that he had one and ran out to the prep room, returning moments later with camera in hand. We stepped away from the operating table to give him room, and he started clicking away, the flashes outlining the jagged edges of the bone in stark relief. He clicked nonstop, leaning this way and that, like a fashion photographer trying to get the best angle, until finally I barked at him that it was enough. I lay the skin back down over Allie's forehead and we went back to the operation, but for the next several minutes Anderson hovered around behind us, taking pictures.

The next procedure was to make an incision along the rim of Allie's lower eyelid to expose the lower orbital rim, then make another incision inside her mouth, along the line where the upper lip joins the gum so we would have access from below. "As you can see," Brandt said when that had been accomplished, "we have now dissected the entire face, down to her teeth. I can pass a retractor through here"—he slid the metal shaft between Allie's lip and upper gums—"and through the coronal incision at her hairline." The end of the retractor poked out from beneath the loose skin lying on her forehead. He moved it back and forth and side to side to demonstrate. "See that?" he said with the air of a job well done. "No obstruction. The skin is completely detached." He moved the retractor again to emphasize the point.

"Well now, Jackson," he continued when everyone had had a chance to see. "Pull her face down, would you?"

I lifted the skin from her forehead and laid it inside out over her chin, the interior of her eyelids about mouth level. A faceless head with opaque eyes stared up from the operating table. A momentary hush fell over the operating room as people took in the sight.

How many operations had I done? I wondered, staring back at her unseeing eyes. How many people had I cut and carved and rearranged, with never a doubt in my mind? It had never bothered me before. I'd never had a problem—

Don't start now, I told myself.

"As you can see," Brandt was saying, the pride evident in his voice, "we now have complete exposure, the entire dermal layer—the face, as it were—removed . . ." I lifted my head and took in the room. Brandt was standing back from the table to let the other doctors get a better view. They filed forward, intently examining our handiwork as he spoke.

" . . . complete exposure . . ." Brandt emphasized, waving his hand over the mass of membrane, tissue and cauterized veins, the audience murmuring appreciatively, nodding, commenting to one another, clearly impressed.

I had the disquieting sense of someone whispering in my ear: Allie was gone, the voice said. Gone forever, and you'll never be able to find her again.

I turned away and asked the nurse for a drink of water. She brought me a bottle with a straw that she slid up under my face mask. The crowd of spectators was shuffling back into place. This part of the demonstration was complete.

The nurse pulled the gauze back up over my nose and mouth, and I turned back to the table.

"Okay," said Brandt, "let's move on."

Keep it together, Jackson, I told myself. You're a doctor. A good one. Just act normal. Just pretend. You can do that. You've done it your whole life.

Henning was changing the CD, and it suddenly blared out an old Beatles tune, "I've just seen a face . . ."

"Mozart, Henning!" Brandt called over to him. "Mozart."

"Sorry," Henning said, switching the CD, "I thought you just meant the classics in general."

The crowd tittered.

"Are we ready?" asked Brandt, looking around the table. I nodded. "Let's start putting her together, shall we?" The nurse wheeled over the tray with its tiny metal plates and screws, arranged neatly by size. The plates were thin bands of titanium, strong but flexible, that widened every few millimeters to an "O" through which the screw passed.

We spent the next couple of hours drilling holes for the screws, fitting the metal plates and attaching them in place. It was laborious work, requiring mostly manual dexterity, and I felt a certain calm return. Brandt worked efficiently, but his arthritis was bothering him and his hands slipped several times while turning the screwdriver. One screw popped out as he was fitting it and got lost in the sinus cavity, forcing us to hunt around inside for several minutes before locating it. After that, he handed the screwdriver over to me and I proceeded under his direction, attaching the bone piece by piece to the long metal bridges that ran above her brow, along the outside of her eye and above her upper teeth.

"Now we've fixed the basic shape of the face," Brandt said, addressing the onlookers. "Next we do the orbital floor, the bone under the eye. Jackson, if you'd lift up the eye, thanks."

I slid a curved retractor under her eye and pulled it up.

"This, again, is much worse than we could see in the CT," Brandt commented. "The bone casing around the eye is extremely fragile and seems to have been splintered by the impact. As you can see, it's left this large hole"—he stood back for people to see—"into which the splinters have fallen. It's unlikely that any of the pieces will be usable, but it's extremely important to get every one, otherwise it's likely to get infected."

We carefully retrieved the fragments from the cavity behind the broken socket, and Brandt explained that we'd be taking a bone graft from her skull to patch up the hole. He marked a roughly rectangular section high on the side of Allie's head, where the skull bone had already been exposed, about an inch long and half an inch wide. "This looks like it should have just the right curve," he said. "Jackson, do you want to do the drilling?"

I took the drill from the tray and began to score along the lines he'd indicated, the mechanical whine turning into a high-pitched scream whenever I pressed the bit into the bone.

"The skull, of course, has two layers of bone," Brandt explained, raising his voice to be heard above the noise, "a double casing for extra protection, so it won't leave an opening."

"Sort of like the *Titanic*," shouted Henning.

"Yeah," one of the residents shouted back. "Just don't run into an iceberg."

"Or an ice pick," returned Henning.

The drill wailed on, a mechanical imitation of agony. The blood and bone sprayed off the churning drill bit onto my gown and splattered against the plastic shield of my face mask. A fine red mist, a pattern of tiny droplets . . . like the pattern sprayed on the wall of that room where Allie was attacked, I thought. I pressed harder along the final cut, the drill shrieking in protest. The nurse reached over to wipe the blood from my mask but only succeeded in smearing the blood before my eyes, as if the whole world had become red with gore. I pressed again, harder. With a final piercing cry, the bit pushed through the bone and the scream subsided into a low whine, a steady, keening lament.

"Jackson. Turn it off, would you?" It was Brandt. "Jackson? We're through drilling for today."

I realized that my hand was still clenched around the drill's grip, pressing the trigger. With a conscious effort, I relaxed my fingers and the drill wound down into silence. I handed it back to the nurse, and she took the plastic face shield from my head.

"Thank you," Brandt said. Then to the crowd: "It's always nice to see someone who loves his work." The residents and students laughed dutifully. "Okay, let's see if it fits."

Brandt took his forceps and had me lift up the eye again as he placed the bone graft over the hole. "Perfect. Now we just lay the eye back down, there, and the weight of the eye will hold the bone in place. We don't have to bolt it. After time, the bone will fuse to the graft."

The operating room felt oppressively hot. I turned to the nurse and asked her to wipe the perspiration that was dripping into my eyes. "Hard work," she said sympathetically, dabbing at my forehead.

"Jackson, when you're ready?" I turned back to Brandt, who was looking impatient.

"Ready," I said, positioning myself again at the operating table.

"Now we can get on with putting in the implants. What do you say?"

"Ready," I repeated, not feeling at all ready. Not wanting to do this. It was the least dangerous part of the entire operation but, I realized, the moment I'd been dreading the most.

The nurse tore open the plastic bag and let the two cheek implants fall on the tray. Brandt picked one up with his gloved hand and began to whittle at the silicon shape with his scalpel.

"The patient's zygoma, or cheekbone," Brandt was saying, "is already slightly pronounced. So I'm reducing the prosthesis in size somewhat. We don't want to make her look like a Mongol tribesman, after all." The audience chuckled on cue. I felt a flash of irritation—at them, at Brandt, at his stupid jokes and their sycophantic chorus. Just fucking get on with it, I thought, clenching my teeth to keep from saying it out loud.

"Usually," Brandt continued, "we have to go through an incision under the eyes to get these implants in and do it half by feel. In this case, however, we can take advantage of the complete exposure of the skeletal frame of the face to adjust the implants perfectly—isn't that right, Jackson?" he added.

I heard the words but didn't answer. I was thinking of Allie, how he was changing her, making her the way *he* wanted and, in the process, taking away the Allie I knew, taking her away from me.

"Isn't that right?" Brandt repeated. "Jackson?"

"What?" I was uselessly checking something on the surgical tray so I wouldn't have to look at him.

"You see the advantage of putting in the implants now?"

Why the hell was he insisting on the point? Was he gloating?

"Jackson?" He wouldn't let it go.

"Yes," I mumbled, my head down—like a subservient chimpanzee, I thought, baring his neck to the alpha male.

"Excuse me?"

"I suppose so—" I began, when Brandt suddenly erupted.

"Damnation!" he cried, flinging his arm violently in the air. I stepped back, thinking his anger was directed at me. The room became deathly still. I imagined everyone was watching me, the source of Brandt's outburst, but as I glanced up, I saw they weren't even looking in my direction. Something else was riveting their attention. I followed their eyes to the other side of the operating table and saw the cheek implant Brandt had been carving. It had bounced across the floor and come to rest under the supply cart. It must have slipped from his hands. One of the medical students reflexively bent down to retrieve it. "Damn it all," Brandt yelled, "leave the bloody thing alone!

"Nurse?" Restraining his voice, he said, "Another package, please." Henning started to make a wisecrack, but Brandt glowered at him and he cut it off in midsentence.

The nurse went to the storage shelf, brought out another package and opened it onto the tray.

"Let's try this again, shall we?" Brandt's hands worked stiffly, and several awkward minutes passed in silence as he struggled with the scalpel against the silicon shapes. Soon, however, he had regained his customary calm and self-assurance, and the atmosphere of the room returned to normal. When he was satisfied that both implants were the right size, he sutured them in place, forcing the needle through the silicon, then through the fascia overlying the cheekbone, pulling the thread through so it held the implant tightly in position.

"Good," said Brandt after the last stitch, holding up the thread for me to cut. He took the skin of Allie's face and pulled it back across the patchwork of metal braces and reconstructed bones. "I think it's going to look rather good," he commented, radiating satisfaction. I looked down at Allie. Her face now lay loosely on her like a mask, but one could clearly see the altered appearance given by the implants. I had the strange idea that she would begin to talk at any moment behind that mask of loose skin, as if being impersonated by someone else. "Yes," Brandt said, "rather good indeed."

I stood back from the table, and the crowd behind me parted to let me through. An overpowering feeling of alienation, like a wave of nausea, clutched at my throat, and for a moment I thought I would be sick. I could feel the perspiration soaking my paper cap and running down my face, my surgical gown sticking under my arms and to my back. I asked the nurse for a towel, and she came over and patted my face dry again. When she was done, I saw Brandt observing me.

"Okay," he said, "we've just got to open up the jaw and take a look, then we're done. Jackson?"

"Sure," I said, thinking he meant for me to take over. I made an effort to collect myself and began to reach for the scalpel.

"Jackson," he said, "you look fatigued. Let's have Anderson do the cutting."

Anderson showed his surprise but was clearly pleased.

"I'm fine," I said. "I'm not tired at all."

"Let's let Anderson have a go, why don't we?" It was polite, but it was a command. "I'll continue solo while Anderson gets scrubbed."

Anderson quickly scuttled off to the prep room, and I moved away from the crowd, pulling off my gloves and removing my hat. Henning cocked an eyebrow in my direction and shrugged, but I didn't respond. I could feel the questioning glances of the others; no doubt they, too, were wondering why Brandt had taken me out of the operation. My eyes burned, but I held my head up, resolutely avoiding the curious stares as I walked to the back of the room and dropped my gloves and mask in the hazardous waste.

Brandt was talking as he cut: "In this case, it's not necessary to completely expose the bone; we just need a good view of the fracture sight . . ."

He'd never taken me out of an operation before.

" . . . as long as the jaw is structurally secure, all we have to worry about is debriding any splinters . . ."

He can't stand it that I questioned his judgment, I thought. That's why he took me out. That's why he made such a point about the implants. To humiliate me.

" . . . my suspicion is that what we saw on the CT were merely what we call 'artifacts,' ghost images . . ."

I leaned against the wall and folded my arms to keep still. You're making too much of this, I told myself. Your nerves are shot. Memorial is a teaching hospital, after all. It isn't uncommon to give other residents a chance.

I glanced quickly around the room. The crowd's attention had returned to the operating table. No one was looking at me. Everything appeared perfectly normal.

Was I projecting? That's what Stern would have said. Projecting my own anger and distress.

With a pang of anxiety, I wondered how obvious that anger and distress had been. Had anyone noticed? I tried to think back over the operation, imagine how I appeared to others, to Brandt.

I'd made no mistakes. I was good. I'd done everything right. Everyone could see that. And Brandt's outburst—it was simply embarrassment at his one weakness, his arthritis.

"Ah, the prodigal returns," said Brandt as Anderson hurried back into the OR. "I was afraid you'd gotten lost."

Titters all around. Anderson looked up and began to explain himself—"What? Me? No . . ."—accompanied by more laughter.

It was all in your mind, Jackson. Everything's okay. It's okay, I said to myself over and over. Just nerves. Only nerves. It's okay.

Still, Brandt had never taken me out before.

Anderson took his position at the operating table opposite Brandt. I didn't like the idea of his working on Allie, touching her, but there was nothing I could do. I wiped the remaining perspiration from my brow with a paper towel, then ran it over my face and around my neck.

"Anderson," Brandt was saying, "let's get a retractor here to keep it open." Anderson took a retractor from the nurse and fumbled around trying to get a good grip on the severed tissue. "Good," Brandt instructed him, "that's right. Good. No! More open. I need it more open. Lock the clamp—okay, that's all right. Just get ahold of it again and pull it open."

After several more attempts, Anderson finally seemed to get it. "Good," said Brandt. "This—try to keep it exposed, Anderson. Pull it back. Back! Thank you—this looked like a possible break on the CT, but up close and personal, as it were, we can see that it's an old fracture that fully healed, most probably due to some past trauma."

I went to look, but couldn't see past the hunched-over bodies around the table. I moved around to the other side but couldn't see inside the incision.

"There's a bit of what looks like calcification. But here"—Brandt reached in, pushing hard against the jawbone with two fingers, and Allie's entire head moved with the pressure—"we can see that it's solid. Just fine. We can close it up and check on the other side."

Anderson released the retractor, and Brandt began making an incision along the gum over the right lower jaw. I still couldn't get a clear view of the bone.

"Pull back, Anderson. No. More. Okay. Just try again. Relax, Anderson. One more time. Yes. That's it. Well, looks very much the same," said Brandt. "Nothing to worry about here." He had the jawbone in his hand and was opening and closing her mouth like one might with a doll. "Complete structural integrity. Must be an old fracture." I walked around the table again, but the view was blocked at every angle. "A few stitches and we'll be done," he said.

He was going to close her up. It suddenly felt vitally important that I see the injury for myself.

The nurse passed Brandt a suture and needle.

"We'll start here, on the jaw."

I saw Anderson's camera on a cart in the back of the room. I grabbed it and walked rapidly through the crowd until I was directly behind Anderson.

"Why don't we get a picture of this?" I said loudly. "Excuse me, Anderson!" He moved his head automatically and made a half step to the side, still holding the retractors as if his life depended on it.

I pointed the camera, but the angle made it difficult to get a clear view through the lens.

"Anderson!" Brandt said. "We're done now, you can let go with the retractors."

Anderson was trying to move back, but I was leaning past him and he couldn't without pushing me out of the way. I could see the incision clearly now, the bone lying exposed. I rapidly clicked off several frames, barely able to make out the image in the viewfinder, hoping at least some of the photos would show me what I needed to see.

"Nurse," Brandt called. "Is that needle ready? Give it to me, please. Take off the retractors, Anderson."

It was no fracture. The bone had been cut cleanly, just as I had thought.

But there were no plates to fix it in place. Just a darker patch where the plates would have been. It might have been calcification of some kind, as Brandt had said, but I'd never seen any like it before.

Anderson elbowed his way back in front of me and removed the clamps that held the skin and muscle out of the way.

"Thank you," said Brandt. "Okay, let's close her up, shall we?"

No, nothing like it. And I could have sworn that I saw a shape that looked like a screw. But it was half dissolved. It made no sense.

Chapter 29

Anderson called me late that afternoon in my office, sounding confused.

"Hey, Jackson, you know what happened to the film in my camera?"

"What's the problem?" I asked. "Didn't the photos come out?"

"No, that's not what I mean. The camera's empty," he explained. "There's no film inside. I thought that possibly you might have it."

"Gee, no. Are you sure you put any in?"

"Oh shit!" he exclaimed. "Probably not. I hate it when that happens."

"I do it all the time."

"Yeah sure, but— Shit, Brandt is going to be pissed."

"I'm sure he'll understand," I said soothingly.

"I'm not. But hey, that was some operation, wasn't it? Brandt really is a genius."

"Yeah."

"And it was really nice of him asking me to assist like that. I hope you didn't mind."

"No, not at all. You did a great job with the retractors." It was petty, but it went right past him anyway. "Well, I gotta go," I said. "Sorry about the film."

"Yeah. See you," he said, and I hung up.

I dropped off the roll of film at a camera store that evening. They advertised custom developing, and with the flash and the harsh lighting of the OR, I was afraid all the detail would be washed out. I told the guy there I was interested in only the last five frames. I drew him a diagram of the jaw and fracture lines I wanted him to bring out, explaining that it didn't matter if the rest was over- or underexposed or out of focus. He said, "Sure thing," like it was a perfectly normal request, and added that he could also try to enhance the image with his computer. He promised to have them ready on Friday.

Chapter 30

A llie no longer needed to be in intensive care, and using a little bit
of pull, I was able to get her a private room in one of the wards.
Her entire upper face was now swollen from the operation, and with
all the cutting and stitching inside her mouth, it would be several
days before she could speak comfortably. I dropped by now and then
to read to her from the newspaper or magazines, but she could concentrate for only short periods, drifting in and out of sleep even
while I was there.

The following days, after evening rounds, I went down to the
morgue to practice for the next stage in Allie's surgery: the repair of
her badly burnt left ear. The procedure involved cutting cartilage
from the rib cage, carving it into a kind of frame and inserting it
under a flap of skin that would be grafted in place, then cut and
molded to fit. We'd wait to see how Allie healed before scheduling
the second operation, probably in a month or so, and Brandt would
no doubt be taking the lead again; but I wanted to have the procedure down anyway. It allowed me to feel connected with Allie. It gave
me something to do.

It took a little explaining the first day to convince the chief
pathologist, a very tall, thin man named Finiker. Eventually, however,
he acquiesced and took me to the "icebox," as he termed it, where he
opened one of the square doors in the bank of storage lockers that
lined the back wall. He gave the metal tray inside a strong pull—
grunting as he did so—and it came rolling out on its metal casters. A
black plastic bag covered the cadaver that lay on top.

"All yours, Dr. Maebry," he said as he unzipped the body bag.
"One John Doe, all bagged, bled and ready for Potter's Field." Huge,
carelessly sewn sutures ran up the cadaver's bloodless skin, traveling

up from his groin to his chest and forking over his sternum into a "Y" that reached to both shoulders.

"You autopsied him?" I asked.

"We autopsy everyone who dies under suspicious circumstances. It's the law. You might not consider a wino falling down dead from acute alcohol poisoning suspicious. I might not, either. But then I don't set policy in this city, Dr. Maebry."

"You can call me Jackson," I said.

"Fine, Jackson, you can call me Dr. Finiker. If this one meets your requirements, I'll have my assistant set you up on Table B. Now, if you'll excuse me, I've got a lot of work to do." He turned to leave.

"I'm going to need him for a few days," I called as Finiker walked out the door.

"Well, no one's waiting around for his funeral," he shouted back. "Just be sure to put him back where you found him. They hate it when we lose bodies around here."

I took the scalpel—none too clean, I thought, but then it hardly mattered here—and made the first incision through the skin over the chest, which parted before the blade and fell open without resistance, as if it no longer cared. I could have simply cut through the sutures and opened him up that way; with his internal organs wrapped in a plastic bag and stuffed back inside, it would have been a simple matter to harvest as much cartilage as I needed. But I wanted to practice the procedure as I would perform it on Allie. I worked several hours that night, the exhaust fans in the ceiling blowing a steady draft on my head, the cold air reeking of formaldehyde and the natural process of human decay that even the morgue's preservatives couldn't keep out completely.

Finiker was still there when I finished, sawing away with his power machinery in the first autopsy room. After I'd cleaned up, I went in to thank him.

"Can't talk now, Dr. Maebry. People are dropping like flies. Dying left and right. Busy, busy, busy." His assistant, who was lowering a circular saw over the corpse's sternum, just shook his head.

"Enjoy," I said.

"Oh, we will," Finiker shouted above the noise of the power saw. "Every day's a holiday in Memorial Morgue!" As I left, I heard the wet, ripping sound of the saw connecting with flesh.

I avoided Finiker after that, but on the third evening he came by while I was working and stood by me silently, watching. I had the cartilage carved and assembled on the tray—it was my fifth attempt, and I was almost satisfied.

"That's supposed to be an ear?" he asked after a while.

"Supposed to be. The inside of one, at least."

"Hmmm," he mused. "Sort of a strange occupation, plastics. Fabricating one body part out of another. Sort of real and not real at the same time, know what I mean? Kind of gives one the creeps," he added.

"I wouldn't think anything would give you the creeps," I said.

"Oh, you mean because I work with *dead people!*" He laughed one of those dry ha-ha laughs. "The truth is, dead people aren't scary. After all, they're dead. Not much they can do to you. Give you a disease, if you're not careful, but generally they're pretty well behaved. Safe, really. It's the live ones that make me nervous."

"I guess you're in the right profession, then," I said, bending down to make another incision over the cadaver's rib cage.

"We've got a power saw if you want," he offered. "Open that sucker up in two seconds, give you as much cartilage as you need."

"No, thanks, I want to practice with the scalpel. I'll have to use it in the operation."

"Suit yourself," he responded apathetically, picking up the tray and examining my work. "So, you're just going to wrap some skin around that, sew it on her head and voilà! she has a new ear?"

"It's a little bit more complicated, but, yes, that's basically what I'm going to do."

"That's truly amazing," he said. "Truly." He set the tray back down on the table with a clatter. "The things you guys do." I couldn't tell if it was his usual sarcasm or if he was honestly impressed. "It's little short of miraculous."

"Well—" I began.

"No, really," he insisted, giving a phlegm-filled cough, no doubt the result of years spent in formaldehyde-filled fifty-degree drafts. "It's goddamned miraculous, all right." He brought out a handkerchief and spat into it. "Too bad you can't bring the dead back to life."

—

Friday morning I picked up the pictures at the photo shop and called Crockett when I got back to the hospital. The technician had done a good job, but as closely as I studied the photos, I couldn't make any sense of them. I told Crockett I wanted his expert opinion on a strange bone growth I'd come across.

"If it's bones, Jackson, I'm your man!" he boomed across the telephone. "Meet me in the cafeteria, I'm dying of hunger."

I found him at one of the vending machines, pushing quarters in the slot and pulling the lever under the Cracker Jacks. He grabbed the box when it came tumbling down, and we walked over to a table by the window. "If I appear to be in a bad mood," he said as we sat down, "it's because I am. I've been filling out insurance forms for the last two hours and I'm thinking of quitting medicine."

He often said that, so I just smiled.

"I'm not kidding. I didn't go to medical school most of my adult life in order to become a bureaucrat. We're all bureaucrats now. Employees in the faceless bureaucracy of the managed care industry. You know why they call it 'managed care,' don't you?"

"Ahh—"

"Because you're lucky if you can *manage* to get any! Get it?" He leaned across the table and hit me hard on the arm to accentuate the punch line. "I made that up myself."

"Funny," I said.

"Christ!" he swore at the Cracker Jack box. "Look at this. It's congealed into one solid piece." He banged the box against the table several times with no effect. "And if the bureaucrats don't get you, the trial lawyers will. Have you been sued yet, Jackson?" He peeled away the side of the carton and started biting off a corner of the hardened brick of candy.

"No. You?"

"Lots of times. I guess it has something to do with my bedside manner. Patients don't seem to find me sympathetic for some reason." He banged the brick against the table several more times, then went back to chewing on the corner. "So what did you want to see me about?"

I handed him the photographs. "It's that patient of mine. The one with severe facial fractures. That's her jaw," I explained as he held them up toward the window to get better light.

"Lousy camera angle," he remarked.

"Best I could get."

"And the lighting's no good."

"I'm not trying to win a prize, Crockett. Can you tell what it is? Brandt thought it was simply calcification of the bone, but it doesn't look like that to me."

"Well, if Brandt thinks—"

"I want *your* opinion. As an expert."

"It's kind of hard to see, but—this is a fracture here?"

"Could be. But it's pretty clean."

"Yeah. And what are these smudges here?"

"That's what I'm asking you."

"Look, Jackson, I can't be certain, and I don't like to go against another doctor's opinion."

"Okay. Okay. Just between you and me."

He sighed. "As I say, I can't be certain, but it looks to me like absorbable plates."

"Absorbable?"

"Yeah. The caralac reabsorbable fixation system, I believe it's called. It's made from a new polymer of— Oh well, I forget, but it reabsorbs into the bone after several months. Could be very useful for certain procedures."

"I've never heard of it."

"It's new. I've only seen a video of it at a conference once. Supposed to come on the market this month, actually. I've got some on order."

"But then it couldn't be that—"

"Could be. The FDA has been conducting trial runs the last couple of years. I think they said several doctors across the country were licensed to use it on an experimental basis. You could probably call them and find out."

"Thanks," I said, taking the photos back.

"Remarkable things they're inventing these days," Crockett mused, gnawing at the candy. "Almost makes medicine fun again."

"Almost," I agreed. I was thinking about the photos and what they meant.

"I remember when—" He stopped talking, made a huge grimace and brought his hand to his mouth. "Screw it! I think I chipped a tooth!" He felt around in his mouth with his fingers. "I did! I chipped my godda—" The rest was garbled as he reached back to his molars to assess the damage. "Maybe I'll call my lawyer," he concluded after withdrawing his hand. "Sue the Cracker Jack company." He got up, still gripping the Cracker Jacks, no doubt as evidence. "See you around, Jackson," he said. "I've got a phone call to make."

He strode off with his hand in his mouth, and I put the pictures back in my pocket. So it wasn't an accident, I thought. Allie had had surgery before.

Chapter 31

I went back to my office and called the FDA. After half an hour or so of negotiating the phone menu, I finally came to a live person who transferred me to someone else, who transferred me back to the first person, who then switched me to another number that rang for several minutes without anyone picking up. I imagined a large building somewhere in Washington with hundreds of empty rooms, phones ringing endlessly, unanswered.

I was about to hang up when a recorded message came on, telling me to give my name, fax number and a detailed inquiry, and someone would get back to me within forty-eight hours. I explained who I was, that I had a patient for whom the reabsorbable fixation system was indicated and that it would be helpful to talk with one of the surgeons involved in the FDA trial who had some experience using the material. I left my fax number and hung up, convinced I would never hear from them again.

—

The library was in a "temporary annex," set up ten years earlier in a couple of trailers on the hospital grounds while the administration raised funds for a permanent building. I walked down there and searched through the stacks until I found what I was looking for: a large blue-bound book titled *Modern Reconstructive Techniques in Cases of Craniofacial Abnormality.*

I'd read it my first year of residency and remembered it now: the before-and-after pictures of patients with terrible congenital deformities—facial features that have grown huge or failed to develop to normal size, misshapen skulls twice as big on one side, bulbous foreheads that look like space aliens' in a science fiction movie. Something gets mixed up in the DNA; the genetic codes that regulate the growth process—signaling when to start and when to stop—misfire, miss their cues. It can happen in any part of the body, and does, but somehow facial deformities seem the worst, perhaps because they're so impossible to hide.

There was a joke we all heard starting out in plastics: What do you call a funny-looking kid who's had craniofacial surgery? The punch line was: A funny-looking kid. That was largely medical school cynicism, however, and not always true. Some abnormalities were easier to treat than others. Some patients would never look entirely normal, but in some cases the results were extraordinary.

In the second year of my residency, I witnessed one such operation on a child with a hugely elongated skull. The surgeons removed the entire cranial vault—everything above the eye and the ear canal—and refashioned it, cutting the bone into sections and carving those sections into smaller pieces that they then refit into the shape of a normal skull. It was as if one had taken the rind off half of a melon, cut it into wedges, skimmed about a third from each wedge and formed it back into a smaller hemisphere. I saw the child a year later when he came back for a postoperative examination. His hair had grown in, and he looked like a normal, happy twelve-year-old. The nurse remarked that it was the first time she had seen him smile.

I flipped through the book, each section with a scientific name indicating a specific abnormality: "A Quantitative Assessment of Sagittal Synostosis and Curzon's Syndrome," "Mask Rhinoplasty: A Treatment for Binder's Syndrome." I kept going until I came to the section titled "Methods for the Correction of Prognathism." The last was the medical term for an overly developed, jutting jaw.

Pictures showed the surgeons making an incision between the lip and the gums on the lower mandible, or jaw, and opening it up to the bone. A diagram demonstrated how the bone would be severed on each side in two places, a section removed and the shortened jaw bolted back in place. On the next page were before-and-after photographs of the patient, a small girl. The first looked grotesque, hardly human, the second like nothing had ever been wrong. The authors concluded with a short statement that craniofacial corrections of prognathism were some of the most consistently successful, giving patients an "entirely normal look."

The position of the plates on the young girl's jaw roughly corresponded to the shadows on Allie's CT.

I looked at the little girl in the photograph, the bottom part of her face jutting out like a wolf's snout, the fear and sadness in her eyes. I tried to imagine Allie like that, but I couldn't bring myself to do it. Something inside me rejected the possibility. It was an accident, my mind kept insisting. An accident.

Chapter 32

I called Anderson and asked if he'd cover for me the next day. He hemmed and hawed until I promised I'd take the next two weekend nights he was on call. Then he readily agreed. "Sure, Jackson. Always ready to help a friend in need."

I got up early the next morning and drove through town to Route 80, crossing the endless expanse of the Bay Bridge and continuing on to the exit for U.S. 5, where I followed the signs pointing south. South toward Fresno and then on to Vidalis, Allie's hometown.

Before long, the strip malls and condo developments gave on to infinite farmland, rows of apricot and almond orchards in perfect straight lines, flashing by like the stuttering frames of an old-fashioned projector. I pulled into the fast lane and accelerated past the tractor trailers, the pickups with loose, flapping fenders and Mexican laborers hunched behind the cab to escape the wind, my old Honda pushing ninety by the time I got to Fresno. The car shuddered in protest as I angled onto the exit and pressed down hard on the brakes to keep from being thrown off the curving ramp.

Ten or so miles farther east, I came to the outskirts of Vidalis. A neon sign on a bank by the side of the road announced that the temperature was 110 degrees. Even with the air conditioner turned all the way up, the air inside my car was stifling.

I slowed in the traffic, passing gas stations, car dealerships, fast-food franchises and farm machinery outlets, and was already on the outskirts on the other side of the town before I realized I'd entered it, the sidewalks ending abruptly before low rows of cabbage and caked soil. I turned and drove through the streets until I found what I was searching for—a low brick building with a flagpole beside the entrance supporting a motionless flag. Underneath was a sign: VIDALIS REGIONAL HIGH SCHOOL.

There wasn't a person in sight, but then I couldn't imagine children hanging around on the close-cropped dusty lawn even on cooler days. I walked up to the front door and peered through the window into the darkened hallway. Patches of light seeped through the classroom doors and reflected off the linoleum floor, but nothing moved inside. The building was empty. I tried the door and found it locked. Of course, I realized, it's August, school is closed for the summer. I laughed at myself. What a stupid mistake.

I deserved this, I thought. I had no right to go snooping into Allie's past.

I rattled the school doors and kicked them in frustration. A car drove by, the sun exploding off its metallic surface into my eyes. The driver slowed down to see what was going on but didn't stop.

Allie was slipping away from me, I could feel it. There was a void between us now, growing wider with each passing day. And in the middle of it all somewhere was her secret. The one she wouldn't share. The one that excluded me.

The sun was moving directly overhead now, extinguishing the last bit of shadow as it climbed, flattening the landscape into two lifeless dimensions.

I rattled the handle again and called out to anyone who might be inside to open the door. Nothing.

—

The interior of my car was burning by the time I got back to it, and I had to turn on the air conditioner and wait several minutes before getting inside. On the way out of town, I stopped at a grocery store and bought a bottle of water. I took it outside to the parking lot, drinking half and pouring the rest over my head. I was dry again a moment later.

I went back in the store to buy another. It seemed pointless, but I asked the woman behind the counter if the high school ever opened during the summer.

"Not until September. This is a farming town. Kids have jobs."

"No summer school?"

"They go to Fresno, the kids that need it." She looked at me suspiciously. "You got business there?"

"I was driving through. I have a friend who went to high school here, and I wanted to look her up in the school yearbook." It sounded odd even to me, but she seemed to find it reasonable.

"Well, you might try at the public library down the street. It's open until four." She handed me my change with a smile. I thanked her, took my water and headed in the direction she pointed.

The library was empty except for an old man at one of the tables. No librarian appeared at the desk, so I found the reference section by myself and searched through the shelves until I saw one lined with large red hardcovers with dates engraved in gold lettering on the bindings. The high school yearbooks.

I picked out the year Allie would have graduated and leafed quickly through the names beginning with "S." Rows of young faces looked out at me, the girls in their best dresses, the boys looking uncomfortable in jackets and ties. I flipped back a page and scanned the pictures: Robyn Sarnes, Saul Schickler, Joan Sherry, Joy Shimomura . . . Stadler . . . Stentina . . . Szosteki. Allie's picture wasn't there. Then I saw a blank gray square in the bottom corner of the page. Her name was printed underneath: Alexandra Sorosh. Under that, her nickname, Allie. No quotation full of adolescent angst, pretentious learning or young hope. No picture. Just the blank space, held ready for the graduation photo that never came.

After the portraits were the group photographs and candid shots: the football team, the 4-H club, happy students wearing costumes at the Halloween dance. Underneath a candid shot of several candy stripers, girls who volunteered as nurses' helpers in the local hospital, I noticed "A. Sorosh," and searched the photograph for her. The printing quality was poor, and it was difficult to make out the features, but by a process of mostly elimination, I found her. She must have been caught by the photographer with the group, no chance to escape. Her face was blurred, as if she'd suddenly moved her head, and she was looking down and away, her golden hair—it looked white in the black-and-white photo—pushed forward, as if to cover as much of her face as possible.

"Can I help you?"

It was the librarian, standing at the end of the stacks, looking pleased that someone was using his library.

"No," I said, closing the book and putting it back. "No, you can't."

—

Back in my car, I thought of something Allie had once said. We were out driving, and she remarked that the street we were on had the same name as the street she grew up on. Unconsciously, the name had become the basis for the mental image I had constructed for her hometown, an image very different from the reality, as it turned out. There was tall grass in my vision, also flowers, and a child running. I could see it so plainly. What was the name? A child running in summer through a field. Summerfield.

I stopped at a gas station to fill my tank and asked the attendant as I was paying if he knew where Summerfield Street was.

"No," he replied, making change. He handed it to me and I said thanks. "There's a Summerfield Place, though, a mile or so out. Just follow Center Street. It's in the development there."

I found the road and drove until I came to what had to be the development, an island of homes in a sea of borderless farms. White-painted brick pillars marked the entrance, but there was no fence or other demarcation. The houses were in fact trailers, but well kept and fixed to permanent foundations, surrounded by neat lawns that must have been watered daily to stay so green. Summerfield Place, despite its name, was a through street running along the eastern edge of the development. There were at least twenty houses that might have been hers.

As I drove by, several teenagers came out of one of the trailer homes, piled into a black Trans-Am with tinted windows and roared off. The heat had forced most people inside, and I saw no other sign of life until I noticed a solitary female figure stooped over on her small patch of lawn, banging away with a wrench at the nozzle of a sprinkler. She was wearing a tank top that was stretched to the limit and spandex shorts that were stretched well beyond. I pulled alongside and rolled down the window. "Hi," I called out.

She turned my way and nodded hello.

"Do you know if a family by the name of Sorosh used to live on this street? It may have been a while ago. In the eighties."

"The Soroshes live a few houses down. Right there." She pointed and began banging again, anxious to get back inside and out of the sun as quickly as possible.

"They *live* there?"

"In the yellow house with white trim." She banged again, and the sprinkler erupted in a geyser of water.

"Thanks," I said, moving on. It must be a coincidence, I thought. Perhaps cousins Allie had never mentioned.

All the trailers seemed to be painted yellow or brown, but I found the one the woman meant. There was a decorative lamppost by the walk and a little sign saying SOROSH. I got out and rang the bell.

The front door opened. Inside, peering out into the sunlight, stood a small, delicate-looking woman—in her early seventies, I guessed. She gave me a friendly half smile, the other half held in reserve in case I turned out to be a salesman.

"Hello, I . . . I'm looking for . . . I have a friend, Alexandra Sorosh—do you know if her family . . ." I stopped my broken questioning as her face lit up in recognition.

"Did you say you're a friend of Allie's?" she asked.

"Yes, I was driving by and—"

"How wonderful!" she exclaimed, her smile becoming complete. "I didn't get your name?"

"Jackson. Jackson Maebry." There was no evident reaction to the name, but she remained just as friendly.

"Well, well. That's so nice. I'm Mary." We shook hands. "Why don't you come in out of the heat."

The front door led directly into a small living room, which, on the far side, became a dining area with an adjacent kitchen. It was all extremely tidy, as if the knickknacks on the tables hadn't been moved, but for the weekly dusting, in years.

"You must be thirsty. Can I get you something? A Coke? We don't have Diet Coke. I know you young people like Diet Coke, but—"

"Real Coke would be just fine," I assured her.

We passed a door, slightly ajar, leading into a darkened room. Inside I caught sight of the lanky figure of a man lying on an unmade bed, his head cocked to the side, motionless, as if anticipating something. A voice from the radio on his bedside table announced the call letters of Fresno's "Smooth Groove EZ Listening" station.

"That's Mr. Sorosh," Mary explained as she quietly closed the door. "He hasn't been the same since his retirement. Heart trouble, they say."

I didn't remember Allie mentioning any grandparents.

Mary sat me down at the table in the dining area and went off into the kitchen for my Coke. Through the window I saw their neat backyard bordered by a low chain-link fence. Beyond the fence a flat expanse of cultivated land stretched out a mile or so before disappearing in the dusty haze that hung above the baking earth.

"Please excuse the mess," she said, placing the glass of Coke before me on a coaster and gathering up a small piece of needlepoint from the table. On the walls were the modestly framed results of her work, pleasant designs with little homilies: "A Stitch in Time," "God Bless Our Happy Home," a longer one called "Footsteps in the Sand."

"We're not used to visitors. We just live here by ourselves now." She sat down so that only the corner of the table separated us, her hands folded together in front of her. "It's so wonderful to meet a friend of Allie's."

I smiled. "How long have you lived here?"

"Oh, almost twenty-five years now. Since shortly after we had Allie. Doesn't seem that long. Almost like yesterday. She used to play right out there. We had a pool then. John"—she nodded in the direction of the closed door—"he built it for her. We took it down, of course, after she left, wasn't much use for it. Are you all right?" she asked, putting her hand on my arm.

"Yes. It must be the heat." I drank down the Coke and wiped my forehead with a napkin she brought out from a drawer under the table. I needed time to take in what she was saying. "So you're—" I stopped. What was I going to ask: So you're the mother Allie told me was dead?

"We had Allie very late," Mary explained, thinking my question was about her age. "She was our miracle child." Her smile turned inward, toward less happy thoughts. "Mr. Sorosh—John—I guess, well, he wasn't expecting . . . and we—well, they were difficult times for us. My! You're all finished!" she exclaimed. "Let me get you another glass of Coke." She picked up my glass and bustled off again to the kitchen.

Through the window, I could see a solitary piece of farm machinery moving across the land in slow circles, a thick cloud of dust rising behind. I thought of Allie facing away from me, stillness all around. "My parents passed away some time ago," she had said. "They were very old." I had moved around to see her face. It was closed to me; in sadness, I had assumed then. In mourning. You always turned away, didn't you, Allie? You weren't a very good liar. Just very good at keeping secrets.

"It's *so* nice your coming to visit," Mary said as she sat back down. "We don't hear much from Allie these days."

"You haven't talked recently?" I asked.

"She's busy, of course, she doesn't have time. We understand that." They didn't know about the assault.

"She's got a full life now. A successful young career woman." She said "career woman" as if it were something exotic that one reads about only in magazines. "She's even been on TV. Have you seen her on TV?"

Sometimes Genederm would send Allie for interviews, on those rare occasions when the head of public affairs wasn't available for the cameras. "She's wonderful," I agreed.

"We haven't seen it, but we have a picture of her. She sent it to us. It's right over here, in the living room." She led me the few steps into the living room, to an end table crowded with framed photographs. The biggest picture was of Allie, a publicity photo taken by a professional photographer.

"Isn't she pretty?" Allie's mother was holding the frame in her hands, which shook slightly, either with age or with emotion. "We're so proud of her," she said with unexpected intensity.

I said something bland to the effect that they had a lot to be proud of. I saw Mary wipe away a tear.

Almost reflexively, I reached over and picked out a small photo that was hidden away in the back of the group. It was of a little girl, about seven or eight years old as best I could judge, sitting alone in the brown grass of her backyard, near the blue siding of the swimming pool. I recognized the fence, the dusty field in the background.

It was like seeing the sibling of someone you knew well: generally different in appearance but with some features so strikingly similar that they might have been physically transposed. The bridge of a nose, the forehead. She must have been swimming—her hair was wet and stringy, just as it gets now, I thought, when she takes a shower. It was Allie.

The pictures in the textbooks had let me know generally what to expect. Her jaw was huge, disproportionate, suitable for a face twice the size, and her mouth was twisted down in a frown—from unhappiness, I wondered, or just the pull of muscles in her face? One of the hardest things for children with severe facial abnormalities, according to the textbook, is that the distortion of features often hides the child's true expression.

They've studied these children and their interaction with others. It isn't simply that people are put off by what they see. It's also what they don't see, those cues that we all—parents especially—are used to picking up on, perhaps are programmed in some basic way to respond to. We communicate so much through subtle changes in expression, a slight curl of the lips, a frown, a smile; a thousand subtle variations of each. And when we don't find them, we become confused and withdraw. So even as infants, children like Allie don't get the same kind of response, the cooing back-and-forth that mothers do instinctively with their offspring. From the earliest moment of awareness, there is a disconnect, a severing of the most important of human bonds.

I looked up from the photo to Mary Sorosh, her face yellowed by the remorseless sunlight forcing its way through the curtains. Motes of dust caught the light as the air inside warmed and rose, despite the air-conditioning. " . . . not like other children—Allie was special," she was saying, but between the words it was as if she was making a confession of guilt. She hadn't expected visitors, and now, with this photo, she had revealed a secret that she shouldn't have. Or maybe it was for some deeper reason.

"I know," I said simply. "I know about Allie."

Her face registered relief. "Mr. Sorosh," Mary confided in a low voice, "he was a good father, but he never could adjust—he just didn't feel the way a father should toward his child . . . He's a *good* man, really . . . and then he lost his job, no insurance, so little money . . ." She was trying to explain herself to me, as if I might be able to give her some kind of absolution. I could see it in her face, the memory of her daughter's long childhood loneliness and hurt, her own failure and inadequacy, so deep that even if she had it to do all over again, she knew she could do no better.

She talked on, something about a doctor in Sacramento, a painful operation, complications—but it was too garbled to get straight, and I didn't have the heart to grill her on the details. I understood the general picture.

"You're a good friend to Allie, I can tell," she said, taking my arm in a frail hug.

I needed to get outside. Away. "I really must go. I'm sorry. I have to get back to the city." I started toward the door, but she only grasped my arm tighter.

"You'll give her our love, won't you, Mr. Maebry?"

"Yes, I will. I promise."

"We haven't heard from her in so long. Tell her to call."

"Yes, of course." I practically had to drag her across the rug to get to the door.

"It's just . . . we're so happy for her. Tell her that."

A shaft of light burst into the room as I opened the door. Mary seemed to wither in the heat as we stood there. She was still clinging to my arm.

"Yes. Yes. I will. Thank you for the Coke," I said, prying her grip loose as gently as I could.

"We're so happy for her," she called out as I walked away.

The air conditioner blew hot air, and the car seat burned through my clothes as I drove off. I knew she was standing in the door waving good-bye, but I didn't turn to look. I didn't want to see.

Chapter 33

Allie was to be discharged from the hospital the next day. I could have prevailed on the administration to keep her a few more days, but she was anxious to leave, and there was no good medical reason to keep her there.

I went by in the morning to help her gather her things, and we drove in silence to her apartment in Berkeley. She leaned against the wall in the hallway as I unlocked the door and then followed me inside.

"God bless our happy home," she muttered to herself as I walked to the window to let in some fresh air. When I turned back, she was struggling with the mirror that hung by the entrance, trying to lower it behind a side table there. It slipped from her hands and fell the final foot to the floor, but there was no sound of shattering glass.

"At least it didn't break," she said, her mouth twitching in what would have been a wry smile but for the sutures and swollen skin. "Enough bad luck as it is."

"Maybe now isn't the best time to be moving furniture," I said. We sat on the couch together, and I took her arm with the cast and put it back in its sling. She was flexing her hand as I did so and wincing. "Does it hurt?" I asked.

"Everything hurts, Jackson."

"I know," I said. I got her two Percocets and helped her take them with a glass of water, then laid her down on the couch and got a blanket.

"There's no food here," I said. "Why don't I get some takeout? It's bound to make you feel better to eat something other than hospital food."

"Okay," she said.

"Chinese?"

"Fine," she agreed without enthusiasm.

"Italian? Vietnamese? Indian?"

"Sure, anything. Just get some beer with it."

"It's not a good idea to—" I began. "Okay, sure, some beer. How about some videos? Anything you want to see?"

She shrugged. "Sure."

"What?"

"I don't know. How about *The Hunchback of Notre Dame?*"

"Come on, Allie."

"Or *The Phantom of the Opera.*" Her head was down and I couldn't see her expression.

"I don't—" I began again.

"Think it's a good idea," she finished my sentence with a bitter laugh. "Get whatever you want. It doesn't matter."

By the time I returned with the food, she had moved to her bedroom and said she wasn't hungry. She just wanted a beer. I brought one in for each of us and helped her sit up on the bed.

"It still hurts, Jacko. Even with the painkillers. Everything hurts."

"You've been through a lot of trauma. It's going to hurt for a while."

Allie tried to sip from the bottle and grimaced. "Sometimes, when I woke up in the hospital, I didn't feel it for the first moment. The pain, you know? And I thought maybe it had all been a bad dream, or it was over. And then the pain would return, and everything hurt again. Everything. Every object I touched—the bed, the sheets when they brushed against my skin. Even the light hurt. So I'd turn away, but it hurt just to look at things. The ceiling, the walls. They were all part of the pain. Do you know what I mean? They were all just different forms of pain."

"Your body is exhausted, Allie, and when it's exhausted, it has less defense against pain. I know it feels overwhelming now, but you just need to rest, give it time.

"I'll stay with you tonight," I added after a moment. "Sleep on the couch." I wondered if she was frightened to be alone, but she'd never mentioned it to me, and I didn't want to upset her by bringing it up. Lost in her thoughts, she didn't answer.

"It's like it's locked inside, Jackson. The pain is locked inside. That's why it won't go away. Like it's this thing inside my soul—you know?—this evil thing deep inside."

"Allie—"

"And it's telling me, it's saying, 'You're just a freak, a hideous, ugly *freak*. Why did you ever think you could be anything else?'"

"Allie, don't say that."

She was crying now, the kind of tears that bring no relief. Neither of us said anything for a while. I finished my beer and wished for more but didn't get up.

Allie handed me hers. "Here, I don't want it."

I drank in silence. It seemed as good a time as any to say what I needed to say. There wasn't going to be a better one. I had some idea it might help.

"Allie, I . . . I know about your earlier operation."

She didn't move or register that she'd heard. Then she asked slowly, "What do you mean?"

"On your jaw. I know you had corrective surgery there."

Again she didn't respond at first. Then: "I didn't want you to know."

"It doesn't matter, Allie, I only brought it up because of what you were saying, and I wanted—"

"How do you know, did someone tell you? It was supposed to be confidential." Her tone was emotionless, frozen. The voice of someone in shock.

"No one told me, Allie. During the operation, I could see." I wasn't going to mention Vidalis now. I wished I'd never gone.

"It's still visible? You can see?" She brought her hand up as if to hide it.

"Inside, yes. I could tell."

"It was supposed to disappear, like it never happened."

"It has, partially. But not completely yet. It doesn't matter, I—"

"You know what I looked like."

"Allie—"

"You *know*," she cried. One more deep, undeserved hurt that she couldn't understand.

I had been meaning to ask her about her doctor, the one in Sacramento, but it didn't matter now. It was just selfish curiosity, I realized, feeling ashamed. I wanted to get away from the subject. As far away as possible.

"It doesn't matter to me, Allie, I thought—"

She shrank away from me as I tried to put my arm around her. I sat back. "Allie, I love you. It doesn't matter what you looked like. All that matters is that we love each other."

A tremor ran through her body. She held her arms tightly to her chest to stop from shaking.

"You never would have loved me like that," she said coldly, as if there was no possibility of contradiction.

I thought of that little girl in her mother's photograph, sitting alone in her backyard in Vidalis. If I could have reached back over time, I would have taken her to me, protected her, loved her. I loved that little girl, and I knew beyond all doubt that I loved the woman she had become; loved her now more than I ever had before.

But—

In my thoughts I could almost hear the prosecution making its case against me. "What you feel *today* isn't the issue, is it? Can you honestly say you would have fallen for someone with such a deformity? Do you want us to believe that you would have learned to love her the way you did? That you would have even given it a chance?" The questions might as well have been rhetorical.

"We love each other *now*. That's all that matters," I insisted, knowing it wasn't all that mattered, sensing that in some irrevocable way I had betrayed her, before we had even met or known of each other's existence, from some broken beginning too far back to ever be set right again. I had betrayed the only woman I had ever loved. The only person who had ever loved me.

"We love each other *now*!" I said, as if repetition might change her mind, justify my treason.

She turned her head away, as best she could with the bandages; out of shame for me or for herself, I didn't know.

"I love you *now*," I pleaded, my words falling into the silence between us like worthless coins dropping down an empty well.

———

I went back the next day after work to keep her company. She slept most of the evening and into the night, but in the early morning the painkillers wore off and I heard her calling to me from the bedroom. I got up off the couch where I'd been sleeping and went in to see her. She'd been crying in her sleep from the pain—her pillow was wet—and she was groggy and disoriented from the drugs, but all that, I knew, would pass. What worried me was her emotional state. Brandt, I thought again, had raised her hopes too high. Last week's surgery wasn't the end of her ordeal, it was just the beginning, and she was coming to understand that as much as she had endured already, and as much as she would have to endure in the future, when it was all over, when everything had been done medically that could be done, things would still never be the same again.

I got her two more pills and she sat up against the headboard, her eyes cast down at the blankets, too exhausted to lift them up. She held the covers tightly to her chin, even though the temperature in Berkeley never fell below eighty that night and the central air-conditioning was no match for the heat.

"Do you want to sleep some more?" I asked.

"No." She shivered and clutched the blankets even tighter.

I got two beers and we sat together without talking. In time the Percocet took the edge off the pain, and she loosened her grip on the blankets enough to accept the beer I offered. She drank with difficulty, holding the mouth of the bottle gingerly to her bruised lips.

"Remember telling me once how you used to feel different as a child?" she asked. "Like you came from this weird family, and you were afraid that if anyone knew, they'd hate you for it. You were just so ashamed, like it was this horrible secret."

"I remember."

"And when you were out in public with your mother, you'd pretend you didn't know her."

"Yeah, I'd stay as far away as I could."

She took a few delicate sips, silent again. Deep in her thoughts. "It's a funny thing," she said after a while.

"That I was embarrassed by my mother? I suppose so. I guess it wasn't right to feel that way, but—"

"No," she interrupted me. "You *were* right. That's what I'm saying."

"What do you mean? I was right to be ashamed?"

She shook her head. "You were right that people would have hated you. They would have if they'd known."

"I'm not sure . . . I don't—"

"Of course they would have," she stated impatiently, as if it was an obvious truth and I was simply being obstinate not to admit it. "You know I'm right."

I didn't know what to say, so remained silent.

She slowly finished the beer, then began again. "Do you know the story of Jesus and the blind man?"

I didn't.

"In the Bible, Jacko. The story in the Bible."

"I haven't really read the Bible," I explained. "Just a couple of excerpts in a literature class in college."

"Anyway," she continued, "our minister gave a sermon on the passage once. I remember it really well, though I guess I wasn't more than seven or eight at the time." The same age as in the photo, I thought. "Jesus sees this blind man begging outside the temple, and he commands the crowd to bring the man to him. So they do. They go out to get him, but the blind man thinks they're simply harassing him again, making fun of him, you know, like they've done all his life. He's kicking and screaming as they carry him in, and the crowd thinks this is really funny. They're laughing at him, and he's pleading with them not to hurt a poor blind man, to just leave him alone. And the more he cries out, the more pitiful he becomes. And the more pitiful he is, the more they jeer at him, of course."

She paused a moment, seeming to reflect on what she'd said. "So, anyway, Jesus smears mud on the blind man's eyes and tells the crowd to take him to the fountain to wash it off. The guy is still whimpering and pleading, and he looks even sillier than before, and the crowd thinks this is just great. It's all a circus to them, the best entertainment they've had in years."

"So what happened then?" I asked.

"They wash the mud from his eyes and he sees again," she said matter-of-factly.

"So it was a miracle, right?" I couldn't understand what she was trying to tell me.

She didn't seem to hear the question and went on along her own train of thought. "After that service, I would sometimes . . . you know, when I was in my bath, I would splash soapy water from the tub into my face and open my eyes as it poured off, letting the soap get into my eyes and feeling it sting—the more it stung, the better—and I would imagine that I was the blind man, seeing for the first time . . .

and then I'd think that maybe the next time I looked in the mirror, I'd be different, too."

"Jesus, Allie." I reached out and held her arm through the blanket.

"It's like that movie *The Hunchback of Notre Dame,* which you wouldn't rent because you thought it would upset me."

"I—"

"When they see the Hunchback, they jeer at him. Point their fingers and laugh and throw things at him. Why do people jeer at deformity? Why do you think, Jackson?" She waited, expecting an answer.

"Because— I don't know. Maybe they're scared, afraid that it could happen to them. It's a way of distancing themselves." It seemed lame even as I said it. The sort of response Stern would have made.

Allie bristled. "That's what people always say. But it doesn't make a lot of sense, not if you think about it. I mean, what's to be afraid of? Sure, maybe they might go blind, or become crazy like your mother, but they're not going to develop a hunchback or become a dwarf. Why do they hate it so much?"

"I don't know."

"I do, though. I know." She held her head up—the first time that evening—and looked directly at me, challenging me to disagree, but then tired of the effort and turned her face back down. "It's like it isn't enough to be cursed by nature. Cursed by God. It's like they feel that the shame isn't enough, isn't deep enough, they need to drive it down deeper into your heart. They have to make sure it's total, complete. Like, if we leave this person alone with his misery, there may be one spark of hope left, one ember. So they have to stamp it out, destroy it, leave nothing but ashes."

"God, Allie, everybody isn't like that."

"No? Maybe not," she said unconvincingly, saying it only to placate me. I felt useless, like a bystander at an accident with no help to offer. All the nice, consoling things I'd meant to say, all the comfort I wanted to bring her, she'd already rejected.

She asked for more beer and I handed her mine. She drank some and went on. "We had this older minister. He was a nice guy, the one who told that story. But he died of cancer. The new one, he was young and really smart. Had a Ph.D., everyone said. He read us this sermon by one of the great ministers from a long time back. A lot of people in the church didn't like it at all. They said it was really morbid. He talked about all these millions of souls, the souls of sinners, and said they were like snowflakes falling into hell."

"That is kind of morbid."

"Maybe," she said. "Maybe that's just what people say when they don't want to think about something. What really got to me was this idea that God had drawn a kind of circle, and that for everyone outside the circle, it didn't matter how hard they tried, how much they wanted to get in. They couldn't. It was fate. And for them, there was nothing to hope for. No compassion, no redemption, nothing. Even if you love them—even if they love you—it doesn't make any difference, because all those human things, all those human feelings, don't matter. They're as good as dead."

"Jesus, Allie, that sounds so cruel."

"I didn't make it up," she said, flashing an angry look at me. "It's just the way it is."

I didn't protest again. I didn't want her to be upset with me. She still gripped the blanket tightly around her body, shivering. I could feel the perspiration dripping under my arms.

"It's a funny thing," she said after a while, as if bringing the conversation around to its beginning.

"What, Allie?"

"How they all have to die in the end."

Again I didn't follow.

"In the movies, Jackson. The Hunchback. The Phantom. It's like no one can figure out what to do with them, so they have to be killed off. They all get crushed or fall off a tower or get burnt up in the end. Sort of like . . ."

"Like what, Allie?"

"Like snowflakes. Falling into hell."

Chapter 34

Allie told me when I called the next day that she wasn't up to a visit; she wanted to spend the next few days alone. I occupied myself with the hospital routine, scheduling two or three operations each day. Evenings, I'd go down to the morgue to practice on my cadaver.

That's where I was when Krista had the Control Center beep me. I called her back at her home number.

"Hey, Jackson," she said cheerfully. I wasn't in the mood for cheerful.

"Hi, Krista. I've been meaning to thank you for looking after Allie while she was in intensive care. It took a load off my mind."

"Actually, that's why I called. Allie has hired me as a private nurse to look after her a couple of hours each day." Typical Krista, I inwardly grumbled, meddling in my life in the most helpful, generous way. One couldn't help but feel guilty for resenting it.

"Is it really necessary?" I asked with obvious irritation.

Krista didn't notice, of course. That was typical, too. "It's no problem," she went on chirpingly. "I moonlight sometimes for extra money. Her insurance covers it, and anyway, we got along in the ICU. She's kinda quiet, but she seems a very nice person. And I feel so sorry for her."

"Well, thanks, Krista. I'll have to take you out sometime to show you my gratitude."

"How about tonight?" she suggested. I immediately regretted my offer.

"Well—"

"You're off now, right? And I don't start my shift until eight. Why don't we meet at the Golden Gate?"

"The bridge?"

"No, silly, the café you and I used to go to all the time, remember? You can have dinner and I'll have breakfast. Just like old times."

She had me. "Okay, sure," I agreed. "I need to clean up first. I'll meet you there in about an hour. Where is it again?"

"That's so like you, Jackson. Such a space cadet."

She gave me the address—just a few blocks from the hospital—and I went to the locker room to shower and change into my street clothes. Krista was already seated when I arrived, and she waved to me from a booth in the back, away from the noisy bar. I could see she was dressed up, complete with makeup and blow-dried hair, and I had the uncomfortable feeling it was for my benefit. Her shift went until the early morning. She wouldn't be seeing anyone else that night except patients.

She stood and held up her cheek for a kiss hello, and I obliged. I had to admit she looked good: a tight skirt, silk blouse just transparent enough to give a hint of the lace bra underneath, long auburn hair. A face that alternated between cute and sexy, depending on her mood, or mine. I marveled again at the fact that after two or three dates, I had somehow lost any physical attraction to her.

She sat down opposite me and leaned across the table to look me in my "big, dark eyes," she said. "You look terrible, Jackson," she concluded, knitting her brow with concern.

I shrugged.

"You've got to take better care of yourself. I bet you've been living on coffee and peanut butter cups and this is the first real meal you'll have had in ages."

"Got me," I admitted. And then, because it was expected: "You look great."

"Thank you. I've taken up swimming. I joined a club. I've lost seven pounds." She made it sound like a rebuke.

"Great."

"It's a real classy place. Lots of cute guys in their tiny Speedos. I think some of them are even heterosexual, which is pretty rare in this town."

"Great."

"I swim three miles, five times a week. I'm really getting into shape. I bought this really cute one-piece swimsuit—a whole size smaller. Too bad you can't see my body now."

"It's a shame," I agreed.

"Well, you make your decisions and you accept the consequences." She said it as if she'd scored a point.

Thankfully, the waitress came by at that moment. Krista ordered a salad and I asked for a burger and fries. Krista insisted that I have a salad, too, and I said all right. When the waitress left, Krista became solicitous again, reaching forward and putting her hand on my arm.

"You've got to take better care of yourself, Jackson," she said.

"I'm okay." I didn't move away, but her touch felt awkward.

"Hardly. I *know* you, remember."

"I'm okay, really."

"Always the same, Jackson. You know what your problem is?"

"I can think of a few," I said, trying to lighten the conversation, but Krista went on even more earnestly.

"Your problem is that you can't get outside of yourself. You worry too much. It's like—what's the expression?—'wheels within wheels,' turning and churning away." She released my arm and made what I supposed was a churning motion with her hands. I used the opportunity to sit back in the booth, out of her reach. "It's so hard sometimes even to make contact with you. It's like you're a thousand miles away."

"Let's not talk about me, okay?"

"And you're so *touchy.*"

"I'm not touchy," I said peevishly, feeling ridiculous that I had to respond at all.

"You see!"

"Okay, that's right, you win. I'm touchy. Can we talk about something else? How are your cats?" Krista loved to talk about her cats. I knew it was my one hope of changing the subject.

"Fine," she said with a toss of her head. "We won't talk about Jackson." She was mad, but she couldn't resist telling me the continuing saga of her cats. Apparently she'd found a new stray and taken him in, making a total, she said, of five. The waitress came with our food and wrote out the check at my request. I dug in, surprised at my own appetite. After a moment I realized that Krista had fallen silent. I looked up from my burger and saw her picking at her salad.

"Allie seems to be doing much better," she said after a while.

"Yes. Thanks again for looking after her in the ICU."

"I was glad to do it. I'm always there for you, Jackson, you know that."

"Thanks," I repeated.

"I mean, we do care about each other, don't we?"

"Yes."

"Don't we?" she insisted.

"Yes, Krista, of course we do." I felt like I was repeating a catechism.

"So." She peered at me intensely and her voice was suddenly bright. "Are you two together? Is she your new girlfriend?"

"She's a good friend," I replied, putting the emphasis on "friend."

"You've been seeing her for a while?" she continued, as if I'd answered yes.

"I've known her for a while."

"Is she the one you dumped me for?" She said it with a smile that she didn't mean.

"I didn't dump you, Krista. It just didn't work out."

"It certainly seemed to me like you dumped me. One minute we're sleeping together, the next you 'just need to be by yourself.' I think that's what you said. I guess you didn't need to be by yourself very long."

"Come on, Krista."

"It's not that I care. I'm over you, believe me. I'm just wondering."

"Look, Allie's got nothing to do with you and me."

"Sure she doesn't."

"Krista . . ." I put down my burger and decided to leave. "I'm really beat, maybe I'll just call it a night. Okay?"

"You're going? You've hardly eaten anything."

I took the check and stood up. "I've barely slept in days, Krista. I'll get this. Maybe we can talk again sometime soon." I began to move out of the booth.

"You know that detective, Rossi?" she asked suddenly, looking up at me with a sly expression. I stopped cold. "He came by to talk to me. I've never been interrogated by a detective before."

I sat back down. "Why was he talking to you?"

"Oh, he wanted to know about Allie. And about you."

"What about me?"

"Just stuff."

"What stuff?"

"Just stuff."

"What kind of *stuff*, Krista?"

"Why are you so upset?" She was smiling again.

"This isn't funny. Just tell me what he asked you."

She went back to picking at her salad. "He asked all sorts of stuff about you. How long you'd been at the hospital. Who your friends were. I said I wasn't sure you had any."

"That's funny. Thanks."

"I'm not going to lie to the police, Jackson." She pretended to be offended, as if I had challenged her integrity.

"Fine, Krista. What else?" I knew she was dying to tell but wanted me to draw it out of her.

"He asked about us. About our relationship."

"What the hell does that— Why did he want to know that?"

"I guess someone else in the hospital mentioned that we were an item."

"What did you say to him?"

"Just that we'd been seeing each other and you broke it off." She paused, then added, "Don't worry, Jackson, I didn't tell him anything bad."

"Anything bad?"

"You know," she said, like two people sharing a secret. "That incident between us."

"What incident?"

She tucked her head down and pouted, angry that I wouldn't play along.

"That *incident*. When you hit me."

For a second I wasn't sure I had heard her right. "Hit you?"

"Yeah, the time we got into an argument and you hit me."

"What the— That's bullshit, Krista. I never hit you."

"Don't tell me you don't remember. When we were breaking up—"

"We were always breaking up."

She ignored me and went right on talking. Her eyes began to tear up, and she dabbed at them with the napkin. "The time you got really mad and I didn't know why. We were in my kitchen, and I'd made a nice meal for you, but you were in this terrible mood, and I kept asking you what was wrong and you wouldn't tell me and you just got madder and madder—"

"Christ! You were hysterical that night. You were swinging kitchen implements at me. You were about to throw a pot. I held your arm, that's all."

"You were really violent, Jackson—"

"I was not."

"You were!" she insisted. "You have a very violent temper. You know that. You used to scream at me."

"I never screamed at you. I may have raised my voice—"

"You used to scream at me all the time. Just like now. You couldn't stand it if I even mentioned your mother—"

"What the fuck does my mother have to do with it?"

"You see! You're screaming at me!" She dissolved into tears, tilting her head to one side and looking at me askance, like a puppy about to be slapped by its master. "All I said was maybe you'd inherited an imbalance of some kind from your mother and you should check it out. I was only trying to be helpful. And you screamed at me just like you're doing now."

"Damn it, Krista!"

She reached up with her hands to cover her face.

"Don't, Jackson," she cried. "Don't hurt me!"

The people in the next booth were staring at us now. I stood up and gathered every bit of self-control I had. "This is bullshit," I said through clenched teeth.

"Don't be mad, Jackson," she pleaded.

"Go to hell!" I walked away, feeling the eyes of everyone in the café on me.

She called out to me as I went out the front door. "I didn't tell him, Jackson. I swear. I won't tell him anything, I promise."

Chapter 35

Monday morning there was a letter in my box at the hospital. Inside I found another card from Krista, this one with a picture of two kittens nestling together in a basket, the word "friendship" printed above in ornate script and for some reason set in quotation marks. This was followed by Krista's handwriting, with its big looping letters and little stars and smiley faces dotting the "i's." She wrote that she was sorry and hoped I wasn't angry. She still cared for me, she said, and wanted me to know that she was still my friend; she was there for me any time I needed a "shoulder to cry on, or just someone to talk to." I dropped the card in the wastebasket. Then I fished it out again, tore it into several pieces and threw it back in.

—

The morning was taken up with the usual rounds and a minor operation to remove two cancerous-looking moles from the face and neck of a fifty-year-old surfer who had spent the last forty years in the sun. Rossi called while I was in surgery and said he'd be coming by later that afternoon. We needed to talk.

I was in my office when he arrived, looming through the door. "Thanks for seeing me on such short notice," he said, taking the seat opposite my desk.

"No problem." I fidgeted in my seat, unable to get comfortable.

He eyed me for a moment before speaking. "Listen. The way these investigations go, it's important for us to gather as much information as possible. Understand?"

"Sure."

"Sort of like when you make a diagnosis, right? You've got to eliminate all the other possibilities. You might do tests for cancer or, I don't know, hemorrhoids, say, just to be on the safe side, right? You gotta be thorough and make sure you don't miss anything." He took out his bottle of nasal spray. "I know, I know, I've got to quit this stuff." He took several snorts in each nostril, then pulled out a Kleenex and honked into it. "Nothing for days!" he said, examining the tissue.

"You should try using the nonmedicated spray for a while," I said. "Wean yourself off."

"Yeah? What's that, sort of a holistic thing?"

"You could say that. It's salt water." I wrote him out the name on my prescription pad and handed it to him. "You can pick it up at any drugstore."

"Thanks." He looked truly appreciative. "I'll do that. Well, okay, here's the story," he said, shifting gears. "We'd like to go by and take a look at your place."

"*My* place?"

"Yeah. We need to take a look through your apartment."

"I don't understand."

"We need to take a look through your apartment," he repeated, slower this time, as if I might not have caught the words.

"You mean you want to *search* it?"

"Basically. Yeah. That's it."

"But why? What can you possibly hope to find there?"

He looked at me like I was being slow to catch on.

"We don't know. Nothing, probably. It's just procedure, as I said. We're just being thorough, Doctor, like when you do a diagnosis, ruling out—"

"But I don't get it. I mean, you're asking my *permission*? Do you have a warrant?"

"No, we don't have a warrant." He looked almost offended.

"I'm not trying to be difficult, I just don't understand—"

"Dr. Maebry. The reason I'm approaching you this way is that I don't want to make it an official thing. If we have to get a warrant for probable cause, that starts a whole process, see? We've got to list your name, address, the reasons for the warrant. It all goes down on a warrant list, which of course is public and could get to the press. And you know what the press is like. Always leaping to conclusions."

"Does this mean you've decided I'm a suspect now?"

"That's the point. I want to clear you of any suspicion. I'm sure what's going to happen is we go in there, find nothing and that's it. We've wiped that off the boards, and we go on and find who really did this."

"But . . . Jesus. What about that guy, that serial rapist you caught? Aren't you looking at him?"

As before, Rossi appeared uninterested in that possibility. "Well, he's one person we're considering."

"*One* person! I'd think he'd be— I'm not a cop—a policeman, I mean—but isn't he a natural suspect?"

"I'm afraid we can't discuss an ongoing investigation with members of the public. I realize this must be upsetting to you—"

"Upsetting! You have no idea!"

"That's why I'm here. We do this thing; we clear the air. That's what we want to do, just clear the air."

"Maybe I should get a lawyer."

"You can do that, sure. But I have to tell you honestly, he'll probably advise you to say no, and then that gets back to what I was saying—we have to go to a judge, get a warrant and, well, it will be weeks before this thing is resolved."

"I don't know."

"Look, it's up to you, Doctor. I'm just trying to move this thing along."

I felt defeated. I could only imagine what the press would do with the story.

"Okay," I said, "I guess. When do you want to do it?"

"Now."

"Right now?"

"That would be best." Rossi pulled a paper out of his pocket and laid it on the table. "If you would sign here," he said, pointing.

"What is it?"

"A 'Consent to Search' form. Just a formality." I signed. Rossi examined the signature and put the paper back in his pocket. "Great. After you, Doctor." He stood and motioned me through the door ahead of him.

—

Rossi drove behind me in his car, and a police van, which had been waiting in the parking lot, followed him. Three men emerged from the van after we parked outside my apartment, Rossi introducing each one in turn. I recognized Mulvane, the San Francisco detective working with him on the case; he said hello and shook my hand. The other two—Pindle, a bald guy with a big smile, and Luntz, a thin, small man with thick glasses—carried large black bags in each hand and just nodded.

I opened the door for them, and they trooped past me into the apartment. Rossi began shuffling through the mess of papers on my desk, while Luntz sat at my computer. "An Apple user," he said, punching the keys rapidly. "I could have told just by looking at you."

On the other side of the room, Pindle was opening the refrigerator and taking out an old pizza carton with a bemused expression on his face. "I wonder what we'd find if we DNA'd this?" he said, then took a whiff and closed it quickly. He stuck his bald head back inside the refrigerator and rummaged around. "Pickles, beer, peanut butter cups—my favorite combination—and some kind of large green mold, exact origin as yet unidentifiable. Hmmm. My acute forensic abilities tell me this guy isn't married."

Rossi looked up briefly from the papers. "Just do the search, Pindle."

I wandered around in a shiftless way, feeling out of place in my own apartment, then sat on the couch awkwardly, until Pindle came over and asked me to get up so he could look under the cushions. Rossi, finding nothing at my desk, went around the divider to my bedroom, where Mulvane was searching.

"Damn it, Mulvane," I heard Rossi growl, "we're guests here. Try not to make such a mess of the place, all right?"

"Hey, it isn't me!" Mulvane protested. "I've just been checking the phone messages. What you see before you is untouched wilderness. Life in a state of nature, so to speak."

"Cute, Mulvane," Rossi said, coming back around the divider with an unconscious look of distaste on his face. The squalor seemed to offend him.

"I've been busy, you know," I began in my own defense. "I haven't had a lot of time to clean up and . . . stuff . . ."

Rossi went on with the search, not listening, but Pindle shook his bald head and winked at me. He was down on his knees, looking under the couch.

"I have this brother," he said as he searched, "real bachelor type before he got married. He goes on a business trip once for about a week, and the smell coming from his apartment is so bad, the landlady calls the police. She's sure there's been a homicide or something. So they break down the door, and I mean they're practically knocked out by this odor. New guy on the force, he starts retching, runs out in the hall and lets out this giant heave—you know, a projectile kind of thing—and splat! It hits the landlady square in the face. He'd had nachos with jalapeño sauce for lunch. Not a pretty sight."

Luntz laughed without taking his eyes off the screen. Rossi just shook his head.

"So, anyway," Pindle continued, "they're all holding hankies to their noses, sure as hell they're going to find something horrible in there. Worse, practically all the lightbulbs are blown. My brother hadn't bothered to change them. And honestly, his place was a rat hole. No light. So they're stumbling around in the dark, tripping over all this crap on the floor, sure each time it's some mutilated corpse."

He was now going through the kitchen drawers and cupboards, putting various items in plastic bags. "Turns out, my brother had gone fishing. Got this real big haul of salmon. He cleans and freezes them and everything but forgets to take out the trash, and all those innards have just been fermenting there for days. Gets pretty hot in the Valley, too. So, the upshot is, this landlady, the next day she files a police brutality report! I kid you not, for being puked on—"

"Whoa!" It was Luntz at the computer. "Rossi, take a look at this."

Rossi huddled over him at the monitor, reading something. I edged closer to see what had caught their attention. The detective at the keyboard was pointing to a line of type on the screen. I peered over Rossi's giant shoulder and saw that it was an e-mail I'd written to Allie the night we'd fought. I thought I'd erased it.

Rossi suddenly stood up straight, and I stumbled back.

"Print it out, Luntz," he said. "And let's take the computer as evidence."

"You're taking my computer?" I asked.

"Yup," Rossi said, not even looking at me.

"Why? Look, that's just a personal e-mail."

"It's evidence now," said Luntz.

"But I erased it. How come—"

"Magic hands," Luntz said, holding up his hands and wiggling his fingers. "Love these Apples. They're so user-friendly."

"I don't see why it's—" I began, but at that moment Mulvane

194

came around the divider from my bedroom holding a hanger with my sport coat in its dry-cleaning bag.

"Bingo," he said. "It's been cleaned, but there's enough blood on this for a transfusion."

Rossi walked over and examined the jacket.

"That's from the hospital," I said.

"Damned bloody places, hospitals," Rossi muttered. He came over to me, took my arm and moved me toward the door. "Maybe you should wait outside, Doctor, until we're finished in here."

"But it's from the hospital. I was wearing it when this patient hemorrhaged."

"You always wear your jacket in surgery?"

"It was during rounds. Unexpected. An emergency procedure."

We were outside by now, and Rossi's giant hand released its grip on my arm.

"I hope you're telling the truth. Just because it's been dry-cleaned, don't count on that destroying the evidence. We can still get DNA off it."

"I'm telling the truth. I swear."

His blue eyes scanned my face. "You might want to consider calling that lawyer now, Doctor."

"Lawyer? You think . . . How . . . ?" He turned and walked inside. "I don't know any lawyers," I said as he closed the door.

I waited there for what seemed like hours, hearing the four of them banging around inside, talking and bantering with one another, though I couldn't make out what they were saying. After a while I went and sat on the curb, wondering how one found a lawyer. In the Yellow Pages? Under "Lawyers, criminal"? Did they have ads like the ambulance chasers': "Have you been unjustly accused of a heinous crime?"

When the detectives finally reappeared, I stood up, expecting them to tell me they'd changed their minds, that it was all a big mistake. Rossi approached, looking grim. Mulvane carried the jacket, in its dry cleaner's bag, and several other items, including what looked like laundry. Pindle just shook his head as he passed by with his black bag and didn't look at me. Luntz carried his electronic gear and my computer. As he walked by, he said he was sorry, they had to take the hard drive, copies weren't usable as evidence. Then he shrugged and got into the van with the others.

Rossi waited until they'd driven off before speaking. He didn't look like he'd changed his mind.

"I think it would be better, Dr. Maebry, if you didn't see Ms. Sorosh from now on."

"I can't not see her! I mean, I have to. She's my patient."

"She'll have to find another doctor, I guess."

"But I have to!"

"Sorry."

He walked toward his car and began to force his bulk inside. I walked over to the driver's-side window. "Can I call her? Allie—Ms. Sorosh?" I asked. "I've got to call her, at least."

The springs of the car seat groaned as he adjusted himself behind the wheel. He stared forward a moment, tapping the wheel with his fingers, then looked me in the face, as if he saw something familiar there. It was the same puzzled look he'd given me down at the precinct. "Yeah," he said. "Sure. I guess that's all right." He turned on the ignition. "Think about getting that lawyer," he said.

"Okay, if you think I should."

"Yeah," he said, just before he drove off. "I think you should."

Chapter 36

In the end I did find a lawyer in the Yellow Pages. I was too embarrassed to ask anyone I knew, and couldn't imagine they'd know too much about criminal defense attorneys, anyway.

His office was down in the Mission District, not far from the city courthouse. Discarded wrappers and other trash swirled about in the wind every time the front door was opened, and you could feel the grit of the lobby floor under your shoes. The directory had lost its glass casing, and many of the little plastic letters were missing. A big display at the top advertised the service of a certain "Tijuana Jones, Bail Bondsman." Underneath was the name I was looking for, Emanuel Lucasian. The elevator didn't work, so I walked up the three flights and knocked on the glass pane of his office door.

"Call me Manny," Lucasian said as we shook hands over his desk. "Have a seat, please." He was dressed ornately, if not quite elegantly, with cuff links the size of quarters, a gold stickpin through his wide tie and a matching but frayed pocket square poking from his jacket pocket. His jet-black hair was pasted flat across the top of his head.

He waited until I was seated, then sat back down behind his desk. "I hope you won't object if I finish my lunch," he said, gesturing at a half-eaten egg-salad sandwich that lay on his desk, the wax paper it came in serving as a plate. "I was in court until just a few moments ago."

"Of course not," I said, settling in and looking around the small office as he ate. He used a plastic knife and fork to cut the sandwich, holding them in the European manner and bringing the food daintily to his mouth with the fork in his left hand.

"So," he began, dabbing the corners of his mouth with a handkerchief he pulled from his coat pocket, "I understand from our brief phone conversation that this visit is purely precautionary?"

"Ah—?"

"What I mean to say is, you have not, as yet, been charged or arrested in connection with any crime?"

"Not yet." I told him about the search, and that Rossi had recommended I get a lawyer.

Lucasian laughed out loud, snapping his handkerchief in the air and wiping away a bit of egg salad that had fallen on his lapel. "Forgive my amusement, Doctor, but it's not Detective Rossi's usual style to give helpful advice to a suspect." He wagged his head from side to side with a bemused smile. "These Irishmen," he said. "Who knows what they're ever really thinking?"

"Irish?" I asked, confused. "We're talking about Detective Rossi, right?"

"Yes, yes. Half Italian, half Irish. A lethal combination, I assure you. Very excitable, and they never forget a grudge." He saw I was still confused and laughed. "The third half, it appears, is black. He's a real melting pot, an incarnation of the American dream—or nightmare, if he doesn't like you."

"So you know him?"

"The good detective and I go a long way back. I was able to manage his son's release on a drug charge. Which in the grand scheme of things probably wasn't the best thing for the boy. The good Lord rest his soul. But the lieutenant is grateful to me anyway."

"His son is dead?"

"Tragically, yes, of a drug overdose. Three weeks after he got out. His other son died defending our country, in a manner of speaking. Killed on maneuvers. Which is about the time Detective Rossi's wife decided to leave him. Our friend Rossi is a man well acquainted with grief, I'm afraid. He was a hard man before, but now, well . . ." He wiped his hands on his handkerchief, put it back in his jacket and folded the wax paper before slipping it into the wastebasket. "But let us get down to the business at hand. Tell me from the beginning. What, in specific detail, is your problem?"

I ran through it for him. He rolled back in his chair, his fingers laced over a round belly that strained against the buttons on his vest, listening to my story with an increasingly pained expression. He let out an audible grunt when I got to the part about agreeing to the search, but otherwise said nothing until I finished.

"Is it bad?" I asked.

"It is, to speak plainly in the vernacular, a large quantity of bull-shit."

"What I said?"

"His case, Doctor. He doesn't have anything substantive on you and is well aware of this fact."

"But he said—"

"He is a detective. He's trying to make the best of what he has. That's his job. Now, assuming, as you tell me, that they don't find a match for the blood on your jacket—"

"It was a patient's."

"So you say. Well, assuming that, unless they find something a lot more solid than they have now, they have no case. Let's run it down, shall we? You had a relationship with this woman, Ms. Sorosh?"

"Yes."

"And you had what we shall call a lovers' quarrel. A rupture. So goes the world. If it were a crime to have a fight with your lover, most of us would be doing life in San Quentin. Unfortunately, she was attacked soon afterward, it seems. That's unlucky but coinciden-tal. Circumstantial evidence. You don't have a good alibi. Unfortu-nate again, but the lack of an airtight alibi is hardly *positive* proof. And apparently there's nothing connecting you to the scene of the crime?" I shook my head. "No physical evidence, otherwise you'd be in jail right now.

"In point of fact, Doctor, Detective Rossi clearly didn't have enough before his visit to your apartment to acquire a search war-rant, which is why he came to you first, in the hope that he could convince you to give up your rights." He screwed up his eyes in a perplexed expression. "Just out of curiosity, did it not occur to you to demand a warrant, or perhaps ask to consult, say, a lawyer?"

"Rossi talked me out of it." I shrugged in embarrassment. "I guess I made a mistake."

"An understatement. Do you not watch television? Police shows, that sort of thing?"

"Not enough, apparently."

"Yes, well"—he cleared his throat—"did the good detective by any chance have you sign a 'Consent to Search' form?"

"He said it was a formality."

"A 'formality' necessitated by our constitution, yes. In any event, it is water under the bridge. A further question, if I may. Did he indicate to you clearly that you were a suspect in this case?"

"Yes. No. I'm not sure. He implied it, I suppose."

"There seems to be some doubt on your part."

"Sorry—"

"No, that's good. I will argue that Lieutenant Rossi misled my client—you—and therefore your consent to the search was not made with full knowledge. Unfortunately, you did sign the form." He sighed. "And given recent Supreme Court decisions, we most likely will lose such an argument in the end. But assuming they found no physical evidence . . ."

"I'm sure there's nothing there."

"Aside from the e-mail."

"Right. But I never sent it to her. I was just blowing off steam. I don't even really remember what I wrote."

"Do you have a copy?"

"No. I thought I'd deleted it, but they were able to retrieve it from my hard drive. They took that as evidence."

"And the phone messages?"

"They took those, too. But there's nothing there, either. Just a message from Allie, calling to make up after our argument."

"Technology, a mixed blessing, is it not? Well, Dr. Maebry, given these facts, I'd say you have very little to worry about. If it were any-one else but Rossi."

"What do you mean?"

"His is a very tenacious personality. How do they say it? 'He always gets his man.' But from the look of things, you are not that man."

"I'm not. I'm innocent. I didn't—*couldn't* have done anything like that."

Lucasian cleared his throat again. "No, no, of course not." He shook his head, a bit theatrically, I thought. "Now I must, I'm afraid, talk business," he continued rapidly, as if quickly passing by a faux pas in the conversation. "I charge a hundred and fifty dollars an hour, plus expenses, which I expect will be minimal. Is that agreeable to you?"

"It's fine, reasonable," I said. "I just don't have much in savings right now."

"But you can always borrow, no?"

"I can do that. Sure."

"Fine. Then it's settled. I will call Mr. Rossi this afternoon and have a little conversation about this affair. Perhaps you could call me tomorrow, and we'll see where we go from there."

"Okay," I agreed. "But there's one more thing I need to bring up."

"I am at your service."

"Detective Rossi said I couldn't see Allie—Ms. Sorosh. I'm her doctor and—"

He laughed. "That's my friend Rossi. Do not worry, Dr. Maebry; unless he is willing to charge you, he may not take any action that impairs your ability to conduct yourself in your profession."

"But what if he goes to the hospital administration?"

"That, as I'm sure the lieutenant is well aware, would constitute defamation, and with the settlement we would surely win from the city of San Francisco, you would never have to practice medicine again." He looked around his office as if imagining what he might do with the money.

"I don't want damages," I said. "I just want to clear this thing up."

"Of course, of course. But it never hurts to give the other side an incentive to do the right thing. We are such fallen creatures, we men. So apt to 'do not what we would, and do what we would not.' Eh?"

"I guess so," I said, not entirely sure what he meant. "How long do you think it will take? Before . . . well, things are cleared up."

"Oh, it all depends on what develops. I will let you know when I talk with Lieutenant Rossi." He stood up, and I stood with him.

"It's just that—" I continued. "You see, I've never been through anything like this before." He gave me a sympathetic nod and I stumbled on. "I mean, being a suspect and all. In a—a *criminal* case." He nodded again, as if to acknowledge that indeed this was a terrible predicament. "I'm a *doctor,*" I blurted out incoherently, "a *surgeon.*" In my thoughts it seemed an important point, but I could hear how ridiculous it sounded spoken out loud. "That's all I've ever done," I added weakly. "I've never . . . It's just—all this is very stressful—I mean, it's a whole new level of anxiety for me."

Lucasian came around the desk and put his hand on my shoulder. "I suggest, Dr. Maebry—and I say this with the utmost compassion for the distress you are now experiencing—that you get used to it."

Chapter 37

When I got back to the hospital, there was a message waiting on my desk saying that Brandt wanted to see me. The "Urgent" box was checked, and the time, one-thirty, was scribbled underneath. It was nearly five.

Eileen was outside Brandt's office, in the process of putting on her coat and getting ready to leave for the evening.

"Where have you been, Jackson? Dr. Brandt has been trying to get in touch with you all afternoon. You're listed on duty today."

"I had to go out. Someone was covering for me."

She huffed in that unmistakable way secretaries have of reflecting their boss's displeasure. "I'll tell him you're here." She pressed the intercom, and I heard Brandt on the other end telling her to send me in. She waved me toward the door, then grabbed her purse and walked out without saying good-bye.

Brandt was on the phone and pointed to the seat opposite his desk. I sat and waited until he hung up. His knuckles were white as he gripped the receiver. He said good-bye to whomever he was talking to and placed the phone back in its cradle with a frown.

"Jackson," he began, his eyes still on the phone, not on me. "This is very disturbing."

I imagined this was the tone that made other residents so fearful of his disapproval. I'd never heard it before. Not directed at me.

"I don't know what you mean," I said.

"This Detective Rossi person dropped by to see me at my private offices this morning." His voice was cold and disdainful, as if he was trying to raise himself above the indignity of having been interviewed by a detective.

It must have been before Rossi called me, I thought. "He's investigating Allie's assault—I—I think I can explain—"

"Explain!" he cried. "I hardly see how!" He collected himself and continued, looking straight at me this time. "In the course of this 'interview,' it became clear that you had been having a . . . *relationship* with Ms. Sorosh. Is this true?"

"We've been seeing each other."

He shook his head in dismay. "I just don't understand you, Jackson. It's so completely unprofessional!"

"I—"

"It didn't occur to you to tell me?" he interrupted. "It didn't cross your mind that it wasn't appropriate to assist me on an operation when—for goodness sake, when *you're having an affair with the patient!*"

"I didn't think it was important," I said feebly.

"I thought you were acting odd during the operation. It's clear now why. How could you jeopardize—" He broke off with emotion. I thought he was going to ask how I could have jeopardized Allie's well-being, but he caught his breath and continued: "How could you jeopardize *my* reputation this way?"

A great shock of white hair fell forward over his brow, and he raked it back from his face with stiff fingers. Several moments passed in which I could hear his breathing, heavy, labored. When he spoke again, his voice was once more under control. Businesslike.

"I don't know what the hospital administration is going to say about this. There are ethical questions involved, and I daresay liability issues. I'll do what I can for you, Jackson, but I have to tell you I'm disappointed. Deeply disappointed."

"But I didn't intend to— It's not unheard of for people to treat patients they know—"

He raised his hand for me to stop. "Please, Jackson. Please. You only make it worse. Of course, I will have to take you off the case. I don't want you treating Ms. Sorosh. Do you understand? You will have nothing to do with her medical treatment from now on."

I stared down at the floor, unable to look up.

"Have I made myself clear?"

I nodded.

"I had such high hopes for you, Jackson. Such high hopes!"

I didn't say anything. My eyes were still fixed on the floor.

"All right," he said brusquely after a few moments. "I don't think we have anything more to discuss."

I could hear his chair rolling to the desk, as if he was turning to other business. He was dismissing me.

I stood up and walked out the door without looking at him.

—

I wandered the halls, feeling like there was some giant black mark of shame on me and hoping I didn't run into anyone I knew. After a time I found myself on the top floor of the south wing, where the hospital had arranged a large room with a view of the ocean for convalescents. Two elderly patients had rolled their IVs in and were sitting in opposite corners dozing off. I took a chair and turned it toward the window so no one could see my face.

Transference. That's what Stern had said. *You transfer the feelings you had—have—for your father on to Brandt. He gives you the feeling of acceptance, of love even, that you wish you had gotten from your father.*

And now, I thought, this ends badly, too.

The sea in the distance was flat as a slab of sheet metal, gray and glinting in the late afternoon sun.

All the time that I had been Brandt's special student—his "protégé," as his wife so aptly called me—I'd wondered why, what it was that he saw in me. And all that time I had known somehow, somewhere in the back of my mind, that it would end like this. I would fail. It was inevitable. He would find me out for what I really was and lose all faith in me. Of course, Stern would say that I'd done it on purpose. Unconsciously played out the trauma of my past in the present. I could imagine Stern taking a certain satisfaction in his theories being so perfectly realized—

"Damn!" I swore out loud, jumping to my feet. Stern! I'd forgotten that I had an appointment with him that evening.

One of the patients started briefly, then nodded back into his slumber. I looked at my watch. My session had started ten minutes before.

I'd missed several sessions and hadn't planned on returning after the last visit. Typically, however, I hadn't gotten around to calling Stern to tell him I was ending treatment. He would say I was leaving a door open so that I could go back, and that was probably true. I didn't have the courage to cut it off cleanly. Worse, I acknowledged to myself as I almost ran through the halls and across the street to Stern's building, I was hoping desperately that he would have some explanation that would make everything all right again, something that would allow me to make sense of what was happening—and if not that, if that wasn't possible, simply a few words of support. I knew it was wretched to place any hope of kindness in Stern, that if I had any sense or any pride I wouldn't go groveling back to him now, but I couldn't help it. I yearned to hear someone, even Stern, say he believed in me. Or, at least, believed me.

He was there, as I knew he would be. I opened the door to his office and he was there, as always. He had his jacket off and was standing by his desk, leafing through a book. It occurred to me I'd never seen him in shirtsleeves before. Nor had I seen him upright, except from the back when he was ushering me to the door at the end of a session.

"Oh, Jackson," he said, surprised.

I thought maybe I'd gotten the time wrong. "I have an appointment?"

"Yes, of course," he said, appearing confused. He turned around and shuffled toward his chair, letting himself down with some difficulty. Without his jacket, one couldn't help but notice his wide, practically girlish hips and the material of his pants hanging loose around his thin legs.

I sat in the patient's chair and tried to think of how to start.

"I know I'm late," I began.

"Um, ah, Jackson. Before we get going . . ." He was fiddling with his tie. A new tic, I thought. "As I say, before we begin . . ." He dropped his tie, then smoothed it out over his stomach and looked around the room, everywhere but at me.

"What?" I prompted.

"Yes, what? Exactly. What?" He clearly made a great effort to go on. "I should tell you that I got a call, I mean a visit, from a certain Detective Rossi."

I didn't say anything.

"Here, in the office, he came by earlier to discuss the, ah, the case he's investigating."

"Allie's assault?"

"Precisely."

I knew what was coming next.

"He wanted to discuss your relationship to the 'victim'—that's the word he used."

"But you can't do that, can you? That's protected, what we talk about here is privileged, a doctor-patient thing." He puffed up his cheeks and blew the air out between his lips. "You didn't talk to him about me, did you?"

"Really, Jackson, don't jump to conclusions. There's really nothing . . . incriminating." He said the last word quietly, as if I might not hear. "Not exactly."

"Incriminating! Damn it, it doesn't matter what you think. You're not allowed. It's *privileged*. Everything that goes on here is *privileged*!"

"Well, that's not entirely accurate," he said, adopting his professorial pose. "It's sort of a gray area of the law, you know. There have been several recent cases where psychiatrists have been subpoenaed to testify—"

"We're nowhere near that. You weren't subpoenaed, for God's sake!"

"No, but the detective made it clear that—"

"I don't care what he said, you had no right!"

I found myself suddenly on the verge of tears. Sensing that, Stern took the opportunity to turn the issue back to me.

"Calm down, Jackson. You're upset, naturally." He said it in his smoothest tone. "I understand this is difficult for you. You're bound to have *feelings* about what has happened. We can talk about it."

"What did you tell him?" I demanded.

"Excuse me?"

"What exactly did you say to Rossi? I want to know."

"I don't know if that's such a good idea—"

"Tell me!" I yelled.

"I, ah, I simply said that you and Alexandra Sorosh had had a short but rather intense relationship"—he nodded as he spoke, as if to emphasize the utter reasonableness of what he was saying—"and that there were many issues from your childhood—your relationship to your mother and father, particularly—that we're working to clarify."

His voice was practically tumescent with compassion. I knew that, coming from Stern, it was completely false. It sickened me. But at the same time I was desperate enough, weak enough, to accept it.

My anger drowned in an overwhelming sense of hopelessness and self-pity. I wiped away my tears, ashamed at myself but unable to stop.

"Did you tell him I'm crazy, too?"

"Now, Jackson." He said it like a schoolteacher saying "There, there" to a little child who has skinned his knee. "We don't have any reason to believe that's true."

"But you *know* me," I pleaded. "You know I could never try to kill Allie. I love her. I could never do something like that."

Stern's eyes moved down toward his tie.

"You know I never could," I said.

"Well, well, after all," he said, as if he'd just hit upon some profound philosophical insight, "what can we ever really know about other people? For that matter, how much do we really know about ourselves?"

Chapter 38

It was late by the time I got to Allie's apartment. I don't know what I expected. My mind was filled with disjointed thoughts tumbling in circles, coming round and round again before I could catch hold. I suppose I expected her to insist that Brandt keep me on the case. Say she wanted me as her doctor. I suppose that was what I wanted.

She had been sleeping and was groggy from the painkillers. She let me in, shuffled back to her bedroom and lay back down in her bed as I spoke to her. When I explained about Brandt, she said simply, "Okay."

"You can ask for me to stay on, Allie. You're the patient. It's up to you. You can choose your doctor."

"But that's not what Peter wants."

"He's overreacting, Allie. If you say you want me, I'm sure he'll see that and accept it."

"I think we should do it his way, Jackson."

"But . . ."

"It's all right, Jackson."

"But I want to be there, make sure everything's done right."

"Peter can do that. Let's do what he wants."

I tried to think of something to convince her but couldn't.

"That detective was here again," she said after a while. "He asked me all sorts of questions." Her eyes were glassy from the drugs, and hooded by sleep. "He asked about you . . . our relationship . . . lot of questions . . . you and the . . . assault . . ." She was drifting in and out, each fragment coming slower, the silent spaces between growing longer. " . . . wanted to know . . . our meeting that day . . . the argument . . ."

"What did you tell him?"

"I . . ."

"What did you tell him about me and the assault?" I asked louder. Her eyes were closed now; her words distant and disembodied, a last communication from the other side of sleep. "I told him . . . I don't . . . remember."

—

I have no clear recollection of where I ended up. I was looking for Tiffany's, the bar I'd been to before, but couldn't find it fast enough. It didn't matter; there were plenty of places just like it, all virtually interchangeable, where there was no pretense about why you'd come. I do remember this guy offering to buy me a drink and pounding on the bar and the bartender telling him to shut up or he'd throw him the fuck out. I remember not even caring when the guy put his arm around me and pushed his drunken face next to mine to tell me something, his horrible sweet breath enveloping me like a shroud. And then I remember he was gone and I was sitting there on the floor trying to get up, the bartender keeping his back to me so he wouldn't see.

Later came the beach. The vermouth spilling in the sand as I tried to pour it into a vodka bottle.

Do you know what makes a great martini, Jackson? Getting the vermouth in that little round hole at the top of the vodka bottle!

This struck me as hilariously funny, but I was beyond laughing. I remember thinking about writing myself a prescription for something stronger. A synthetic opiate, like Demerol. A few Valiums. Maybe a shot or two of morphine. Mix them together in a nice oblivion cocktail. Not enough to kill me. Not intentionally, at least. But Rossi was probably checking on every move I made. I was his prime suspect now. His only suspect. Jackson Maebry, M.D. Doctor, surgeon, violent felon and psycho case. Oh yes, and prescription-drug abuser.

Screw Rossi. Drink your martini, Jackson.

They all suspected me now. Rossi. Brandt, probably. Stern.

Try to forget. Just forget.

And Allie? Did she suspect me now, too?

Oh God!

Drink, Jackson! Keep it down! Good, that's better now, isn't it? Much better . . .

It took a while to figure out what it was. A halo of light in the mist, shadows playing against the overhanging sky.

Surfers, I decided, having a party. If I forced my eyes into focus, I could just make out a circle of dark forms, almost indistinguishable from the shadows, tall yellow flames rising in the center. There was music, too, faint fragments of melody that escaped the wind, beautiful and somehow very sad. Sad like mourning.

I remember that part. The feel of my cheek on the wet sand and the notes trembling in the wind for their brief span, the shadows flying up from the flames, as melancholy and transient as the music. And I remember the sound of waves cracking, low and insistent, like a command; the exhalation of surf and the white foam that lolled negligently on the sand before drawing back into the blackness, willing me to follow. And all the time the music, sweet and seductive, like the smell of decay on the bum's breath, his face next to mine, tugging at me, pulling me closer. I remember looking out to the sea and thinking how easy it would be to comply, to swim out until the cold cramped my limbs and acute hypothermia annihilated what little consciousness I had left. I'd hardly even feel it.

Not a bad offer, I decided, all things considered, and I reached over and took the bottle of vodka and drank until the alcohol bit into my throat and made me gag. I waited until the gagging stopped and then drank more. I listened to the sweet sound of death and drank and kept drinking, until I was sure I'd drunk too much to answer its call.

—

Stern, I suppose, would call it "disordered thinking," a "temporary psychosis," and no doubt he would be right. Especially the voices. That's a sure sign, they say.

I've tried each time to exorcise the memory from my mind, but I realize now that he's always with me, he's never left my side. He's my constant companion, my fallen guardian angel, eyes full of hate and loathing, just as they were all those years ago. And the voice, the voice is the same, too, taunting me, mocking my cries for help, "Dad-dy! Dad-dy!"

The first time, of course, was no delusion. I was eight. Mother, as usual, had closed herself up in her room, a Billie Holiday record on the stereo to accompany her descent into self-pity, the sound of sickness seeping through the walls and infecting everything it touched. I don't know why I opened the door. I must have heard something besides the usual tears. Something frightening.

I forced myself to go inside and saw her there, half naked, bloody. She was biting herself, deliberately, methodically; biting the flesh of her arms, the anorexic, dried flesh that still produced enough blood to stain her nightgown red. I ran downstairs to Father's office—the one to which he retreated as soon as he came home and where he was never supposed to be disturbed—and rattled the locked door, crying for him to come out. I yelled and beat on the door, and when he ignored my pleas, I started breaking things against it, smashing anything I could get my hands on, anything an eight-year-old could reach. Calling out, "Dad-dy! Dad-dy!"

Then I heard his voice: "Dad-dy. Dad-dy." He was standing there, mocking me, though I'd stopped dead in my rampage, just sobbing now, my fury—my hysteria, as he called it—replaced by humiliation and defeat. He grabbed my arm as if to restrain me and began dragging me down the hall to the back door, like he was hauling out the trash, all the time telling me to shut up, grow up, he didn't want to hear my goddamned crying anymore. When we reached the kitchen, I broke away and grabbed the first thing that came to hand—one of those heavy glass ashtrays that lay all over the house, full of Mother's half-burnt and forgotten cigarette butts—and hit him hard in the face.

That's when he said it. The first time. "You're sick, Jackson," he said, as if he were looking at something particularly repulsive. "You're crazy. Just like your mother."

He says it all the time now.

You're crazy, Jackson, he says to me now, *just like your mother. I feel sorry for you.* But I know he feels only disgust.

"If you hate me so much, why don't you just leave me alone?"

Because you're crazy!

He's always there for me now, right by my side, as real as damnation, as corporeal as hate.

Chapter 39

H ey! You there!"

I thought it was the beach patrol telling me to move on.

"Yo, Jackson! What's going on?"

They know my name?

"You're sick or what? It's the middle of the day."

It was hard to focus my eyes, especially with all the movement. I made an immense effort and was able to pull together the multiple images into one big blur: feet.

Danny's little feet, in their huge sneakers, were bouncing up and down on the mattress next to my head. I must have made it back to the apartment somehow.

"What do ya want to bet that if I jump real hard, I can bounce you out of bed?"

"Oh my God! Danny, stop, please."

He was jumping with all his might, slapping his hands against the low ceiling on the way up and coming down as hard as he could on the mattress.

"Oh my God! Please stop!"

"What will you give me?"

"Anything, anything at all."

He didn't stop. I rolled out of bed and slumped in the chair, trying to control a wave of nausea by remaining as horizontal as I could.

Danny plopped down cross-legged in the middle of the bed, then jumped up with a yelp and stood on the side of the mattress, wiping the seat of his pants with his hands.

"Scaggly! It's wet. Man, it's beer! Yuck!"

I took a beer bottle from the nightstand, where it stood with several empties, and twisted off the top.

"What ya doin', Jackson?" He was still now, eyeing me with a ten-year-old's disdain.

"Nothing, Danny," I croaked.

"You've been drinking."

"Not so much."

"A lot."

"What the hell are you, from A.A.?"

"What's that?" He looked hurt. The alcohol had given my voice a hard edge.

"Sorry, I'm not feeling well."

"Yeah, I guess nobody is. Sandra's been drinking since yesterday afternoon. She throws up on the kitchen floor and doesn't even clean it up. Scaggsville!"

He watched as I drank. "How come you drink so much, Jackson?"

"I don't. Not so much. Just now and then."

"Yeah, that's what Sandra says, too. She says she only drinks 'socially.'" He was clearly repeating a word he'd heard but didn't know the meaning of.

"A society of one," I said.

"Sometimes she says she drinks to forget."

"Sounds reasonable." I finished the beer and stumbled to the refrigerator in hope of finding more. There wasn't any, but I found three unopened bottles lying loose on the couch.

"So what's she got to forget?" he said, following me around the divider.

"I don't know, Danny." I propped my head up on the arm of the couch so I could drink. "Lots of things, probably."

He came up next to me and just stood there, watching. It was beginning to bother me.

"Billy Derwinski says he can drink a whole case of beer in ten minutes." He was speaking loudly, as if challenging me.

"Keep it down, Danny, my head hurts."

"He can drink a whole case and then a quart of bourbon. Just like that!" He snapped his fingers. "That's what he said."

"No, he can't."

"He can, too! I saw him! And he can drive a car afterward like it's nothing."

"That's stupid, Danny."

"You're stupid!" he said angrily.

I finished the beer and reached for another.

"He can, too!"

"Give me a break, Danny, I'm trying—"

"Gimme that," he yelled, grabbing the beer and taking a gulp.

"Danny!" I struggled to my feet and tried to catch him, but he moved quickly out of reach. He held the bottle away from me and took another gulp and started to choke.

"Enough, Danny," I said, lunging at the bottle and prying it from his grasp. The bottle fell to the floor with a clunk.

"Fuck you, Jackson! Fuck you!" He was choking and sobbing now. "You're a fucking drunk!"

I held my head and tried not to fall down.

"You're a drunk and a liar! Just like Dad. Just like Sandra."

"I never lied to you, Danny."

"You did, too! You did, too!" he shouted, his little body seething with emotion. "You said I could see Allie and you lied!"

"Jesus." I sat back down and tried to get my head to stop spinning.

"You're just a scaggly drunk! Fuck you! Fuck you!" His voice broke into a high-pitched squeal. "I hate you! I hate all of you!" Then he ran out the door, banging it so hard I thought it would break.

I went over and picked up the bottle lying on the floor. There was still some beer remaining, and I drank it down.

Yeah. Fuck me, I thought.

—

. . . the man behind the counter wanted to see the money before he'd hand over the bottle.

"I've got money," I said, drawing myself up with the inebriated dignity of a wino.

"Give me the money," he said, "then you get the Stoli . . ."

. . . the water turned cold. I sat in the shower stall drinking the vodka, until the shivering became so violent the glass lip of the bottle rattled against my teeth . . .

. . . it wouldn't stay down. Such a waste, I thought, resting my head against the toilet bowl and wondering why the water was so red . . .

—

A woman in a white uniform was shaking me, then I realized she was taking my pulse and feeling my forehead to see if I had a temperature.

"Hello, Nurse."

"Jackson, what the hell is going on?" It was Krista.

"Am I in the hospital?"

"No, but maybe you should be." It wasn't her usual sympathetic tone.

She helped prop me up on the pillows, then put a blanket over my body and handed me some coffee. "This is how you like it, right?" she said. "Hot tap water and instant coffee? Disgusting, but I think you need it." The caffeine slowed the gyrations in my head, and I could see I was still in my apartment. Krista walked around my bed, picking things up off the floor.

"It's cold," I said.

"The coffee?"

"Me."

"I'll turn the heater on." She went over and turned it on high. Warm air filled the room. It felt good for my body but bad for my head, like it was floating and spinning at the same time.

"Everything's bloody," Krista said, holding up a stained shirt.

"I know. There's blood in the bathroom, too. I saw it."

"Jackson, it's you. You cut yourself badly on the leg. I'm surprised you didn't bleed to death."

I pulled the cover up and saw a bandage wrapped around my right shin.

"Did you do that?" I asked.

"Yes. You broke a vodka bottle in the bathroom and must have rolled on it or something." The idea seemed to make her angry. "Drink the coffee. Then drink some tomato juice."

I looked over and saw a glass on the nightstand. "Uggh."

"What the hell did you think you were doing?"

"I was drinking. I'm pretty sure."

"No kidding." She took the coffee cup and went to the sink to make another. I considered the tomato juice and decided against it. She came back and handed me the cup.

"How long have you been here?" I asked. *"Why* are you here?"

"You called me, remember?"

"No."

"You called about an hour ago. Asked me to bring a prescription pad. Said you needed something urgently."

"Did you bring it?"

"Of course not. You were obviously drunk."

"Oh."

"What were you trying to do, kill yourself?"

"No. Not really."

"Not *really*? Just sort of ?"

"I'm fine now. I am."

"Are you sure?" She paused and glanced rapidly around the apartment, just as she would after straightening up for a patient on a busy day. "Because I've really got to go. I'm on duty. Someone's covering for me, but I have to get back to the hospital."

"It's night already?"

"Ten o'clock."

"Saturday, right?"

"How long have you been drunk?"

"Just one day."

She was anxious to leave, and it wasn't only because she had to get back to work. She's still mad at me about the other day, I thought dimly.

"You're not going to do anything stupid?" she said. "No more drinking?"

"I don't know. I don't think I have the constitution to be a good drunk."

That provoked her for some reason, and she picked up her bag as if getting ready to go. "This is all about her, isn't it? Allie Sorosh."

"In a way, yes."

She shook her head angrily. "You are really sick, you know that, Jackson?"

"It's the alcohol," I said. "I'll get over it."

"No, I mean mentally sick. There's something really wrong with you."

"I'll make a note of that and mention it to my shrink."

"Always so clever, aren't you?" She screwed up her face in an attempt at sarcasm. "You think you're so smart, don't you! Jackson's so smart! You think you can hide behind that, but you can't."

"I'm not really feeling up to this," I said, but she went on as if I hadn't spoken.

"You think you're so smart and everyone else is so dumb, but I'm not so dumb I didn't know you were cheating on me with her. I knew it all along—"

"I wasn't cheating—"

"I saw you! I saw you two together and I knew it. I knew she was just your type, a thin little stuck-up upper-class snob—" She flounced her head back and forth in imitation of an upper-class snob.

"She's Polish—" I began, but then thought maybe that wasn't right. "Or Hungarian or something . . ." It didn't matter; Krista was on one of her tirades and wasn't listening, anyway.

"Just the kind of superficial snob you'd go for. And taking her out to all those fancy places! You never took me out to eat at Aqua. I guess I was just the cheap date, good enough to screw but not good enough to spend any money on—"

"Krista—"

"I can't believe I ever fell for your lies! You were just *using* me! When I think of what I did for you—"

I held my hands to my head and prayed for her to stop. To my astonishment, she did. I looked up to see a startled expression on her face, as if she'd seen something shocking. Or remembered it. Then she clutched her bag to her breast and darted out the door.

Chapter 40

A couple of beers the next morning took the edge off my hangover, though my body rebelled against any further poisoning and I had to work to get them down.

Lucasian had left a message on my machine at some point the previous day. I first called in sick at the hospital—apparently I'd done so the day before as well, though I had no recollection of it—then dialed Lucasian's number shortly after nine.

"Ah, Dr. Maebry. You sound unwell."

"It was a forty-eight-hour thing. I'm getting better."

"I am glad to hear that. I had a talk with our friend Rossi yesterday. So far, as I surmised, he has mainly his suspicions and little else. I made it clear that it would be inadvisable to interfere with your professional duties."

"Thanks, but they've taken me off the case." I could feel my headache coming back and opened another beer.

"For what reason?" Lucasian asked.

"Rossi interviewed my boss, and it came out that I'd been seeing Allie."

"Unfortunate. Did Detective Rossi imply in any way that you were a suspect in this investigation?"

"I don't know." It was a huge effort simply to get the words out, a bigger effort just to think. "I don't think so, no. But Brandt—my boss—may have figured it out from what he said."

"Is this Brandt also involved in Ms. Sorosh's treatment?"

"Yes. He's the lead plastic surgeon."

"Then I am afraid there's little we can do about that. It would seem a legitimate part of Mr. Rossi's investigation." I was silent for a time, taking it in, slowly processing the information. "Dr. Maebry?"

"Yeah, sorry. He also talked to my psychiatrist. And other people I know."

"You have been seeking professional help?"

"Yes."

"For a long period of time?"

"A while. Six or seven months." I couldn't really figure it out at that moment. "Is that bad?"

"I suppose that depends on the particular professional." Lucasian laughed good-naturedly. I laughed, too, though it sounded more like someone clearing his throat. Then I coughed, which sent a stabbing pain through my head.

"I don't think my shrink is good at keeping confidences."

"Unfortunate again."

"I thought— Isn't everything I said to him privileged?"

"We can certainly make that case, should they attempt to introduce any of what Mr. Rossi learned from him in court, but I suspect that the lieutenant was just fishing for leads in his investigation."

"He's allowed to do that?"

"It's a question of what he can get away with. Mr. Rossi will always step right up to the edge of the envelope, as they say. If your therapist had refused, there probably would have been little Rossi could do, but it appears your therapist is not the strongest of individuals."

"No, he's not." My head was throbbing now.

"I have also asked the detective for a copy of the e-mail that you sent—ah, didn't send, to Ms. Sorosh. It should be here today."

I dreaded having to read it again. I couldn't think about that now. I drank more of my beer.

"Dr. Maebry, are you unwell?"

"Yeah, I mean no," I rasped. "I'll be okay. How about the DNA on my jacket. Has that come back yet?"

"I'm afraid that will take some time. Two weeks or so, minimum. And it was sent to the state laboratory, which always has a backlog. I'm sure the police are as anxious as we are to expedite the process."

"I'm sure." I just wanted to lie down again and hold my head until the throbbing stopped. "So, ah, there's nothing else we can do?"

"Nothing but wait, I'm afraid, and practice the virtue of patience."

I gripped the receiver tightly against my temple and forced down the nausea rising in my throat. "Yeah, okay . . . You know, it's kind of hard to be patient with something like this hanging over you."

"If it were easy, Dr. Maebry, it wouldn't be a virtue."

—

I lay around the rest of the day, recovering. By nightfall, I felt well enough to put something solid in my stomach, so I walked out to the 7-Eleven to buy several doughnuts and peanut butter cups. And beer. As a gesture toward sobriety, I also picked up a six-pack of Coke. I came back and sat on the tiny lawn in a plastic chair Danny used as a goalpost when playing street hockey. I ate my dinner and watched the cars roll by, their tires making tearing sounds on the wet pavement. I was too exhausted to think clearly and just let my mind wander the way it usually does after a drunk, memories of the last two days dribbling back into consciousness, dim and barely real, except for the overwhelming feeling of self-loathing they carried with them.

When I'd finished the last of the synthetic pastries and wiped the jelly from my face, I got up and walked back to the house. A pale blue light played behind Sandra's drawn curtains, and when she opened the door, I could see the television on behind her, the volume turned low, a constant mumbling sound. The last few days hadn't been kind to her, either. It showed mostly in her eyes. They were grayer even than her hair, and filled with fatigue.

"I was hoping to find Danny," I said. I didn't remember everything that happened, but I knew it was bad. "We had an argument. I wanted to make it up to him."

She motioned me inside. "He didn't come back last night." She turned the TV down further, but not all the way off, then walked to the kitchen and brought back a bottle of wine and sat next to me on the couch.

"Do you know where he is?" I asked.

"Probably at his father's," she said, pulling out the cork.

"I didn't know he had a father."

"It's usually required, Jackson. Want something to drink?"

"Maybe later. I've got supplies." I took a beer out of my 7-Eleven bag.

"It's not your fault, Jackson," she said after she'd finished her first glass. "Danny does this whenever I go on a bender. Runs off and stays with his father. He must have been pretty mad, because he hates it there. And the SOB hates having him. Gets in the way of his lifestyle, he says. Danny will be back sooner or later."

"Are you okay now?" I asked.

"Define okay. Sure I am. I will be. I just get too involved some-times." I guessed she wasn't talking about Danny. "I had what you might call a cathartic experience. That's the result." She gestured in the direction of her sculpture, now squashed into a malformed lump of clay.

"You didn't like it?"

"Like? I never really *like* what I do," she mused. "No, that wasn't the reason. It got away from me."

"Got away?" It felt like she was talking in riddles, and I didn't have the mental energy to untangle them.

"It's hard to explain, Jackson."

"Okay," I said.

"It is a shame," she said. "It really was very good in the end."

"Why did you destroy it, then?"

She glanced over at the battered clay and grimaced, then swal-lowed the rest of her wine as if it were medicine. "Artists are cruel, Jackson. They do what they have to do."

—

I left a note on Danny's bed saying I wanted to make it up to him and that I'd get tickets and take him to any game he wanted. Then I tore it up and wrote another that just said "Sorry" and signed my name.

As I was leaving, Sandra asked me about the police. She must have spied them through the window when they came to search my apartment.

"It's about the assault on my girlfriend. They—the truth is, they consider me a suspect."

I imagined all sorts of things she might say, but all she did was ask me if they'd be coming back.

"I don't think so. They got what they needed."

"Good," she said. Then, "Are you going to be okay, Jackson?"

"Define okay," I said.

She smiled. A haggard smile, as much to say she was sorry, she'd like to help, but was too busy wrestling with her own demons to take on mine. "I'm here if you need me," she offered anyway, without much conviction.

She closed the door behind me, and as I looked back, I could see the weak light of the TV flickering behind the curtains, playing wearily on the fabric. Like a fire burning in rubble, I thought, with little left to consume.

Chapter 41

The message light was blinking on my machine again. I pressed the play button.

"Hello, Dr. Maebry. It is Emanuel Lucasian on this end. Would you be so good as to give me a call when you return? Do not trouble yourself as to the hour. It is important we speak tonight." He'd left his home number and I called immediately.

A woman answered, distracted by a babbling infant that she must have been carrying in her arms; as soon as she realized it was business, she called out "Manny!" in a loud voice and then "No, Anton, not the phone!" This was followed by a young boy's laughter and the generalized commotion of scampering feet and high voices.

"May I help you?" It was Lucasian.

"It's Jackson Maebry—"

"Here, Koyana, eat this instead," he cooed. "That's a good girl." Then back to me, "You must excuse us, it is dinnertime here."

"Oh, sorry," I apologized, "I didn't mean to disturb you."

"How can one disturb chaos?" He laughed. "Do not concern yourself. Thank you for calling. Excuse me, let me take the other phone." After a while I heard a second extension being picked up, and Lucasian called to still another child to hang up the other phone. There was breathing on the line, followed by giggles. Lucasian yelled several more times without effect before a sharp motherly reprimand produced a dropped receiver. There were more scampering feet. Then a firm click as the phone was hung up.

"There, we have attained a momentary peace," he said.

"How many children do you have?" I asked. I hadn't imagined him with children.

"We have not taken a census recently, but at last count there were nine, I believe."

"All yours?"

"That is a personal question." He laughed again. "But my wife assures me that such is the case. Now, Dr. Maebry, I talked with our friend Lieutenant Rossi, and it seems that we will need to put in an appearance at his office tomorrow. I said we would be there at ten o'clock. Is that all right with you?"

"I can make it. Why?"

"I don't want to concern you too greatly, but several issues have arisen."

"What?" I asked, dreading the answer.

"For one, the jacket. The DNA tests are not complete yet, of course, but the blood type was found to be a match for Ms. Sorosh. O negative, I believe. This is of course not conclusive, as some seven percent of the population has the same blood type. Neither is it exculpatory, unfortunately."

"It was a patient's," I said feebly.

"There is also the matter of the e-mail—"

"Which I never sent!"

"Do not be upset, Dr. Maebry. I'm sure we will clear it up tomorrow. Mr. Rossi still does not have sufficient grounds to charge you, I am sure, otherwise we would be facing an arrest tomorrow, not a friendly office chat. Let us meet with him tomorrow and see what he wants."

"Okay, I'll be there."

"Excellent." He was about to say good-bye.

"There's one other thing," I said quickly. It had been lurking in the back of my mind all day, but my memory of the last two days was still hazy and I hadn't really been able to think it through. "This may sound strange, but . . ."

"Yes, Doctor?"

"I don't know what this means. But I was seeing this girl, this woman—she's a nurse at the hospital—before I met Allie, and—I think she was jealous. Of me and Allie, you know?"

"Yes?"

"Well . . ."

"You think she might be the assailant?"

"It's hard to believe, but . . ." I thought of her complaint about my taking Allie to that restaurant. Aqua. How did she know? "She may have been following us," I said, wondering if I sounded paranoid. "She knew we'd been to this place, this restaurant, together. It's called Aqua. That doesn't matter, obviously. The name, I mean. But . . . well . . . it occurred to me that she might have followed us there. Of course it could have been a coincidence, she may have seen us by chance." It sounded less compelling spoken out loud.

"I see," he said. He asked me for Krista's name and a few other facts about her. "I will bring it up with Detective Rossi."

"Thanks. Do you think—I mean, I don't really know anything, it just seemed important to mention it."

"It is certainly worth looking into." I wasn't sure if he was just humoring me.

"Okay."

"Tomorrow then," he said in a bright voice. "Now I must return to my brood."

—

I drove down after rounds the next morning and waited for him, sitting uncomfortably on a wooden chair in the lobby, facing the woman behind the Plexiglas window. Lucasian arrived shortly afterward, straightening his suit—the same one he'd worn at our first meeting, I noticed, though the tie and pocket square were a different color—and wiping his forehead with his handkerchief. His black hair glistened in the artificial light.

"Allow me to do most of the talking, Doctor," he said as we rode the elevator up. "If I feel it is appropriate for you to speak, I will indicate so. We don't need to give the detective more information than is necessary."

Rossi waved us in from the cramped reception area and led us to an empty room in the back. He shook Lucasian's hand warmly, then mine. "How's the family, Manny?" he asked as we all took our seats.

"Splendid! Three have colds, one a broken arm, and another poured his lunch milk into the school fish tank, which did not have a positive effect on the fish's health. We have been obliged to make reparations."

"I don't see how you have the time for your practice," Rossi said. I could hear a note of envy in his voice.

"My wife is a saint. Or, as she would tell you, a martyr. So, Lieutenant, my client is a busy man, with many ailing patients dependent upon his care. How may we help you?"

Rossi adjusted his bulk in the chair and took on a businesslike expression. "As I mentioned, the blood type on the jacket matched the victim's—"

"As it would with a million other people in the San Francisco area."

"Maybe." Rossi scowled. "I've also been speaking with others in the hospital who have given me cause to be concerned that Dr. Maebry may pose a danger to the victim."

"Others? Really, Detective, we must be more specific."

Rossi looked as if he was deciding whether to divulge the information.

"Detective," Lucasian said, "we are talking about my client's reputation and livelihood. We want to be reasonable, but it would be a shame indeed if your department were to overstep itself and charge someone without adequate cause. If that were to happen, and my client was then exonerated, as he surely would be—"

"Okay, Manny," Rossi interrupted. "We're not talking about charging anyone yet. We're talking about taking precautions. Safeguarding the victim from any further danger."

"A commendable impulse, certainly. But you have not to this moment given us any substantive reason why you believe my client poses such a danger."

"For one, there is a nurse who attended the patient, a Ms. Fal"—Rossi consulted his notes—"Feltin."

"Diane," I said under my breath.

"She says that Dr. Maebry was acting strangely—"

"Strangely!" I burst out. "For Christ's sake, she's incompetent!"

Lucasian gave me a hard look.

"The head nurse," Rossi said, "thinks she's reliable."

"It's a union," I protested. "They always stick up for each other."

"Allow me, Doctor," Lucasian said sternly, laying his hand on my leg.

"She says," Rossi continued, "that Dr. Maebry was giving Ms. Sorosh a lot of medication, more than was called for. Keeping her overly sedated."

"She was in a highly anxious state—"

"Please, Doctor!" Lucasian squeezed my leg hard enough to hurt. I was surprised at his strength.

Rossi frowned. "It's not far-fetched to conclude that the doctor was trying to keep her knocked out, medicated and confused, so that she wouldn't remember."

"I believe the woman has amnesia, is this not right?" Lucasian asked. Rossi nodded reluctantly. "It would then seem somewhat *redundant* on my client's part to give her drugs to not remember."

"He may not have known she had amnesia at that time."

"*May* not? Why not? It is fairly common in such cases, so I am told."

"Common but not universal," said Rossi, insisting on the point. "Anyway, there is also the e-mail." He picked up a piece of paper and handed it to Lucasian. "That's your copy."

Lucasian read it, and Rossi gave another copy to me. I folded it without looking at it and put it in my pocket. "A bit florid, perhaps," Lucasian said, "but I see nothing out of the ordinary."

"And the phone message, in which Ms. Sorosh refers to an argument they had shortly before the attack."

Lucasian let out an expression that sounded like "Pffui." "My wife and I had an argument just last night," he said. "I can't even remember what it was about."

"Manny," Rossi insisted, "the e-mail—he makes threats."

Lucasian waved his hand dismissively. "Only a suspicious mind would read it that way. They had a lovers' quarrel. That is all."

"Lovers' quarrels can end badly."

"And most of them end in bed in passionate reconciliation. It is a much remarked-upon occurrence. I'm sure all of us have had the experience."

Rossi smiled at Lucasian, then remembered my presence and frowned again.

"Detective," Lucasian went on in a mollifying tone, "I am not telling you anything of which you are not already aware when I say you do not have much to go on here. We do understand, however, your need, as you say, to take all necessary precautions. And while your concern about my client is misplaced, as I am sure you will discover on your own in short order, we are willing to submit that Dr. Maebry will voluntarily agree that he shall no longer attend to Ms.

Sorosh as her physician, either in her rehabilitation from this or in future operations, until he is fully exonerated." Lucasian gave me a sideways glance and continued. "I must stress that this action will be, as I say, voluntary on my client's part, simply a demonstration of his desire to cooperate with your department. It reflects no prejudice on him in any way; indeed, it redounds to his sense of civic-mindedness—"

"Okay, okay, Manny. I get your point," Rossi broke in.

"Of course, there will be nothing said to the hospital that could in any way injure his professional standing there?"

Rossi nodded once, frowning even more deeply than before. "Agreed, Manny, if he keeps to the bargain."

"He will." Lucasian clapped his hands on his knees and stood up. "It is a pleasure doing business with you, Detective." I got up as Rossi lumbered around to our side of the desk.

"What about Krista?" I said to Lucasian, afraid he had forgotten.

Lucasian seemed reluctant to bring it up. "This is the woman I mentioned to you earlier on the phone. The nurse, Ms. Generis."

"We've looked into it, Manny. Nothing there. But we always keep an open mind."

———

A strong wind from the bay battered us as we huddled outside on the sidewalk. One particularly violent blast managed to unglue Lucasian's hair from his head, and he pulled out a comb and slicked it back as we talked.

"I trust you are content with the bargain we just made," he said.

"I'm not sure I understand it."

"Detective Rossi was skillfully playing a weak hand, but I think we were even more skillful, no? He wanted to protect Ms. Sorosh from the danger he imagines you represent as her doctor. Without some assurance, it's possible that he might have gone ahead with an arrest and taken the consequences if—I should say *when*—his mistake became apparent. So we bargained away something that we no longer had—your attendance as a physician on Ms. Sorosh—though he clearly was not aware of this."

"You think he would have arrested me otherwise?"

We were interrupted by a blaring siren. A squad car nearby lit up in a blaze of flashing lights and sped off.

"I think it highly probable. Detective Rossi is a man who plays his hunches, and right now you are his hunch."

"Why, though? Why me?"

"The detective has not let me in on all of his thinking, but from our conversations, I gather he is convinced that Ms. Sorosh was attacked by someone she knew."

"Why does that mean *me*?" I complained. "What about Krista?"

"He has apparently ruled her out. I suspect she has an alibi."

"How do we know it's real?" I argued. "Maybe she's lying. I mean—"

"Dr. Maebry, I have learned from experience to repose a certain degree of faith in Lieutenant Rossi's abilities. He is an excellent investigator, and his honesty is above question. This does not mean, of course, that he is infallible. There may come a time when we'll wish to hire a private investigator of our own to check up on Ms. Generis, but I do not believe the time is now."

"Okay," I said. "If you think so. But I still don't see . . . Why couldn't it have been a stranger?"

"First, there was no robbery. Her purse had a large amount of cash remaining. Second, the location. It's not a place she normally frequented. It is a significant distance from where she lived or worked. She must have had some reason for going there, which suggests she was acquainted with her assailant. Perhaps they had scheduled a rendezvous."

"Or she could have been kidnapped."

"Her car was at the scene of the crime, which would tend to indicate that she came of her own free will."

"She might have been tricked or threatened," I insisted. "Maybe someone else drove the car."

"And walked home?"

I felt foolish, and he could see it.

"What you say is not inconceivable. There might have been two assailants working in tandem. It is a possibility." He clearly didn't think it was much of one. "There were, however, no marks indicating she had been restrained, and if the assailant—or assailants—had a gun, it seems unlikely he or they would have resorted to, well, such a crude use of force. The detective feels that the pattern of injuries suggests that it was something personal, a crime of passion."

"And that points to me?"

"It might," he said, looking contemplative. "But a young woman—beautiful by all accounts, in the prime of life—such a woman could very likely inspire passion in more than one man. Or . . ."

"Or what?" I asked.

He shrugged. "This is, after all, San Francisco. Passion takes on—how shall I say it?—an almost infinite variety of forms in this city."

Chapter 42

S hortly after returning to the hospital, I passed Crockett in the hall walking the other way.

"Oh, Jackson," he said, stopping short and looking unhappily in my direction.

"Good morning to you, too," I said.

He consulted his watch and growled some kind of epithet under his breath. "Listen, Jackson. You got a moment? Good," he said, taking my arm before I had time to answer. "Let's get something to eat. It's almost lunchtime."

I walked silently down the hall with him to the cafeteria, where he piled his tray with food. I took a greasy wedge of pizza and a Coke and we sat down in a still empty section of the room. He sat silently for a while, shoveling large forkfuls of what looked like pot roast and mashed potatoes into his mouth, appearing increasingly discontented as he ate.

"You know," he said, still chewing, "they did a study feeding hospital food to rats. They all died of malnutrition. I don't know why I bother to eat it." He finished it off anyway, then pushed the tray away and took up his dessert. "At least they can't screw up Jell-O," he sighed as he spooned it down.

I ate my pizza and waited.

"We had a meeting of the surgery board this morning. I'm on it, you know."

"I didn't."

"Yeah, inasmuch as I'm now the new head of ortho."

"Congratulations."

"Yeah, yeah. More work, same money. But I'm a sucker for prestige. So anyway, your boss is on it, too, of course, and well, we were discussing the new plastics slot opening up."

"Oh."

"What the hell happened between you and Brandt, anyway?"

"What do you mean?"

"He's pissed about something. You had been a shoo-in, but he just started going on about 'grave doubts' and 'serious concerns' about your conduct. The man is pompous enough to be a U.S. senator."

"Oh," I said. Brandt had promised to do what he could for me. Apparently he'd changed his mind. "So did the board make a decision?"

"Not yet, probably not for several weeks."

"But you think—"

"Basically, Jackson, you're screwed." He considered me as I took it in. "What's the story? You were his star. Everybody knew it."

"It's about Allie Sorosh, a patient. I assisted on her surgery. Those photos I showed you were of her operation. We had a relationship, and he was angry that I didn't tell him. He said it was unprofessional and took me off the case."

"Crap! I put in my mom's hip replacement. Set my uncle's fractured tibia. Seems like people in my family reach a certain age, all they do is fall down." Crockett scratched at the bottom of the Styrofoam cup with his plastic spoon to get the last of the Jell-O, then leaned back and looked at me with another sigh. "Listen, Jackson, I like you."

"Thanks." I laughed; he was so clearly uncomfortable saying it.

"Yeah, well, I'm trying to be sensitive. My wife says I'm not sensitive enough. Says I've got to open up to my Venus potential or some horseshit like that. We've been going to this group counseling. We all hold hands in a circle and tell each other how much we love them."

"It's hard to imagine."

"Wait till you get married; you'll find yourself doing a lot of shit you couldn't possibly imagine now. Look, the point is, I'm sorry about this thing with Brandt. It's a raw deal, but personally I'm not surprised."

"Why not?"

"You've heard the expression 'All surgeons are assholes, but some are bigger assholes than others'? Maybe that's not an expression, but it should be. Brandt is one of the biggest of them all. Don't repeat that. I mean, most of us aren't so hot on people skills. I'll admit that. Take me, for instance."

"For instance."

"Yeah, well, I do what I do and I'm good at it, but—listen, you know why I became a surgeon? I didn't want to get drafted and go to Vietnam. I was studying philosophy—you think that's funny? It's true; I was a philosophy major. Plato, Hegel, Kant, all those guys. But while it might have been good for my soul, philosophy wasn't going to keep me out of the war. So I went to medical school, and I wasn't in any rush to get out, so I went into surgery. And I chose orthopedics because I like to fix things. That's it. Really. I'm good at what I do, but I don't have any pretensions about it. Brandt, on the other hand, thinks he's an artist."

Crockett scratched absentmindedly again at the empty Jell-O cup. "Which makes his patients what, exactly? Get my point? I mean, Jesus, have you seen his nails? Perfectly manicured. How many men do you know outside the Mafia who manicure their nails? Brandt's nails are always perfect. Everything about him is perfect, his grammar, his clothes. Most doctors are slobs, like you and me, right? I've seen him come out of an eight-hour operation looking like he just got dressed in the morning. I don't think the man has sweat glands.

"I'm not putting down plastic surgery. I think every woman should wear forty-two-D-cup bras—except they don't need bras, do they; they've got interior suspension. Okay, okay, I know plastics is more than that. My point is—what the hell is my point? Oh, Brandt. He's a control freak. A total control freak. He's wound so tight, I bet he hasn't had a decent bowel movement in years. If you catch my drift."

"We always got on. Until now."

"Ever wonder why? Lots of young, bright doctors have come through Brandt's plastics program. You're good, but so were they. About half of them left early. None of them did he take a shine to like you. Why do you think that is?"

I shrugged.

"Because he thought he could remake you in his own image, turn you into a little Brandt. He knew he could shape you like . . . like—" He searched for the simile. "Putty."

"I didn't know I was that spineless."

"I'm not criticizing you, Jackson."

"Sure."

"I'm trying to be sensitive."

"I appreciate the effort."

"Well, I'm new at it." He laughed, and I tried to smile.

"All I'm saying is, you've got to stop being such a pushover. Stick up for yourself. Otherwise, Brandt is going to flatten you like a steamroller. We'll all be sorry for you and all that, but there won't be much we can do except scrape you off the pavement after he's done and hose down the grease stain."

"Pretty graphic."

"Yeah, well, I have a way with words. He's really pissed with you, Jackson, for whatever reason, and I'll tell you: someone like Brandt, booting you out of the plastics department is the least he could do to you."

"You think he'd do that?"

"Yeah," he said simply. "I do." He examined his watch, then looked straight at me, suddenly serious, as if only now had he gotten to the real point of our talk. "Listen, did you ever study philosophy?"

"Just a philosophy-of-science course as part of premed."

"Well, you might have run across him then: William of Occam?" I shook my head. "He was a monk philosopher sometime in the Middle Ages. Primarily he was interested in distinguishing between faith and reason—yeah, right, pretty arcane, but in the process he established one of the most important rules of logical deduction. It's called Occam's razor. I guess because it forces you to draw clean, sharp distinctions, sort of like a scalpel. What it says, basically, is that one should never assume multiplicity if singularity will suffice."

"I don't have a clue what you're talking about," I said.

"Another way of putting it is: The simpler explanation is almost always the right one. It's a basic axiom of science. Including medicine. If someone comes into the emergency room with a knife sticking out of his head, complaining of a headache, you don't start looking for a brain tumor or checking his metabolic function, right?"

"Right."

"You assume it's probably the knife in his head. Follow me so far?"

"Yeah. Probably the knife. Sure."

"Okay. But what if it isn't? What if it's not the knife causing the pain?"

"I don't know, a knife in the head's gotta hurt."

"I'm making an *analogy*, Jackson. Maybe it's only a superficial wound. Maybe the knife has nothing to do with it; he's had the headache for weeks, and the next week he comes in looking pale and his breath smells like almonds. And it turns out his wife has been poisoning him gradually with arsenic for the last month."

"Who stuck him with the knife?"

"Who knows? Maybe he was mugged, maybe she did it, maybe it's pure coincidence. Try not to be so literal, we're talking philosophy."

"Okay. Where are we going with this, Crockett?"

"I'm getting there. So what we have here is the *corollary* to Occam's razor." He enunciated each word like a professor with a slow pupil: "If the simplest mode of explanation doesn't work, you have to move to the next level of complexity." He paused, eyebrows raised, waiting for the concept to sink in. It didn't.

"If you say so," I agreed anyway, no less bewildered than before.

"Look. They used to think the world was flat, right? Made sense, really. A straight line was the shortest distance between two points. It was the simplest explanation of what they saw. Nice and neat, and it works beautifully, until you start sailing around the world and end up where you began."

"Uh-huh."

"So they figure out the earth is round, and all the people in China are standing upside down. Pretty weird until you get used to the idea, but we think it's normal now. Or take quantum physics. They thought it would all get simpler as they explored further into the atom, but it just gets more and more *weird*. It's like some new particle or force is discovered every year. Quarks, strong forces, weak forces. No one expected it. A lot of scientists refused to believe it because it violated their sense of the way things *should* be."

"Yeah?"

"What I'm saying is, the world is a much stranger place than we usually think."

"Actually, it's always seemed pretty strange to me."

"Things are never as simple as we think. Especially when people are involved. Things often don't turn out the way we expect."

"Right."

"The simplest explanation isn't always the right one," he repeated.

"Okay."

He nodded as if he'd come to the end of the discussion.

"That's it?" I asked. "The simplest explanation isn't necessarily right?"

"Exactly!" he exclaimed, as if we'd finally clarified the point. "Well—" He pushed back his chair and looked at his watch again. "I gotta get up to the OR and crack some bones. Glad we had the chance to have this little chat."

He stood up with his tray. "Think about it, Jackson," he said, then walked over to dump his trash and left the room.

—

Outside my office window, the swallows gyrated under the clear canopy, dazed and panicked by repeated collisions with the glass.

Crockett was right. I was a pushover. A wimp. I was trapped like those damned birds and I was too confused to find my way free, too weak to try. Old indecisive, wishy-washy Jackson. It had even been a joke in prep school. Someone would ask a question and the other guys would answer, "Maebry yes, Maebry no." Everyone thought it was terribly amusing.

It was true. I had no real sense of myself. Or, more accurately, I was so unhappy with whatever tenuous sense of myself I did possess that I'd gladly give it up for someone else's idea of what I should be. I was—as everybody apparently thought—like putty, a lump of clay in their hands, becoming whatever they desired me to be. For Stern, an example of psychoanalytic principles at work; for Rossi, a suspect; for Brandt, someone he could remake in his own image. And I had obliged them. Always obliged. So why shouldn't they think the worst of me now? I had so little character of my own that they could easily believe whatever they wanted. Before I was a good patient, a star pupil, an exemplary citizen. Now I was vicious and deranged. And who was I to object, who was I to say that it wasn't true? Who was I, exactly?

I got up and went to the men's room and splashed cold water on my face, contemplating the person staring back at me from the mirror. He looked like he'd gotten lost there and hoped no one would notice his presence. I could always get drunk again, I thought. Get drunk and forget. At least for a time. It was an appealing idea. And proof that I was what everyone thought, a weakling.

You can't just sit here and let things happen to you, I told myself. You have to take charge. You have to *do* something.

Oh boy! My reflection smirked back at me. *You're actually going to do something? That's taking charge, all right!*

I threw more cold water on my face and turned from the mirror. *What, Jackson? What! What are you going to do?*

I leaned my head against the cold tile and heard a lone, crazy voice crying in an empty men's room. "What are you going to do? What are you going to do?"

Chapter 43

I could hear her pushing back the cover on the peephole, and once I was inside, she carefully locked the door behind us and attached the chain. Whether it was from fear of intruders or just another level of protection from the world in general, I didn't know. The windows were still closed, and the whirring air conditioner did little to move the air. The apartment felt sealed, like a storage locker.

Who else could I go to besides Allie?

She walked ahead of me to the couch and sat with her head down. She wore large sunglasses and a scarf over her head, tied under her chin.

"I brought you some things," I said, placing my shopping bag on the counter that separated the living room from the kitchen.

"That wasn't necessary."

"Just necessities: caviar, champagne." I held up the bottle.

"Thanks, Jacko." I caught a brief smile. She could never refuse champagne.

I poured two glasses, brought them to where she was sitting and joined her on the couch. She accepted the glass and raised it to her lips, but her mouth was obviously still hurting. Most of the champagne spilled, forming a dark stain on her sweatshirt.

"Damn," she muttered helplessly. I got a napkin from the kitchen and knelt before her. I could see she was crying.

"Here, let me—"

"Don't." She lowered her head and pulled away from me. I handed her the napkin and sat back where I'd been.

"It just takes time, Allie."

"I know."

"But it will keep getting better."

"Until the next operation. And the one after that. How many more will there be? Three, four?"

"It depends how the skin grafts take; it's hard to say now."

She readjusted her glasses and pulled down on the scarf to make it cover more of her face. I took a deep breath and started. I knew it wouldn't be pleasant.

"Allie," I asked, "has your memory come back at all? Do you remember anything, anything at all about the assault?"

"No, nothing. I told you."

"Allie, I know you don't want to talk about it. I wouldn't ask if it weren't important. What about the day or two before? Has nothing come back to you?"

"No!" It was sharp, angry.

"I don't want to upset you, but you've got to try—"

"It's just like that detective," she said bitterly. "He keeps coming by and calling me up. I told him I don't remember. Why does he keep asking me? It's like he doesn't believe me. Like he thinks I'm lying or something."

"He's trying to find the person who did this, Allie."

"I wish he wouldn't come here. I wish he'd stop bothering me."

"Allie, whoever it was is still out there, and he could be dangerous. You don't have any idea who it might have been? Anyone you knew?"

"No!" she cried, visibly agitated. "I told you. I told that detective! I don't *remember*! I have no idea why I was up on Mercury Drive or whatever it's called, in that house. I have no idea why I would have been in Marin at all. I can't remember anything about that day. I can't, Jackson, I can't!"

I got up to pour another glass of champagne, then came over and refilled her glass, too. I waited a moment, then continued. "Isn't there anyone you can think of that it might have been? An acquaintance?"

"Why do you keep asking that?"

"Allie . . . I have to ask because—" She jerked up onto her feet, furious that I was still pressing the subject. "Allie, I *have* to. Rossi thinks—" I was about to tell her what had happened: the search, the lawyer; that I was Rossi's chief, if not only, suspect. But I froze in midsentence. What if she believed it, just as the others did? What if she suspected me already?

Allie didn't notice, however. The mention of Rossi's name had only reminded her of how angry she was. "I told that—that *person* a hundred times I can't remember!"

"Okay, Allie," I said, relieved, as if I'd stepped back just in time from the edge of a precipice. "I'm sorry I brought it up."

"I don't remember!"

"Okay, Allie," I said, as soothingly as I could. "Okay."

"I don't!" Her voice was lower now, plaintive. "I wish he'd just leave me alone. I wish everybody would go away and leave me alone."

"Everybody," I knew, included me.

Chapter 44

I stood at a pay phone in a coffee shop in Berkeley and paged through my address book to find Paula and Brian's number. I hadn't heard from either of them since my last strange phone conversation with Paula, but I had to talk to her now. She was the only one who knew about the other men in Allie's life before me, the ones she never talked about, the ones she wouldn't tell me about now. I'd pushed as hard as I dared, possibly too hard. Possibly more than she would forgive.

Paula didn't sound pleased to be hearing from me again. "It's really not a good time" was all she said. When I asked when it would be, she said she was very busy these days and couldn't say.

"It's important, Paula," I insisted. "I just need to come by for a few minutes, please."

"Sorry, it's not possible." She was adamant. Only when I threatened to drive down anyway did she grudgingly agree. "But you better make it here quick, Jackson," she said. "I've got an appointment later and I can't wait for you." Always an appointment, I thought. I promised to hurry.

I found the house again without too much difficulty and was greeted by the maid, who led me through the foyer and down into the living room. It had been completely redecorated since the party, all in varying shades of white and beige. Paula's young daughter sat in the middle of a vast pale rug, looking like a small splotch of color on an overexposed black-and-white photograph.

She came up to me as I sat on the couch and held out a doll in her little hands. "This is Barbie. I have twelve of them," she told me proudly.

"Pleased to meet you, Barbie Number Twelve," I said, shaking the doll's hand with my fingers.

"That's not her name! She's Poolside Barbie!"

"Oh. And what's your name?" I asked.

"Halley," she said, tucking her face in her shoulder, suddenly shy.

"Hello, Halley, I'm Jackson." Her face opened in a big smile, and she took my hand, then dropped it abruptly as Paula entered from the kitchen. She was wearing leggings and a large sweatshirt, her hair pulled back in a ponytail.

"Halley," she said sternly, "go into the kitchen and play with Marguerite."

Halley bundled up her dolls as if she'd done something wrong and went out the way Paula had come in.

"Bye, Halley," I said as she left.

She turned to me and smiled. "Bye," she said back, then looked at her mother and scampered out. Paula walked over to the bar without speaking and got a bottled water. She didn't offer me anything.

"I'm sorry to impose, Paula, but I need to talk to you about Allie."

"Jackson—" She said my name as if it were particularly exasperating. "What's the point?"

"The point! What's going on, Paula? What's the problem?"

She shot a glance at her watch. "I said I didn't have time. I'm already late for ballet class."

"Do you realize how badly Allie was injured?"

"Of course. I tried to call her at the hospital, and they said she didn't want any visitors." She realized that wasn't a satisfactory answer and tried again. "Listen, when we heard from the people at Genederm about Allie, I was really broken up. I'm sorry for her and all that, but . . ." She had started apologetically but broke off in irritation.

"Did you two have a falling-out?"

"You mean you don't know?" she said in surprise, then more distantly, "No, I guess you wouldn't."

"Allie didn't tell me anything. All I know is the four of us went out a couple of times after the party, and then we stopped seeing each other. That was four months ago."

"I haven't seen her since then, Jackson. We haven't even talked."

"But you were her best friend."

She didn't say anything, merely took a swig from the water bottle.

"What about at Genederm, didn't you see each other there?"

"I quit. Shit, I don't need the money." She waved her bottle in an arc around the room to demonstrate the point.

"What did you two fight about?"

She stood at the bar, fidgeting. "Why don't you ask her?"

"She has amnesia," I said.

"Amnesia—like in the movies? You're kidding."

"No."

"She doesn't remember anything?"

I let her think that. She shook her head and gave a snorting little laugh. "Boy, I wish I could forget the last four months. No, make that four years."

"Listen, Paula, I'm just trying to figure out what happened, why Allie was attacked. You used to hang out together all the time—"

"So?" She brushed at her hair with her hand, but as it was already tightly pulled back, all she touched was air.

"I thought that you might be able to tell me about some of the people she knew. Friends. Guys. You know."

"What for?"

"In case they had anything to do with it."

"Like they attacked her?" She snorted again. It was an especially unpleasant sound. "That's ridiculous, Jackson."

"Maybe, I don't know. But you and Allie got around—"

"You could say that." Another snort.

"And, well, I know Allie did drugs sometimes."

"So what, Jackson? What does that have to do with shit?"

"I thought that maybe Allie got involved with someone and . . ."

She let the sentence hang in the air for a moment. "Involved?" she asked sarcastically. "However do you mean, Jackson? Another boyfriend?" She smiled a not very nice smile.

I colored. "You know what I'm saying, maybe she was buying drugs and, well, got into trouble."

Paula laughed. "What an imagination!"

"It's possible," I protested.

"Jackson, Allie didn't have to buy drugs. She could get whatever she wanted free from almost any bartender in the city."

"Okay, friends then. I know she had boyfriends before me."

She looked at me with undisguised contempt. "You really don't have a clue, do you?"

"Okay, Paula, I'm clueless, but I need to know—"

Something outside distracted Paula, and she turned to see what it was. "Fucking shit!" she burst out, slamming her bottle of water on the counter. "Fucking goddamn shit! Hubby's home. Why can't he work late like other men?" She turned to me as if I was a problem she didn't know what to do with. "I think you should leave now, Jackson."

"I need to get a few names," I persisted, but she was already striding over to the entrance, slinging a workout bag over her shoulder as she went. I got up and followed her. "Paula, just a few names."

She turned her head toward me with a sudden movement when she reached the door. "I want you to leave, Jackson," she hissed. "Get it? I want you out of here!" Then, equally suddenly, she put on her smiley face and turned to Brian as he came through the door, greeting him with a gush of words.

"Hello, darling. I didn't know you'd be home so early. Jackson Maebry's here, you remember Jackson, don't you? Unfortunately, he was just leaving. Bye, Jackson." She shot me a nasty glare. "Bye, darling," she said to Brian, "I'm late for class." She gave him a peck on the cheek and rushed out before he had a chance to embrace her.

Brian smiled at me, his arms still out, as if he was used to it.

"Hey, Jackson. Haven't seen you for a while." He threw his computer case down on a side bench and came over and shook my hand. "Do you have to go right away?"

"Not really," I said.

"Great!" We walked back to the living room. "Want a beer?"

I said yes, and he got two from the bar and threw me one—which I managed to catch—before plopping down in one of the overstuffed armchairs.

"How do you like the new look?" he asked, rolling his eyes about the room. "Paula had it done. One of the hottest interior designers on the West Coast did it. You know, that guy, what's-his-name."

"It's nice," I lied.

"It's like living in an igloo," he said. "Every time I come home, I think I'm going snow-blind. So, it's good to see you, Jackson. What brings you down the peninsula?"

"I wanted to talk to Paula about Allie."

"Oh, yeah. I heard. God, that was terrible. How is she?"

I told him and he shook his head. He appeared honestly upset at the news. "Jeez. I had no idea. We spoke with that detective, but he didn't go into details. Paula said— I don't know, somehow I got the impression it wasn't that serious. Jeez!" He shook his head. "Is there anything we can do?"

"Not right now. Brandt's taking care of the surgery. I've been assisting." Phrased that way, the statement was accurate, at least.

"Well, Brandt's a genius, they say."

"Yeah," I said. "So what's going on with Paula? She didn't even want to talk about Allie."

He screwed up his face and was about to answer when Halley came running into the room screaming "Daddy," and jumped into his lap. He held her and asked her how her day was, and they talked about her teacher and a boy in school with whom she'd had a fight: all the pressing issues of her day.

"You've met Jackson, haven't you, Halley?" he asked.

She turned and nodded, then hid her face in his chest.

"She's shy." He caressed her hair, and she looked up and smiled at me again. "She looks just like her mother, doesn't she?" Brian said proudly.

"She's very cute," I agreed. I thought of what Allie had said: that Halley wasn't his child. She was probably right. They didn't look anything like each other.

"Halley," Brian said to her, "Jackson and I have to talk. It will just be a little while, and then we'll play together, okay?"

"Uh-huh." She nodded again enthusiastically, gave him a kiss and ran out.

Brian looked with dismay at a wet spot on the couch where his beer had spilled when Halley jumped on him. "Paula will be angry with me." He got up to get another beer, grunting as he fell back on the couch. "To be honest, Jackson, I don't think Paula and Allie are on the best of terms."

"Apparently not. How come?"

"Oh, I don't know." He rubbed his round face. "Some woman thing, probably."

"Paula was Allie's closest friend."

"Was is the operative word."

"What happened, Brian?"

He sighed, feeling the bald spot on the back of his head, exhaling deeply like a balloon running out of air. "Paula didn't want to tell me, but I sort of figured it out. I mean, she and Allie were inseparable, right? They used to go out all the time together. Then, suddenly, she didn't even want to hear Allie's name. She'd get mad if I brought it up. So I didn't. I mean, it's been—what?—three months now since we last got together."

"Longer. But Allie didn't say anything. I thought you guys were busy."

"No more than usual." He closed his eyes as if the subject might go away, then opened them again. I was still there, waiting.

"I think what it was, is . . ." He rubbed his fingers around his bald spot again. "Simply put, I think Paula believes Allie stole her boyfriend." He gave one of his boyish smiles and then looked away, embarrassed. I realized the embarrassment was more for me than for himself.

"Her *boyfriend*? I don't get it."

"Come on, Jackson. That's the way it is with Paula. I know it."

"You mean she was seeing someone else?"

He shrugged and gave a little smile. Easygoing Brian.

"And Allie?" I felt that I had to go through it step by step, make sure I was getting it right. "Allie was seeing this guy, too? When?" I'd been tearing myself up with my suspicions, but at least I'd been able to tell myself that's all they were. Suspicions.

"God, I don't know. I sort of put it together." Like it was just one of those things. "Hey," he said in that mild, completely inoffensive voice, "you look about finished with that beer, how about another one?"

I wanted to shout at him. "You don't know when?"

"I'm sure it was before you and Allie. Paula just found out about it later and—"

"How do you know?"

"I put it together, kind of—"

"I mean how do you know it was before *me*?"

"It was, Jackson. I'm sure. Pretty sure."

"Who was it?" I asked, feeling as if something cold and hard was bearing down on me.

"Jeez, I don't know. Probably one of their club friends. The pretty boys. You know those guys constantly falling all over them." It was the first time I'd heard bitterness in his voice.

He looked down, his round shoulders slumping even farther than usual. "What am I supposed to do? I love Paula. Or I did. I loved her a lot when we got married. It's different now, but . . . I guess it all doesn't matter to me as much as having her with me." He said it as if he wanted my approval. "And after all"—he had a different kind of smile now, a bit sheepish, but proud, too, the kind of smile that wells up from somewhere deep inside—"she is the mother of my child."

—

I drove west over the hills and down toward the shore, past the produce farms and horse ranches, through the sparse beach communities whose residents apparently didn't care that this section of coastline was perpetually shrouded in mist. By the time I got to the beach, the light was already failing, a premature, fog-induced twilight, and the wet air hung about my body like damp clothing. I turned in to a small parking lot near the ocean. There was only one other car there, an ancient Mustang with red tape covering one of its fractured taillights. A trail of bluish smoke escaped through the driver's-side window and crept along the corroded exterior. The red tip of a joint flared brightly, then faded. The boy inside faced straight ahead, his eyes barely open: they weren't seeing much, anyway.

I parked so I could see the water and pulled out the copy of the e-mail Rossi had handed me. My letter to Allie. The paper wilted in the dampness, its surface wet and slimy in my fingers. I didn't want to turn on the dome light. I could still make out the type. A different font than I used. As if someone else had written the letter, using my life as material. An official header indicated that it was now police evidence. A series of numbers followed, probably specifying the case file. The one for Jackson Maebry, unnamed suspect. So far.

Dear Allie,

You said it doesn't matter, but it does, it matters more than anything in the entire world. I have given everything to you that I have to give, which may not seem like much, fine. But you took it, or accepted it, and there's no way to give it back . . .

Jesus! It was embarrassing. I could imagine sitting on the witness stand, reading it out to twelve stone-faced jurors. I skimmed through the next section, barely able to make myself read on, phrases like: *"cutting away pieces of my heart . . . smashing my love like a hammer . . ."* What had Lucasian said—"florid"? I skipped further on.

You said we could start new, leave the dead past behind, throw it away, but now I feel—God, I hope it isn't true—that you want to leave me behind, throw me away like a mistake with all those other discarded things. But that can't happen. I won't let it. Allie, is there someone else? Do you love someone else? Is that why you said no to my proposal and handed me back my ring. Is it that guy at the club last weekend with his hands all over you? That was his voice on the answering machine, wasn't it? You have so many goddamned friends, but we never see them together except when we bump into them by mistake. They must think I'm a real idiot. You're not where you say you'll be and you refuse to tell me where you've been. So many secrets. Do you keep secrets from someone you say you love? Maybe. Maybe especially from them. But maybe I was just along for the ride and now you don't need me anymore but it's too late. I don't like it here where you left me. Alone. I can't live without you and you can't live without me. You won't, even if you think you will. Lots of people play at love, but I don't. Because I know it's a matter of life and death, and I won't be left to die here without you. We are connected now, we can't live without each other, and I won't die alone . . .

That was it. The end. I'd never finished it. Never even read it until now. I'd pressed the delete key and watched it vanish, like so many things about ourselves that in the light of morning we want to pretend never were. Even in the state I was in, I knew it was crazy and never would have sent it. Maybe that's what Lucasian would say to the jury: he was in a "state." He was very upset, crazy when he wrote it. Temporarily, of course.

I folded the limp paper and put it back in my pocket.

Brian was sure that whomever Paula and Allie had fought over had been before my time. But how did he know? He didn't, obviously. He didn't really want to know. He lived inside an illusion and wasn't interested in complicating it too much. In a way, I envied him. I'd live there, too, if I could; escape into some comforting illusion and never come out again.

Who could it be? I racked my mind for the names. Andy, Bart, Mike—a couple of Mikes. The pretty boys, as Brian said, with blond hair and bland manners. There were thousands of their kind all over San Francisco, all over California. Where the hell did they all come from?

They weren't important, Allie would say, just guys she liked to "hang with." Bartenders who gave her free drinks, club owners who would invite us to the "private" section of their clubs. I never really bothered to learn their names, I could hardly distinguish one face from another in my memory. They were all so interchangeable. So tan and young and easygoing and nice. That was the most infuriating thing, how nice they were. How nicely they'd smile and serve our drinks and make nice, easygoing small talk with Allie, and I knew they were always waiting. Waiting for their chance with her.

It was completely dark now, the ocean and beach beyond the fence an indistinguishable wall of black. It was as if nothing existed but our two cars—islands of debris in a drowned world.

The heavy smoke from the Mustang curled in the watery currents. The boy inside was still working diligently on his own personal illusion. Someplace he could escape to. Someplace, he probably believed, where everything would be all right again.

Chapter 45

I was at my desk in the hospital the next day when the secretary announced a caller over my intercom. It took a moment to register that she had said Helen Brandt was on the line.

"Hello? Mrs. Brandt?" I couldn't imagine what she wanted.

"Don't be so formal, Jackson. Are you trying to make me feel old?"

I mumbled something to the effect of "No."

She laughed. "Call me Helen, sweetie," she said. "So I suppose I should congratulate you." I thought maybe she was being sarcastic.

"Congratulate me?"

"The protégé has been officially promoted, or will be, so I hear."

She didn't know.

"I don't think so. Actually, ah—"

"Don't be modest," she broke in. "Peter asked me to set up a dinner with you and some of the other doctors in the practice. He's going to make the announcement that you're joining them. Of course, he wants people from the hospital and Genederm there, too, and some media types. He's always doing business."

"Helen—"

"'Helen.' How nice that sounds! Much better than Mrs. Brandt. How's next Saturday for you? Eight o'clock, our place?"

"Helen, I don't think it's a good idea. The thing is . . . I'm pretty sure Dr. Brandt has changed his mind."

"He didn't say anything to me about it." She sounded put out.

"When did he tell you to set up the dinner?"

"About a week ago, maybe longer. But I just got back from a week with my girlfriends at a spa. I went on this marvelous diet and must have gained three pounds— What's going on?"

"I think things have changed, that's all."

"What's changed? Don't be so damned cagey."

"Okay. He's not putting me up for the position at the hospital any longer. He didn't say that to me, but it's what I hear. He and I . . . Listen, we haven't spoken for a few days, but I'm pretty sure he's no longer interested in having me join his practice. Maybe you should speak to him."

"Tell me what this is about, Jackson."

I might as well, I decided; she'd learn soon enough anyway.

"He took me off the Sorosh case." She didn't say anything, and I thought she might have forgotten the name. "Allie Sorosh. The woman who was attacked. She works in PR at Genederm. He didn't tell you?"

"I've got better things to do than talk about his damn patients all day," she snapped.

"Sorry," I said, not sure what I was apologizing for.

"Why did he take you off the case?"

"We'd been seeing each other, Allie and I, and he was angry that I hadn't told him. He said it was unprofessional for me to operate— Mrs. Brandt? I mean, Helen?"

She was laughing. She broke off abruptly and asked: "Who's her surgeon now?"

"Dr. Brandt has been the lead surgeon from the start," I said, confused by her reaction. "I was just assisting. He'll find someone else, I'm sure. . . . We did the first skeletal reconstruction last week. Of her face. It was very successful, though, ah . . ." I sputtered out, wondering if she was listening.

"I'm positive this is all a misunderstanding," she said. "We can work it out."

"I'm not so sure—"

"Trust Auntie Helen, Jackson." She was back in her flirtatious mode. "Why don't you come out to see me and we'll talk about it. Are you free this afternoon?"

"I'm on call—" Maybe she really could smooth things over with Brandt, I thought. She probably could, if anyone could. "I'm free this evening," I added quickly.

"This evening, then. Our place. Peter's at some meeting. He never gets home until after ten anyway."

"Okay. If you think it's a good idea."

"See you at six," she said, and hung up.

—

The sidewalks of Pacific Heights were empty, silent but for the ever-present wind. I rang the bell and waited, and rang again. There was a rattle inside, and then Helen swung the door open, struggling with a large number of shopping bags she was holding in her hands.

"Hello, Jackson," she said, as if I'd arrived for a business meeting. "Hortensia!" she yelled in no particular direction, then turned around and loudly called out again for her maid. I caught the door before it closed on me and stepped into the foyer as a meek-looking woman shuffled out from a back room.

"Grab these, would you," Helen said, unloading the bags in her arms, "and get the rest out of the car in the garage. I've got to change." She barely gave the maid time to get hold of the bags before she hurried on, adding as she exited, "Oh, and get Dr. Maebry a beer or something."

I waited in the hall, shuffling my feet, until Hortensia came back with the beer. She'd poured it into a crystal glass and held it out for me on a silver tray, then departed again without looking me in the eye.

The house appeared cavernous with no one in it: all shining surfaces, mirrors and glass. Like a giant vacuum bottle, I thought. A low bench and a couple of chairs perched uncomfortably on the marble floor of the foyer while several plants shrank against the walls. Helen didn't return for some time, so I walked through the living room and out the French doors onto the porch. I leaned against the rail, looked out toward the bay and waited.

I don't know how long after—maybe ten, fifteen minutes—I turned back and saw Helen standing in the living room. She had changed from a black pantsuit into a long green dress that hung straight from her shoulders and pooled gracefully about her feet. Her arms were unmoving at her sides, and she wore a blank expression, as if she couldn't remember why I was there. She made a noticeable effort to rouse herself as I came in from the porch, and walked forward to greet me. By the time we reached each other, her face had taken on a welcoming smile. A moment later it even appeared genuine.

"Well, I see you've got a beer," she said.

"Yes, thanks."

She reached over to adjust the collar of my coat—not knowing what to expect, I'd dressed up for the evening—then tightened my tie and let her hands rest there. "I thought we'd just have a light dinner here," she said. "I've been shopping all afternoon and spent the morning at the health club with my personal sadist, and I'm totally wiped out. I hope that's all right."

"Yes, of course."

"We'll have a nice relaxed evening at home. Just the two of us."

"Sure. Okay."

She tilted her head to the side as if considering an amusing thought. I complimented her dress in order to fill the gap.

"Do you like it? I bought it today," she said, taking a step back and holding herself in such a way that demanded I look. She gathered up her loose hair and held it on top of her head, walked several steps away from me, twirled around and walked back, like she was on a fashion runway.

"It's very . . . elegant," I said.

That was apparently the wrong word. "This?" She laughed. "No, it's for relaxing." She tossed her hair back with a graceful motion, and it settled perfectly in place, lightly brushing against her neck, as if never disturbed. "But it's nice to have someone to appreciate it. I could go naked and Peter wouldn't notice."

"I can't believe that. I mean—"

She laughed again. "Actually, it's true, it's been a long time since he noticed me in that way. Am I embarrassing you?"

"No," I said, meaning yes.

She had my arm now and was leading me through the living room and past the swinging door into the kitchen. "It's like a painting you hang on the wall and then never really see again. I'm invisible to him— Thank you, Hortensia," she said to the maid as we entered. "You can go now."

"Yes, *Señora*," Hortensia said, hurriedly putting on her coat and leaving by the back door.

"Why don't we get rid of that beer," Helen said, taking the glass from my hand, "and open a bottle of wine." She pulled out a metal drawer and handed me a corkscrew. I took the bottle from the cooler on the table but got the wrong angle with the screw and stripped the cork.

"Let me," Helen said with a trace of annoyance. She forced the screw in, gave it a violent twist and pulled out the shredded cork, picking out the remaining pieces and flicking them off her fingers. "Well?"

"Oh," I said, and held out the glasses for her to pour.

"Cheers," she toasted, and we both drank. Helen finished hers, then reached over with a dissatisfied expression and wiped away a bit of cork that had stuck to my lip.

"Are you hungry? We've got some salmon, salad. Sushi."

"Not really."

"Neither am I. Sit with me here," she said, and patted a high stool by the counter. We perched there together, and she was already refilling her wineglass before I'd completely gained my balance.

"Peter's a very busy man," she said, continuing the conversation of before. "He likes his life to be well ordered, and I suppose I serve that function for him." She drank down the wine and rapidly refilled the glass. "I used to serve other functions as well." She laughed. "Once in a rare while, I still do. Even invisible objects, I guess, have their uses. See, that's from a week ago." She held out her arms toward me and pulled her bracelets back so I could see the rope burns circling her wrists. "They're clearer on my ankles." She let her shoe drop and lifted her foot into my lap. "Peter likes to be in control," she said, leaning toward me and lightly running her fingertip along the burn. "I guess I'm lucky it's not very frequent." She looked up coyly from under her hair. "I'm embarrassing you again, aren't I?"

"No, it's okay."

"You're not shocked? Just a little?"

She could see that I was.

She drew her finger up her leg to where the dress parted above her thigh. I stared into my wineglass and tried to focus my attention there.

"Peter says I heal well because I'm so blond and fair-skinned. The less pigment in your skin, you know, the less you scar. What am I saying?" She laughed. "Of course you know that."

She sat back and brought her leg down, resting her foot on the crossbar of my stool, touching my foot. She drank down her wine and emptied the bottle in her glass. "Why don't you get another bottle from the refrigerator. And take off your coat and tie, you make me feel like a teacher seducing her student."

When I brought the bottle back, she was resting her head on her hand, her elbow on the counter, holding the wineglass against her cheek. I opened it successfully this time and filled her empty glass. Somehow we were sitting closer than before. She brought her hand up and undid the top button of my shirt, pursed her lips and undid the next.

"There, that's more relaxed. You needn't worry, he won't be back for hours."

"I'm not. I just—"

"Just what?" she said, flashing her eyes at me, but she became unsteady on her seat and had to hold on to the counter to keep from falling.

"I'm not sure I feel comfortable . . . being here."

She ignored me. "Don't feel bad, Jackson. Peter is like that with everyone." She said it as if we'd been discussing him all along. "He loses interest. That's all. You've heard his artist speech? —Ha!" she exclaimed, when she saw from my expression that I had. "Of course you've heard it. Well, he *is* an artist, the bastard. He finishes you and you're done. You hang there on a wall and he never sees you again. Unless he's in the mood for one of his little amusements. Or until the paint starts peeling and it's time for the next operation." She leaned forward with her head to one side and pulled her hair back behind her ear. "Can you see that? The scar?"

"It's barely visible."

"What about that?" she said, parting her hair above her forehead. "Can you see that scar?"

"Yes. Just. It's very well done."

"Of course it is, Peter's an artist!" She said the word as if it was a curse. "And I'm a perfect subject for his skill. So blond and fair-skinned. I think that's why he married me, actually."

She let her hair fall back and ran her hand down her cheek, tracing the contour of her collarbone with her fingers. She'd had a full bottle of wine but seemed even drunker than one would expect from that.

"I was beautiful once . . ." she said, her hand sliding down toward her breasts.

"You are," I answered, saying what was expected of me.

"I *am,*" she insisted, as if I'd contradicted her. "Lots of men think so. I could have any man I want. I could have any of them just by saying yes. Young men, too. I could!"

"I'm sure," I said, trying to soothe her.

"Fuck you!" She flung her head back defiantly, then rolled her eyes and held on to me so as not to fall.

"Maybe I should go," I said when she'd regained her balance.

"You think I'm drunk?"

"I think maybe you should lie down."

"I'm not drunk, it's the pills . . . I don't usually take them, really."

I helped her off the seat and held her as we walked.

"I'll just lie down on my bed."

"That's a good idea," I said.

Her bedroom was on the lower level, past Brandt's study, where Burton, the dog, lay curled up asleep on his favorite chair. I could tell, even before she told me, that Helen slept alone; there was no evidence of anything masculine in her room, but it was hardly feminine, either. It reminded me of the hallway: hard, cold. A vacuum of the spirit. On the wall were huge framed photographs, all life-size portraits. All of her.

She lay down but held my arm and pulled me down so that I had to sit beside her. "Don't be mad," she mewed.

"I'm not. It's okay."

"I'm sorry, I really am."

"Don't be. It's okay."

"The truth is that I do take pills. All the time. I guess I took too many."

"Prescription?"

She giggled. "Of course, Peter prescribes anything I want."

"What are they?"

"I call them my invisible pills. The more I take, the more invisible I am. See." She wriggled around and opened a drawer, taking out a plastic pill bottle.

The label said Xanax. Two milligrams. The doctor was listed as Peter Brandt.

"How many of these do you take?"

"Two or three a day. Usually. Ambien at night."

"How many today?"

"Lots. Why so interested, Jackson?"

"It's not a good idea. You know that."

"Oh! I love it when you talk like a doctor. So authoritative." She put her hand on my chest and began to work her fingers in between the buttons. I put the pill bottle in my pants pocket, just to be safe.

"Were you telling me the truth? Do you think I'm beautiful?"

"Of course you are," I said, trying to move away.

"Do you?" She held on tight and pulled me closer. "Come to me, Jackson." She grabbed hold of my hand and put it on her breast.

"Helen—"

She pulled harder.

"Helen, stop."

"It's all right, Jackson. Come to me."

I jerked my arm to get free of her grasp, but not hard enough. She clutched my hand and moved her body to press against my chest. Her face was next to mine now, and she moved forward suddenly to kiss me. I turned to avoid it, and my forehead collided forcefully with her nose. It made a crunching sound.

She let go and I stood up, dazed.

"You bastard!" she cried. "You hurt me! You fucking bastard!"

"I'm sorry."

She pushed herself away on the bed, holding her face. "You son of a bitch! You stupid little boy!"

"Let me see—"

"Get away!" Her nose was already beginning to swell.

"I didn't mean to hurt you—"

"You stupid, naive little piece of shit! You think you're being loyal to Allie? Don't you know your precious girlfriend is fucking Peter?"

"What are you talking about?"

She laughed as if she'd scored a victory. "I guess she hasn't told you, has she? Left the little protégé in the dark."

"I don't believe you. You're just angry—"

"God, you are so stupid! Where do you think Peter is right now? He's with her. He's fucking her right now." She started to laugh again, but it came out as tears, and she began to weep.

"I'm leaving," I said, and started toward the door.

She stopped crying suddenly, the hard edge of her vindictiveness cutting through the self-pity, the tears frozen on her face. "Poor, poor Allie. Fuck her! I wish she'd died, the little bitch. She deserves what she got."

"Good-bye, Helen," I said.

"Go on, go back to your beautiful little bitch. But she's not so beautiful anymore, is she?"

I slammed the door and heard a crash in the room behind me, then the door being flung open again.

"She's not so beautiful anymore!" she shrieked as I ran up the stairs. I grabbed my coat and tie from the kitchen and made my way to the front door. I turned when I got there and saw Helen at the top of the stairs, gripping the railing, her face contorted into something unrecognizable. "The fucking whore's not so beautiful now!" she screamed. The sound filled the empty rooms, a violent echo resounding off the glassy surfaces of the hallway where I stood, but like everything else there, it was instantly swallowed up in the vacuum and died. Even so much hate couldn't keep it alive.

Chapter 46

After I left Helen, and for the next several evenings whenever I could get free from work, I would wait outside the door to Allie's condo. Sometimes I'd sit in my car across the street, sometimes in a coffee shop a few doors down, until the looks from the owner would send me back outside. For several nights running, I got back to the hospital after four A.M.; I didn't feel like going back to my apartment and slept in any spare bed I could find. I'd get up at seven the next morning for rounds, then be out the next night, sitting, waiting. Sometimes Allie would appear, her head covered by a shawl, and walk hurriedly down the street, and I would slump down in my seat but wouldn't take my eyes off her. Once Krista came by and spent the better part of an evening there. Otherwise, nothing much happened—nothing but endless, hollow hours, the dark car like a little pocket of shame in which I lay, as if naked and paralyzed, sick of myself, disgusted with what I was doing.

She didn't want me to come over, she said, the few times she forgot to screen her calls on the answering machine and actually picked up; she was tired, not feeling well. Didn't want visitors. I would insist, however, and bring her things, and we would make conversation about something, until after a few minutes I had exhausted all I could think of to say and would leave, wishing I hadn't come. Most of the things I did then I wished I hadn't.

So I would go back to my car and wait. For days I waited with no result. Until finally, almost as if I'd willed it, he came.

But for the suit and tie, which looked out of place in Berkeley, and the shock of white hair, which was too well groomed to belong to a professor, it was an unexceptional occurrence: a man walks down the street from his car, rings the intercom and is buzzed in. Perhaps it was an innocent visit. If I waited, he might come out after a short while, having simply dropped in to see how his patient was doing.

Brandt didn't come out. Not for the eternity I waited, maybe an hour, possibly two. Sometimes, as I sat there in the dark, I thought I could hear Helen's screams in my ears, cries of abandonment and loss coming from somewhere deeper than where jealousy resides. The empty place where nothing else is left. Nothing but rage.

I tried to reach Lucasian, but the message on his office machine said he was away on business, and when I spoke to his wife at home, she mentioned a "family matter" he had to attend to in a place that sounded eastern European. I asked her to have him call me when he returned, but the truth was, I wasn't eager to tell him about Helen. It meant telling him about Brandt and Allie. I would because I had to. And I'd endure the humiliation because I had no choice. Enough humiliation, I thought, and maybe you even begin to get used to it.

—

The hospital hardly felt real to me, but I was able to function almost by rote. I operated and consulted with patients, and since Brandt never scheduled me for his operations, it was easy to avoid him. I'd been taken off Residents' Clinic. Anderson was running it now. If I'd gone to the administration, they probably would have given an explanation, but I didn't ask and none was offered. I could imagine why.

One evening several days later, I was sifting through the accumulating pile of papers in my in box, desultorily filling out insurance forms, waiting for it to be dark enough to drive out to Allie's. In my preoccupation, I wrote "zygoma" rather than "melanoma," and that in the wrong box. My Wite-Out was dry cement, so I got up and walked out to the central office in search of another bottle.

It was after ten o'clock and the secretaries were all long gone, the lights out and their desks all cleared off. I made my way in the semi-darkness to the supply closet. It was, of course, locked, but as I turned back, I noticed a paper in the fax tray. The letterhead was an official-looking seal with three big letters: FDA.

According to the printout, the fax had come through at two-thirty that afternoon, and apparently no one had bothered to retrieve it. There was no cover sheet, no note from the sender; just an off-kilter copy of what I soon realized was the protocol for the tests on reabsorbable fixation plates. The one I had called to ask about.

I walked back to my desk and read it through, about seven or eight pages. A third- or fourth-generation Xerox, it wasn't easy to read. And even for a doctor, the language was almost impenetrably bureaucratic, but I was able to gather that the trials had begun five years earlier and make out the names of the department heads assigned to head up the protocol. Some were vaguely familiar, no doubt big names in medicine. The participating hospitals were listed, too, spread across the country in cities like Memphis, Baltimore and Madison, Wisconsin. Two in New York. They were listed alphabetically by name, and at first I thought I'd simply overlooked the one in Sacramento—the one in which, according to her mother, Allie's surgery had been performed—but it wasn't there. It was highly unlikely that a doctor would have had access to the reabsorbable plates outside the protocol. Impossible, really. But unless this was an administrative error of some kind, Allie hadn't had her surgery done in Sacramento. Only two hospitals listed were in California. One was a famous plastic surgery center in Los Angeles. The other was St. Mary's Hospital in Palo Alto.

Genederm was headquartered in Palo Alto.

It probably didn't mean anything. San Francisco was known as the plastics capital of the world, with more plastic surgeons per square foot than any other region of the country. It was natural to choose a hospital in the area. Still.

I looked up Paula and Brian's number and called their house. The maid answered, and I asked for Brian. I could hear her footsteps receding down the hall and what sounded like a door opening to loud voices.

"Hello?" It was Brian.

"Brian, it's Jackson."

"Oh, hello." His geniality was more strained than usual. I heard Paula in the background asking who it was and "What the hell does *he* want?" when Brian told her it was me, followed by muffled sounds as a hand was put over the receiver.

"Brian?" I called into the phone. "I need to talk to you."

"Yes, Jackson, what was that?" Again an angry exchange of words through the muffled receiver. Finally I heard Brian say, "Please, Paula" and "Excuse me!" and then a door banging.

"Brian—" I began.

Another extension picked up, and Paula came on: "Leave us

alone, Jackson. We don't want you calling here. Do you understand that?"

"Paula—" Brian tried to break in, but she was yelling now.

"Just leave us alone! We don't want to see you, ever again! Get it?"

"Jesus Christ, Paula! Just hang up." Brian wasn't accustomed to raising his voice, and it cracked under the strain, the last few words squeaking out like an adolescent boy's.

"Brian, I'm warning you—" Paula slammed down the receiver, and I thought the line had gone dead until I heard Brian's labored breathing on the other end.

"Sorry, Jackson. Bad moment." He inhaled again, as if he wasn't sure he was getting enough oxygen. "Actually, it's been a bad week. Paula thinks, well, she thinks you've been telling me something, I guess. Some secret—"

"I need to talk, Brian," I said. "Can we get together?"

"Ah, well—"

"It's about Allie, and her treatment." That was more or less true. "It's urgent, otherwise I wouldn't ask."

"Here?" he asked. "I'm not sure that's such a good idea."

"No, Genederm," I said. "I'll meet you there."

"It's kind of late, Jackson."

"It's urgent, Brian."

"What could I tell you that's so important?"

"Trust me, it is. Okay?"

"Well—" He considered, no doubt realizing it would give him a reason to get out of the house. "Oh, hey, why not? I'll meet you in about half an hour."

"It may take me a bit longer; I'm in the city."

"No problem," he said. "I'll wait for you in my office."

———

The Genederm building was a shiny skin of mirrored glass, surrounded by sculptured shrubbery from which spotlights illuminated the company logo high above the entrance. The guard behind the desk buzzed me in and, after calling up to Brian's office, told me how to get there. Brian's was the only door open. I found him inside, sitting in front of a laptop computer, intently playing a video game.

"With . . . you . . . soon," he said. "Aghh!"

I sat down and watched him struggle with the game, furiously punching the keypad and saying "Fuck" and "Shit" and "Damn" several times in rapid succession, then throwing his hands up in defeat. The game over, the program reverted to its default setting and the screen filled with some kind of creature in a leering devil's mask cutting the heads off people in medieval costumes.

"Hey, Jackson," he greeted me. He looked even younger than usual, his eyes puffy and bloodshot, like a small child who'd been distracted by a new toy and forgotten what he was crying about. "Killer game. So what's up?"

"I need to look at Allie's medical insurance files. I was hoping you could help me."

"Unh, sure. Why? Is this about, you know, the other night? What we talked about?"

"No, Brian. It's medical. She had reconstructive surgery some time ago, and it's important to get the name of the doctor who performed it. It could be very important to how we treat her."

"Allie had plastic surgery before?"

"Reconstructive," I emphasized.

"Oh, like, you mean, an accident? I didn't know. Can't she tell you who it was?"

Sure, I thought. If I could ask her. And if she'd tell me the truth.

"Brian," I said, "she's got amnesia."

"Oh, yeah, right." He fiddled with the keys of his computer. "The problem is, these things are confidential."

I rolled my eyes. "About as confidential as someone's credit rating."

"Yeah, right. That's true." He laughed. "Did she sign some kind of release or something?"

"Come on, Brian. I'm her doctor." I gambled that he didn't know Brandt had taken me off the case. "I just need to take a quick look."

He shrugged. "Everybody's gone, you know, and I wouldn't know where to find it. Anyway, this place is locked up pretty tight at night. Even during the day, security is really tight. You wouldn't believe how much spying goes on in the Valley."

"Don't you have everything on computer?" I asked. "I've heard you're real good with those."

He raised his eyebrows and laughed again. "Yeah. Used to be, at least." He wheeled over in his chair to another computer and started opening up programs. "This one's connected to the mainframe. I suppose the files are in there somewhere." As he worked, I watched the video devil on the laptop swing his ax at the men in medieval costumes. They never seemed to learn, running up one after another to have their heads chopped off.

"This may take a while," he said. "I've never really explored our personnel files before." He was typing rapidly as he spoke. "If you want, you can try the game."

I looked into the leering devil's face. "I don't think so."

"You should. It's new. It's called Dante's Inferno." He said it as if he'd never heard the name before. "The idea is to descend through the seven rings of hell. The first ones are the minor vices and venial sins. They're no sweat, but the mortal ones are a bitch. I can never seem to get that far."

"It takes practice, I guess."

"Yeah," he responded, his focus on the search.

"What happens if you get all the way to the bottom ring of hell?" I asked.

"Beats me. Become ruler of the underworld, I guess—Yes! Here it is. That was easy. This stuff isn't secure at all!"

He punched a few keys, and the printer began to whir. It spit out several pieces of paper, and he handed them to me.

"We've got pretty good health coverage here," Brian went on as I read, "even covers acupuncture, aromatherapy, alternative-medicine sorts of things. Ever been Rolfed? Hurts like hell, but . . ."

Allie's file began three years earlier, when she had started at Gene-derm. One of the first entries was for a visit at St. Mary's Hospital in Palo Alto, a follow-up for an operation performed about six months before she'd joined the company. The operation was listed as a "sagittal mandibular ramus osteotomy/reduction"—the shortening of a protruding lower jaw. The reimbursed physician was identified as Peter Brandt.

So he'd lied. That was clear. Brandt knew all about the reabsorbable plates in Allie's jaw because he'd put them there. He'd lied to cover it up. And he'd taken me out of the operation so I wouldn't see the evidence. It made sense; it was the bad conscience of someone covering up an affair. You lie about all sorts of unnecessary things because you never know what fact, what stray bit of information, will set off a chain of revelations that leads back to your guilt.

"Find anything helpful?" Brian asked. He was back at his computer game, making his way through the minor vices.

I thought of Helen, her fashionably emaciated body given unaccustomed strength by passion—a passion she'd been storing up for three years or more, until she was so filled with anger that she could tear Allie apart with a claw hammer. Maybe that's what Brandt was keeping hidden. Somewhere deep inside, he knew he was responsible, he knew what he'd unleashed. Though he probably couldn't admit it to himself. It was so unfair, after all. Everyone in San Francisco has affairs. It was so unjust that this should happen to him, someone who led such an exemplary life in every other way.

Brian let out another string of expletives. "Fucked again! I always get hung up on sex, and that's small potatoes in this game."

"I didn't know Brandt worked at St. Mary's," I said.

"Yeah, I think so," Brian answered with half his attention. "A few years ago, when we first started up. He was doing some research there. How come you ask?"

"I know it was Brandt," I said simply.

He was working the game ball furiously. "Damn, gluttony! That should be an easy one." He let his hands fall off the keyboard into his lap and stared at the screen.

"It was Brandt who was having an affair with Paula," I said. "He's the one that Allie stole. That's what their fight was about. Isn't that right, Brian?"

"Son of a bitch!" he swore under his breath. He was still looking at the monitor, but he wasn't talking about the game anymore. "What does this have to do with—"

"Brian, I know."

"Jackson." He lifted his hands in some indeterminate gesture and let them fall again in his lap. "Shit. Okay," he exhaled. "Yes. Probably. I mean, sure, definitely." He looked up at me. "I told you, that was *before*—before you and Allie."

"I don't think so."

"I told you, I'm guessing. Paula doesn't tell me what she does. It's not like she denies anything, either." He gave a dry laugh. "She simply won't discuss it. She says it's none of my business. Do you believe that? Actually, she says it's none of my *fucking* business. For emphasis, you know. 'It's none of your *fucking* business, Brian.'" He said it with a flip of the head, the way Paula would. It was a pretty good imitation.

"Is that what you and Paula were fighting about?"

"Well—" He twisted his face sardonically. "It's one of the subjects that comes up."

"Why's Paula so pissed at *me*?"

"I don't know. She seems to think you're telling me secrets about her or something. When she and Allie had that falling-out, she got really paranoid, kept saying that Allie was spreading lies about her and I shouldn't believe anything she told me. But shit! Like, what's left to tell?"

I thought of Allie, her face turned toward the black window of my car, my promise not to reveal the truth about Halley.

"You think I'm a total dweeb, Jackson, don't you? Putting up with all of this shit."

"No." Not too different from me, in fact. "Total" was probably overstating it.

"But the thing that kills me is Brandt." He shook his head, saying the name with all the bitterness he'd been holding inside till now. Brian did care, after all, and it was making him uncomfortable. He squirmed in his seat, like a schoolboy hoping to be excused from a lesson in life. "I'm sure it doesn't trouble him for a moment to steal the wife of his, like, *partner,* after all. Christ!"

I wanted to go. Get away from there. I'd confirmed what I already knew. Brandt and Allie were having an affair before I came along. Maybe after I came along, too. And now I knew why Allie was so psychologically dependent on him. He had given her a new life once. He could do it again.

Brian was still talking, but I didn't have the strength to listen anymore. Not now. I'd forced him to open up, and now I didn't want to deal with it. He'd have to work out his own screwed-up life. I had to rescue mine.

"It sucks, Brian, but—" I straightened the papers and got up as if to leave. He didn't notice. He was too wrapped up in what he was saying and went on talking. I sat back in my chair.

"I mean—what do they call it? Right *du seigneur?*" He pronounced it "senior." "Like that movie, remember? The king takes whatever pretty woman he wants and to hell with the husband. But you know what really galls me? He's so condescending. I try to talk to him about the research, and he acts like I'm some computer nerd who couldn't understand. Which may be true. I'm a dweeb and a nerd. But it's my money, mostly. Or was, anyway." He smiled then. Brian had a secret, too.

"What do you mean 'was'?"

"That's why we went public. You didn't know? Yeah, I wanted to get out, and I don't care so very much at this point about maximizing my earnings. So let the genius run this company for a while. See how well he does. I'm through."

"Since when?"

"Soon. I've cleared most of my shares." He shrugged. "It's not revenge, exactly. It's not personal." He smiled again. "Okay, it is personal. But there are other reasons. We've got some pretty smart guys working in our labs, but we're not going to go anywhere without a lot more capital. Brandt is the celebrity; we can't raise it without him. And he's been so—*weird* lately. You can't rely on him, like he's too busy to raise money. Christ, we had a huge meeting with the big money people at this biotech conference in L.A., and he didn't even show. Suddenly he's, like, *gone*. I couldn't find him all day. And when he finally reappears, he's so damned distracted. And he got drunk later. In public. Never seen him drunk before. Not that it seemed to make much of a difference. You couldn't really tell, I guess, he just got more stuck-up—except his fly was open the whole time. Damned if I was going to tell him."

He laughed, remembering the scene, then shook his head. "It was pretty fucked up, I'll tell you. And lately, I don't know what he's doing. I haven't seen him here, except to—"

"Hold it, Brian," I interrupted. "He missed the meeting? When?"

"Huh? Oh, this was back several weeks ago. In August."

"Which meeting? Which meeting did he miss at the conference? When was it?"

"The second day, first full day, really. It was a weekend conference in L.A. We started Friday night with a dinner—"

"It was on Saturday?"

"Yeah, I guess. Yeah, definitely. It was Saturday."

Chapter 47

Allie, it's me. Jackson." The intercom crackled with static. "Allie!" I yelled into the box, "let me in!"

I was standing at the door of her condo complex, my car parked illegally, the shifting shadows of the homeless in the playground behind me. A glass bottle crashed onto the pavement, and immediately the door buzzer exploded as if in response. I pushed through the entrance and ran up the stairs to the second floor, knocking loudly on Allie's door. I waited for what seemed like forever, then knocked again, and when there was still no answer, I banged until the door rattled in its frame.

"What is it?" It was Allie speaking through the door.

"Allie, I've got to talk. Allie? Open the door." It suddenly occurred to me that Brandt might be inside. Inside with her. Then I heard the locks snap open, and the door swung in on her darkened apartment. Allie was walking away from me as I entered, tying a scarf around her head. She was alone.

"It's awfully late, Jackson."

In my urgency, I hadn't thought of what I was going to say, and now I didn't know how to begin. I reached over to the light switch and turned it on. Allie dropped her head into her hands to cover her eyes. Instinctively, I stepped toward her.

"Don't!"

I froze in the middle of the floor. "Do you want the light off?" She didn't answer, but I went back and switched off the light. She sat down on the corner of her couch, facing away. I went over to the chair, as far away as I could sit. It seemed to make her more comfortable.

"I'm sorry to come by so late." I noticed then that she was still dressed. "Were you asleep?" I asked anyway, needing to say something.

"I was out earlier."

"Good," I said, "it's important to get out—"

"I went over to Krista's."

"Oh. How come?"

"What do you mean?" She was suddenly challenging.

"I don't know, I . . ."

"She's become a good friend," she said. "We see each other a lot. She knows what I look like, so it doesn't matter."

"That's great," I said, trying to sound like I meant it.

"Yeah. It's great." It would have been sarcastic if there had been any inflection in her voice. "We just talk. You know, like girls. You never told me you two were seeing each other."

Damn Krista, I thought. I should have expected it, though.

"That was before, Allie. Before us."

"I know. She told me."

"It wasn't important. It never meant anything."

"She seemed to think it did."

I took back whatever kind thoughts I still had for Krista. It didn't take long; there weren't many left.

"I need a drink," I said. I walked over to the refrigerator and opened it. The half-finished bottle of champagne was all it contained. That and the caviar I'd brought before, still untouched.

"Have you been eating anything?" I asked. "There's no food here."

"I'm not that hungry these days."

"You've got to eat, Allie. You won't heal if you're weak."

"I'm okay," she said, as if telling me to mind my own business.

I poured the rest of the champagne in a tumbler and took a taste. It was flat but would still serve its purpose.

"You drink too much, Jackson," she said as I filled the glass to the top. It was the first time since I'd known her that she'd criticized my behavior. She sounded like Krista.

"I know," I said, "I drink to forget." The phrase had stuck in my mind. I meant it as a joke, but it came out tired and heavy. And angry.

"I don't have that problem," Allie said.

"Sorry, Allie." Somehow we'd gotten on to another sore point. Everything was a sore point these days.

I stood at the counter in silence until I'd finished the glass. Finally,

I began telling her what I'd come to say. I spoke slowly because I wanted to say it right, but as I approached each word, I realized there was no way to soften the meaning.

I told her about Helen. Or as much as I could get out. I told her about my meeting with Brian. I said I knew she had been seeing Brandt. That they had been lovers.

Allie gave no response, not even the slightest movement to indicate that she'd heard what I said. My words seemed to die before they made it across the room, like talking into a phone after someone has hung up on you.

I asked her how much she remembered from before the attack. She didn't say anything. I asked a second time, and reluctantly, as if it was inevitable now, she answered. She said she remembered about Brandt. It had started a while ago. Years ago. About three, she said. A few months after the jaw surgery.

"What about the doctor in Sacramento?" I asked.

"He messed up." She spoke from the shadows, her head bent, the scarf hiding much of her face. "I was thirteen. I couldn't eat solid food for a year. Good way to lose weight."

"What happened?"

"Two operations and he couldn't get it right. They had to wire my mouth shut the second time. Feed me through a tube."

"Jesus," I said. "Allie—"

"Yeah, I was a skinny freak, and I still had a funny-looking jaw. I almost died. The doctor said it was my fault. I didn't have the will to survive."

"My God, he sounds incompetent."

"Sure, if we'd known anything, we could have sued him and retired on the settlement. But we were just ignorant white trash. Anyway, he was right. I didn't have the will to live. Then."

"When— How did you find Brandt?"

"There was an article on him in *People* magazine, 'Miracle Doctor,' they called him. I came up to St. Mary's and he saw me. I didn't even have an appointment. I was going to make one with his secretary, but he noticed me in the waiting area and took me into his examining room. He—" She broke off, choking back tears. "He put me in front of this white screen he had—you know, like in a photographer's studio—and took photographs of me. He sat with me, and he—he *touched* me, Jackson. He held my face in his hands and *looked straight at me.* He looked at me and told me he could make me beautiful."

I held on to the counter and wished for more to drink, but the bottle was empty.

"No one had ever touched me like that," she said, as if he was holding her now. "I never had a boyfriend. Obviously! My dad—he never held me like that. He never even . . . you know, once I fell down and cut my lip, and he instinctively picked me up and . . ." I could hear her inhale, holding back the emotion. "I saw him, when he thought I wasn't looking, washing his hands."

"Washing the blood off?"

"No, just washing. There wasn't much blood. It was that he'd touched something . . . unclean." Her hand went unconsciously to her mouth and lightly felt her lips. "Mama said—" She sighed deeply, then started again. "Mama, she tried to make it all right." I'd never heard her call her mother "Mama" before. It was always "my mother," distant, third-person. Her voice sounded different, too, like I had imagined the voice of the little girl in the photograph, hidden behind the other pictures in the stifling trailer home in Vidalis. "Mama, she always said that it was because he felt *guilty*, Daddy did. He thought it was his fault I was the way I was. That's why he didn't want to look at me. I shouldn't blame him for it." Her accent had also changed. Just slightly. Broader. More rural. "But she was wrong about Daddy. She was. Daddy didn't feel guilty, he felt embarrassed. He was *ashamed* of me. He couldn't bear to think that he had produced such a monster."

"Allie, I'm sorry." It was all I could think to say. "I'm so sorry." But she was too far away in her thoughts to hear.

"I actually *heard* him say it one time, when they were arguing. He said it would have been better if I'd . . . never—" She couldn't bring herself to finish the sentence.

"You should have told me, Allie."

"I didn't want you to know, Jackson. Of all people, I didn't want you to know."

"Allie I love you, more than anyone else, ever. More than my life. Didn't you *trust* me?"

She was silent. That question had been asked before. Asked and answered.

I didn't want to go on, but I had to. I asked again how much of her recent memory had come back.

"Some," she said.

"Tell me how much you remember, Allie. Do you remember the assault?"

She stood up and walked over to the window, pulling on the cord to close the blinds tighter. "No," she said, her back to me.

"Do you know why you were there, in Marin?"

"No."

"Do you have any idea who it might have been? Do you know who attacked you?"

"I don't remember anything at all, not for several days before."

"You don't have any idea?"

"No!"

"Allie, listen. Brandt wasn't at the conference in L.A. on Saturday. The day you were attacked."

No reaction, except that she seemed to draw herself up, her body suddenly still, rigid.

"He wasn't in L.A. He was here, with you. Brandt attacked you."

"That's crazy."

I thought she simply didn't understand. "That's why he lied to me about your CT scans. Don't you see? He pretended he didn't know anything about the reabsorbable plates. And it was him all along. He was your doctor."

"He was doing it for me. I didn't want anyone to know about the operation."

I thought of Sandra, the sculpture she'd beaten into a mangled lump of clay. Artists are cruel, Sandra said. Except in Brandt's case, Allie was his raw material. It seemed so obvious.

"He—Jesus!—he didn't tell me because he didn't want anyone to know about his relationship with you!"

"Of course not. He's married." Her voice was calm, matter-of-fact, as if we were talking about people we hardly knew and events that we'd read about in the newspaper.

"Why don't you see this, Allie? *He wasn't in L.A. the day you were attacked!* You were going to leave him and he couldn't stand that. But he didn't know you were leaving him for *me*. That's why he got so furious when he found out from Rossi that we'd been seeing each other. That's why he took me off the case. He was jealous."

"I think you're the jealous one." She turned and looked straight at me.

It was the first time in several days I'd gotten a good look at her face. The swelling was gone. Pale pink lines crisscrossed her almost translucent skin where the sutures had been removed. One could clearly see her features now, and in some detached part of my mind I found myself admiring Brandt's handiwork. So perfectly natural. The cheekbones so "right," so fitting for her face. So different. For a moment I was back in the operating room: Allie looking up at me from behind the loose mask of skin that covered her reconstructed bones. Changed into Brandt's creation. Taken from me. I closed my eyes tight and shook my head violently to banish the vision.

Allie didn't notice. She was perched now on the edge of an armchair, coolly proceeding with the conversation as if she'd just had an interesting idea she wanted to share with me. "I've been thinking. Paula was really hysterical when we broke up. She made threats and things—"

"You mean when she and Brandt broke up?" I asked, not sure I'd heard right.

She was silent. Then she said, "I thought Brian told you."

"He said—he thought Paula was jealous because of Brandt. Because you took him away from her."

Allie looked at me closer. "Paula was never seeing Brandt."

I felt like I was losing my way. "But Brian said—"

"Brian doesn't get it. He never did and he never will." She paused a moment. "Paula wasn't jealous of Brandt, she was jealous of you."

"Me?"

"Jackson!" she said, exasperated, as if I was being obtuse.

"You and Paula? You were . . ."

"Lovers, Jackson."

I was too surprised to know how I felt about it. "Was it serious?"

"Serious?" she said with a shrug. "What does that mean?"

"It means— Jesus Christ, Allie!" *Serious like us,* I wanted to say. *Serious like two people in love. The way we were in love.* That's what I wanted to say, but everything seemed skewed now, altered in some way I didn't understand, and I suddenly felt uncertain—even of that.

"Okay . . . okay," I said, battling my confusion, "but still, it doesn't make sense. Paula helped get you and me together."

"So? Oh, Jackson—" She smiled indulgently, like she would at a little boy. "It wasn't the sex. Paula isn't too—particular—about that. She wanted to get me away from Brandt. That's why she put us together. She never thought I'd fall in love with—" She stopped herself. "She never thought you'd be more than a fling."

"I'm glad people think so highly of me," I said angrily. I couldn't help it.

"That's Paula," Allie said, as if it was no concern of hers. "That's the way she is."

I tried to switch gears. "And you're saying you think Paula attacked you?"

"Could be. Why not?"

"Do you really think that, or—"

"Sure," she said. "Brian is Paula's meal ticket. She likes having money, a lot of money. And if Brian ever found out about Halley, that she isn't his child—"

"Did you threaten to tell him?"

"I don't know. *She* was threatening to tell Brandt about *you*. We were pretty angry, making accusations back and forth. But if she thought so—sure, it definitely could have been her." She seemed pleased with the deduction.

"It's possible, but that doesn't change anything. I've got to go to Rossi. Let him figure it out. I've got to tell him what I know."

"No!" she shouted, shattering the strange calm of the last few moments. She stood up and took a step toward me, her body shaking with a violent tension she could barely contain.

"I have to—"

"No!" she screamed. "You won't! You won't do that!"

"But I've got to tell him about Brandt. For God's sake, he may have tried to kill you!"

"Stop it! Just stop it!" She lifted her hands to her head as if to cover her ears.

"Allie—" I walked around the counter toward her.

"You can't, Jackson." She tried to get control of her voice, only barely succeeding. "You can't say anything to Rossi about Brandt. Brandt's fanatical about his reputation. If he even thought he might get drawn into this, he'd refuse to operate again. He wouldn't let himself get involved in any way."

"But—"

"He's the only one who can give me my life back!"

"There are lots of other plastic surgeons—"

"He's the only one! He's the only one who can do it!"

"He's no god, Allie. We can find someone else—"

"No! No! No!" she cried. "There's no one else!" She paused. "He said he'd use the Genederm skin on me. It's better than grafts, he said, it—"

"For God's sake, it hasn't even been approved. He's using you as a guinea pig."

She stepped back, putting more distance between us. "Go to hell!"

"I'm sorry, I didn't mean—"

"If you go to that detective," she said, glaring, "I'll never talk to you again. I'll never talk to you or see you ever again."

"Allie, this doesn't make sense." She jerked her body angrily as if about to reply. "Wait—wait a second, Allie. Listen, Palfrey said—what I mean to say is, you suffered this huge trauma, your head— No! Wait, listen to me! Your head was badly beaten. You spent days in a coma. It's probably affected your brain chemistry. It would be strange if it hadn't. Your judgment is bound to be off. It is, Allie! I can tell. You're just not yourself. You're not acting like yourself."

Her eyes burned into me the whole time I spoke. When she spoke, her voice was cold with fury. "If you go to that detective, Jackson, I'll hate you. Do you understand? You'll be as good as dead to me."

"Allie—"

"Dead!" she screamed, raising her arms. After a moment she let them fall and turned away. "I am very serious," she said in a steely voice. Without looking back, she walked into her bedroom and closed the door.

I must have stared at the door for twenty minutes or more. Then I walked over and knocked. When I opened the door I found her, sitting on her bed. The rage had fallen away. She looked very small somehow, like someone seen from a great distance. I sat beside her.

"Promise you won't speak to the detective," she said.

"Okay."

"Promise!"

"I promise."

She breathed deeply, as if for the first time; her chest filled with air, and her body slumped as she exhaled.

"What about us, Allie?" I asked. She raised her head, looking toward some distant place. "We loved each other. That was real, wasn't it? Despite everything . . . else?"

She nodded. A tear formed in the corner of her eye but didn't fall.

I reached to take her hand, and she let me. I held it close, like precious salvage from a wreck. "It wasn't just me that felt that way? You loved me, too?"

The blinds were pulled tight, the windows securely shut. Outside, it was two in the morning; inside, it was infinitely later.

"You did. You loved me, too," I repeated.

"Yes, Jackson," she said. "I loved you."

It was only when I thought back on it later that I realized we'd been speaking in the past tense.

Chapter 48

I had been so certain. All the pieces fit so perfectly: Brandt's affair with Allie, his feigned ignorance of the earlier operation and his anger when he found out about Allie and me. But the more I thought about it, the less certainty I felt. It was like those two-dimensional drawings of cubes that shift perspective as you look at them. What was front is now back, what was solid is suddenly no more real than a mirage. Brandt wasn't at the conference. But he could have been anywhere. He was jealous, no doubt. But so was Paula, in a way I hadn't even imagined. And Paula had another motivation that might have been just as strong. For her it was probably stronger—Brian's bank account. In fact, as far as jealousy was concerned, it was a fairly large club. Not only Brandt and Paula, but also Helen and Krista—my previous suspects.

And, as Allie insisted on pointing out, me. Jackson Maebry.

—

Lucasian called the next day and apologized for being "out of the pocket" for the past week. He'd already checked with the police: the DNA results still hadn't come back, and he assumed Rossi hadn't found anything else or we would have heard from him.

I asked if everything I said to him was confidential. "You know, the attorney-client-privilege thing. Is that absolute?"

"In general. As an officer of the court, however, I am obliged to tell the authorities if I come upon information about criminal activity."

"Oh."

He changed his tone, as if he wanted me to pay particular attention to what he was saying. "Dr. Maebry. You are innocent of this crime. That is what you have told me. All of our discussions have been based on this predicate, you might say *fact*. Therefore, all of our discussions are certainly privileged. Do you understand?"

"Yes." I did, more or less. I wanted to tell him what I knew of Brandt; but if he went to the police with the information and it turned out not to be true, Allie would never forgive me.

"Dr. Maebry. Is there something you want to tell me?"

I needed to think. There was time. I hadn't been arrested yet. The DNA test would come back at some point and clear me. Without it, they wouldn't have enough to arrest me. Lucasian had said so.

"No. Nothing. I was just wondering."

"You may, of course, call if there is anything you wish to discuss."

"Yes. Thank you."

"Have courage, Doctor."

"Sure. Okay."

I no longer kept watch outside Allie's. I slept in the hospital a couple more nights out of habit, then went home for the first time since I'd begun my vigil. It was late in the evening, but the light was still on in Sandra's house, so I stopped in to see her. She was a good way through her nightly half-gallon when I got there, listening to the ancient, scratched record of *White Bird* she always played before tuning out completely. There was no evidence of the destroyed sculpture, and no evidence of Danny. Sandra had tried to reach Danny's father, but he was rarely in—or conscious when he was—and he never returned her calls. After a week of trying, the bleary voice of a woman had answered the phone, and said something like "Oh yeah, the kid. He's been around." That, however, was the only coherent information Sandra could get, and several days had passed since then. I looked in Danny's room and saw the message I'd left, lying undisturbed on his pillow.

My own apartment disgusted me. It wasn't the mess; I was used to that. It was too full of other people's footprints, their touch; of their ideas about who I was and what I'd done. Too full of memories.

I went back to Sandra's and borrowed her mop and broom, a large sponge, some kind of ammonia cleaning fluid and a box of large garbage bags. I gathered everything in my apartment that was movable and stuffed it in the bags: the food in my refrigerator, the fraying mats that served as rugs, every book, magazine and newspaper, all the remaining blankets and bedclothes. I stripped the stained cover from the couch and found several pieces of pizza and a couple of Danny's baseball cards under the cushions. I kept the cards. I emptied my drawers. I cleaned the dishes and went through my closets, leaving only a few clothes that I had to have. There weren't many, anyway. When I was done, there were six full large garbage bags, which I bound up and hauled out to the curb.

Then I scrubbed everything, the floors, the kitchen and bathtub, even the walls, as far as I could reach. When I was finished, the place was as empty and sterile as I could make it. By the time I took the cleaning things back to Sandra, she was sound asleep. I went back to my place, got a sleeping bag out of the closet, which I hadn't used since an aborted camping trip over a year back, and spread it on the bare mattress.

It felt good. I felt good: clean for the first time in weeks.

Before I lay down, I hit the play button on my answering machine. The light had been blinking all evening, but I hadn't bothered to listen, assuming it was Lucasian responding to my call from that afternoon. The mechanical voice announced there was one message, but it was from early the evening before. And it wasn't Lucasian. It was Krista.

"Jackson, where are you?" she began. "It's the middle of the night, and I know you're not on call." Spying on me again, Krista? I thought to myself. "I really need to talk to you, I really do. Oh!" she whined on the tape. "It's really, *really* important!"

I ejected the cassette from the machine, ripped the tape out and tore it into several pieces. Then I walked outside to the trash, undid one of the big black bags and threw it in with the other garbage. I didn't care what Krista had to say. I didn't want to know, and I didn't want any more messages from anyone. Especially her. If I wanted to speak to Lucasian, I'd call him, as many times as necessary to reach him. I was tired and wanted to sleep. That was all. Just sleep.

And I did, better than I had in months, as if my mind had been stripped as bare as the apartment. I covered myself with my sleeping bag and lay in the dark and smelled the ammonia vapors that filled the room. Disinfecting. Cleaning. Making it all like new.

—

Shortly after I got in the next morning, Henning approached me in the locker room, acting like Peter Lorre playing a conspirator in a silent movie. He stuck his head around the lockers to see if anyone was there, then into the empty shower stalls.

"Holy shit, Jackson!" he said in a stage whisper.

"What's up?"

"What's up, you ask? Why don't you tell me? Taking you off clinic and giving it to Anderson, for God's sake!" He looked right and left as he spoke. "They're reaming you pretty good. Like a pig on a spit, in one end and out the other." He made the appropriate hand gestures.

"That's about right," I agreed.

"So what's going on, anyway?"

"Long story."

"Man, they're acting like you killed someone."

"Maybe they think I did. Or tried to."

"Funny," he said, then suddenly became serious. "By the way, I guess you heard?"

"Guess I heard what?"

"About that nurse? Krista something-or-other."

"Krista Generis?"

"Yeah. You knew her?"

"Sure."

"Sorry."

"Sorry for what?"

"I guess you haven't heard. She died. Heart attack, apparently. Jesus, what was she, twenty-something? She was in really good shape, too, you could tell. A body like that doesn't come without a lot of work. Wasn't bad-looking, either, for a nurse. Shit, twenty-whatever. But I guess it happens. One day you're— Jackson?"

I was feeling queasy and sat down.

"Are you okay?"

"A heart attack?"

"That's what I heard. Overheard. I hang out in the nurses' lounge a lot. Haven't gotten a date yet, though. Bought one lunch once, but all she wanted to talk about was my chakras. Seems mine are misaligned. I suggested she realign them for me."

"When?"

"Anytime. I'm always up for being realigned."

"When did Krista *die,* Henning?"

"Oh. Sorry. They didn't find her till late yesterday. They assume she died sometime the night before." That was the night she'd left the phone message. "She lived close to here, so they brought her to the

ER, but she was DOA so they just sent her right down to the morgue. You sure you're okay?"

"Yeah. I'm okay."

"Just goes to show," Henning said, "you better live it up while you can, 'cause any day the Big Guy upstairs is gonna call a code on you and"—he made a clucking sound with his tongue, like a plug being pulled from its socket—"bye-bye, life support! Well. Gotta go, Jackson. Good luck with this admin screwup." He left, shaking his head, and had probably forgotten about Krista before he was out of the locker room.

I walked around to the back of the hospital and down the steep asphalt ramp to the morgue entrance. It was constructed much like the loading platform at the emergency room, but fewer ambulances came here, mostly just hearses.

Finiker was sitting at the desk in his office, eating an Egg McMuffin with one hand and filling out forms in pen with the other. I greeted him from the doorway.

"Ah, Dr. Maebry," he greeted me back. "What brings you to the catacombs this fine morning?"

"You had a—what do you call it, a patient?—brought in yesterday."

"A *body*, Doctor. We call it 'a body.' Sometimes 'the deceased.' 'Cadaver' is good, too. 'Dead person' or 'corpse' will do in a pinch."

"The name is Krista Generis."

He looked blank.

"Woman. About twenty-six years old. She was a nurse here at Memorial."

"Oh. Yes?"

"Do you have her here? Her body, I mean."

"Last I looked."

"Did you autopsy her yet?"

"Yup. Stayed up until almost midnight, as a matter of fact. She's all bagged and ready to go."

"Can I see her?"

"Was she a patient of yours?" He knit his brows, a succession of furrows creasing his bald head to the crown. "I didn't notice any excess plastic in the body, or any of the other materials of your trade, for that matter."

"I was consulting," I lied. "She was thinking of surgery, and we'd run some tests. Blood work and such, to get ready for the operation. I just want to know if we missed anything that we should have caught."

"How thorough of you. Hard to believe she wanted plastic surgery, though. There was nothing about her body that was exactly, well, lacking. But I suppose it's the thing to do these days. Never big enough. Never firm enough. Can't leave it to nature, can we? You'd be amazed how much silicon I find here. Then again, maybe you wouldn't."

He dug through his pile and pulled out a folder, then pushed his chair back with a violent scraping sound and walked past me out of the office. I followed him to the "icebox" and waited as he examined the tags hanging from the square doors lining the walls.

"Here we are. Krista Generis." He pulled the handle down, swung open the door and heaved the tray out on its casters. "One white female." He examined his chart. "Twenty-nine years old, actually." He unzipped the bag and pulled down the plastic so that her entire body was exposed. It wasn't exactly white now. It was colorless.

The same large black "Y" ran up her abdomen and spread out across her chest, even more carelessly sutured than usual. It looked like the skullcap had barely even been sewn back in place. As little affection as I felt for Krista, it seemed wrong that her body hadn't been treated with more respect.

Finiker must have noticed my expression. "The family said she was to be cremated," he said defensively. "No open casket, public viewing, that sort of thing. It was late, the end of a busy day."

"What was the cause of death?" I asked.

"A good question."

I sighed. "And the answer?"

"I would have to say cardiac arrest. Of course, technically speaking, cardiac arrest is almost always the cause of death. Unless your brain gives out first, but this is a matter of some legal controversy, as you know. In general, however, your heart stops pumping, you die." I endured the unneeded medical lesson in silence. "The question is," Finiker concluded, "why did her heart stop pumping?"

"Okay, why?"

"I don't really know. It happens sometimes. There were no anatomical abnormalities. She was, as I mentioned, an excellent physical specimen. I examined her heart carefully. Fine organ. Very strong."

"What was it, something electrical?"

"That's what one assumes. Arrhythmia. Faulty wiring, the signals to the heart misfire. Unfortunately, there's no real way to test that now. You can't do an electrocardiogram on a cadaver."

"You didn't find anything else?"

"We always find something else. A lot else, as a matter of fact. The question is, was any of it enough to kill her? The answer is no."

"What did you find?"

He leafed through his folder. "Stomach contents, let's see. Looked like she just had a Big Mac, or it may have been Burger King, can't tell for sure. A small amount of caffeine in the blood, probably had a Coke with the cheeseburger. Also, her alcohol level was significant, point-oh-eight. Legally drunk in this state."

"Cuba Libre," I said.

He looked up, puzzled by the non sequitur. "I suppose it will happen eventually."

"No. It's a drink. Her favorite. Rum and Coke."

"Oh. You have quite an intimate knowledge of your patients' habits, Doctor." His brow furrowed all the way up to his crown again. "Let's see, blood? Yes. Positive for Zolpidem—probably Ambien, a sleeping medication."

"Maybe it was the mixture, the drugs and the alcohol together."

"Not enough of either. The only danger of a point-oh-eight alcohol level is from the highway patrol. And the Zolpidem, I'd guess it was twenty milligrams at most. Though it's hard to tell because it passes through the body so quickly."

"Isn't the recommended dose more like five milligrams?"

"Five to ten. Maybe she forgot and took a second pill by mistake. It didn't kill her. People have swallowed twenty times that amount and recovered. Even with the alcohol, it didn't kill her."

"Anything else?"

"We did the normal tox scan. Nothing. As to her general health, let's see. Hemoglobin, normal. Cholesterol, a bit high. Too many Big Macs, I guess. Damn healthy female, actually."

"There were no signs of—violence?"

"You mean like rope marks around the neck, stabbing wounds to the heart, contusions suggesting she'd been hit with the proverbial 'blunt instrument'? I think I might have noticed. No, Doctor, nothing so gothic. There were, let's see"—he flipped to another page in his report—"there was a fair degree of mucosal inflammation and some discharge. I assume she had a cold or maybe the flu; a bruise on her left shin, looks like it must have hurt; a vaginal yeast infection, unpleasant, I hear, but rarely fatal; a needle mark on her left arm, hypodermic needle or intravenous, can't tell from the size—"

"What about that?"

"What about it? She probably gave blood. Or had tests recently. Or was irrigating herself, taking in fluids by IV to ward off the flu. Most of the unpleasant flu symptoms are due to dehydration. It's not uncommon for nurses to do that. I've done it myself one or two times. It wasn't drugs. The Zolpidem was ingested, still a residue in the GI tract."

"She just seems awfully young for a heart attack," I said, as much to myself as to Finiker.

"I had a twelve-year-old in here a couple of months ago. Same diagnosis. As they say, stuff happens." After a moment he added in a different tone: "This nurse, was she a friend of yours?"

I started. "Yes, I—knew her."

Finiker's face took on an unaccustomed expression. I realized after a moment that it was sympathy. "I'm sorry, Maebry." He said it like he meant it. "There really is nothing left to find."

"Yeah. Okay. Thanks."

"That's the frustrating thing," he said, returning to his usual ironic tone. He zipped up the body bag with one well-practiced movement. "Even with all the advances in medical knowledge, we haven't been able to do anything about the death rate, have we?"

"The what?" I asked.

"The *death rate,* Dr. Maebry. It's still one per person."

He rolled the tray back in and swung the metal door closed with a thud.

Chapter 49

Residents' Clinic was later that morning. I had the opportunity to assist Anderson, but I begged off and had the rest of the day free.

I went to my office and closed the door, studiously ignoring the looks from the secretaries, who had become aware of my decline in status and wanted nothing more than to get me to talk so they could find out all the gossip. My desk drawer was crammed with forms, some of which had gotten wedged inside, and several tore as I yanked them out. I piled the papers on top of the desk and felt around in the back of the drawer with my hand, pulling out old pens, stickers, paper clips and other junk, until finally I found the key I was looking for. The one to Krista's apartment that I'd never gotten around to returning.

Even if I hadn't destroyed Krista's message, it wouldn't have meant much to the police. She could have been talking about anything or anyone, and no one was putting much stock in my suspicions these days. All I had to go on was a perverse faith in Krista—that she was enough of a busybody to have actually found out something important.

I drove up the hill beyond Sunset Heights, about half a mile east of Memorial, and parked in a space the street from Krista's apartment. Inside, it was little changed since I'd seen it last, except that it was even more packed with ornate pillows, stuffed animals (mostly different versions of Garfield), knickknacks (mostly ceramic cats) and bowls full of potpourri, which did little to hide the smell of the real cats, who were either in hiding or had been taken in by a neighbor. Or whoever found her body.

It was developing into a hot day, and the apartment was already baking. I drew up the blinds and opened the windows to let in some air. Cat hairs floated in the shaft of sunlight that made it over the facing condo, barely twenty feet away. The dirty footprints of the rescue squad led directly over the white pile carpet into the bedroom, clustering around the still unmade bed. In the haste of the rescue attempt, someone had knocked over a large ceramic cat—one of her favorites, I remembered—which had fallen onto the floor. Despite the thick carpet, it had cracked into several pieces. I picked them up and put them back on her bureau.

There was no desk in the apartment, but the drawer of her night table held her phone and address book. All the names and numbers were written in Krista's childish hand, with big curlicues and smiley faces. My name had a big black line drawn through it. I held the book by its binding and shook it, and several pieces of paper fell out on the bed. There was a receipt from Victoria's Secret, a prescription for birth control pills and a note concerning "Benny," with a date by it, the name itself underlined three times and followed by several exclamation points. I supposed he was a new boyfriend. And then there was one that said simply "Kathy" and "Valparaiso Realty," and under it two telephone numbers. One, I assumed, belonged to Kathy. The other was mine.

I put the papers back in the address book and went into her bathroom. The medicine chest was as overstuffed as the rest of the apartment: aspirin, Tylenol, a lotion called Youthful Radiance, several bottles each of cream, shampoo and hair spray, plus makeup and the instruments for its application—the usual feminine articles. There was also a prescription bottle. I picked it up and read the label: Zoloft, 100 milligrams. An antidepressant.

Krista, always happy and bubbling, telling me how important it was to "look on the bright side," to be "thankful for life's blessings," as if one could live by clichés; it never would have occurred to me that Krista could have suffered from depression. But then, I'd been missing a lot lately.

I looked under the sink. In the closet. No other prescriptions. No Ambien. Not even any over-the-counter sleeping pills. I walked back to the bedroom and tried to think what else I should look for. She didn't have an answering machine; she used voice mail and I didn't know her code. She didn't have a computer. The only things Krista ever wrote were cards.

And her diary.

I hadn't noticed it because it didn't look like a book. It was sitting right on her bureau, next to the pieces of the ceramic cat. It was covered with padded cloth and embroidery and had a fringe like a little pillow. There was a tiny clasp with a lock, but I got her nail file and pried it open easily.

It was hard to read; drawings of cats and bunny rabbits crowded the writing, and the big loops of the letters made them all look the same. Punctuation was random—except for the exclamation points at the end of each phrase—and the capitalization was used mostly for emphasis. There were stickers—more cats—and sometimes pictures of TV and movie stars pasted in as well. A lot of the notations didn't use names, just pronouns: "HE said . . ." or nicknames, like "Dreamlover" and "The Jerk" (I guessed the latter was me). I usually had to decipher the entire sentence to see what and whom it was about, and wasn't often sure.

Finally, however, I found Allie's name. Most of the notations were single lines: *Went to Allie's we really pigged out on sushi and HAAAGEN DAAS can you get faaaaat from sushi??? . . . Allie out of hospital loooong talk she thinks I like her but she has NO IDEA!* An earlier notation contained my name: *Jackson called I WONDER IF . . . !!!* It was dated a couple of days after Allie's assault, when I had called Krista to ask her to check in on Allie.

I turned through the pages from the time Allie was in the hospital. One line said, *DR. B. came by AGAIN!!! He must work late A LOT!* From another, I made out that Krista had been listening to Allie and Brandt's conversations over the intercom. *HOW NAUGHTY!* she wrote. *I bet Jackson has NO IDEA????*

I did now.

As I read on, it became apparent that Krista had been spying on Allie and Brandt, just as, I supposed, she had spied on Allie and me. After several pages, the handwriting changed, becoming more angular. One of the last entries, dated just the week before, read, *MEAN to Allie I told her she was a FREAK it really hurt her GOOD I DON'T CARE she's such a bitch and so STUCK UP!!! GOD I hate her!! Exactly the kind the Jerk would like COLD I'm ten times the woman she is I feel so bad NEVER NEVER NEVER stop taking the BIG Z!!!!*—this was underlined several times—*never let it happen again NEVER.* On the other side of the paper was a stick figure with another of Krista's little round faces, this time with "X's" for eyes and a blacked "O," like a gaping hole, for the mouth. Across it all was scrawled the word "bitch," and the pen seemed to have been stabbed into the paper in several places. It was frightening, a graphic record of uncontrolled rage. I wondered if I should add Krista back to my list of suspects.

The final entry was another reference to me. *WHERE IS THAT JERKOFF??? Kathy at Valparaiso called! I was right! Oh MY GOD!!! WHERE IS HE!!!! Not home probably drunk again won't he be SUR-PRISED!* The date wasn't clear, but I assumed the entry was from two nights ago, when she called my answering machine.

At that moment a shadow fell across the room, as if a cloud had blotted out the sun. Then a low voice, like a rumble. "Dr. Maebry?"

I looked up to see a huge shape filling the doorway and started so violently I dropped the diary.

"Dr. Maebry. I'm afraid I am going to have to place you under arrest."

Chapter 50

Rossi bent down to pick up the diary, closing it softly and putting it in his outside coat pocket. Mulvane, his partner, was behind him. When I started to speak, Rossi held a finger to his lips.

"This is where I read you your rights, Doctor. Judges in this part of the country seem to take spontaneous confessions as proof of coercion. Police brutality, that kind of thing."

He took out a card and read it, slowly enunciating every word. "Okay," he said, putting the card back, "you can talk now if you like. We're open for confession."

I stood up. Rossi's bulk towered over me, just a few inches away. I sat back down on the bed. "Confession of what? I don't have anything to confess."

"Well, we've got two ex-girlfriends, one beaten almost to death, the other in the morgue. Not to mention breaking and entering."

"I had a key."

Mulvane coughed into his hand.

"I think I better call my lawyer," I said.

"Right," said Rossi. "You can do that at the station house. Now, if you'll excuse me." He took me securely by the arm, pulling me up and turning me around. He snapped a pair of handcuffs over my wrists, asking if they were comfortable, then patted me down and quickly went through my pockets, looking through my wallet and taking my key ring and the key to Krista's apartment. "Escort Dr. Maebry outside, Mulvane."

Mulvane came up, shrugging his shoulders as if to say "What can you do, it's our job," and led me out. We walked awkwardly down the stairs, me in front, and he held my head down as he sat me in the back of Rossi's car. He took the front passenger's seat. "You got enough room back there?" he asked. I said it was tight, and he moved his seat forward. We sat there sweating in the heat for about ten minutes until Rossi came out and got behind the wheel. The springs creaked as he settled in.

"What about my car?" I asked as we drove off. "I don't want it to be towed."

Mulvane turned around and smiled. "Don't worry, Doc, parking violations don't go on your record."

"But—"

"We're impounding it," Rossi said. "Evidence."

"Do you know where it is?"

Mulvane gave me a look and said, "Duh!" like it was a stupid question.

"You mean you've been following me?" I asked.

"Hither and thither," Mulvane said.

"How long?"

"Long enough," he answered, and turned back.

We drove north and picked up Route 101 at the access ramp to the Golden Gate.

"Where are we going?" I asked. I'd assume they'd take me downtown to "the Hall."

"San Rafael," Mulvane said. "The Marin County Jail. The crime was in Marin, so that's where we'll book you. Ever been there? To the Civic Center, I mean."

"No."

"You're in for a treat."

No one spoke as we drove up 101. At the end of the exit ramp, we stopped at a light and saw the Civic Center towering above, a sort of fifties-modern fantasy of the future, all saucers and spires and little spikes and portholes and spindly legs. It looked like a set for an out-of-date science-fiction movie.

"It's by that architect guy," Mulvane explained, as we moved on. "You know, that famous one, Frank Lloyd Weber."

"Wright," Rossi corrected him.

" 'Course I'm right," Mulvane said.

The county jail, Mulvane informed me, was underground, carved out of the hill we were circling. At the far end, we drove down a steep ramp and waited for a guard to open the gate.

"By the way, Doctor," Rossi said, half turning in his seat to address me over his shoulder. "I have to thank you for your advice. I used that stuff you suggested, the nonmedicated nose spray."

"Oh, did it work?"

"Yeah. The first couple of days were hell, but now—" He inhaled deeply through his nose to demonstrate, sounding like he was going to suck in the entire car. His shoulders expanded even wider than usual and actually knocked into Mulvane. "I can breathe again," he said after he exhaled. "I can even smell things. Including, unfortunately, Mulvane here."

"Very funny," Mulvane said.

Rossi laughed, then took another deep breath and let it out. "Man," he said. "It's good to be alive."

The guard waved us on and we drove under the hill, the metal gates clattering shut behind us.

—

The holding cell was empty when they led me into it. There were no windows, of course; no windows in the entire place.

Lucasian arrived shortly before noon, an hour or so after I left a message on his office machine. I immediately launched into an explanation, but he waved his hands up and down and gestured with his head toward the uniformed officer, who was still within earshot.

"Oh," I said, "sorry."

"At least," he said, sighing, "you called your lawyer before you started talking this time?" He arched an eyebrow waiting for confirmation.

"Pretty much."

His eyebrows changed positions on his face, one going farther up, the other down. "Well, I suppose this is progress. We will discuss the case at our leisure after we get you out of here."

"Am I going to have to spend the night in this cell?"

"We shall see. It's early yet. It depends how active the criminal element has been today, or should I say how conscientious the police have been in tracking them down. If we are lucky, we'll be able to have you home this evening. In the meantime," he added, "why don't you try cleaning your face a bit."

After the fingerprinting, an officer had given me some paper that felt like newsprint and didn't even begin to get the ink off. I'd been sitting with my head in my hands and must have smeared ink all over my face.

Lucasian handed me his handkerchief. "Perhaps they'll let you use the men's room."

They did, a guard standing by the door to watch as I ran cold water on the handkerchief—there was no hot water, or soap in the dispenser—and tried to scrub the ink off my face and hands.

"It's a bitch to get off, isn't it," the guard said, more as an observation than a gesture of sympathy. "It's indelible, of course. Soaks right into the pores."

"Yeah," I agreed.

"That's understandable. I can see that—the ink part," he continued in an abstract way. "But the paper they give you to wipe your hands. It's waxed. Did you notice? Like it was designed not to be effective. After all, they could give you an alcohol wipe, or even a plain paper towel. At first I thought it was some administrative thing and no one had given it any thought. But it's the same at every precinct. It's purposeful. And I finally figured out why."

I glanced over at him. He was leaning against the wall, idly scuffing the floor with one foot.

"Why?" I asked, turning back to the mirror. There was ink on my shirt collar as well, which for some reason particularly depressed me.

"It's a way to humiliate the detainees. We're not allowed to use torture. Can't even slap prisoners around anymore. So we figure out all sorts of little ways to humiliate them. Knock them down a notch or two."

"That doesn't seem right."

He gave an indifferent shrug, as if that wasn't the point.

But it didn't seem right. None of it did. I didn't know which was worse, being arrested and very possibly ending up in jail, or being publicly accused of brutally attacking the woman I loved. All this time—all the "interviews" with Rossi and conversations with Lucasian, the search of my apartment, all the anxiety and waiting—none of it had prepared me. I never really thought it would happen.

I could feel the bottom of my stomach dropping out, like when a plane goes into free fall. I braced myself with both arms on the sides of the sink and heard myself groan.

The guard didn't hear or, more likely, didn't care.

"I'm innocent, you know," I said.

He straightened and turned his unfocused eyes in my direction. "Yeah, so, are we all done in here?" he asked.

There were no paper towels, so I dried my face with my shirttail and tucked the soggy material back in my pants. The guard led me back to my cell.

———

Lucasian came back an hour later, saying everything was set for my arraignment. The guard accompanied us down a long corridor and into the courtroom through a side door. Several people were milling around, casually conversing with their neighbors and appearing to pay little attention to the judge, a gray-haired woman of about fifty, I guessed.

Lucasian walked over to the lectern, and the guard guided me over to his side. "If you'll permit me, Your Honor. I'm Emanuel Lucasian, counsel for Dr. Maebry."

She squinted at him. "You're not from Marin?"

"No, Your Honor, San Francisco."

"All right, do we have the paperwork?"

I looked over and saw Rossi leaning down, talking to a man sitting at a side desk. Papers exchanged hands. I realized he must be the D.A.

"One moment, Your Honor," the man said. "Right. Okay." He began reading from one of the papers. "We've got assault with a deadly weapon. Assault with intent to do grievous harm. Attempted murder. Ah . . ." He followed his finger down the page. "Arson. Interference with—oh, sorry, I skipped a line. Obstruction of justice. Trespassing. Interference with law enforcement personnel in the investigation of a crime." He flipped the paper over. "That appears to be it. The people may have more later."

"All right," the judge said. "Do the people have a bail recommendation?"

"He tried to murder a young woman, Your Honor. It's possible he may have committed another murder to cover up this initial crime. The people ask that bail be set at two hundred thousand dollars."

"Murder!" I whispered to Lucasian. He waved his hand for me to be quiet.

"Do you have any evidence of this murder?" the judge asked.

"I understand"—the D.A. glanced at Rossi, who nodded—"I understand that we are gathering it now, Your Honor."

"In other words, no." The judge turned to Lucasian. "Your turn, Counsel."

"Your Honor, Dr. Maebry"—he pronounced the word "doctor" with exaggerated deference—"is the chief resident in reconstructive surgery at San Francisco Memorial Hospital, a position of great responsibility, and as such he performs a vital service to our community. He has patients who at this very moment are depending on his care. He has never been arrested, nor convicted of any crime. I daresay, apart from an occasional parking ticket, he has never in his life run afoul of our colleagues in law enforcement. He is highly educated, has a sterling reputation in the medical field and comes from a good and respected family in the university town of Princeton, New Jersey. Your Honor, the State's case is based on evidence that is hardly even circumstantial. It is an amalgam of hearsay, supposition, flights of imaginative fantasy—"

"Your Honor—" The D.A. made a halfhearted attempt to interrupt. I saw Rossi smiling.

"I am certain," Lucasian said quickly, "that my client will be cleared of these charges in very short order—"

The judge held up her hand for him to stop. "Of course, Counsel. That goes without saying."

"In the meantime," Lucasian continued, "it is of the utmost importance that Dr. Maebry be allowed to return to the care and succor of his patients at San Francisco Memorial Hospital."

"Succor?" the D.A. said, shaking his head.

"Indeed," Lucasian said. "At this very moment, patients languish in their hospital beds, waiting—"

"All right, I get the idea," the judge interrupted. "How about a hundred thousand? Given the gravity of the charges on the one hand, and the defendant's standing in the community on the other, I think that's reasonable." She looked from the D.A. to Lucasian.

"Yes. Thank you, Your Honor," Lucasian said quickly.

The D.A. nodded.

"Good. Shall we set a date?" the judge said.

Lucasian huddled with the D.A. at the judge's bench. "That's it?" I asked when he came back. "I can go now?"

"Once I arrange things. You'll have to wait in the cell a little while longer. We'll have you out of here soon."

I was escorted out back down the long corridor and was standing in the vast parking lot with Lucasian a half hour later. His hair shone with a deep gloss in the hot afternoon sun, like the melting macadam that stuck to the soles of our shoes.

"What about the bail?" I asked him.

"I settled that, no charge for now."

"Thank you."

"It is common practice in the defense bar with those clients in whom we are able to repose our trust."

"Thank you," I said again, "for saying that."

He nodded deprecatingly. "I imagine you will need a ride?"

"They took my car for evidence."

"Well, come with me. We will discuss our business on the way home, it will be more relaxing." He took my arm and led me past a chain-link fence to where his car was parked. It was an immaculate white Cadillac from the early eighties, the kind that still had tiny tail fins.

"We can thank Lieutenant Rossi," he said as we drove onto the highway, "for expediting the arraignment hearing back there. A defendant like you—normally you would be a big fish, they would want to make the most of it."

"How so?"

"A professional. A *doctor.*" He said it again with exaggerated respect. "If I may say, a person of Caucasian descent. Charged with the attempted murder of a beautiful young woman. This is prime fodder for the tabloids. Not to mention the local news, to the extent that one can make a distinction these days. The police do not generally shy away from such excellent publicity."

"Then why did Rossi help out?"

"As strange as it may seem, Doctor, I believe he likes you. One doesn't think of members of his profession being led by their hearts, but Lieutenant Rossi is getting to that point in life where—well, perhaps one has different priorities. It happens to us all." He sighed, and smiled to himself. "I suspect, in fact, that you remind him of his late son."

"Which, the one in the army?"

"It was the air force, as a matter of fact. No, I would suppose the other son. The one with the drug problem."

Lucasian drove in no particular hurry. We crossed the Golden Gate, and I gave him directions to my apartment.

"Dr. Maebry—" he said, after we'd been silent a time.

"I know, I know," I said. "I should explain what I was doing in Krista's apartment . . . I was just . . ." I stopped. I still needed to think about this. We passed Sunset Boulevard, and I told him where to turn onto my street.

When it was clear I wouldn't go on, he spoke again. "As I mentioned before, if at some point it seems appropriate, we may want to hire an investigator of our own, privately, to check on Ms. Generis's alibi, but private investigating is something best left to professionals."

"Right. Of course. Sorry. But were they saying in the arraignment that Krista may have been murdered?" It occurred to me that if she had been, I once again had no alibi. I was asleep at the hospital the night she died. I doubted anyone had seen me.

"As far as I am aware," Lucasian said, "Ms. Generis's death is still officially listed as due to natural causes. I imagine that, due to your somewhat—ah—suspicious activities in her apartment, Detective Rossi and the D.A. were simply playing their strongest hand."

"That's a relief," I said.

"I'm afraid that what I'm about to say is not, however. The lab has finally come through with the tests. It seems that you were correct. The blood on the jacket did not belong to Ms. Sorosh."

"Then why . . ."

"Unfortunately, some other articles that they also found in your apartment—a towel, I believe, possibly bedclothes, a shirt—did contain blood with her DNA."

"But—that doesn't mean anything," I objected. "She probably cut herself cooking. Maybe she had—you know, it was that time of the month. God, I mean—I don't do the wash that often. I know this sounds . . . complicated . . ."

"Dr. Maebry," he said sympathetically, "life is always complicated."

We came to my apartment and stopped.

"Thank you," I said again. "I think you're the only one who believes me."

"I am your lawyer, Doctor. It is my job to believe you."

Chapter 51

The efficient-sounding woman who answered the phone at Valparaiso Realty said Kathy was out "showing" but probably would be back soon. Was it urgent? she asked. Should she page her? I said no, I'd drive up and hopefully be there before five. She gave me the address in Mill Valley. Not far, I thought, from where Allie was attacked.

I went next door and asked Sandra if I could borrow her pickup truck. She handed me the keys without asking why.

"You drive a stick?" she asked.

"I think I did once. Maybe. How hard can it be?"

"Okay, but there's no real second gear, so you have to rev it fast in first and go immediately to third. And be sure if you're parking it on a hill to put it in reverse if you're facing down, and turn the wheels to the curb."

I stalled out at the first few intersections but eventually made it up the hill to Pacific Heights. Brandt's private office was only a few blocks from his home and easily could have been mistaken for a private residence itself. A discreet metal plaque engraved with the doctors' names was the only indication otherwise.

I knew Brandt's schedule called for him to be at the hospital that afternoon, and I'd never been inside before, so I was fairly certain no one would recognize me. I scanned the doctors' business cards on the receptionist's desk and chose a name I didn't know, explaining to the woman there that the doctor had been recommended to me by a friend. She asked me if I wanted to wait, but I said that wasn't necessary, I'd just take some information and think it over. She gave me several brochures with résumés and photographs of the various partners in the practice. Before I left, she managed to fit in a short pitch about how wonderful the doctors were.

It was easier driving downhill, and in a few minutes I was on the Golden Gate. I turned off Route 101 at the same exit I'd taken on my previous trip to Mercurtor Drive, then made my way through Almonte and Hempstead to Mill Valley. Valparaiso Realty was a white clapboard colonial-style house that might have been copied from a Norman Rockwell painting, set on a tiny plot of grass wedged between a strip mall on one side and a condo development on the other.

Inside, several women and one man sat behind faux mahogany desks. The walls were covered with a floral-pattern wallpaper and hung with large portraits of generic ancestors, the kind who would have owned a country home and horses if they had ever existed.

I stopped in front of the desk with a nameplate that said Kathy Poolpat and greeted the woman who was sitting there. She was a tiny woman, barely five feet, as far as one could tell when she was sitting, impeccably dressed in a powder-blue pantsuit with a little cream-colored bow under her chin. She smiled a big smile and said hello back to me.

"You're Kathy, I assume?"

"Oh, yes! Yes, I am!" she said perkily, as if it was a great pleasure to be asked. "Please, won't you have a seat."

"I called earlier—"

"Oh, yes!" she agreed wholeheartedly before I had a chance to give my name. I gave it anyway.

"My friend, Krista Generis . . ." I paused, watching how she would react to the name. "She called earlier."

"Yes, that's right." She nodded again or, rather, kept nodding.

"She didn't come by here?"

"No, no," she said, changing her head movement to a horizontal wag. "I would have remembered, I'm sure of that. I never forget a person once I meet them," she added proudly.

"You just talked with her, then, on the phone?"

Her head was still for a moment, not sure which way to move, but the pleasant smile remained fixed on her face. "I think so. I can check if you'd like."

"I'd be grateful if you would. I'd just like to make sure."

She was too eager to oblige to notice that the request was a bit odd. She got out a leather appointment book and started searching through the pages.

"It would have been about two days ago, maybe three," I said.

"Yup. Here it is. She called. Wanted to know if we handled the new houses on Mercurtor Drive. I said indeed we did. She said she was going to come by."

"She was calling for me."

Kathy nodded, waiting for the next statement she could agree with.

"Do you think we could drive up there and take a look?"

"Yes, certainly," she agreed. "Oh, you mean this afternoon?"

"If it's not too late."

"Oh no, not at all."

"You see, the lease on my condo runs out soon and, well"—I smiled broadly myself—"I've decided to buy."

"Oh, yes!" she said. "There's nothing like owning one's own home. That feeling of satisfaction." She gave herself a little squeeze, as if thinking about it did in fact give her a feeling of satisfaction. "And it's such a beautiful spot, very secluded, and such a beautiful view." In a more confidential tone, she went on, "And it's rare to have new homes here come on the market. It's only because the builder was held up in court over some zoning dispute and the original buyers dropped out. You've come at exactly the right moment. Well, well, let me see if Marsha can cover for me." She went over to Marsha's desk and apparently worked things out, then bustled together her things and walked out with me, talking all the time.

"Shall we take my car, or would you rather drive?"

"Perhaps you should drive," I said, glancing over at the pickup.

"Yes, yes, I'll drive, it's better that way, it will give you a chance to look around, and it's such beautiful country up there."

We got in her car, a large Buick that she navigated out of the shopping center about as easily as an aircraft carrier, gaining thorough control of the machine only when we made it to the highway and she could steer in a straight line. Her seat was pulled as far forward as it would go, and she sat on a pillow to give herself extra height. She talked all the way up to Mercurtor Drive, agreeing with me enthusiastically whenever I ventured a comment.

We parked by the unfinished foundation and walked up the muddy incline to where the other two houses were being built. Not much had changed, except that the police tape had been taken down.

"A beautiful spot," I said.

"Oh, yes. Beautiful!" She began walking toward the other house, which was further along in construction. "I know you're just going to fall in love—"

"Actually, I'm more interested in this one," I said, pointing to the one in which Allie had been attacked.

"Oh, yes. This one is even better situated."

"Have you had a lot of people come to look at it?"

"You love it already, don't you?" She laughed. "Yes, quite a few. Some are very interested. But you know, with the court case and the delay and all—"

"How much is it?" I asked.

"How much? Yes, yes. Well—" She looked it up in a folder she was carrying. "It's listed at two million five." When I looked surprised, she added, "Just between us, we might be able to get it for less. The builder is anxious to sell as quickly as possible and"—she winked conspiratorially—"we could probably convince him to knock off a couple hundred thousand."

"I wasn't thinking of going above two million," I said, "but for something this beautiful"—I tossed my hand in the air—"what's a few hundred thousand dollars, more or less!"

We smiled big smiles at each other.

"Can we look inside?" I asked.

"Of course. Of course. You won't believe the view!"

She accompanied me to the house, and we climbed up a ramp to the unfinished wood floor. We walked around the lower level, then Kathy followed me up the stairs into the master bedroom, where we stood by the window and admired the view. The last one Allie had seen before she was attacked. The damaged section of the floor had been replaced and new plasterboard put up on the walls. I wondered if the charred and bloodstained supports had been replaced, too, or just covered over.

On the drive back, I asked Kathy about her children, the dancing lessons, baseball practice. It wasn't very hard to get her talking, and I encouraged it. As we neared town, I interjected a question, as if it was an afterthought.

"Someone at my hospital—I'm a doctor, by the way. A surgeon."

"Oh, yes, isn't that marvelous!"

"Yes, well, I have a colleague who I think mentioned he'd been interested in one of the houses himself. His name is Brandt. Peter Brandt. Did you show it to him?"

"Brandt?" she pondered. "I don't think so."

"I ask because, well"—I chuckled—"I don't want to be bidding against him for the same house, do I?"

She chuckled, too. "No, I guess not."

"He's an older man, early sixties."

"No, no." She knitted her brow, distressed that she couldn't answer yes. "I don't *think* anyone named Brandt."

"Tall. Shock of white hair. Distinguished-looking."

She shook her head unhappily. When we got back to Valparaiso Realty, I asked her to wait a moment, went over to the pickup and came back with one of the brochures from Brandt's private practice. The one with a handsome four-color photo of him on the cover.

"Oh, yes," she said when I showed it to her. "I recognize him. I never forget someone if I meet them in person. He was here six weeks ago or more. But I don't remember him saying his name was Brandt."

"He's very famous, and he likes to be discreet, so he sometimes uses a pseudonym." She nodded to indicate that she understood perfectly.

"Have you talked to a Detective Rossi?" I asked.

This question seemed to make her less happy. A look of confusion vied with the ever-present smile.

"A large black man," I continued, "with blue eyes. It would have been about the same time."

"Yeeees. I don't talk to that many detectives. I remember when I do."

"Of course." I tried to laugh like it was inconsequential. "Was it recently that he came by?"

"A month ago, I'd say." Her eyes became hooded; the look of confusion won out and the smile left her face completely. "You know, Mr. Maebry, I mean Doctor, if you have these questions, maybe you should talk to our manager, Mrs.—"

"No, no, that's not necessary. Here, let's start the paperwork, I'm anxious to get this process moving as fast as possible."

"You mean you've decided already? You want to buy?" She was all smiles again.

"Well, I probably should think about it overnight, but can't we get the ball rolling in the meantime?"

"Yes, yes, we certainly can!" We started walking together toward the door.

"Just one more question," I said. "Did the detective ask about Dr. Brandt?"

She stopped. "He asked who I'd shown the houses to, and I told him. But I didn't know Dr. Brandt's real name."

"Of course," I said. "What a silly question." I laughed again. Or made as good an imitation of a laugh as I could. She smiled, unsure. "Well, it's no big deal," I continued. "Thank you for your time." I shook her hand and began to walk away.

"But don't you want to fill out the papers?"

"I'm sorry," I said, "I just remembered something I have to do. I'll come back soon." I waved good-bye, and she raised her little hand to wave back.

"Yes, yes, all right," she said, perplexed again.

As I was getting into the pickup, she called after me. "Dr. Maebry! Dr. Maebry!" She came running up to my window, her hand outstretched. "I forgot to give you my card."

Chapter 52

Rossi might have inquired about Brandt at the real estate office, I thought, as he would in a general way about the others who had visited the house, but he wouldn't have brought a picture or been able to track down a fictitious name. Assuming he'd even tried. Brandt wasn't a suspect, after all. I was.

But now Rossi had Krista's diary. I wondered how long it would take him to decipher it and make a return visit to Valparaiso Realty. It didn't prove Brandt's guilt, but it tied him to the scene of the crime. It clearly made him a suspect now, too. Assuming Rossi was still interested in other suspects.

The pickup slowed to a crawl as it battled a strong headwind on the bridge. I downshifted to first to keep from stalling and inched along as the lower, sleeker cars zoomed past. When I eventually chugged home, there was a note from Sandra on my door asking me to come by. I found her sitting out on the small deck behind her kitchen, nursing a mug of tea and wearing a bathrobe as if she'd just gotten up in the morning. The wind howled between the buildings, stinging my face with salt spray from the ocean two blocks away.

"It's about Danny," she said as I sat down in the beach chair opposite her. Her hair was coiled loosely around something that looked like chopsticks. A gust of wind hit us, and she pulled her bathrobe tighter.

"Have you heard from him?"

"No."

"He's still with his father?"

She pulled at her robe again, but it was as tight as it would go.

"I caught him again on the phone today in one of his rare moments between drunks." She snorted. "I guess I'm not one to talk about drunks. Anyway, Danny's not there. Hasn't been for days."

"Have you called Danny's school?"

"None of his teachers have seen him for a week or more."

"Have you called the police?"

She shook her head.

"You really should—"

"I can't," she said, suddenly emotional. Her face was creased with lines I'd never seen before. "They'll take him away from me. They did once already."

"Sandra, he's not here *now*. You've got to think about him. He's only ten years old. You can't just let him—" I stopped. The creases cut deeper into her face, and her mouth opened to cry out, but there was no sound. "Listen, I'm going to go look for him. But you've got to call the police."

She caught her breath and nodded. "Okay."

"Where do you think he might be?" I asked. "Where would he go? Favorite hangouts, that kind of thing."

"The beach, maybe. Any place with a video game. God, I don't know, Jackson. He doesn't tell me where he goes."

"Any friends who might take him in?"

"Maybe," she said, unsure. She didn't know his friends.

"I'm going to try and find him," I said, getting up.

"Jackson." She held her hand up to her brow to protect her face from the salt spray. Or perhaps from my look. "You don't think I'm much of a mother, do you?"

"Maybe not," I said. "Maybe I'm not much of a friend, either."

—

I drove Sandra's pickup along the coast, stopping at all the beach spots, parking lots, rest areas, anything that looked like it might be a hangout. Sometimes there would be a huddled figure on the sand, hood up, head down below the knees. If it looked anything like him, I'd walk over and say "Danny" loudly, then say "Sorry" as the head came up from its shelter and stared at me.

I passed by playgrounds, peering through chain-link fences, getting dirty looks from mothers tending their children. I looked behind school buildings for the kind of dead zones that grown-ups never visit so kids naturally gravitate to them. I stopped by all the convenience stores, especially any store with a video machine, and showed his photo to the people who worked there. No one recognized him, even in the video arcade where I knew he must have dropped hundreds of quarters into the machines. He was just another ten-year-old with a baseball cap turned backward, baggy pants and a plaid shirt, two sizes too big and untucked. They all looked the same.

It was dark by the time I got to the Haight, where kids not much older than Danny hung around in small groups, sitting on dirty doorsteps or on the sidewalk itself, clustering outside bars and the lighted windows of head shops. They all had knapsacks and were smoking, mostly cigarettes, sometimes marijuana, which they didn't seem concerned about hiding. In the shadows of a side street, I saw two boys and a man in his twenties exchanging something for money. Small packets of folded white paper. Possibly cocaine or, more likely, crack, which is cheaper. Maybe Ecstasy, or even LSD, which I'd heard from Lieberman was making yet another comeback with the preteens in San Francisco—he'd seen his share in the emergency room. A squad car rolled by, not a hundred feet away. The patrol officers kept their faces pointed straight ahead. Unseeing. More likely uncaring.

Most of the kids responded to my questions with the kind of affectless, blank stares common to adolescents and drug users alike. The storeowners and bartenders were scarcely better. Before I'd even finished describing Danny or shown his picture, they were sure they hadn't seen him.

I was sitting in a booth at the back of a bar, drinking a beer and trying to figure out what to do next, when a girl approached me and leaned her pelvis against the edge of the table. "Hi," she said.

If I'd had to guess, I would have placed her age around sixteen, possibly younger. She wasn't so much thin as emaciated. The top of her shorts clung slightly above her pubic region, looking as though they might lose their grip at any moment. She had green hair, on the side that wasn't shaved; that side had black stubble, like a three-day-old beard sprouting out of her skull. Three rings were clipped in her nose, and several more rings that looked like staples ran up the outside cartilage of her ear. She clicked something against her teeth, then smiled and stuck out her tongue so I could see the silver stud impaled there.

"Are you looking for someone?" she asked in a voice that somehow seemed bruised.

I assumed she had overheard me asking about Danny and might

know where he was. "Yes," I said. "I am." I started to reach in my pocket for the photo, and she slid into the booth next to me.

"Later," she said, putting her hand on my leg.

"Later?"

"Yeah. You know." She moved her hand up my leg. "Not here."

I took out the photo and showed it to her. "I'm looking for him. The boy in the picture. His name is Danny. Have you seen him?"

"Oh." She slid her hand away. "You're into boys. If you want, I could probably get someone to fix you up—"

"No. You don't understand. He's missing. I'm looking for him. I want to bring him back home." I pointed to the photo again. "Have you seen him anywhere?"

She took the picture for a second look, shook her head and handed it back to me.

"Do you know where he might be? Where I might look for him?"

"You might try the shelter," she said, wiggling out of the booth and pulling up her shorts. "You know, for runaways."

"Where's that?"

"A couple of blocks north. Bordering the park there. It's called Clarion House. It's like, you know, a church."

"Thanks," I said.

She walked a few steps away, then turned. "I hope you find him," she said, and was gone.

—

Clarion House wasn't a church. It was attached to something that had probably been one once, but was now a "community center," with a big rainbow painted over the door and a street mural covering the side. Inside, there was a bulletin board with notices for lost cats, home-made jewelry, acupuncture classes and announcements for various events, including "Days of Rage/Nights in the Cage," which appeared to be a theater group, and "Come with the Coven, a Lesbian-Wiccan Celebration of Womb-Person Power." There was a small sign posted below that that said Clarion House and pointed to a door on the right.

I wandered through the building, finding no one until I bumped into a thirty-something man with a limp ponytail and an untended beard exiting the men's room.

"I'm looking for Clarion House." I said.

"This is it," he said, zipping up his jeans as he walked past me.

I followed him down the hall. "I'm trying to find a young boy," I said to his back. "Ten years old. I think he's run away from home. Could he have come here?"

The man went into a small office and sat behind a desk, seeming not to have heard what I said. I stepped inside and asked again. He took a pack of cigarettes out of his shirt pocket, tapped one out and lit up. The prematurely gray hairs of his beard were stained a dirty yellow, and the cigarette almost seemed to disappear in its bushy recesses. He smoked like a recovered junkie, sucking in the fumes as deeply as he could and holding it there to pump the nicotine into his system. Trying to make up for the drug he was missing.

"Have you told the police?" he said finally as he exhaled.

"His mother just called them." I handed the photo over the desk to him. "The police don't seem to care that much about what goes on around here," I commented.

"San Francisco is a very tolerant community." I couldn't tell if he was being ironic. He glanced at the photo and flipped it onto his desk. "How long has he been gone?"

"About two weeks. I'm not sure."

"You're not sure," he repeated meaningfully. "He ever run away before?"

"I don't know. Maybe."

He took a strong pull on his cigarette. You could see the red cinder glowing and hear the paper crinkling as it burned halfway to his fingers. "Know why he ran out?" he asked after a long exhale.

"No. I guess . . . His mother is an alcoholic and . . ."

He peered at me dully through the smoke. "And you?" he asked with a tired sort of leer.

"I'm a *doctor*," I said incoherently.

"His doctor or hers?"

"Listen, I'm just a friend. I live next door. I'm trying to help find the kid."

He looked me up and down, took another drag that finished the cigarette, then shook his head as he stubbed it out in a dirty coffee cup. "Haven't seen him."

"Maybe someone else who works here has?"

"I'll ask around."

The way he said it made me doubt he would. I wrote out my number and Sandra's on a piece of paper, anyway, and handed it to him. His hand was shaking slightly as he took it. He dropped it next to the photo and pulled out another cigarette.

"You might take a look around Castro," he said as he lit up.

"What?"

"It's the gay district—" he began to explain.

"I know what it is. He's only ten years old."

He shrugged. "Right."

"Look," I said, "maybe I could talk to the guy who runs this place."

"That's me. Father Michael."

"You're a priest?" I asked, showing my surprise.

"Yeah." The corners of his mouth twitched around his cigarette in a distorted smile. "Father Michael, pastor of the Church of Perpetual Twilight." The leer widened into a yellowish grin, and he jerked his head up at the wall behind him. Next to a poster that said "Heaven is a state of mind" was a framed document with the Vatican logo at the top and large letters indicating it was from the archdiocese of San Francisco. I couldn't make out the rest. Maybe he really was a priest. Maybe the paper was a joke. It hardly mattered.

Beads of sweat were appearing on his forehead. His entire face looked clammy. I realized I was wrong about him being recovered. He was just a junkie. He sucked viciously at his cigarette and tapped his fingers loudly on the desk, waiting for me to leave. "Well?" he asked. His other hand was playing with the desk drawer; he was hardly able to restrain himself from reaching inside. He needed it bad.

"I guess I'm holding you up," I said, slowly picking up the photo and putting it in my pocket. "One more question before I go."

"What?" he asked impatiently.

"I was just wondering which side you're on."

He spat out a fleck of tobacco that caught in his beard. "There are sides?" he sneered.

"Sure."

"And I suppose you know which is which."

"Sometimes it's pretty clear," I said, and left him to his next fix.

Chapter 53

It was after five A.M. by the time I drove home, the streets taking on the anemic colors of dawn and a dirty wind agitating the trash left in the gutters. A few stragglers hurried to make it home before the day began. I understood their haste. Some things are better left in the dark.

I'd visited every late-night arcade I could find, every cheap all-night cafeteria and twenty-four-hour movie house showing porno and kung fu, where I'd knock about the seats in the dark and get yelled at when I stared too long into the shadows. I left Castro for last, but the bar owners and club bouncers were even less helpful than in the Haight, and I got nowhere.

Sandra was waiting for me at the door when I got back. She was sober and looked so bad I thought of suggesting that she take a drink. She looked even worse when I said I'd had no luck and gave her a brief, edited version of my itinerary the night before. The police had nothing, she told me, but had added Danny's name and description to their files. I didn't say what I was thinking: that if they looked as hard for Danny as they did for all the other runaways I'd seen that night, the first place they were going to find him was in San Quentin, doing time as an adult. If he lived that long.

We drank some coffee and sat together but didn't talk much. I said I'd look again after I got some sleep, then went into my place, curled up in my sleeping bag and watched the clock, waiting for it to be seven-thirty so I could call Lucasian at home. I wasn't sure what I was going to say. I hadn't gotten any further in my thoughts than the decision to call him.

I woke at ten, immediately called his office and left a message. He called back a little after eleven.

"Dr. Maebry," he said simply when I picked up. "Hello." He was unusually subdued.

"There's something I need to talk to you about," I said.

"Yes, of course. I'm afraid at the moment . . ." The sentence trailed off. He cleared his throat and began again. "You should know that I have just been down to the main precinct. They informed me that Lieutenant Rossi has passed away."

"He's dead?"

"I am afraid so." I could hear the sadness in his voice.

"How? When?"

"Last night, in his car. He was parked in the alley behind some nightclub. Rush, I believe, is the name. Or perhaps Rash. He was found this morning by a traffic patrolman, slumped in his seat. Apparently a heart attack. He never was the same after his children died."

"Did he have a history of heart trouble?" I asked.

"I wouldn't know his medical history, Doctor. But losing your children—it must be a terrible blow to the heart, in a feeling man. And of course, his wife . . . Perhaps I should try to locate her," he said, more to himself than to me, "it might be less distressing hearing the news from a friend than from the precinct captain."

"There was nothing . . . else?"

"Nothing else? You mean medically? Perhaps. He was not in good condition. It is hard for a single man of that age to care for himself."

"Do you know where they took the body?"

"Apparently to your hospital, Doctor. The nightclub is not far from Memorial. They took him first to the emergency room, but they tell me he was already dead by the time they got there."

We made an appointment for me to come by the next day, and he hung up.

—

"Another *friend*, Dr. Maebry?" Finiker asked, his brow furrowing as usual like a plowed field. At least he remembered my name.

"In a sense," I said. "I knew him."

"You don't seem very lucky in your choice of friends."

Rossi's body lay before us, the black suture lines running up his massive chest, his dark skin looking pale.

"You've already autopsied him?"

"Just finished. He was brought in early this morning. Law

enforcement gets top priority. I suppose you want another run-down?"

"If you would."

"Basically, the man was a disaster waiting to happen. I'm surprised any blood made it through those arteries at all, they're so clogged. Cirrhosis of the liver—"

"Alcoholic?"

"Don't think so. His arteries would have been cleaner then. Best arteries in the world belong to alcoholics. No, this is almost certainly the result of hepatitis, apparently contracted in the war."

"The war?"

"According to the records, he served in Vietnam. Wounded twice. Patched up on the spot, as it were." He pointed to a mass of scars on his leg and groin area. "Looks like fieldwork, no? He had nodules on his prostate, possibly early stages of cancer, which is pretty well universal in men over fifty, though he hadn't been for an exam in, let's see"—he flipped through the pages in his report to Rossi's medical records—"well, never, if these records are correct. If he'd let it go longer, he might have been in trouble. What else?" He turned back to the autopsy information. "Let's see: somewhat inflamed sinuses, scarred septum, could indicate drug usage—"

"Nose spray."

"Is that slang for something? I have trouble keeping up with the vernacular of the younger generation."

"No. He had a cold a while back, then got hooked on nasal spray."

"You don't say. There wasn't any in his personal effects."

"He'd been off it for a few days."

"Well, it would certainly comport with the large amount of anti-histamine in his blood."

"What else?"

"In his blood? No alcohol. Small amount of caffeine. A fair amount of Ambien. Also Alprazolam."

"What?"

"It's a benzodiazepine, generic name—"

"I know what it is. Don't you think it strange he'd take sleeping pills while he was driving around in his car?"

"Why so strange? Maybe he got a call after he'd gone to bed. Maybe he was camping in his car for the night, didn't want to go home." He shrugged. "Most people who come in here have some kind of drug in their veins. It's the culture. Doesn't mean it killed them."

"How much was it?"

"For the Ambien, maybe thirty milligrams. I'd say a milligram, maybe, of Alprazolam."

"Seems like an awful lot."

"Yeah, but he was a big guy. Three hundred eighty-five pounds, stripped naked. It wasn't easy moving him around, I'll tell you."

Krista had taken a high dose of Ambien, too, I thought. And there was no prescription bottle in her apartment. It's a common drug. Still.

"Is that all there is?" I asked.

"No, but that's all the serious stuff. It was his heart, Doctor. Believe me."

"Can I take a look?" I held out my hand for the chart, and he gave it to me.

"Be my guest," he said. "I'll be in my office."

Finiker left, and I read through the notes. He had dictated them into a microphone while doing the autopsy, and they'd been transcribed automatically by the computer. The result was that much of it didn't make sense as written, and I had to sound it out phonetically to decipher what it meant. "Prostrate glance" and "Venus trophy" were fairly easy ("prostate gland" and "venous atrophy," respectively), but I couldn't make out some of the others for the longest time. When I came to it, though, I knew what it was.

I dropped the report on the table and pulled Rossi's right arm out of the bag. There, on the inside of his arm, were three needle holes. It looked as if whoever had injected him had missed the first two times before finally hitting the vein.

I stood in Finiker's doorway again. "There was nothing out of the ordinary in his blood?"

He looked up from his reports. "I told you. Nothing."

"He was injected with something. There are needle marks over his vein."

"Yes. I noted that. So what? He probably gave blood or had a blood test done. Something like that."

"Rossi didn't give blood. And he hated hospitals. That's why he'd never had blood work done to check on his prostate."

"I don't know what to tell you, Doctor. I'm not a detective. Are you finished with the body now? I've got dead people lined up into the hall, and it's not polite to keep them waiting."

—

Lieberman was by the admitting desk gabbing with one of the nurses. It was slow in emergency that afternoon.

"Maebry! What brings you down here?"

"I need to talk," I said. "In your office."

"Follow me," he said, leading me in and closing the door before we sat down. "What's up?"

"You studied cardiology before going into emergency medicine, right?"

"Yeah, but the hours were too steady and the pay was too good. Why?"

"This is kind of a strange question."

He smiled. "I would expect no less from you."

"What would be the easiest way to induce a heart attack—artificially, I mean?" I was pretty sure I knew the answer but wanted to be positive.

"You have it in for someone, Jackson?"

"Someone I know died of a heart attack." I didn't say it was two people. That would have sounded too strange. "I think it may have been induced somehow. But there was nothing in the blood. Nothing that could have killed him."

"How old was he?"

"Mid-fifties."

"Sounds pretty natural to me. But okay, assuming it wasn't. You could use electric shock. That's what happens when they electrocute you—"

"No, what I mean is, so that there would be no trace. Something that wouldn't show up in the autopsy. What about potassium chloride?"

"Sure, KCl. That would work. It's available at every nursing station in the hospital, as you know. A big enough dose would stop the heart cold."

"How big?"

"About ten or twenty cc's, I'd imagine, if you gave it all at once. You could administer it through an IV very easily."

"What about a large hypodermic?"

"Sure, probably."

"But wouldn't a dose that large show up in an autopsy?"

"Not unless you autopsied the guy right away, like in the first ten or twenty minutes, *and* you knew what you were looking for. Potassium chloride is absorbed quickly by the body, it's naturally occurring in practically every cell, so there would be nothing suspicious."

"Wouldn't the levels be elevated?"

"Not really. Not enough to detect. The tests aren't that fine. I don't see it, though."

"Why not?"

"Twenty cc's is a pretty large dose. And you have to administer it intravenously. The person injecting it would have to know what they were doing. You know how hard it is sometimes to hit the vein just right, even when you've had practice. You'd need a pretty compliant victim."

"What if the victim was asleep?"

"Sure, if he didn't wake up and ask you what the hell you were doing."

"Maybe he was drugged."

"Yeah. That's true. A couple of black beauties. That's what we used to call barbiturates in college. Not much of those around these days, though."

"Or maybe just a lot of Ambien?"

"Use it myself, actually. You know what this schedule does to your sleeping patterns. But you'd have to get them to take it first. And, of course, you'd find it in their blood."

"That's easy. Mix it in a drink. A mixed drink, like a rum and Coke, to disguise the taste. Or coffee and milk. Decaffeinated, so it doesn't counteract the effect."

"I usually take mine with a beer. Ten minutes later I'm out like a light."

"Thanks," I said, getting up.

"Jackson. You really think . . ."

"I don't know. It's probably nothing. I was just curious."

"Maybe we've got one of those 'angels of mercy' on our staff," he said as I walked to the door. "You know, like you read about sometimes. Going around knocking off terminal patients."

"This wasn't terminal," I said. "And mercy had nothing to do with it."

—

I put a note in Brandt's mailbox. I knew he'd get in before the end of the day. Eileen was very thorough; Brandt demanded it. The note said simply: "I know what you did." In place of a signature, I wrote the letters "KCl." He'd know who left it for him.

Chapter 54

I called her from my office. "Allie, we've got to talk."
She started to make some excuse, as I knew she would.

"Listen to me!" I shouted, and she fell silent, waiting. "Please. Things have changed. We have to talk."

"What's changed?" she asked, sounding like she didn't want to know.

I would have preferred not to tell her over the phone, but she clearly didn't want to see me. "I've been arrested, for one. They think I'm the person who attacked you."

"Oh." I waited for her to say something in my defense, such as "That's absurd" or "That's impossible," but all she said was: "How come?"

"Thanks for the vote of confidence."

"It doesn't help to be sarcastic, Jackson." She was right, but it seemed unfair to scold me, considering the situation. "You're not in prison now?"

"I got out on bail. That's just part of it. There's no question that Brandt was the one who attacked you—"

"But the police don't think so—"

"Yeah, they think *I* did it. I know *Brandt* is the one, and I think he killed Krista because she found out something, and now Rossi, too."

It was as if the line had gone silent.

"Allie? Allie? You know about Krista, don't you?"

"Yes," she said finally. "The hospital told me. They said it was a heart attack."

"That's what the pathologist said, but— Listen to me, Allie, first Krista and then Rossi—"

"Listen to *yourself*, Jackson. You're not making any sense. Krista died of a heart attack. And this man, Rossi—I mean, even if he was killed. He's a cop. Lots of people might want to do him in."

"For God's sake, Allie!"

"Jackson. You're upset. I understand—"

"Damn right I'm upset. But it's not just about me. Brandt is dangerous. I've got to go to the police."

"I told you I don't want that!"

"He's killed two people! We've got to do something. He's crazy—"

"You're one to talk about crazy!"

It was the way she said it as much as what she said—cold and final, as if she'd taken a knife and severed whatever ties still held us together.

"Yeah. Maybe I'm crazy, too. A paranoid schizophrenic. Maybe you don't love me anymore. You certainly don't seem to care. I just . . . I . . ." Saying it into the phone, when she wouldn't see me, was like the final humiliation. I was using all my self-control to keep my voice from breaking and just kept stuttering, "I . . . I . . ." There was nothing else I could think to say.

After a moment she answered, in a different voice. "I care about you, Jackson, I do."

I snuffled back the tears.

"I do care, very much," she said soothingly.

"Jesus!" I groaned.

"You're upset now—"

"Allie! For God's sake. Yes, I'm upset. That's not the point—"

"Don't yell at me!" she commanded, her voice sharp again. "I'm trying to be your friend."

My friend. From loving me to caring about me; now she was my friend.

"Okay," I said.

"I understand what you must be going through." She was soothing again.

"Okay."

"Listen, Jackson. Don't make any decisions right now. We'll talk, all right? Tonight. I'll come to your place. Okay? Before you say anything to anyone?"

Confusion filled my head and I felt suddenly very tired. So tired it was an effort even to hold up the phone.

"Okay, Jackson? You'll wait till we talk?"

Of course I would. I'd do anything she asked me. "Yes," I agreed. "I'll wait."

—

The fog came in early, a wet, low-hanging wall advancing up the hill from the ocean, forcing the cabdriver to turn on his wipers to clear the windshield. Back home, the fog was so thick I couldn't see Sandra's door from my own.

I entered my apartment unnoticed. There was still some light outside, but it was trapped in the haze, illuminating nothing but the white of the fog itself. After a time the sun set—it must have been setting, because the white in the windows turned black—and it became as dark outside as in.

I don't know how long I'd been sitting there or how late it was when I heard Allie's voice, as if it had materialized out of the night. Or just my desires.

"Jackson?"

"I'm here."

Her shadow was standing in front of me hugging itself. "It's freezing in here. Why don't you turn on the heater?"

"Sure," I said, not moving. She went over herself and turned it on. The kerosene flame burned behind the metal slats.

"And all the windows are open! It's like we're underwater." She turned on the overhead light. It was harsh and sudden, like an assault.

"What happened to your apartment? It's practically empty."

"I cleaned it out."

"I'll say."

"Why don't you turn off the light?" I said.

She turned it off and carefully made her way to the couch, sitting beside me with her back to the glowing flame of the heater, her face swallowed up in shadow. I felt her hand touch my arm, then work its way down to my hand, which she lifted from my side and held in her lap.

"How much do you remember, Allie? I mean, really remember?"

I heard her draw in her breath.

"Do you remember the assault?"

"I don't remember the actual assault. Or really much about getting there."

"Brandt took you?"

318

"He flew up from L.A. and we drove there. I followed him in my car."

"You were seeing him?"

"I had been, Jackson. When we met, you and me, and then . . . for a while."

"And Paula?"

"That was never important, Jackson. Not to me."

"Is that why you were crying that night? In Brian's room?"

"That was because of Helen, seeing them together."

"You were jealous of Helen?"

"Yes. At the time."

"What about me?"

"Jackson, I had just met you."

"You were seeing him the whole time you were with me?"

"It wasn't like that—"

"He was taking you to see the house? He was going to buy it for you?"

"He didn't want me to leave him. The house was persuasion."

"You were going to—leave him?"

"Yes, that's why I went with him. To tell him for the final time. We'd argued about it before he left for the conference. But I don't remember much after that. Just driving to the house. He said he had something to show me. He insisted."

"Why were you leaving him?"

"You know that, Jackson."

"Why?"

"You. I was going to marry you."

"But you turned me down."

"You never listened to what I said, did you?"

"You said it was too soon."

"I just needed a little more time."

"And in time . . . ?"

"Yes."

She lifted my hand from her lap and laid it against the right side of her face so that I could feel her skin, my fingertips against her cheek, the corner of her mouth. Then she found my other hand and brought it to the other side, to the raised pattern of lines where we'd sewn her lacerated skin back together.

"You're healing, Allie, getting better." I leaned forward to where my hand touched her lips and kissed her.

"Not too hard, Jacko, it still hurts. There, that's right."

She pressed her lips back against mine, so lightly it could have been a dream, and I could smell her breath as she sighed. I moved my other hand down the side of her face. I wanted to feel her skin, her scars, everything that belonged to her. With my other hand, I traced the curve of her neck, then the contours of her side.

"Careful." She spoke with her lips brushing mine. "My ribs."

I slowly unbuttoned her dress from the neck down and put my hand inside, gently touching her breasts. Then down farther, to the burn scars on her abdomen, and to the curved bone of her hip.

"We should talk," I said.

"Tomorrow, Jackson. Tomorrow."

"We have to go to the police, Allie—"

"I know," she said. "We'll do what we have to do."

I felt a strange sensation—sharp, almost painful, like damaged nerves healing after a long paralysis. It was hope.

"Tomorrow?" I said.

"Yes," she answered, "tomorrow."

She led me to the bed and stepped out of her dress, and we wrapped ourselves in the sleeping bag. I felt the warmth of her body against me, her cold feet on mine, and I realized I was happy again. Happy for the first time since that night in the emergency room. And I thought: I won't lose her again. Whatever it takes. I won't lose her. Never again.

"It's going to be okay," I said, believing it.

"It's going to be okay," she said.

"We'll start over again, Allie. From the beginning. Just like new."

"Yes, Jackson," she said. "Just like new."

———

I let it go. Like an injured animal gathered up by a child that takes the first opportunity to struggle free. I let it go, piece by piece, item by item, like an inventory of unfulfilled desires, a storehouse of fears, resentments and obligations never met. I gave it all up: like dreams to daylight, substance to fire. Like the last hope of rescue. I let go and felt the deep currents carry me out into the void and pull me under.

Chapter 55

Screaming. Someone was screaming. Calling my name.

It's Danny, I thought. Screaming like I'd never heard before. So far away and still so loud . . .

There's nothing to worry about, I assured him. I'm not drunk again. I'm okay. Everything's going to be fine. No need to worry. But then I realized the conversation was happening only inside my head.

Danny was still screaming, pulling on me now, yanking at my arms, my legs, lifting me onto a stretcher, I could hardly believe he was so strong. Then several men held him back and he yelled my name one time as they closed the ambulance door. They put a mask over my face and someone was yelling at me to breathe and someone else was talking into the radio about carbon monoxide poisoning. "It's from the space heater," I wanted to say, but I was very tired, too tired to speak, and I couldn't talk with the mask on, anyway. My head throbbed with pain, like it was exploding inside. "Breathe," the person yelled, but it seemed like too much work. Maybe I'd just go back to sleep.

They were shaking me, yelling in my ear, and I just wished that they would stop, leave me in peace. Then I thought of Allie and that maybe they'd missed her and I had to tell them. I forced out her name, but the pain racked my body. My eyes erupted in phosphorous-white light and I groaned, and even that hurt. I felt myself starting to vomit, and someone yelled, "Jesus Christ!" and I kept throwing up as he yelled, "Jesus Christ! Get the NG tube in! NOW!" Then I gagged and started choking. I couldn't breathe. My lungs strained against my chest, and strained again, but no air came. . . .

—

"Let's get an IV going stat." A command. I was in the emergency room and they were putting in an IV. "Keep him down! Keep him down!" I was struggling to sit up, trying to tell them not to give me an IV, Brandt would kill me, but there was something in my throat and I could gasp only "No!" as they forced my head back down on the bed.

I jerked away as the needle pierced my skin, but my arm was held fast. I wrenched my shoulders and kicked my legs against the bands that held them, but the grip on my arm remained steady and I could feel the catheter being pushed up my vein, then quickly bandaged in place. I twisted my torso and tried to yank it out, writhing against the restraints as the strength ebbed from my body. Then all I could do was kick my legs against their bonds. I kicked and kicked and kept kicking. Until I couldn't kick anymore.

—

A wave of nausea spread out through my limbs and then washed back into my chest and up my throat. I tried again to tell them not to put in the IV, but the nausea caught me first. I heaved up in bed and tried to turn over to the side but wasn't quick enough. My whole body spasmed, then spasmed again, as if trying to expel my internal organs one at a time; then it stopped, and I fell back on the bed and hardly had time to feel the next wave building before my muscles convulsed again into a knot. Somebody was holding me, or making an effort to, but there was nothing he could do but lay his hands on my shoulders as I retched, over and over, until my muscles were too exhausted to tighten anymore, and the only effect was a constant, spastic twitching running through my limbs.

"They're only dry heaves." The words came through the swimming nausea of my head and body like a voice underwater. "Relax now. There."

A familiar voice.

I lay still until the twitching stopped. When I felt enough strength come back, I turned my head on the pillow. A white coat. A doctor.

"They tell me you almost didn't make it. If that boy hadn't found you when he did— Another minute or two . . ."

My ears were ringing and my head was pounding from the inside. I could barely move my head now, enough to see a suit and tie above the top button. I couldn't see the face, but I recognized the tie. It belonged to Brandt.

"Don't!" It took an enormous effort to get the word out.

"What did you say, Jackson?" He leaned down toward me, toward the IV.

"Don't!" I rasped.

"You've been intubated. Your vocal cords are raw. You shouldn't try to speak."

"Nurse!" I summoned all my energy and called as loudly as I could. It came out a hoarse whisper. "Nurse! Help me!"

"Quiet, Jackson. Don't thrash around so—"

I passed out and came to looking up into his face. He was holding something over my nose and mouth. Trying to smother me.

I gasped for breath. Nothing. Again my chest heaved, straining for air, and I felt a steady stream of oxygen flow into my lungs. It flooded my brain: cool, clean, pure. I drew the oxygen in again and again, until the pressure began to lessen inside my head and I could feel life coming back into my extremities.

I lay there for several minutes, taking deep breaths from the mask, Brandt looking down at me, me looking up at him, just breathing, breathing. He waited until I relaxed, then took the mask away.

"Oxygen's a wonderful antidote for carbon monoxide poisoning," he said.

I felt stronger now. Strong enough to talk, almost. I ground out the words: "Why are you here?"

He straightened up as if surprised. "I was concerned, Jackson. I heard—"

"Sure," I croaked. "You were concerned—" I fumbled for the mask, and he let me take it. I put it over my face and gulped in the oxygen. "You were . . . concerned," I choked out between gasps, "I . . . might . . ." I had to take another draft of oxygen to finish the sentence. " . . . tell someone."

"Tell someone?"

"I know . . . what you did. You mur—" I began, cut off as my throat constricted around the word. I gagged, my head pounding again from the effort of speaking. "Murderer!" I rasped out, the sound of my own voice like a hammer inside my skull.

"Jackson, what are you talking about? You must still be delirious."

More gulps of oxygen. "I know what . . . I'm saying. You killed Rossi . . . because . . ." I couldn't go on. The pain was forcing the nausea back up into my throat.

"What do you mean? Detective Rossi is dead? I wasn't aware."

"Right, and you . . . weren't—" The pain spiked higher with each word. " . . . aware of Krista . . . either?"

"Krista? You mean Alexandra's friend? The nurse? I heard that she died of a heart attack."

"Brought on by . . . an injection of potassium chloride . . . just like Rossi." The nausea crested and I retched again, forcing tears from my eyes, leaving my body trembling under the blanket. I sucked desperately at the oxygen, but even that movement sent shards of pain tearing through my head.

"Jackson, I really don't— Look, you're in no condition—you've suffered severe oxygen depravation of the brain, it's natural to be confused."

"I'm not so confused I don't . . . know . . . you tried to kill Allie."

The pounding in my head was so violent now I could hardly see. I'd used up all my remaining strength getting out that last sentence. It required a supreme effort of will just to hold the oxygen mask in place.

Brandt loomed over me. I couldn't focus enough to make out the look in his eyes.

"You shouldn't be talking," he said.

The IV began to beep, and I saw him glance down at the control panel. Deciding what to do.

This is crazy, I realized in a belated flash of lucidity. Threatening him when I'm so vulnerable. Completely at his mercy.

He reached for the IV and I started to scream for the nurse again, but he quickly pressed a few buttons on the pump, and the alarm stopped beeping as the pressure came back up.

"You shouldn't try to talk," he said. "You need to rest." He gazed down at me for several moments before speaking again. "I'll send in the nurse."

Then he walked out the door and was gone.

Chapter 56

The first chance I got, I asked the nurse about Allie. I had to explain to her that Allie was the person I had been brought to the hospital with. Another case of carbon monoxide poisoning. She said she didn't think there was anyone else. I was brought in alone.

I had her call the admitting desk in the ER to make sure. I made them put one of the doctors on the line while the nurse held the phone for me. He confirmed it. There was no one else with me. I was the only CO poisoning patient that day. The only one that month, he assured me, consulting his records.

Allie must have left after I fell asleep. I let my head sink into the pillow and felt my body relax. She'd been anxious about her upcoming operation. Probably she couldn't sleep. "Lucky," I said to myself, drifting back into unconsciousness. We deserve to be lucky once in a while. The two of us, Allie and me.

Lieberman came by later. I'd recovered enough to sit up. He flashed his penlight in my eyes, took my pulse and checked my reflexes. "How's your head?"

"It hurts, but it's getting better."

"Nausea?"

"Almost gone."

"I'd like to keep you under observation for a few more hours," he said, "but we'll probably have you outta here before tonight."

"So I'm okay?" I asked.

He ahemmed. "Well, nothing serious, probably. Oxygen deprivation no doubt caused some damage to the brain, but in your case that seems to be a vestigial organ, anyway."

"Sorry, Lieberman," I said, "my mind's not moving fast enough to catch your wit."

"I'm just wondering what the hell you thought you were doing. And I'm also wondering if, when I let you out of here, you're going to decide to go for a car ride in your garage with the garage door closed."

"I wasn't trying to commit suicide. It was an accident."

I knew it wasn't. I never close the windows. Not all the way. Brandt must have gotten my note and followed me home.

"Pretty dumb-ass accident, Maebry. I gotta tell you, I'm worried. You come to me with some—how can I say this?—*paranoid* notion about someone secretly murdering people, then the next thing I know you're in my ER raving like a lunatic. I mean both parts of that: 'raving' and 'lunatic.' Granted you were delirious, but I'm wondering how much of that was induced by the carbon monoxide poisoning, and how much is just your—well, normally abnormal self."

"Did I say anything?"

"You said a lot, all of it incoherent. Something about some other person."

"Was I brought in alone?" I wanted to be absolutely sure.

"Yes."

"They found me that way—alone?"

"Of course. There was a kid, apparently, who called. Who else would there be?" He looked at me dubiously.

"No one. Never mind. I was just checking. I didn't say anything about the IV, did I?"

"No. Something about how someone was trying to kill you and— Jesus! You thought we were going to kill you, put potassium chloride in the IV?"

"Not you."

"The angel of mercy?"

"No. I told you that's not it."

His manner altered. "Listen, Jackson. Have you ever considered seeing a shrink?"

"Been there, done that. I'm not crazy, Lieberman. It only sounds like it."

"Uh-huh." It was a skeptical grunt, but it also signaled the end of the conversation. Lieberman hadn't gone into emergency medicine because he liked to dwell on psychological issues. We'd just about exhausted his emotional attention span.

"Fine," he said, pocketing his penlight and getting ready to leave. "I've said my piece. I want to check on you in another couple of hours, then we'll probably release you."

"Thanks."

"Maybe life isn't exciting enough for you, Jackson. That offer to join me in the ER still stands. You've gotta be a little crazy to do ER, anyway."

"I'm persona non grata in this hospital these days, Lieberman. I don't think the administration is going to want me in the ER or anywhere else."

"Yeah, I heard about that. Screw the administration. I run the ER, not the surgeons. If you want to, I can get you in. See you later," he said as he walked out.

A short while afterward I saw Danny's head poking around the door. Sandra's followed above it.

"Hey, Jackson," Danny said, his eyes panning the room warily. "Is it all right for us to come in?"

"Yeah, Danny, come in."

Sandra looked as if she had dressed especially to come to the hospital, even done her hair. She could have been a middle-aged member of the PTA. Danny was in his cleanest clothes, too, wearing pants that actually fit him. He ran up to the bed, then stopped suddenly two steps away.

"It's okay, Danny, I'm fine."

He approached cautiously, and when he was near enough, I grabbed his head and gave it a bear hug. He laughed and squirmed out of my grip.

"You saved my life," I said.

He shrugged and shuffled his feet, looking down at the floor in embarrassment.

"You did. You saved my life, Danny. They said that if you hadn't found me when you did and called 911, I would have been dead in a matter of minutes. You came just in time."

"You looked really *weird*, Jackson," he said, his eyes wide, like it was the most amazing thing that had ever happened to him. "Like, you were, you were—" He was so excited he was having trouble getting it out. "You were *red*, like, like *really* red."

"It's carbon monoxide poisoning. It makes your skin turn bright red."

"So how come? What happened?"

"The heater needs ventilation, otherwise the carbon monoxide builds up. I must have turned it on with the windows closed."

"Boy, that was kind of dumb, huh?"

"Yeah, Danny, kind of dumb."

What was dumb was leaving that note for Brandt. I hadn't thought through how he'd react. I simply wanted him to feel some of the panic and desperation I'd been living with for so long. Apparently I'd succeeded.

Sandra, who had been hanging back, came up to my bed now. "We brought you some clothes," she said, lifting a shopping bag for me to see and setting it down in a nearby chair. "Jackson . . . I'm so sorry. I knew that space heater wasn't a good idea—"

"Forget it, Sandra. It wasn't your fault. The heater's not the problem. I was stupid."

"I feel so awful."

"It's fine. I'm fine." I changed the subject. "Hey, Danny, you're back. We were worried about you, you know."

He bent his head and shrugged again.

"Where were you all this time?"

Sandra put her hand on his shoulder. "He was with 'friends,'" she explained. "It isn't going to happen again," she added, referring more to herself, it seemed, than to Danny.

"I was crashing for a while with these surfer guys I know." He said it as if it were no big deal. But he knew it was.

"Okay, Danny," I said, "we'll talk about it later. No more running out, okay?"

"Ye-*ah*," he muttered under his breath, rolling his eyes back in his head the way ten-year-olds do when under duress.

"Ye-*ah*?" I knuckled him in the shoulder. "Say it like you mean it!"

"Ow! Okay. Yeah!" he answered loudly.

"That's more like it," I said, and we both laughed.

"Come on, Danny," said Sandra. "It's time to go." She began to lead him out with her arm around his shoulders, but he slipped out from under before they got to the door and came back to the bed.

"What about Allie, Jackson?" he whispered, serious again.

"She's okay, Danny. We'll see her soon. It's been a hard time for everybody, but it's over now. Everything's going to be fine. Just like it was."

His face lit up. "Really?"

"Really, Danny." Just a few things to take care of, I thought. One sociopathic surgeon who needed to be brought to justice. It would all be over soon.

"Come on, Danny," Sandra said.

"See ya, Jackson," he said, walking to his mother and waving good-bye.

"See ya, Danny," I said.

"Stay cool!" he yelled back.

Sandra took him by the shoulder and pulled him out of the room.

"Bye, Jackson," he called from around the corner.

"Bye, Danny," I called after him.

—

Lieberman came again later in the afternoon and discharged me after having me walk back and forth across the room.

"Maybe you shouldn't drive right away," he said.

"I didn't come by car, remember. Anyway, I've got some things to do in the hospital."

"Well, I'd stay out of the OR," he advised. "And I wouldn't make any important business decisions today. It will be another twenty-four hours before you're fully recovered. From the effects of the carbon monoxide poisoning, at least. Other issues I'm not qualified to discuss."

"I get the point."

"Take it easy for a while. Get some rest."

"Okay."

"And keep your windows open," he said as he left.

—

Eileen gave a start when she saw me. She didn't know how to react.

"He's expecting me," I said, opening the door to Brandt's office without waiting for a reply.

Brandt was sitting in his chair, his arms hanging limply by his sides, as if he'd lost something but couldn't remember what it was. When he saw me, he reached over to press the intercom and told Eileen to take the rest of the day off. That done, his hand fell back to his side. "I see you've recovered," he said. His eyes glanced up to my face briefly, then down at his desk.

"I know you were the one who attacked Allie," I stated.

He didn't deny it. He didn't say anything, so I continued. This time I could talk without gasping for air.

"You lied to me about Allie's scans. You knew about the reabsorbable plates because you were her doctor. You put them in. You did her reconstruction."

"She asked me to keep it a secret—"

"You weren't at the biotech conference that Saturday," I went on. "Brian told me so. You were going to buy her that house in Marin, where she was attacked."

He seemed to collapse into himself, suddenly frail, an old man.

"The house where *you* attacked her. Nice present."

"It's probably hard for you to understand," he said in a weak voice, his hands opening, palms up, as if in supplication.

"Understand! Jesus!"

"I loved Alexandra. I still do."

"If you call it love," I said. "She's more like a possession to you. She was your creation, and you couldn't let her go. When she refused your house—your *bribe*—and told you she was leaving you for someone else, you tried to destroy her so no one could have her."

He covered his face with a gnarled hand. I realized now why it had been hurting him so much. He'd inflamed the arthritis attacking Allie.

"It's like a dream. A terrible dream," he moaned, tears welling in his eyes, imploring my sympathy. "You have to believe, I never intended . . . Never. I can hardly believe it even happened."

"It didn't just *happen*. You did it!"

He shrank farther in his chair and held his hand to his chest. "Please, you must understand—" He broke off, taking a labored breath as if the strain was too much for his heart. "Jackson, please try to understand. I ask only that you try to judge what *happened* with compassion. This has all been so terrible for me. You can't imagine what I've been through."

I was too stunned to answer. He wanted sympathy for *his* suffering. As if *he* were the victim.

"Jackson, you must believe me. I'm not a bad person."

I laughed. I couldn't help it. At that moment he hardly seemed to me to be a person at all—just a grasping, narcissistic maw of self-pity.

"That isn't all," I continued. "You killed Krista. She found out about the house—I guess she overheard you and Allie on the inter-com one night. So she did some checking on her own, and you had to get rid of her. And then Rossi, you killed him, too."

He shook his head. "No."

"Come on! I know you did. Once Rossi got Krista's diary and realized what was going on—you knew you were caught. It would have been easy to check up on the plane tickets from L.A. to San Francisco. And only someone with medical training would know that KCl can induce cardiac arrest and then leave the body without a trace."

"Potassium chloride? So that's what that note was about. It was you—"

"Quit pretending. You knew exactly what it was about."

He was shaking his head. "You think I killed that Krista woman?"

"Of course."

"And then that detective, too, to cover up . . ." He didn't finish the sentence.

"Why don't you say it?" I spat at him. "You can't, can you? To cover up the fact that you smashed Allie's face in with a hammer and tried to burn her while she was still alive."

"You must think I'm a monster." As if it were unfair to think such a thing.

"I'll tell you what I think—what I *know*. You tried to *murder* Allie, and then you did murder two other people to hide your crime."

"No, no, no," he repeated to himself. "That's not right."

I wanted to bash his proud head against the desk and make him admit the truth. "I saw the needle marks on their arms!" I cried. "You injected them with potassium chloride to induce cardiac arrest. Very ingenious on your part, but you didn't know that Rossi never went near a hospital—"

"No," he said again, more forcefully. "Whatever you think of me—whatever I may have done in a moment of . . . passion, I'm not a cold-blooded killer. I never could have done that."

"No? Just rip Allie apart with a hammer, but you'd never kill someone silently in his sleep! Don't give me this crap about 'passion.' Your only passion is for yourself."

For the first time he looked me directly in the eye. "If what you accuse me of is true," he said, "then why didn't I do the same to you this morning? We were alone for almost half an hour. It would have been simple enough to inject a lethal dose of potassium chloride into your IV while you were lying unconscious. For that matter, I could have done the same to Alexandra when she was comatose, if I were really so ruthless."

"I interrupted you that first night when you came back early from L.A. You were probably thinking of doing just that, but then I saw you there—"

"There were many other opportunities."

"Like last night."

"Last night?" For a moment his expression turned blank.

"I know it was you! You got my note and followed Allie to my apartment, and when she left, you closed the windows."

He was either a good actor or he genuinely didn't follow what I was saying. He seemed to mull it over a short time. Then he surprised me. He smiled. "Do you mean the carbon monoxide poisoning, Jackson?" He wagged his head at the absurdity of it. "Is there anything you *don't* want to accuse me of?" Something occurred to him, and he actually chuckled as his tongue darted out over his lips. "You say Alexandra was there, in the apartment with you?" The smile turned into a grin. The grin of someone who's just turned the tables on an adversary.

"All I know," I insisted, "is that you wanted her back, you wanted to make her yours again, and when you realized she didn't remember the attack, you thought you could get away with it—"

He glanced up sharply, a haughty gleam in his eye. I halted in midsentence. "You wanted her back," I repeated, no longer so sure of myself.

"Yes," he said, the grin transforming into a leer. "Yes, I did want her back. And now I have her, don't I?"

Chapter 57

Crockett found me later in my office, the phone in my hand. I'd dialed Mulvane's number at police headquarters several times but always hung up before anyone came on the line.

"Jackson, glad I found you." Crockett plopped down in the chair. "I only just heard."

He commiserated with me briefly over my near brush with death, then told me the news. The board had officially decided to give the plastics position to Anderson. They were also terminating my fellowship at the end of the year. A year early.

"There wasn't anything I could do. Brandt insisted. Sorry," he said. "Maybe this wasn't the best time to tell you."

"As good a time as any. Anyway, Lieberman promised me work down in the ER if I wanted it."

"Great way to grow old fast," he said. Then in a different tone: "So, remember that reabsorbable hardware? You ever contact the FDA?"

"Yeah. Brandt was on the list. He knew what it was all the time."

"I'm not surprised," he said. "What's up with the old SOB?"

I felt at the bandage on my inner arm where they'd put in the IV needle. "I don't know anymore. I thought I did, but—"

Somehow I knew Brandt wasn't lying. Not about the windows, at least. He had seized upon the accusation too readily. I'd overreached and he'd taken his opportunity. By some calculation in his cold heart, he'd won. His gloating was too authentic.

"But what, Jackson?" Crockett asked.

"I don't know. Remember what you told me about that monk guy?"

"Yeah, William of Occam."

"The point is that the simplest explanation is always the best. Right?"

"Right."

"Except when it isn't."

"That's the idea. If the simpler explanation doesn't work to explain all the facts, then you proceed to the next level of complexity and see if that works."

"Makes sense," I said, trying to think it through but unable to get past the first step. It was like those math problems with more than one variable that had always stymied me in school. "But—what I don't understand—how do you know what the next level is?"

"Beats the shit out of me, Jackson," he said. "I'm only a doctor."

Chapter 58

I gave up on calling Mulvane. I figured he'd be contacting me soon enough anyway. I dialed Lucasian's office, relieved to find him out. At least I wouldn't have to lie to him. I left a message saying I wouldn't be able to make our meeting that day. Maybe never, I thought.

Before leaving, I glanced around the room to see if there was anything critical that needed my attention. Only insurance forms. Nothing urgent. Nothing that couldn't be done just as well by someone else.

I walked home. It helped to clear my head. The weather was warm and sunny, and I could tell there wouldn't be any fog that night. I brought a towel to the beach, lay in the sand between the dunes and let myself drift off into sleep. If I'm right, I thought, I won't ever know. I liked it that way.

—

The cold woke me when the sun went down. I bought some heavy dark rum and piña colada mix from the liquor store, took it back home and made a call.

"Allie," I said into her answering machine. "I was hoping to see you again. I know tomorrow is your operation. I thought maybe you wouldn't want to be alone tonight."

She called me back almost immediately, as I'd known she would. I said I'd like to come over. She said she was sick of being holed up in her apartment and that she'd come to my place. She was there about an hour later. She hovered in the entrance, as if unsure whether to come inside.

I walked toward her and she came up to me. Despite the injuries, her body moved as it used to. The way it had moved the first time I met her at the party and watched her drift over the lawn—like a dream of something beautiful. Four, five months had passed since then, so little time to live a life.

I held her lightly by the arms and looked into her face. Allie's face. Different but the same.

I kissed her. She let me.

"Let's make love," I said.

"Later," she said.

"Now." I led her around the partition to my bed. She put down the overnight case she'd been carrying, and we sat together. I kissed her again. She put her hands on my chest and gently pushed me away.

"Later," she said. She laid her hand on the sleeping bag and caressed it gently.

"You left last night without saying good-bye."

"I didn't want to wake you. And I don't like going out in the daytime." She looked unconsciously around the room, as if checking on something.

"Let's have a drink," I said. "I've got rum and piña colada mix. You want to make some?"

She nodded and walked out past the partition to the kitchen area. I heard her opening and closing cabinets and finally calling to me, asking where the pitcher was.

"Same place."

"Same place as what?"

"Same place as before."

"Where's that?"

"I don't know," I said, and she knocked about some more looking for it. The overnight bag was by my feet. I knew what it contained but leaned over anyway and felt inside, under the clothes, until I found it. A plastic bag with several bottles of potassium chloride. Forty megs, about ten cc's each. More than enough. Inside her cosmetic bag, lying innocently among the makeup jars, compacts and brushes, was a syringe and hypodermic needle. I assumed she had the Ambien, or whatever sleeping medication she was using, with her now in the kitchen. I closed the zipper and sat back on the bed, drawing the sleeping bag around my body. Suddenly cold.

Allie came in a short while later with the two drinks and handed me one. "There's no crushed ice."

"Doesn't matter." I took a large drink. "It's good."

"I'm going to change," she said. She picked up her bag.

"Change here," I said. "Let me watch you."

"No, Jackson, not the way I look."

"Okay."

She went into the bathroom and emerged a while later wearing sweatpants and an extra-large sweatshirt with a hood and big pockets. It said LIFE'S A BEACH. She picked up my glass. "That was quick; you finished it."

"I was thirsty."

"I'll get you another."

"Fine," I said.

"I'm very tired," I said after I'd drunk the second glass. "I'm going to lie down a second."

Allie helped me adjust the sleeping bag so I was comfortable, then started to take off my clothes.

"I love you," I whispered as she leaned over to undo my shirt buttons. She started when I spoke. She began to smile, but the smile extinguished itself almost before it appeared, like a match being lit in the wind, leaving only a trail of vapor. She undid my belt buckle and slid the pants over my legs.

"You do that very well, Ms. Sorosh." My mouth opened wide in a yawn that didn't end for a long time. "Just like a nurse."

Her face was streaked with tears. "I was a candy striper in school," she said. "I spent three afternoons a week in the hospital helping the nurses. Didn't I tell you that?" Her voice came to me just this side of sleep.

"Did you? I guess I forgot."

I closed my eyes and passed over to the other side.

Chapter 59

The alarm went off at six A.M., a high-pitched siren loud enough to wake the dead. Perhaps it did.

I let it play itself out and listened to the room become still again. Allie was gone. As if she'd never been there.

I felt thirsty and reached for the piña colada I hadn't finished the night before. It was gone, too. Like Allie. Both our glasses were gone.

It didn't seem to make sense. I was alive. That wasn't how it was supposed to be.

The sun had risen, and bright morning light streamed through my windows. Yes, I was almost certainly alive.

I wasn't sure how I felt about that. So I just lay there for a long time, not feeling, not thinking, until my body and brain roused themselves enough that I could sit up. I slumped against the headboard and stared at the hospital bandage on my inner arm for several minutes before pulling it off. Underneath, there were two or three needle marks, surrounded by a fair-size bruise.

In itself, that didn't mean anything. Nothing conclusive. It might have taken the ER crew several tries to hit the vein when they put in my IV. It often does. Especially with a delirious patient. For some reason, I hadn't looked the day before.

Did I imagine the potassium chloride in Allie's overnight bag? Was it just another hallucination? I remembered it so clearly. Holding the little glass vials. Reading the labels. Rummaging through her makeup kit. I looked at my hands. There was lipstick on my fingers. Unmistakable. Allie's lipstick. That was no hallucination. Allie hadn't been wearing makeup.

I got to my feet and walked over to the door. Outside, it was a normal day. Surf crashing in the distance. Gulls screeching overhead. A lone car grumbled by on the street. Sandra's curtains were drawn shut. I was still sedated from the drugs, but felt reasonably lucid otherwise.

I went to the bathroom and turned on the fluorescent light above the mirror, examining my body for any other veins that Allie might have used. My neck. My groin and pelvic region. She might have missed the vein or been unable to get a good shot into it, injecting most of the potassium chloride into muscle tissue, where it would do no harm. Even if some entered a vein, the farther away from the heart, the less effective it would be. Producing only a mild shock to the heart. Easily mistakable for the real thing. But not fatal.

That was one explanation why I was alive. The simplest one.

I looked at the backs of my legs, behind the knees. Between my toes. Anywhere one can administer a hypodermic to a vein. There are many such places. Ask any junkie. They'll shoot drugs directly into their eyeballs if every other vein has been used up.

I searched the entire surface of my body. Even looked inside my mouth. Nothing visible. No soreness. Nothing at all. The bandage on my shin—the one Krista had placed over my cut—was old and dirty and clearly hadn't been removed. I took it off anyway. The wound was scarring over. It hadn't been touched.

Allie hadn't tried to kill me and failed. She hadn't tried at all. If she'd used my arm, I wouldn't be around to wonder why I was alive. If she'd tried to inject the potassium chloride somewhere else, it would have left a mark. There wasn't one.

I wondered if I was disappointed.

I had told myself that if I was right, I'd be dead. I hadn't really considered the other alternative.

If the simplest explanation doesn't account for the facts, then you have to move on to the next level of complexity.

Okay. And what the hell is that?

Maybe I was wrong about Allie. For a moment I hoped it was true. There might be some innocent explanation . . .

Get serious, I told myself. Women don't carry potassium chloride and syringes around on dates for the hell of it. Allie had come prepared to kill me. That was pretty obvious. But she hadn't done it. Why?

What was the next simplest explanation? The next level of complexity?

She had already killed—twice. She'd killed to protect Brandt—or to protect what she thought only he could give her, a new life without the old pain. If Brandt hadn't changed her in that original operation, she might have endured the way she was now. But he'd given her hope and then taken it away. Human beings can endure almost anything if they have to, but not that. Not the final loss of hope. So she'd killed Krista and Rossi. And tried, the night before, to kill me by closing the windows and leaving the heater on.

But . . .

I resisted the thought. It was too much what I might have wished. I'd fooled myself too long. It was time, I told myself again, to get serious. Assemble all the facts and figure out the simplest explanation that accounts for each and every one. Wishes don't count. Just facts. Still . . .

What was it that Crockett said? Something about people screwing up the whole equation. That it's never as simple as we think, especially when people are involved.

Perhaps more so when there's love.

It wasn't a sure thing, after all. The heater. The carbon monoxide poisoning. The apartment was drafty, even with the door and all the windows shut. Like attempted suicides who take only half the bottle of sedatives, or leave a note hoping to be found before it's too late, maybe a part of her didn't want me to die. Or at least wanted to leave an element to chance. And last night, when it came to a way she was certain would work, one she'd used twice before, she couldn't bring herself to do it. Even though she believed it was her final hope.

This was not what I wanted. I had longed to be released from the conflict, to find the only permanent resolution possible in this world, death. But it wasn't to be. Nothing so simple as that.

I would go to the police. She knew it. I would tell them about Brandt and what he had done. Today's operation would be his last. And Allie? It would be her last operation, too, most likely. Because I would also tell them about her. She knew I would. I had to.

—

Several cups of coffee at the diner helped to banish the remaining effects of the sedative. After the fourth refill, the waitress put the pot on the counter next to me and told me to help myself. I ordered a huge breakfast of eggs, ham, fried potatoes and waffles with syrup, which I ate as if I was starving. Then I went to the men's room and threw it all up in the toilet. I washed my mouth out as well as I could at the sink and went back to the counter for more coffee. A few more cups and I began to feel better. Better, it's a relative term.

By the time I got to the OR, the first round of operations had already begun. I scrubbed and found a nurse to help me with my sterile gown. There wasn't an audience this time, just the necessary personnel clustered around the operating table. Brandt looked up when I entered and nodded, almost as if he had been waiting for me. It was over now. He knew it.

He told his assistant that I'd be taking over for him, and I assumed his place beside the patient. Brandt indicated the lines marked on her skin for grafting, and the sections of cartilage already taken from her rib cage.

The nurse held out the tray for him, but he gestured in my direction, and she brought it to me. I took the scalpel in my hand and felt with my other hand the uncovered scars on Allie's face. The scalpel moved smoothly along her skin, the flesh parting gracefully like two lips breathing a sigh of longing.

The blade was sharp, perfectly formed, my hand steady with exactly the right amount of pressure. It cut through the layers of tissue, making fresh wounds in her face where so many had been cut before. I cut her so she would heal. But neither I, nor anyone else, would ever be able to cut deeply enough.

Epilogue

The steel doors open and shut, making a noise like an airlock. What's in here is too dangerous to be let out.

I see Allie standing beyond the bars. She still wears a shawl to hide her scars, though she has healed well in the last year. Outwardly, at least. The guards frisk her. She lets them, passively, her arms by her sides. She doesn't see me yet.

Sometimes I think she was right. Dig down beneath the veneer of humanity and all you find is a nightmare of viciousness and horror. That's the reality beneath the comforting lies we tell ourselves about love and compassion: the pit of humankind where the misshapen are mocked, the broken are crushed and the lonely are exiled without hope of return. To those who have much, more will be given. To those who don't, whatever little they have will be taken away. That's what I think sometimes. And yet . . .

I had another dream several days ago. Though I was awake, so perhaps I should call it a vision. It was of the earth stripped bare; stripped of everything that lived on it, like skin dissected from bone. All that was left was naked rock, until that, too, dissolved into insubstantiality, leaving only that which was there before: a pure love, the origin of it all. Harder than any stone.

Stern, in his careless, self-serving way, had almost hit on the truth. We thirst after knowledge, but we can't really bear it. We desperately want to know about others, but we run from knowledge of ourselves.

Even if the police had believed what I told them, there wasn't much of a case to be made. Lucasian explained that to me with a weariness of the world that he bore, I thought, with remarkably little resentment. Brandt had indeed flown up the Saturday Allie was attacked. They had his credit card receipts for the plane fare up and back. He had inquired at the real estate office about buying the house on Mercurtor Drive. But Allie didn't remember the attack. She probably never would. And there was no physical evidence to connect Brandt to the scene of the crime. He'd left no fingerprints. The gas tank handle had been wiped clean, and carpets, it turns out, don't pick up prints well. The actual hammer—or whatever weapon he had used—was never recovered. He'd apparently had the presence of mind to discard it somewhere it would never be found. The sea, perhaps.

The rest of the case was circumstantial and pointed as logically to me, I was informed by the D.A., as anyone else. I had no good alibi for the time of the assault. Nor did I have an alibi for the nights Krista and Rossi were killed. I'd been sleeping in the hospital one night, where no one had noticed me, and wandering around the city looking for Danny the other. A few of the bartenders I'd spoken to said they remembered me, but what did that prove? The police were never convinced, in fact, that Krista and Rossi had been murdered, that it wasn't just my fevered fantasy. The coroner's report found no evidence of foul play in either case. As far as the D.A. was concerned, my story might have been simply the paranoid suspicions of a jealous lover. As far as the D.A. was concerned, I made a better suspect than a witness. It's all a question of what level of complexity you stop at.

—

They are finished with the search. Allie sees me and walks my way. She visits me regularly now.

I wanted to heal others; now I want to be healed. They have a name for my sickness. Several names, in fact, all with the word "psychosis" in them. It's not exactly schizophrenia, according to the doctors. They're almost sure it isn't, "though the boundaries aren't as clearly defined as one might wish," they explain. Seems the break was precipitated by psychological trauma. Too much stress, they say. Not enough sleep. Too much alcohol. Too much tragedy.

Eventually, the indictment against me was dropped. Lucasian managed a plea bargain of sorts. The D.A. didn't want to proceed with a weak case against someone who had just been certified psychotic by his own doctors, and Stern readily offered up the notes of our sessions as proof that I had been legally insane all along. The fact that Stern almost certainly believed me guilty seemed to make him even more eager to help, and he has insisted on continuing our sessions here. I had no choice in the matter. I finally gave up trying to dissuade him, which he took as a sign of progress, and we reached a kind of unspoken compact not to bring up the subject of innocence and guilt. As Stern explained, such things were immaterial to our "therapeutic goals."

I agreed to be confined in a state facility until the doctors pronounce me cured. My confinement is "without prejudice," Lucasian explained. Once I'm released, I can resume my "normal life," assuming there's a market for surgeons with a history of severe mental illness. I ask how much longer it will be until I'm free. The doctors are encouraging. The antipsychotic medication seems to be working. A month or two longer. Maybe more.

Brandt retired. The D.A.'s investigation was too upsetting for someone who did, after all, have a conscience. Or maybe he simply couldn't stand the social embarrassment. He has moved somewhere else, where he lives in obscurity with other wealthy people. No accounting, no retribution. Not for him. Not in this life.

I stand up from the table as Allie approaches, and we embrace. The medication makes me awkward, as if I'm moving inside someone else's body, but I can still feel her touch. We sit quietly as she lifts the shawl from her head. Her hair is pulled back tightly but still breaks free in irresistible curls. I can see the ear we reconstructed. It looks almost natural. She said in an earlier visit that she might eventually have more surgery, but not now. Perhaps because she won't go forward without Brandt, or maybe it no longer seems so important to her.

There is something different this time. I know it before she speaks. She has come to tell me something, she says. Something she's been thinking about for a long time. Her face is drawn in sorrow. Sorrow for me. Sorrow for what she must do.

"Tell me, Allie," I say.

———

We are closer now. Shorn of our illusions, there is less to keep us apart. Two people whose deepest fears have been realized. My insanity. Her disfigurement. The worst has happened. And we are still alive.

"I love you, Jackson," she says.

"I know."

"All this time . . . Do you believe that? Always. Even when . . ."

"Yes, Allie, I do."

Her head is bowed. She takes my hand and pulls it close. I feel her warm tears falling on my skin.

"I'm so sorry . . ."

"I'll be out soon," I say. "According to the doctors, I'll even be reasonably normal."

"I would love you any way you were, Jackson."

"We can start over again, like new."

She leans her head against my hand and weeps. "Forgive me, darling. I wish I could. With all my heart, I wish—"

"Allie," I say, "listen—"

"I can't live like this, Jackson," she cries softly. "I can't." She wipes the tears with our joined hands. She forces herself to continue. "I'm going to go to the police. I'm going to tell them about Krista and Rossi. What I did."

"Allie—"

"They didn't deserve to die. I . . ." She struggles with the words. They are hard words to say. "I *killed* them."

"Please, Allie. The police had their chance. They dropped the case. You don't have to—"

"Oh God! Jackson. I tried to kill *you.*"

"It's over, Allie. In the past—"

"Oh God, no! It isn't over." She grips my hand hard enough to hurt. "It's not over."

I tell her what I have told her before. She was suffering at the time from a massive head injury. Her brain chemistry was violently disrupted. It's an established medical fact that it happens, even with injuries much less severe. It's a legitimate defense. No court in the country would ever convict her. She was temporarily insane.

She wipes her eyes with my sleeve. She looks up at me sadly. "I know, Jackson. It doesn't matter."

"It's all true, Allie. You weren't yourself. You didn't know what you were doing—"

She shakes her head.

"It was my fault," I say. "I pushed you over the edge. That night. When I insisted on going to Rossi."

"And what else could you have done?"

I have no answer.

"Give it time, Allie."

"I can't," she moans. She rocks slowly back and forth, holding herself; the tears falling, accompanied by short, shallow breaths. "I can't," she cries in a weak voice, "Oh, Jackson. I'm so sorry."

My heart sinks.

"I'm so sorry, Jackson. I just couldn't bear it any longer."

It's done, I realize. She's already been to see Lucasian. Turned herself in.

The drugs give my expression a frozen appearance, but I can feel it breaking. I move to her, putting my hands to her face, burning with tears. The last warmth in a world of ice, and soon she, too, will be taken away.

"He is so *kind,*" she says of Lucasian, as if kindness is not something she deserves. "He is such a caring, *good* man." She marvels that someone so good would ever help her.

"Yes," I say. "He is. All of that."

Lucasian, she explains, advised her much as I had: that given the "extremity of her injuries" and the "severe psychological and physiological trauma" she experienced, she should plead to insanity. It was her decision not to, she emphasizes, afraid that I might blame him.

That was yesterday. He has already arranged a time in the afternoon when he will take her to surrender to the police. Lucasian believes they'll go lightly on her. Given her injuries. Given that she's turning herself in. Twelve years. Maybe ten. Less with parole.

Allie looks at me and her face becomes even sadder. Infinitely sad. She speaks tenderly. She voices what I am thinking. "And what about my Jackson?"

Despite the drugs, the tears stream down my face.

"Darling Jackson. What a terrible thing I am doing!"

"No." I shake my head.

"It's as if I'm murdering again. Killing the only one I have ever loved."

I only wish she were.

"I am so sorry," she says, weeping with me, pleading forgiveness for what she cannot help. "I am so sorry. Hold me, Jackson," she says. "Hold me."

I do.

—

"Write it down," Stern said. And I have. All that I can remember. All that I am able to understand.

Everything I've recorded here is true, as far as I can know it, though I know something truer: That all that we love on this earth will die, everything whole will be shattered, and all we think we have will be taken from us. Other people may be able to live with that, without hope that somehow, somewhere, it will all be made right, but I am not strong enough.

It is a terrible thing when justice is denied, but if we are honest with ourselves, we know that it can be even more terrible still when it succeeds. Allie will go to jail. As she must. She understands that better than I. There is no other way.

And me? How will I live?

I look out the wire cage covering my window and think of the other cage that will separate us now, locking her in, me out. Two prisoners before the flood, calling out for mercy. But who will ever hear our cries?

Everything I've written is true, but I also know that what we call truth, like justice, is only a faint echo of a summons we heard long ago, and our human approximations, as necessary as they are, are just that, approximations. Like the beauty of music or children's voices. Like our human passions. They are only approximations. They can never fill the longing we feel. They are the longing.

I still love her. And I will wait for her as she has waited for me. For she is my longing. She is my hope.

I love her despite, even because of, what I know. As I love her scars. Because I know that when the world is dissolved and blows away like the fragments of a dream, there is, there, a deeper wound at the center of it all. And only love will bring it to healing.

Acknowledgments

I have tried to make the medical aspects of this novel, particularly those involving plastic surgery, as accurate and realistic as possible. To the extent I have succeeded, I owe a debt of gratitude to the many extraordinary doctors who generously gave of their time and professional expertise. I particularly would like to thank Dr. Stephen Hardy, Associate Professor of Plastic Surgery at the University of Wisconsin, whose heroic work in pediatric cranio-facial surgery was a literary and personal inspiration, as were the insightful comments of Dr. Jeffrey Fischman, Assistant Clinical Professor of Plastic Surgery at Mt. Sinai Hospital in New York. Dr. Jim Zafier and Dr. Bruce Champagne taught me my way around the ER and Intensive Care Unit, respectively, Bruce also performing yeoman's work correcting the many medical errors in my draft. Thomas Chippendale, M.D., Ph.D., gave me invaluable coaching on neurological issues. I also drew extensively from several medical texts, including *Clinics in Plastic Surgery: Oculoplastic Surgery, Vol. 15/2,* and the EF Teleplast video *Management of Craniomaxillofacial Trauma,* with Joseph S. Gruss, M.D. On matters of law and forensics, I relied on the sage counsel of my cousin Eddie Hayes, my good friend Victoria Pittman-Waller, and Jimmy Harkins, a detective with the NYPD. I'd also like to thank the members of the SFPD and their very helpful public affairs office. Needless to say, any remaining errors—medical, legal and other—are solely my responsibility.

A multitude of friends provided encouragement and editorial suggestions in the early stages. My old allies from the political trenches, Peter Robinson, Tony Dolan, Bob Reilly, Mark Klugmann and Ralph Benko, lent their considerable knowledge and talents to the enterprise. Other invaluable readers include Mark Davis, Patricia

McNeill, Milari Madison, Carsten and Britta Oblaender, Ned and Petey Perkins, Simon and Penny Linder, Andreas Gutzeit, Michael Dobson and the many enthusiastic members of my wife's book club. Special thanks go to my mother, Mary Ellen Gilder, a voracious and particularly perceptive reader, and my immensely knowledgeable brother, David.

On the professional side, the novel was greatly improved by the helpful advice, trenchant editorial suggestions and general emotional support of my agent, Matt Williams—who must accept a large measure of responsibility for discovering this fledgling novelist—as well as his colleague, Betsey Lerner, and their boss, David Gernert. I was especially fortunate in my editors at Simon & Schuster, Nicole Graev and Jon Malki, and my copy editor, Beth Thomas.

Finally, though words hardly seem adequate, I want to thank my wife, Anne-Lee, who was there at the inception and by my side at every stage of creation, a true collaborator, inspiring me with her faith, comforting me with her love and never, ever, losing heart, even when the author sometimes lost his. This novel never would have been written without her.

About the Author

Joshua Gilder served in the White House as a senior speechwriter for President Ronald Reagan, penning some of the most memorable speeches of his administration, including "Go Ahead, Make My Day!" and the address to students at Moscow State University. He later served under George Bush (the elder) as Principal Deputy Assistant Secretary of State for Human Rights, before leaving to cofound a successful D.C. consulting firm. He has written articles for *The Wall Street Journal, Crisis, New York* magazine, *The New Criterion* and *World News Daily,* among other publications. He lives in Bethesda, Maryland, with his wife, Anne-Lee, and young son, Max.